A Beautiful Pawn in the Hands of Fate

Marie came through the French doors back into the drawing room. It had filled with men in blue uniforms. Glass shattered as they brutally pillaged the premises with methodical efficiency. Some had started placing pots of combustibles in the corners.

She started running down the dark front stairs. Everywhere it was getting as bright as day. The whole of Washington Street was beginning to take fire.

A wave of hopelessness came over Marie. How impotent a girl was all by herself! In a daze of pain and need she turned down the burning street to begin an agonizing search for the lone, gray-coated soldier in this wild inferno.

Bantam Books by Elizabeth Boatwright Coker
Ask your bookseller for the books you have missed

DAUGHTER OF STRANGERS
INDIA ALLAN
LA BELLE

La Belle

A NOVEL
BASED ON THE LIFE OF
THE NOTORIOUS SOUTHERN BELLE,
MARIE BOOZER

Elizabeth Boatwright Coker

LA BELLE

A Bantam Book / published by arrangement with
Mockingbird Press

PRINTING HISTORY

Mockingbird edition published April 1976
Bantam edition / April 1978

ISBN 0-553-10881-6

Published simultaneously in the United States and Canada

PRINTED IN THE UNITED STATES OF AMERICA

The Boozer coach, with the glass windows partly folded back on hinges, "exploited" a rare vision. A mother and daughter—Mrs. Feaster and Marie Boozer—the one rich, dark in coloring and costume, the other (occupying the whole front seat) a girl of golden hair, rose shades, blue orbs, healthy, poised, delicious, pressing into the soft cushions, wrapped in ceil blue and swan's-down, leghorn hat, from which white plumes fell, curling under upon the white and pink throat. It was an angel's *seeming*—and she, beautiful as Venus, the goddess of the chariot.

MRS. THOMAS TAYLOR,
South Carolina Women in the Confederacy

AUTHOR'S NOTE

Like all great beauties, Marie Boozer was a combination of classic features, exquisite flesh, and that ineffable essence, or natural perfume, without which no woman, whatever her physical perfection, can take her place in beauty's ranks.

The truth about Marie, as always with the lovely and the lost, has been so lacquered by gossip, legend, and anecdote that it has been difficult to separate the real woman from the mythical one. Thus while seeking out the mirror view of her I could never fail to be influenced by the spell she cast. To this day people in Columbia still speak of Marie and her mother with as much current curiosity, envy, admiration, and opprobrium as they do of the fiery General Sherman who once visited their city. It is almost as if these handsome ladies had just passed by in their crystal coach. My "real life" information about Marie has come from many and varied sources and people, not all of them reliable. To establish a frame for her, I have used, at the top of each chapter, a documented quote from daily newspapers, diaries, letters, memoirs, records, legal papers, and history books. In addition, Marie's adoption papers, Dave Boozer's will, and Marie's letter to Julian Selby follow the wording of the originals. All these tell of a beautiful and exciting woman who in her short life traveled an exceeding long road. The renowned Dr. Babcock, of the South Carolina State Hospital, is said to have remarked on returning home from a trip across Europe in the early nineteen hundreds, "I came on Marie's trail everywhere I went and am sore afraid that our little Columbia girl has been guilty of sinning in many languages."

COLUMBIA, SOUTH CAROLINA

December 1846

In late December of 1846, when our drama begins, a poor child-woman, twice widowed at sixteen, is living in a simple boardinghouse kept by an aged schoolmaster and his wife, on Richland Street, near the corner of Sumter, in Columbia, South Carolina. It is a tottering steep frame house hot in summer and cold in winter. The widow's room is at the top, close under the roof, dark and without ornament. Light and air penetrate into this place through the chimney and through a small window in which all the panes rattle loosely in their decaying frames.

There is another room on this top half-story occupied by two students from the Upcountry, attending the South Carolina College. On the floor below four or five accountants and cotton clerks share two bedrooms and a sitting room, in which they play cards until all hours. At times the widow, whose name is Amelia Burton, plays at cards with the men, snapping her black eyes and stealing puffs off their cigars. She is keen company. But, since she always wins, the clerks have lately fallen into the habit of making up their game before she finishes helping the Negro cook wash and put away the supper dishes. For in these ways Amelia pays for her board and lonely lodging.

On this, our opening night, the widow has come with more than her usual loathing up the narrow stairs to her attic room. It is almost eight o'clock. She sits on her lumpy bed, trembling, afraid of the persistent recurring cramps in her abdomen and the low hurting in her back. Fear is a new emotion for Amelia. She hates this fear that comes up from below, from her bowels, and climbs through her stomach to her throat like a chilly wave, unnerving and weakening her legs, her arms, her determination to get away.

She hates many things: the slapping of the cards downstairs; the students in the next room droning out a Latin verse; the ringing of the new Trinity Church bells down Sumter Street; the faint strains of a fiddle played by old Scipio, the slew-footed West Indian barber, in the house of John Suder, the French dancing master; the clear voices of the tall, thin, fine-faced Carolinians marching, singing, in the torchlit street on their way to fight a war in Mexico.

Amelia goes over and leans far out of the tiny window watching the torches make evil shadows march behind the soldiers. A crazy old Negro is jumping around like a puppet, waving a collard leaf for a flag, under the gas lamp on the corner.

Amelia hates the crazy old black man as she hates everything about this town to which Peter Burton, that disgusting, elderly, dry-goods clerk, pretending to be a prosperous Carolina merchant, lured her from Philadelphia, and then died in wild convulsions on a strange Sunday morning four months ago.

The aching that has plagued her all evening suddenly changes into such a shocking, agonizing spasm that Amelia sinks to her knees on the cold bare floor. Her envenomed scream stabs the ears of the marching soldiers and the card players and the students and starts the crazy old Negro on the street corner howling like a dog against the hateful sound. The northern wind, rushing icily through the palmetto and oak trees, crescends and the big clock in the belfry of the Town Hall pounds out the hour of eight.

PART ONE

NEWBERRY, SOUTH CAROLINA

1846–1849

> The mother of the too famous beauty, Boozer, . . .
> has been married three times, and yet by all showing
> she did not begin to marry soon enough. Witness the
> existence of Boozer.
>
> *Mary Boykin Chesnut,*
> A Diary from Dixie

1

As the clock struck half past eight, Mr. David Boozer of Newberry, visiting lecturer in practical medicine at the South Carolina College, had abruptly concluded a discourse on the most efficient manner to deliver a difficult calf from a pure bred heifer as opposed to delivering a difficult calf from a heifer of the common herd. The young gentlemen had just clattered away, when two youths from Newberry, students at the college, burst into the classroom.

"Thank the Lord, Mr. Big Dave," they gasped, "you're here!"

"What the devil," Big Dave sputtered, "are you young scoundrels up to?"

"There's a girl barely sixteen years old having a baby

in our boardinghouse and we can't find a doctor anywhere. Come quickly."

"Not on your life. I dismissed my class so I could go and hear Governor Johnson bid farewell to the Palmetto Legion before they take off for Mexico. Wish I was young enough to go along. Yes, just wish I was."

One of the students grabbed him by the shoulder. "Oh do! Mr. Dave, hurry, for the Lord's sake, hurry. The old people who own our boardinghouse have gone to Charleston for a visit. We're all by ourselves. Just us boys and her—"

"Can't you leave me alone?" Big Dave shouted testily.

"Her—hollering like a sick cow—ooooh—aaaah—ooow!"

"She's got shiny black hair and bright black eyes and a mouth shaped like a heart and the whitest, creamiest skin you ever saw."

"She swears the baby is coming two months early."

"She's a widow woman and poor as a church mouse but mighty pretty and young and going ooooh—aaaah—"

"Oh, rest your rattling." Big Dave jammed his bell-crowned beaver hat uncomfortably upon his enormous Swiss head and turned his back on the excited boys, but he knew where he was headed. "Well, now why don't the boardinghouse lady just send for a midwife? Whole thing sounds sordid and none of my affair." He opened a bag on the desk in front of him and checked the contents, then, his old fashioned claw-hammer tailed coat flying out behind, rushed into the hallway, the boys following.

Sancho Cooper, the African infidel, who waited on the boys at the college was ready with Big Dave's buggy when he came running down the stairs into the bitter night.

"My Lord," Big Dave shouted, looking down at the boys, "you thought I was a soft-hearted old fool and would swallow your mad tale! But I have no intention of missing Governor Johnson's speech. Pierce Butler is from near Newberry and my good friend. I couldn't miss it." He picked up the reins then called back to

the boys, "You say the girl is all alone and already at
the screaming stage?"

The horse galloped all the way to the boardinghouse.

The clock in the Town Hall was striking four. Weary
and elated, Big Dave sat in front of the wide kitchen
fireplace staring down at the miracle of flesh he held
in his hands. She was pink and perfect and, rather
than premature, had probably been cradled an extra
month in her mother's womb. Would she be brunette
or blonde? The tuft of hair that showed was bold. The
eyes were shut but the very long thick eyelashes were
light. No, she would not be dark like her mother. A
pretty nose—not the usual baby button. He leaned
over and kissed it lightly. And the mouth was exquisite. As if she realized Big Dave's adoration, the infant
yawned and stretched herself and her dainty toes
pushed strongly against Big Dave's thick tender fingers.

"You ack like you witched, Mister Big Dave," the
Negro midwife spoke from the head of the narrow cot
where she was sponging Amelia's face with a rag wrung
out in half-wine half-water.

"No, not that," he said softly.

"You sho' pult that young'un out quick at the last.
Wonder this'un's still here but blue as she turnt, her
pulsk is hitting back sho' as shooting."

"Foot-first delivery is usually fatal to one or the other," Big Dave said, wrapping a shawl around the enchanting little creature's girl-nakedness. He rose from
the stool and, holding the infant close against his rumpled shirt front, went over and looked closely at Amelia.

"Did you have to be so brutal?" she asked hoarsely.

"To save the baby, yes. Would you like a little
laudanum?"

Amelia gulped down the potion the midwife fixed
and turned her face away from Big Dave. "You might
have killed me," she said hatefully.

"Is there anyone you would like me to notify?"

"There is no one."

"Who is going to take care of you? The midwife will

leave as soon as she gets you cleaned up unless you can pay her to stay."

"There is no one," Amelia repeated, closing her eyes, "no one."

"Can you look after yourself and this child?"

Amelia's black eyes slithered open and, with a shock, comprehended the sincere pity that Big Dave betrayed with all his being. "I don't know, sir," she whispered weakly, schemingly.

"You're nothing but a child yourself," he said tenderly.

Amelia managed to agree with a pathetic sort of sob.

The midwife made a sound halfway between a snort and a giggle.

Big Dave held the baby girl closer. "Would you like to come home with me to Newberry?" he cried from the depths of his kindly heart.

The laudanum was easing Amelia. Home! How long since the word had had any meaning. Why, home meant a wide feather bed, servants, petticoats that rustled, wine with your dinner, polished card tables, fiddles and flutes and dances with tall, thin, fine-faced soldiers!

"Is he rich?" she whispered to the Negro woman.

The midwife leaned over Amelia and this time she giggled lewdly, "Big old farm, big old house, lotsa big old country niggers, all the big old widderwomen in the Up-country trying to ketch um. Looks lak you gonna land on yo' foots too, gal. Same like that pretty little baby there did. You better grab Mr. Dave quick cause you is mighty tore up inside; you go have trouble when you gits older."

"How will we get to your home?" Amelia was truly drowsy now. She held out her thin arms and Big Dave handed her the baby, grinning fatuously as a new father. "I have no money."

"I'll drive you and the baby there in a coach piled with feather cushions as soon as you are able."

Amelia whimpered a little, nodding. The child felt good against her swelling breast. A good child. A good omen. She would keep the child fast and never let her get away. Already the child had proved she was an extraordinary female.

"Mary. I'll name you Mary," she whispered to the goldy head, "and if you *are* as beautiful as that foolish old man declares, our fortune is made!"

And the infant opened her rosy mouth and began to cry lustily and hungrily.

She shall from henceforth be known and recognized
by the name Mary Sarah Amelia Boozer. . . .

Chancellor Job Johnstone,
November 21, 1848

2

Big Dave was not rich but he was moderately wealthy.
He owned Birdfield's Hotel in Newberry, several lots
in the town, hundreds of acres of cotton, tobacco, corn
and pinelands and plenty of Negroes to work his fields.
His plantation dwelling was similar to an English basement house.

The first story was of brick finished with stucco and
the two upper stories and attic were of clapboards. The
interior woodwork, rather finely carved, had been
done by a Mr. Schoppert of Newberry. Big Dave's
slaves had made the brick, and all the lumber for the
house had been cut from his acres. The lime for mor-
taring and plastering had been imported and brought
from Charleston in wagons. There wasn't much of a
flower garden, since no woman had lived at Aveliegh
in so long, but there was a handsome English sundial
between the house and the long brick kitchen.

Big Dave was a godly, churchgoing man who never
drank, danced, or gambled at cards. He was a well-
known figure throughout the Upcountry with no reputation for wenching, though a widower for many years.
He went about dressed in plain, sober clothes; his
beard was usually cut in time; and in the country he
wore a broad-brimmed Panama hat pulled square on
his coarse white hair. He had, in 1827, married Elizabeth Wallace, of the district, and sired two sons, but
they were all dead now and when he wed the Yankee
woman and brought her and her baby into his home
there was a small war of tattling tongues.

Big Dave doted on the child who insisted on calling

herself, not Mary, but Marie. As she emerged from babyhood with laughing eyes, red cheeks and dancing feet, he spoiled her outrageously. He bought her china dolls, stuffed her with sweets, threw her in the air till she shrieked with joy, and showed off her accomplishments to every visitor.

Marie loved to follow the shadow around the sundial and Big Dave would say her hair was the true sun and that big yellow ball up in the sky just an imitation of it.

Newberry often heard more of the battles between the parents over the rearing of Marie than it did of the glorious exploits of their own sons fighting a war with Mexico. When the beautiful Pierce Butler was killed, leading the Palmetto Regiment at Churubusco, and his flag-draped body came home to Edgefield, it was of secondary importance to the fact that Mary A. P. Burton had petitioned her "next friend, David Boozer, she being an infant, born in Columbia, and since the intermarriage of her mother and the said friend it is now desirable to both the petitioner's mother and her stepfather that her present name Mary Adele Peter Burton should be altered to that of Mary Sarah Amelia Boozer "

As soon as the adoption was made legal, Amelia constantly nagged Big Dave about bringing his will up to date. So in March 1849 Big Dave had his friend, Judge Belton O'Neall, draw up a completely new will:

THE STATE OF SOUTH CAROLINA,
Newberry District.

I, David Boozer, make the following disposition of my estate to take effect at my death as my last will and testament.

FIRST. I direct all my just debts to be paid. . . .

SECOND. I desire my Executors to enclose a graveyard at Aveliegh Church from 45 to 50 yards square with a wall of split rock from 4½ to 5 feet high, so as to include the grave of my first wife as well as my own with sufficient space also for the grave of my present wife; and to erect over the area included by the wall a covered wooden building of the most lasting material, to be finished and painted in appropriate style and in the most endurable manner. And I appropriate $1000 out of my estate to these purposes.

THIRD. . . . My wife Amelia is to have during her life the free use and the right to dispose of the clear profits of the estate, charged with the maintenance and education of her daughter, Mary S. A. Boozer (formerly called Mary Burton). . . .

FOURTH. I authorize my Executors to sell. . . .

FIFTH. When the said Mary S. A. Boozer shall come of age or marry, my Executors will give off to her to be settled to her sole and separate use my negro man Stobo and his wife Hannah. . . .

SIXTH. After the death of my wife I gave my whole estate to the said Mary S. A. Boozer to be settled to her sole and separate use not subject to the control nor liable for the debts of any husband she may ever have

SEVENTH. If I should have any child or children born after the making of this will I wish such child and each one of such children to have equal enjoyment and benefit from and share of my estate with the said Mary S. A. . . .

EIGHTH. If the said Mary S. A. should die leaving no issue then living all the property given to her by this will shall return to my estate and go to my next of kin . . .

NINTH. I appoint my friends the Hon. John Belton O'Neall and George Gallman executors of this my last will and testament.

In witness whereof I have hereunto set my hand and seal this 23rd day of March 1849.

/s/ *David Boozer* (Seal)

Signed and published by the said David Boozer as and for his last Will and testament in the presence of us who have at his request and in his presence subscribed our names as witnesses thereto also in the presence of each other.

/s/ *John S. Carwile*
/s/ *John B. Carwile*
/s/ *Thomas H. Pope*

As time passed, Amelia and Big Dave quarreled; Marie and Big Dave never. In the three years they were together, Marie and Big Dave never said any but loving words. Amelia went often into the town. The family were seldom together, except at teatime. While they ate a hearty meal, Amelia shuffled and clicked a deck of cards. If the child or Big Dave tried to talk to her, Amelia would put a red queen on a black king and say, "How stupid you two are. Hush, can't you, I've wagered something special on this game of solitaire."

Marie didn't understand until many years later that Amelia was staking this or that decision on whether *she* or the cards won the game!

One afternoon in May, 1849, Amelia took Marie into town in the carriage, black Stobo driving. Amelia ordered Stobo to stop at Birdfield's Hotel "just a minute to get the child some candy." They went into the parlor where three men in tall beaver hats and long, tight, fawn-colored pants and black frock coats were sitting at a round table. They called Marie "Sugar" and smelled of the wine Amelia so often drank at teatime.

Marie smiled at the men, especially a tall one Amelia called "Hugh Huger." He had wonderful sensitive hands and Marie liked the way they felt on her hair. He said to Amelia, "What a pretty child. What a dear, darling, little thing."

"You Santa Claus?" Marie asked pleasantly.

"No. I am a doctor."

"I don't wike doctors. I go find Stobo now."

Amelia leaned down and pinched Marie's cheek. She said in an excited way, "You'll like this one, Mistress Mary, this is my very best friend, Dr. Hugh Huger Toland. I bet his pocket is full of sugar plums."

Dr. Toland bowed gravely and Marie allowed him to pick her up and sit her on his knee.

There was always lots of money on the table and after each card game Amelia would laugh and pick up the money and stuff it into her reticule.

After a while, Marie heard Big Dave calling out her name.

"I is here, Big Dave," she shouted, "come see me quick. I is ate a whole cone full of candy."

He ran in followed by Stobo and the minister of the Aveliegh Presbyterian Church. Big Dave snatched Marie off Dr. Toland's lap and hugged her tight, and Amelia screamed, "How dare you follow me?" to Big Dave, and "You damned nigger!" to Stobo, and terrible mean things to the preacher. And the preacher who was very young and horrified said, "Woman, I'll put you out of the church."

Amelia laughed and ran her eyes all over the young preacher's body and flicked her cigar ash onto the preacher's tie and he wiped it off as if it were pure fire and then Big Dave said apologetically to the preacher, "Mrs. Boozer is just a child herself. Don't put her out of the church."

Amelia was wearing a necklace of silver ornaments set in black marble, wrought by the Indians. Big Dave had turned it up in a ploughed field one day. The heavy necklace rattled as her shoulders shook with her vehement laughing. Big Dave handed Marie to Stobo and took Amelia by the arm and jerked her up from the chair. Two of the card players had disappeared. Dr. Toland said, "I would like to explain this to you, Mr. Boozer."

Big Dave said, "We've nothing to say to each other. Stop laughing, Mrs. Boozer."

Amelia said, "How sick I am of you! I can't bear the sight of you."

The preacher said to Big Dave, "Do you want me to go home with you, Mr. Boozer?"

"No. I can manage my wife," Big Dave said sadly.

"Well, I'll come to the farm tomorrow. And let me tell you I am mighty surprised to have found you in such company, Dr. Toland. Mighty surprised."

When they got outside a crowd of ladies and gentlemen were standing in a group but they scattered like chickens and Big Dave pushed Amelia into the carriage and told Stobo to drive her straight home.

Dr. Toland tried again to say something to Big Dave but Big Dave ignored him and lifted Marie on his

horse's neck and climbed up in the saddle and hugged
her hard against him and she was suddenly happy and
safe and warm and the air smelled living and fresh of
elderberry blossoms and greening over-cup oaks and
honeysuckle and not of cigar smoke and sour wine.
Big Dave pressed his cheek down on her head for a
minute and she reached up and patted his rough head.

As the horse singlefooted down the sandy street Marie tried to comfort Big Dave. She sang,

> "Buzzard and butterfly
> Pickin' out 'e eye
> And po' wittle thing
> Cwying Mammy!
>
> Mammy! Mammy!
> Po' wittle thing
> Cwying Mammy."

And everybody along the way seeing the pretty child
singing up to Big Dave, who was looking proud and
tall in the saddle, waved at her and smiled and none of
them ever forgot that picture for soon they saw Big
Dave looking very, very different.

From that day dark tales sifted from the Boozer farm
into the town. The Dutch Fork people were superstitious folk and firmly believed in witches. They were
positive that evil forces were at work to destroy the
lovable, foolish man. It was told and retold, first by
Stobo and black Hannah, then by the country people
and the townfolk, that one June afternoon Amelia was
sitting at a table playing solitaire on the piazza and all
the while nagging at Big Dave about moving into the
town. Marie was playing hopscotch at the foot of the
steps and Big Dave heavy as an ox was hopping with
her.

"Not ever into the town," he bellowed up to Amelia,
"not ever—ever—ever! Not even *if* Hell freezes over."

Marie laughed at Big Dave's clumsy feet mashing
down a clump of toadstools. Amelia slapped down a
deuce of clubs, saying contemptuously, "Oh, fiddle

foot!" and flashed her black eyes toward a beautiful stand of piney woods.

That night a raging fire consumed every one of the virgin monarchs.

On a morning in late summer Amelia was buying a jug of corn whiskey from one of the covered wagons that came down regularly from North Carolina peddling the stuff through the upper part of South Carolina. Big Dave was leading Marie on his big horse up and down in front of the coach house and he called to the wagoner to get the devil off his farm and never come back or he'd give him a hiding with his buggy whip.

Amelia coolly counted out the money from her reticule, told the North Carolinian to be sure and come by next time, picked out a jug and, shrugging her pretty shoulders, walked back to the house by way of a large field, golden green with sweet, ripe tobacco. A hawk swooped wide and Amelia watched it until it disappeared. Even after it was lost in the horizon she stood there in the hot sun staring away at nothing over and beyond the fragrant plants.

During the night, worms stripped every valuable leaf off the tall green stalks.

This was told too and people came to see, and it was a true thing that had happened.

Then in the autumn, on a windy afternoon, Amelia drove herself in the one-seated buggy to a tavern in the town. She was brazenly wearing a red dress cut so low over the bosom that wagers were made in the courthouse as to whether a man could see the whole business while standing on the street or whether he had to be passing her on horseback and looking down.

The next Sunday the preacher turned Amelia publicly out of the Aveliegh Presbyterian Church for wearing unseemly clothes on the street and for gambling at cards with strangers in a tavern.

Big Dave began to waste away. His thick white hair thinned and his round blue eyes seemed covered with a film.

In November, Stobo drove Amelia in the carriage to

Columbia to sell Big Dave's cotton. Big Dave wasn't feeling well enough to go himself.

Instead of finishing the business in a few days Amelia was gone two whole weeks and during that time drove all the way to Charleston. It also happened that Dr. Hugh Huger Toland was doing some special surgery in Charleston that November. But Big Dave never knew about that. Unless Stobo told him, which was not likely. However, he suspected something for Amelia returned with a whole trunkful of beautiful new frocks and bonnets.

"Where did you get the money to buy those clothes?" Big Dave asked her when she came out on a Sunday to go to town in an expensive white silk and lace dress ornamented with solid gold buttons and a white silk and lace bonnet.

"From the cotton money."

"That's a lie. The factor has sent me every penny of the cotton money. You are carrying on with Dr. Toland. I've heard things. I won't have my name or this child's name soiled by you."

In December, on Marie's third birthday, Stobo drove him and the child to town to the bank. Marie stayed in the carriage while Big Dave went in the bank and transferred his whole cash account of $25,000 into Marie's name. Then he went to confer with Judge O'Neall in his law office. Marie remembered a little about this later, but only that the leather on the chair scratched her leg and that the Judge's whiskers tickled when he kissed her cheek. She didn't remember Judge O'Neall urging Big Dave, for his personal safety, to rewrite his will. Nor did she remember Big Dave saying, well, yes, but he'd try and reason once more with Amelia.

Amelia was not yet twenty, Big Dave said wearily, maybe later she would behave more decorously. Maybe being a Philadelphian, she was just bored with Southern country life; maybe he should try living in the town; maybe that would satisfy her. The child was such a gay sunny little thing that he spent his entire time playing with her. Maybe he should take Amelia to some parties where she could play at dropping the glove, or grinding the bottle, or brother I am bob'd, or throwing long bullets. Maybe if he took her to watch some wrestling or jumping or running races or let her shoot for a hanging beef on Saturdays she would mend her wild ways. When she chose she was a mighty attractive female, but that was seldom. And he hoped there was nothing too serious between her and Hugh Toland. Hugh's wife was just sickly—that was why he enjoyed being with a woman so strong as Amelia.

Judge O'Neall listened to Big Dave and then he put his hand on his friend's shoulder and said, gravely, "Don't fool yourself, David."

"Why not, Judge?"

"There are too many 'maybes' and, actually, not a soul in Newberry would play at games with Amelia. Those who aren't convinced she's having an affair with Hugh Toland are convinced she is a witch. Come on now, let's rewrite your will. If Amelia knew you'd not hesitate to turn her out penniless and she had no hold on your property, she'd change her ways. She's a handsome woman, I'll grant you, but there's nothing kind about her. Try being cruel and you'll see her come to hand mighty quick. I have an idea that being poor is all in this world Amelia Boozer is afraid of; that money is the one thing she craves or respects."

"I know you're right, Judge, and I'll surely come back in tomorrow and tend to it. But Mary can't sit still any longer now can you, sugar-pie? Say good-by to Judge O'Neall, Mary Sarah."

Having been born with a flair for charming the men, Marie ran and held her face up for the Judge to tie her bonnet ribbons. Big Dave had sent to New Orleans for the lace bonnet that set off her face like a halo. "Why this child has sky-colored eyes! Real spirit-eyes!" Judge O'Neall made a one-sided bow. "I've never been flattered with such a come-hither look in one so young."

"Where have you been?" Amelia asked Marie when they returned.

"Out," Marie answered, starting to greet fat, shaky,

jovial black Hannah and give her a paper cone of peppermints she'd fetched her from the town.

"Who did you see in the town?" Amelia knelt down and her sharp eyes bored into Marie's soft ones.

"Nobody."

"Yes—you *did*, you naughty girl. Tell me or I'll shake it out of you."

"Man. Man wikes Big Dave. Man hates you and I hate you."

Marie ran away to Hannah who petted her and began greedily sucking a peppermint.

Amelia went onto the piazza. Stobo was passing the steps. Stobo was a smallish, glossy Negro with sharp Jewish features and straight black hair. Big Dave had sent him to the Lowcountry to one of the big plantations when he was a boy to be trained as a coachman and butler. Consequently, Stobo felt and acted superior to all the other Negroes and most of the white people here in the Upcountry. He was a very lonesome man.

"Where is Mr. Dave?" Amelia asked.

"Out in the coach house, mending the door handle."

"Where'd you all go in the town?"

"See the judge."

"Oh—Judge O'Neall?"

"That's the one."

Stobo watched Amelia run, lithe and swift, to the coach house and go in and close the door. He heard her talking, loud and ugly. He heard Big Dave curse her. Then he walked away. Such things were not unusual here on this plantation. Mr. Dave should have married better. Someone from the Lowcountry where his mother had been raised. This was one mean Yankee woman.

Stobo was grooming the horses, the cook was chopping kindling wood, Hannah and Marie were upstairs, the field hands were ploughing under cotton stalks and singing very loud, when the shotgun went off. For a while they all got quiet and listened, then, hearing nothing further, went on about their ways.

Pretty soon two of Big Dave's nephews came by to see their uncle about some hound dog puppies. Amelia called to them from over by the well to take her into town if they were going that way. She put on a green shawl and a green bonnet and drove off with them in their carriage laughing and talking.

At the dusking Amelia returned, called to Stobo who was setting the supper table, told him to put on two extra plates for the boys and asked had his master come in and if not when had he last been seen?

"You the last one seen him in the coach house," Stobo said insolently. Then his shiny brown face turned ashy gray, his hooked nose flattened and his dry thin hands grew cold and moist as Amelia fixed her eyes on his, paralyzing his will, shattering his nerve, draining his blood, softening his bones.

"I did *not* see him in the coach house. You go this minute and find out if he's still there. The boys want to talk to him."

Big Dave was still there. The upper half of his head had been blown off and a double-barreled shotgun was clutched in his stiffening hands.

At the funeral the relatives and the friends of the much loved David Boozer drew away from the widow brazenly wearing the white silk and fancy lace dress with the gold buttons, as if by the merest contact with her they would wither away as the sensitive briar will do when a hand touches it. For Big Dave couldn't have shot himself with that double-barreled gun he was holding when Stobo found him. His arms weren't long enough.

Amelia could not be shaken from her story that she'd been to the town that afternoon and never been near the coach house so there was no inquest. But there was a church trial in the Aveliegh Presbyterian Church in Newberry immediately after the funeral and Amelia was accused by the minister of murdering her husband. But due to the testimony of the two young nephews who had driven Amelia to town that afternoon; and to the fact that Dr. Hugh Huger Toland came from Columbia and defended her, saying he had been playing cards with her in the hotel during the time Big Dave must have shot himself, she was cleared of the murder. And Stobo never opened up his lips to say one word against her.

At Amelia's request, the executor sold Birdfield's Hotel in the town for a nice sum. Then, taking her daughter, the Boozer carriage and the two slaves who belonged to Marie, Hannah, the nurse, and Stobo, the coachman, Amelia moved away from the open hate and hostility of the people of Newberry, back to Columbia where Judge O'Neall, for the child's sake, used his influence and enabled Amelia to engage rooms in a good boardinghouse.

In the meantime public opinion in Columbia became so bitter against Dr. Toland that he packed up his sad, but forgiving, young family and moved West to San Francisco where he was appointed chief surgeon at the Marine Hospital and where he spent the remainder of his useful, famous life.

As for Amelia, in 1853 she met Jacob Feaster of Fairfield, a healthy, young gentleman of property and fine family, who had a room in the exclusive establishment. Jacob had heard the gossip about Amelia and Hugh Toland, but her black eyes captivated him and he began to ask her to go driving with him in the evenings. Suddenly one warm evening he proposed to her. He worried all night and then decided he was up to his ears in love with her. And they were married at once.

After a dying consumptive of fifteen, a dull clerk of fifty and a foolish farmer of sixty, the normal Jacob was a welcome husband for Amelia. Perhaps she really loved him. For a time anyway. She put a rebellious Marie to board in the Female Academy in Columbia and moved with Jacob Feaster to Alston and thence to Greenville. There she bore him two children and to all outward appearances settled down, as Big Dave had so hoped she would, to live an ordinary life.

PART TWO

COLUMBIA, SOUTH CAROLINA

1856–1865

Certainly one gentleman of the old school still remembers the beautiful Marie for he made mud pies with her and more than once threw down bat and ball and gazed admiringly as she dashed by on a handsome mount.

THE COUNTESS POURTALÈS,
by *"Felix Old Boy"*

3

The terrible death of her beloved Big Dave, and her consciousness of being "different" in background, *and* an heiress, cast its spell on Marie Boozer's childhood. Perhaps that was why, at the Academy, she was so boisterous. Certainly she walked her own willful path, and had her own way, unruffled by rules, threats or even the punishments by the preceptor, Mr. Muller.

But when she was ten the preceptor took it upon himself to give her a lecture on what the future held for a young lady who walked on the upstairs piazza banister-rail like a cat in her bare feet and waved at the Arsenal cadets who watched widemouthed in the street below; who was not afraid to run out in the dark or to speak to strangers.

This future sounded so enchanting to Marie that, when the preceptor excused her to go and write in her copybook a hundred times "I am a naughty girl," she merely walked through the door into the garden, climbed the iron fence and, minus her bonnet, went skipping away down the street toward the railroad station.

In the station she met a big, brown-eyed boy in a straw bowler, with a basket of lunch.

"Where are *you* going?" she asked boldly.

"To Greenville. Where are you going?"

"I," Marie bragged, "am running away from the Academy and going to my mama in Greenville. We can have fun there together, can't we? You must give me your ticket and tell the conductor you have lost yours. You have a hat on so he'll know you're respectable. Mr. Muller says I am not respectable. Even *with* a bonnet!"

The children laughed and the boy, Willie C., opened his basket and she ate all of his tea cakes and both fried chicken wings before the cars came and, hand in hand, they climbed aboard.

When she reached Greenville, Willie's father drove her to the house where the Feasters lived.

Amelia Feaster, flashily handsome in rustling crinoline petticoats and high-heeled red shoes and dangling gold earrings, with the inevitable cigar between her two forefingers met Marie in the parlor where a delighted Stobo had fetched her.

She sat down in front of Marie and turned upon her the magnetic power of a pair of black eyes that had always weakened the will of her opponent.

But Marie had magnetic eyes too: blue-gray and aflame now with stubborn determination. In a pale-blue pinafore that covered a deeper blue frock, her gold hair blown wild by the wind, her cheeks scarlet, her head erect, she returned her mother's gaze with one in which there was already a threat of rivalry.

Amelia went on at length about the sin of stupidity; she explained that a little girl, who was also an heiress, must never let the opportunity slip to better herself so that she could grow up and marry a millionaire and wear diamonds and sables and ride to balls in six-horse coaches; if a little girl *did* let her opportunities waste, Amelia quoted from the Bible: "so shall thy poverty come as one that traveleth"; and paused, for the result.

"I have traveleth," Marie said, still staring across at her mother, "to see my mama's shiny black eyes, my new brother and my little sister and especially my handsome, rich papa!"

And what could Amelia Feaster reply to that by way of rebuke or reprimand? She turned to her husband, "Come here! Greet my wicked daughter. . . . That's right. Be friends."

With a sweet smile, Jacob put his arms around Marie and said, "I'm delighted. I've worried about you being away from your family. Have you been unhappy?"

The next two years Marie ran wild in Greenville. There were high hills to gallop her horse over; fascinating games to play in the streets and on cool green lawns with manly, goggling boys; stick hockey; pistol shooting (Marie had a remarkable eye); pop-the-whip. There were thick woods all around where boys and a girl, provided she was a tom-boy, could take a lunch and find arrowheads and pull off their shoes and wade in the rocky brooks and hunt for chinquapins. And if Amelia Feaster had suddenly become too respectable a matron to countenance such a hoyden for a daughter, why Jacob and Hannah and Stobo kept these escapades from her. Amelia thought Marie an odd one at any rate and rarely bothered to ask where she had been or who she had been playing with.

But one spring day when Marie was twelve, Amelia looked down from the upstairs piazza and saw her lying on the grass under a tulip tree beside a husky youth. The sunshine flickering on Marie's yellow hair made leafy patterns on her bare throat and pointed up the fact that her muslin dress had all at once got far too tight across her chest. The boy was nibbling at a peach and exchanging a juicy kiss with Marie for every other nibble.

For an instant Amelia was powerless. Then her eyes began to spark ominously. She hit the banister with her fist and called, "Marie, come upstairs."

Marie's voice floated back, rippling with merriment. "No, I won't. Willie and I are going to find more peaches."

And when Amelia looked again there was no one under the leafy tree and she had to squint her eyes to see that tufts of grass were slowly rising in stiff spears from where the two young ones had been lying.

Mr. Feaster was a worthy, clever man, employed in the commissary storehouses, but he was principally known as the fourth husband of a quite noted woman whom he married as Mrs. Boozer, formerly Mrs. Burton, formerly Mrs. Somebody else—a Philadelphia woman by birth.

James G. Gibbes, Philadelphia Times,
September 20, 1880

4

Amelia sent Stobo downtown in the buggy for her husband. "Tell him to come home at once. Stop whatever he's doing. It's terribly important."

A younger son of a plantation family, Jacob Feaster was at the time making an excellent salary managing a large warehouse in Greenville. When he married Amelia Boozer his family in Fairfield, friends of the Newberry Boozers, had been outspoken in their disapproval. Later it had astonished them when they had learned of the birth of a daughter, and that Amelia was well liked in Greenville and active in woman-ways in the life of the town. And when a son was born, they relented and wrote to Jacob, though it did not lessen their dislike of his wife.

Jacob reached home this afternoon to find Amelia waiting for him. She turned away impatiently when he leaned forward to kiss her cheek. Jacob handed Stobo his gray beaver hat and sighed deeply. After seven years of marriage, he was beginning to ponder on the nature of his wife's affection for him.

Physically Jacob Feaster was a medium-sized man with a good pair of shoulders but a poor carriage of them. His expression was mild and his smile of an unusual sweetness. His hair and eyes were soft and honey-colored. His nose was straight, his lips sensitive and his chin on the tender side. Only his thick neck and his strong hips betrayed the passion of which he was capable and which had interested Amelia Feaster with her malicious smile and her glittery eyes for a little while. But Amelia was not by nature a warm woman nor an affectionate one, and before Jay was weaned she had begun to resort to the usual backache and headache excuses. And Jacob, being a lazy sort of man, to whom discord was hateful, gave in to her on that as he did on other things so that he could enjoy a peaceful kind of life.

Now, though she had rebuffed his caress, she looked so glad to see him that Jacob knew she was going to ask him to do something he wasn't going to approve. Without even a how was your work today, Amelia said, "I have to talk to you—now. Come in the parlor."

"All right. What is it this time—a new dress? You know I like to give you dresses. Come on, kiss me. You are looking very handsome this afternoon and I have a yearning to—"

Amelia's mouth tightened. "I am going to leave Greenville. There's no future here for the children. Marie's already being fast with boys. I saw her today kissing that big Willie C. in the yard. I know her kind. And I'll die if she doesn't marry well. A rich man. And there aren't any rich men in Greenville."

Appalled by Amelia's ugly tone of voice and the way she looked at him as if he were a total stranger—which is a shocking experience for a young husband of twenty-seven—Jacob sat down suddenly.

Amelia stopped. She collected her thoughts and controlled her vehemence. She fetched a pillow and put it behind Jacob's head and pecked him with her lips on his soft chin.

Jacob said tiredly, "What do you want me to do?"

"Move back to Columbia. All the prominent people in the state come and go there. I thought first of Charleston. But Charleston wouldn't do. We'd never get into society there. They're as snobbish as Philadelphians. But Columbia is full of people from everywhere. Marie could meet the richest young men in the state and—"

Jacob sighed. It was an evil day.

"Amelia—we aren't society people. I am an ordinary man and my life is ordinary and it pleases me to remain ordinary."

"That's not true. The Feasters *are* society people. You are just lazy."

"What you are suggesting is impossible."

"You can easily get work in Columbia."

"Then I'll be blunt."

"Go ahead."

"You have been talked about in Columbia."

"Oh foot! Years ago. Nobody ever really accused me of—"

"They accused you of having an affair with Hugh Toland. He had to leave Columbia on account of their talking. And, believe me, he was more popular there than you ever were. You haven't a chance of crashing into Columbia society." Jacob was angry now. He found Amelia almost repulsive with her set white face, her high-necked wool jacket with green pleats on the breast, her skirt with rippling stripes like a snake's skin. She was staring at him steadily and her eyes were so terrible that he suddenly dreaded to look at her.

"You must, Jacob," she whispered, breathing erratically against his cheek. "Say that you will or I will die. If you will, I promise you that I'll never refuse to sleep with you again. Never. I'll do any way you like. And I'll be so good in Columbia. So happy. Wait and see. Do this for me Jacob—just this and—" She was tearing open her jacket. Coal black eyes—lips red as rubies—her breath coming hotly—her bare breasts—

At this time Columbia was a small but beautiful town situated on a ridge of high land just below the confluence of the Broad and Saluda rivers and on the eastern side of the Congaree. It had been conceived and built for the capital city of South Carolina when Charleston's accessibility to the enemy by sea and inaccessibility to the patriots of the Up and Backcountry by land had been demonstrated during the Revolutionary War.

Accordingly, in 1796 the plantation of Thomas and James Taylor having been chosen as *the* spot (Mr. Taylor remarked some years later that "a damned good cotton plantation had been spoiled to build a damned poor town") a two-mile square was laid out as the township of Columbia. The streets running north and south were named for Revolutionary generals, those east and west for the fruits of the field and the forest. In ten years the capital city was an accomplished fact with wide, tree-shaded streets, and many beautiful dwelling houses designed by or in the style of the South Carolina architect, Robert Mills, and his teacher, Benjamin Latrobe. There were whole squares of lush semitropical parks and gardens. And there was an unusually large number of lavishly appointed hotels, boardinghouses, public houses, taverns, livery stables and shops, so that the legislators could live in the manner to which some of them had been accustomed, when the governing body convened in session.

During the sittings of the legislature, Columbia was gay as a carnival, at other times it assumed the sleepy tranquillity of a village. But, with its aura of eminent political figures, so picturesquely headed by Charles Pinckney, John C. Calhoun, Preston Brooks and the three Wade Hamptons, its classic old State House on a beautiful eminence of monarchal oaks giving it an air of antiquity, its Wren-like Town Hall and columned Court House, the rising *new* State House of marble and domes, in sixty years it had attained a dignity and an air of high society both, and of both it was fiercely proud.

Jacob easily found a good position in Columbia managing several government storehouses and he rented a house from Mr. Bausket on the corner of Washington Street and Sumter one block down from the Town Hall on Main. It was a typical square colonial brick building with four stories including the basement. Charm was given the house by deep piazzas on both the first and second floors with iron balcony railings decorated with brass knobs at intervals, and an iron railing surrounding the flat copper roof like a crown.

Unlike the houses of the period, the staircase up to the second story was at the eastern side of the hall, hidden from view, being concealed in a small room, known as the staircase room. The wide halls, both upstairs and down, were flanked on the west side by two twenty-five-foot square rooms with high ceilings and French windows.

The house slaves lived in the basement. The dining room and a study were on the first floor; a drawing room and a bedroom on the second floor; and the stairs came out of the little side room and curved prettily from the second to the top story which was divided into three bedrooms and a nursery.

The drawing room was filled with new-style Victorian furniture all covered in red velvet, and there were heavy claret-colored draperies suspended from elaborately carved gilt cornices at the French windows. The black marble mantel, with a deep fireplace, had for ornament two alabaster vases holding red and blue wax flower bouquets under glass bells and a tall brass clock with naked cupids leaping over monkeys' backs and swinging in vine swings. The floors were of checkered wood and waxed and there were handsome bas-reliefs on the walls and ceiling, in a garland rose design bordered with moldings of gold.

To top such grandeur, Amelia designed, and had Mr. P. F. Frazee, the Yankee coachmaker, build, a pot-bellied, painted coach with hinged glass windows and silver lamps and brass handles and all the inside lined in sky-blue satin. This equipage was so much gaudier than elegant that it was called by respectable Columbians "the showbox," or the "glass case." Jacob cringed whenever he was forced to drive about the town in it with his wife.

In settling the Feaster family properly, Amelia spent a lot of Marie's money and all of Jacob's. She was delighted with her surroundings and so full of confidence that she bought an oversize silver card tray and put it on the hall table to be ready to hold all the little engraved white visiting cards that would be dropped there by the great ladies of the town.

But Jacob was bereft of confidence, knowing what was going to come about. For he went downtown every-day and he heard the whispers and the rumors, or at least sensed them, in the guarded remarks of his former friends and his working associates. He knew he had been unwise to let Amelia influence him, but he had hoped the move would perhaps be the beginning of a change back to their former relationship. Instead the change had been inside him and her.

This new Amelia, Jacob realized, just went to show you. Went to show you, as his sister had said at the time he had married in such haste, that you should never wed a woman whose chimney smoke you could not see from your own back door.

Nature and environment were very kind to Mary, for in addition to growing rapidly in the direction of being a great beauty, her stepfather gave her his undivided parental affections and lavished wealth and opportunities on her with unstinted hands, yielding to her every caprice, . . . and soon she became the most beautiful and accomplished young lady in the city, this being conceded by both sexes, impossible as it may seem.

HERALD & NEWS *of Newberry, S. C.,*
August 6, 1909

5

There was an exclusive girls' school in the town run by Madame Togno, a shrewd French woman. Jacob Feaster wisely went alone to see if Madame would undertake the task of fashioning a lady out of his stepdaughter. His manners correct and his Fairfield background proper, Madame agreed to interview the supplicant *and* the mother the next afternoon.

It was a sickeningly hot day but from the tips of her gray, glove-kid slippers laced around her ankles to the one pink rose on her floppy leghorn hat, Marie, trembling with pleasure, was *corsage á la Watteau* in pale-pink muslin with yards of mull flounces and a crushed sash of gray satin binding her waist.

"Lord!" exclaimed Amelia, "I must say the outfit was worth the price."

The Negro woman in blue homespun and a high, starched turban who opened Madame Togno's door to them curtsied to Marie and nodded her head at Amelia, taking her for the child's governess.

After a few minutes in the parlor with Madame, Marie was summoned by the Negro woman to come and get some lemonade and ginger cakes. Marie sat on a gilded cane sofa in the wide, restful hall papered with scenes from towering Greek ruins, in soft browny-cream tones, and watched a waving pattern of lines and shadows swaying with the motion of the tall pine outside the fan-shaped transom.

Marie's dreams soared. This house would be her stepping stone into the world she was destined to inhabit. All her life she had felt she was a changeling left by fate on the wrong doorstep. Big Dave Boozer hadn't been her real father. Amelia wasn't her real mother. Amelia was the black-haired Jay and Evie's mother. Amelia had stolen her away from her real mother. *Her* mother had light hair and gentle eyes. *Her* mother was soft-voiced and sweet and smelled of violets. *Her* mother wore white muslin tea-gowns with long trains decorated in knots of pale-pink ribbon. *Her* mother. . . .

She tiptoed to the door of the parlor and listened to Amelia airily explaining to Madame Togno how yesterday she had had a letter from her cousin Drexel in Philadelphia and from her cousin Biddle only last week and before classes started she planned to take Marie to visit her uncle Pew in Swarthmore. And, Amelia went on, she simply adored living in the South except that she could never like hominy for breakfast and rice for dinner every day. She hated watermelons and sweet potatoes and greasy turnip greens. She would not eat hot buttered biscuits without discretion and ruin *her* figure! And, oh, Law! but she missed the opera and dancing at the Assembly and hearing the lectures to which she had been accustomed in Philadelphia.

Madame Togno listened incredulously while a flybrush boy with a bunch of peacock feathers brushed flies off the iced tea and fondant cakes. Finally, when Amelia's tales swelled too fantastically, Madame Togno jerkily opened a blue enamel watch pinned on her scant bosom and harshly said *Tiens!* it was twenty minutes past four and the very rich Colonel Preston, uncle-in-law of the fabulously rich Wade Hampton, III, was bringing his daughters at four-thirty which, *bon chance,* was now, to speak about entering them in her school. And *they* had been in Paris for years, simply years!

Hearing a bustle at her gates Madame called her

daughter, Ascèlie, to greet Colonel Preston while she directed Amelia and Marie *Vite! Vite!* out through the back door. Amelia resolutely continued chattering, but Madame was made of as tough material as she. So finally Amelia gave way in the face of Madame's cold silence and said a formal good-by and that she did hope Marie would prove a tractable pupil and—then Madame wearied and desperately opened the door to the hall leading onto the front piazza where Colonel John S. Preston, the six-foot-four Beau Brummel of Columbia, immaculate in a white linen suit and fine ruffled shirt, was coming up the steps followed by his daughters, Sally Buchanan and Mary.

Colonel Preston stared at Amelia who held out her fingers to him. He took a pair of spectacles from his pocket, put them on and then quickly removed them and pushed disdainfully past her. In his haste, he walked straight into Marie.

"Oh—Oh—do excuse this clumsy big gentleman— Oh dear—whose pretty little miss are you?" Colonel Preston took off his wide-brimmed Panama hat and resting on his gold-headed cane, bowed gracefully to Marie. Tossing her curls invitingly, Marie put one shapely foot forward, caught a flounce in a hot, white-kid-gloved hand and made a curtsy, all the while looking up out of the corner of her eyes as if she desired to say *My* what a handsome man you are!

Instead she said, "*I* am Mary Sarah Boozer of Newberry, and I think I am going to study here."

"Ah!" he nodded pleasantly, as if he were accustomed to little girls who looked invitingly at him. "Tell your papa he'd better keep you under lock and key when you get a little older or I will come and steal you away." He disappeared into the dark hall, his enormous patent-leather pumps twinkling with a sort of delicacy.

Behind Colonel Preston, his daughter, Sally Buchanan, or Buck, as she was called, wearing a cool, purple-flowered calico dress and a plain Scotch tam-o'-shanter, glowered at Marie Boozer. Marie jumped down two steps, turned, and triumphantly stuck out a pointed tongue at Mistress Buck who, until this moment, had been the undisputed budding beauty of Columbia.

Inside, a shaken Madame Togno said, as she sipped a glass of fairly old Madeira, *"Hélas,* Colonel Preston, I must ask you to gossip with me a moment and tell me what you've heard of Jacob Feaster's wife. She has affected me uncomfortably."

"Oh—I hear *she* is quite notoriously wicked. Quite. Poisoned poor old Peter Burton, her no. 2 husband. Then when she lived in Newberry she gambled—had an affair with you-know-who and finally shot Big Dave Boozer's head off; but reformed since Jacob Feaster got ahold of her and is now said to be the wiliest social climber in the state."

"Then you would advise me not to take the daughter as a pupil? I didn't want to in the first place. Her eyes disturbed me, taking on the color of everything she looked at. Poor Mr. Feaster was such a nice young man—"

"No, Lord no, take the daughter by all means. She was the child we passed on the piazza?"

"Yes—what did you think of her?"

"I thought she was unbelievably beautiful."

Meanwhile, as they stepped over a pair of Colonel Preston's small, liveried black footmen playing marbles under the giant pine tree and passed his graceful French landau and climbed in the ponderous "showbox," Marie kept trilling loudly, "Where is my uncle Pew? And why haven't I ever met my cousin Biddle or my cousin Drexel?"

"Shut up. Someone may hear you!"

"But what about my cousins and my uncle?" Marie insisted stubbornly. "Why haven't I—"

Yanking one of Marie's curls, Amelia drew her close and whispered into her ear, "You haven't because they don't exist. But you must have family connections to *be* somebody in this town. It's just a little joke we'll play on Madame. And you must promise not to tell Papa Feaster what I said to Madame Togno. It'll be our little secret, hey? Don't you like to have clever little secrets with Mama?"

Marie wasn't sure. This was suddenly a new Mama; a too close Mama. Marie pouted out her mouth and stared at the high-stepping sorrels frantically thrashing their bobbed tails at the gnats and yellow flies swarming about their sweaty hindquarters.

"So, if you study hard and make friends with the rich, aristocratic girls you'll meet at Madame Togno's, that is, *if* you get in, you'll be invited to all the balls when you grow up and marry a count and take Mama to Paris and Rome and—"

"Will I go to the Assembly in Philadelphia where you used to dance?"

"I never danced at the Assembly. You know I was married the first time before I was fourteen. What a fool I was! But your grandmother was the belle of Philadelphia. When she was young she was so startlingly beautiful that her family made her go veiled whenever she went on the street. Even veiled, crowds followed after her. At one of the balls she wore a diamond tiara and everybody thought she was the Queen of Sweden; or some queen."

"Was that your mother?"

Amelia laughed; a bitter laugh. "No, not my mother."

"Grandma Burton?"

"What?"

"Wasn't my real father's name Peter Burton?"

"Oh—shut up. Did you see him snub me? Did you?"

"Who?"

"Colonel Preston, ninny."

"Yes, I did. You've never met him before and you pretended you had. And all those things you told Madame Togno were lies. That about my grandmother is a lie too." Marie hid her face in her hands and wept with mortification and indignation.

For once, Amelia did not exert herself to pinch or slap Marie. She slapped at a mosquito and hummed *Old Rosin the Beau*.

Sucking her thumb, five-year-old Evie was waiting at the gate when the coach stopped in a spray of sand. "Did you get in?" she shrieked, grabbing at Marie's skirt. "Did you get in? Hannah said she bet you didn't."

Amelia, sounding cross, said, "Dry up. How would we know yet? Where is your father?"

Evie said to Marie, "I knew you wouldn't. I knew you wouldn't."

Holding little Jay on one shoulder, and Jay's big yellow tomcat on the other Jacob was waiting behind the green curtain of vines on the piazza. Marie ran and flung her arms around his waist. "If she takes me in her school, it will be because of you. O, I do love you, Papa Feaster."

Amelia kicked at the cat and said to Marie, "Take off those clothes. You're getting cat hair on that frock!"

Jacob put Marie from him gently, "Such a red-faced little one. Put on your linen riding dress and let's take a gallop down Mill Creek Road and cut across Millwood. We might catch a glimpse of Mr. Hampton exercising one of his race horses. Perhaps he'll ask us to stop for tea. It's shady all the way so you won't get sunburned."

Marie, her anger dissipated in the face of Jacob's gentleness, ran inside as if she were borne on wings. Jacob called to Stobo to fetch the saddle horses. Amelia began unplaiting her long hair and said she would change into a muslin sacque.

"Don't take your hair down on the front piazza."

"What difference does it make?"

Jacob looked at Amelia, not with anger but with open astonishment. "Tomorrow it will be all over Columbia that you were out on the front piazza with your hair down."

"Better that than to have them whispering I was mooning in the hall by an empty card tray." She snatched at the combs holding the figure-eight knot on her neck.

"You mustn't," Jacob said in an imploring voice. "I tell you, my dear, you mustn't do this. Come into the hall. I will continue to beg Sister to come from Winnsboro and introduce you to some of her friends."

"I met one of her friends yesterday morning," Amelia said, looking angrily at Jacob's perturbed face.

"Who? Where?"

"It was too awful," Amelia whispered, with a look of intense pain, "too awful!"

"Well—tell me—" Jacob was angry and he reproached himself for he knew he had been at fault to have allowed Amelia to persuade him to leave Greenville. What could he say to her? Yet he must say something. After all she was his wife. They faced a long time together. To say outright to her, "I told you how it would be. And it is." He had not the heart. Nor could he say, "I'm sorry. I love you." For search as he might, there was mighty little spark of that left. Lust at times but no more love. And so he listened quietly while the words gushed out.

"The handle of the coach door came loose yesterday while Stobo and I were driving home from Mrs. Smith's shop. We stopped by Mr. Frazee's to have him tighten it. It was beginning to rain a little so Mr. Frazee directed Stobo to pull inside the workroom. While he was tightening the screws, Mrs. Goodwyn and Sally drove in. Something was wrong with the axle of her carriage. It began to rain hard. I leaned out of the coach and said, 'I'm leaving now, Mrs. Goodwyn, and will be happy to drive you and Sally home.'"

"That was friendly of you. Why—"

"Mrs. Goodwyn acted as if I'd invited her to accompany me to a bawdy house. She said, 'Mercy, no! No! oh, no!' and turned and flew out of the coach house dragging Sally with her. It was pouring down rain by that time. Mr. Frazee said she looked like a chicken with its head wrung off the way she went jerking out of the coach house."

Jacob said slowly, "Evidently she was one of poor Mrs. Toland's friends."

"You promised never to mention that name to me again. That is the past. It's the present that's so wrong. I have come to hate this house and this street and the people. I am sick of our dull, dreary life. I want to be invited to the big white houses on Sumter Street and to the Preston mansion and to dance and play cards and—"

Jacob stammered, "I—Amelia—I understand. But

if Marie is accepted in Madame Togno's school and if you'll just be quiet and genteel for a few years things will change. Marie will do well in the school and then Evie can get in and of course Jay will be invited everywhere and—"

Jacob suddenly fell silent realizing that he was saying nothing, that his expression was stupid and his voice strained. And Amelia, he knew, could read the truth in his eyes, for she pinched her lips into a tight little heart, looked at him with dislike and contempt.

"I'm going to send Stobo around to Mr. Frazee's and invite him to come and play cards with us this evening. He told me yesterday a man from Philadelphia was in town. Perhaps he'll bring him. That will make four of us. I'm hungry for a good card game."

"No. No, Amelia. I do realize that you are bored in Columbia and that you have been hurt. But Mr. Frazee is suspected of being an abolitionist. A friend of his from up North might be one of those underground railroad people who are encouraging our slaves to run away. I won't permit you to become intimate with such people. Feeling in Columbia is growing against them. I wish to heaven I'd never allowed you to have Frazee build that coach. Mr. Carroll could have made just as outlandish a one. And Carroll's a Southerner."

Amelia replied dryly and coldly, and very rudely, "Southerner! Southerner! You don't seem to realize that a person from up North can get mighty tired of Southerners, do you?"

Jacob uttered a choked sound of outrage, "Yes. I realize it. It works both ways." He went inside, slamming the door behind him.

"Good riddance," Amelia said loudly.

She sat on the joggling board and began tearing her hair out of the smooth plaits. Across the street Henry Timrod, the poet, coming out of the newspaper office stared with open-mouthed curiosity as she shook the heavy rope of her plait in his direction. He only saw the masses of black hair not the humiliation and the hate which was making Amelia do this bizarre thing. Loosing her hair on the front piazza because she had

come back to Columbia planning to be respectable
and rich and happy and yesterday had been cut by a
silly woman; and Madame Togno had treated her today
as if she had been dirt under her feet; Colonel Preston had looked at her as indifferently as if she had no
sex at all; Jacob Feaster had spoken to her, just now,
as if she were one of Dutch Rose's girls from the Holy
Land down Main Street. So she was loosing her hair
on the piazza because she hated this whole town and
everybody in it and someday she would find a way to
pay it all back.

She was consumed with jealousy, anger, and frus-
trated ambition. She wanted to stamp her feet on the
floor and scream aloud. Stamp and scream. She had
planned so well when she had bewitched the old man
and made a fool of him. Yet here she was right back in
a town she hated and that hated her. Where had she
lost her senses? Oh—she knew all right. In Greenville
when she had been witless enough to think the people
who had pursued Hugh Toland out of town would
welcome her. Almost every day she could see Jacob
blush with shame for her. See him humbled by her
past conduct. And yet if he had been richer none of
this would have occurred. If a person had money
enough they could love whom they liked and no one
would continue to hold it against them. If one were
rich enough they could befuddle old men and get rid
of them and it would not be considered a sin at all.
Money, as she had always known, was the important
thing. Plenty of money.

She was independent, clever, bold and, yes, she would
face it, a bit depraved. Not excessively so. Just a little.
And there was no reason for her to grow stale; nor to
live like everyone else. She would live by her own
rules. Never forgetting her objective. But she must not
let her nerves give way again as they had done a few
minutes ago with Jacob. She would make no further
attempts to get "in."

She would concentrate on getting "out." But how
would she ever have enough money to get away? Certainly Jacob, who was content to be an ordinary

man, would never make a fortune. It went back, as it always did, to Marie.

It grew more evident every day that Marie was going to be a great beauty. And more—in addition to her angel face, she had the power to please and a soft heart. It would be easy to use Marie as her pawn to checkmate fate. She was almost positive Madame was going to take Marie in the school. That automatically meant Marie would be in society. That was all she need bother about right now. What she herself did on the quiet from now on was nobody's business but her own.

Across the street Julian Selby, the young newspaper editor appeared with the poet, Timrod, and looked over toward her piazza. With trembling fingers Amelia quickly fastened her hair up and caught it with the wire combs. She came to the steps so that the poet could see that her hair was *not* loose on the piazza. She waved at Julian Selby. He was an attractive young man.

For a moment she considered calling and inviting him and the poet to come over and have a glass of Madeira with her. But remembering Jacob's plea that she not invite Mr. Frazee and his friend and knowing how annoyed he would be if she did, she summoned Stobo and directed him to follow her upstairs and take a note from her to Mr. Frazee inviting him and his friend to come to her house for a game of cards that evening.

6

Marie was accepted in Madame Togno's school and
entered on a girlhood tinted with gentility. She learned
how to enter and leave a room with grace; to pour tea
with charm; to play with a fan and talk frizzle frazzle
for hours in French or German or Italian as well as in
English; to use and understand the globes; to read
every novel she could lay her hands on, especially
French novels; best of all to take dancing lessons
from Madame Feugas and Monsieur Berger, two of the
most skillful teachers in the South.

But during the recreation and leisure hours things
were different.

The first day one of the girls said, "I hear your
mother has been married four times. Where does she
bury her dead?"

Marie did not answer but ran away and shinnied up
the tall pine tree by the piazza.

Never, never would she speak to that dreadful girl
again! Even though her father *was* a senator.

Beyond the Jail, on the next square, she spied a
group of Arsenal cadets playing a game of ball on a
wooded knoll. With fiery cheeks and an angry heart,
she climbed down and ran across the way.

The cadets received her with derision and disbelief
when she told them how straight she could throw a
ball. "You're too soft and curly."

"I'm not. I'm not," she cried, biting her lip. "Let me

play with you. You must—you must. I'm not like other girls. See—how strong I am. Feel my muscle. And look how fast I can run!"

"We'll take a vote."

"Oh, wonderful—I knew you all would let me play."

From then on, she joined them frequently and on the days she didn't come they sneaked around the Jail and perched on Madame Togno's fence to see what had happened to their gay, rebellious comrade.

So, swiftly, two years passed with Marie resolutely holding her own in the school.

She held her own because she was obsessed with the desire to grow up and have fun all over the world and be a grand lady and marry a man she loved as much as she had loved Big Dave and be happy and beloved forever and ever. Amen.

And because the boys appeared wherever *she* appeared the other girls in the school invited her to their houses to tea parties and dances and candy pulls. Oh, Marie realized *why* they included her in their social affairs. Already she had an instinctive understanding of her sex and she knew that the girls, rather than accepting her as one of them, grew more wary of her as her hair turned even a brighter yellow, her breasts thrust out and her ankles proved to be slenderer and shapelier than the marble Venus's ankles in the art history books. "Just watch how *I* can make the boys look at *me!*" she would whisper to herself when one of those superior girls flaunted a governor or a signer to compare with plain Big Dave Boozer. And too, at that time Marie looked older than she was—and this was another mark against her. For of what use the figure of a woman when everyone knew she could not be more than fourteen at the most?

"You must act your age," Madame cautioned her. "And lessen your flamboyant appearance by behaving shyly and modestly and remaining at all times in the background. Never forget beauty is of the soul and not of the face."

Her quickness in her studies, her lightness in the dance also widened the bridge between these girls and Marie. But she never held herself back nor was she

ever lonely for if she had any free time she would be off
on her thoroughbred gelding Tulip, purchased from
Mr. Wade Hampton, in wind, rain or sun seeking
pleasure and gaiety somewhere with someone. And
packs of bewitched males gathered on street corners
to admire her riding by and followed her up and down
the city ways.

Thus it came about that on an early November
day, in 1860, Marie again sat on the gilded cane sofa
in Madame Togno's hall and clasped and unclasped her
chilly hands. This was her last hour in the school.
The school she had entered with such a determination
to be good and clever and ladylike. She rose and went
to the wall and studied herself a long time in a round
mirror. So this was the way a "fast girl" looked: a girl
with red cheeks and, today, big green eyes, and a green
velvet riding costume, a white silk scarf knotted at
her throat. And a green hat with a flowing green chif-
fon veil.

She heard Madame in the parlor ask the Negress
with the high turban if Stobo had fetched the horse
yet. If Marie Boozer had gone for good. She tightened
the scarf at her throat. In minutes now her association
with this lovely house would be over. She closed her
eyes and remembered the way the parlor had looked
the first day: old Plato sitting on the mantel, the pink
Dresden clock ticking happily, the sun striking on the
finial of the gilt harp, the smell of rose and lilac leaves.

On arriving this morning, when she had gone to take
off her hat in the cloakroom a scared-faced Mary
Preston had handed her the letter. Marie was glad it
had been Mary and not Buck. Mary was kind and
sorry. Buck would have been triumphant.

Marie sat on a footstool and read the letter:

Dear Mistress Mary,

I have sent a communication to your stepfather in the
city advising him that your fast behavior of yesterday
makes it imperative for me to refuse to consider you any
longer as a pupil in my school. Your stepfather will,
naturally, receive a refund on your tuition and your marks
will be scrupulously recorded so that you will not have
any trouble, scholastically, in entering another school.

I will not elaborate your ruthlessly riding your horse over my new rye grass with a horde of shouting South Carolina College students and Arsenal cadets leaping about like apes to catch hold of your horse's bridle. Had you given them no encouragement this escapade could never have occurred. Last evening I received no less than ten visits from outraged mothers whose precious daughters had been roughly shoved and almost trampled underfoot as they sought to enter my gate. And to top the whole, when you dared Buck Preston to mount your wicked horse and jump him over the fence and he reared and she was thrown, you laughed! Yes—you were heard to laugh. Be it to Buck's generosity she insists she was not injured and the whole affair was in fun. But endangering the lives and limbs of my best pupils does not amuse me.

Therefore I must ask you to consider yourself expelled from my school and to leave on the instant. Regardless of your superior standing in your classes. I am unable, being an ambitious woman, to tolerate such a hazard as you. However, I shall always hold your ability in regard.

> And I remain your friend,
> *Madame Togno.*

Marie put the letter back in the envelope. Stobo was waiting outside with Tulip. She could see him through the side glass of the door. The tall-turbaned Negress, her eyes hooded against Marie, opened the front door. Madame did not come to say good-by. The letter was a lie and Madame knew it. It wasn't the admirers or daring Buck Preston to ride Tulip. Madame had made up her mind the first day—when she met Amelia— not to keep Marie in her school. Until now, she'd not been able to find any excuse to get rid of her. Just yesterday, for the first time, Marie had been carried away and done a foolish thing. She pulled on her chamois gauntlets and straightened her back.

"You should of known better than to cut up with this woman," Stobo grumbled as he held out his hands for Marie to step in to mount Tulip. "She's as tough as your ma and that's going some."

"Don't fuss, Stobo. You'll make me cry."

They rode down the street. The air smelled of winter and the gray sky made harsher the outlines of the leafless trees.

Amelia was standing in the hall with Jacob when

she reached home. "Marie, what are you doing home at this hour? How pale you are. Are you ill? Come in—come in. We are all excited. Mr. Frazee just called by fetching a telegram that said Abraham Lincoln has been elected President of the United States."

Jacob Feaster spoke up, "And that means all the radicals from up North will be down here at once inciting our slaves to John Brown raids and what have you. It makes me sick."

"And it makes me happy. Come in, Marie, the wind is blowing."

Marie entered and said, "I've been expelled from Madame's school."

Amelia said, "Prosperity, that's what it means. And interesting people."

"It means South Carolina will probably secede from the United States."

"Foot! It wouldn't dare."

"Didn't you all hear what I said?" Marie looked incredulously from Jacob to Amelia.

"Sorry, darling." Absent-mindedly Jacob took the letter Marie handed him and put it in his pocket. He put on his hat and started for the front door. "I don't think I'll be home for dinner. I want to hear the talk at the State House."

"I'll get up a card game for tonight. I feel lucky."

They didn't care whether she had been expelled or not! They weren't even interested in her. Neither of them. Marie ran into the staircase room and started up the stairs. Amelia called after her, "It's terribly thrilling. Secession or not doesn't matter a whit to me. This election means change. That matters. It means all kinds of important men coming and going for us to be introduced to. That's what it means."

Marie ran on up to the third story and into her room. The big room, so comfortably furnished, suffocated her today. Amelia was following her saying, "It means Jacob can now make a lot of money. And money will give us an opportunity to show you off properly. Who cares about that snobbish old school? Why are you crying? You are so emotional. All we need—you and I—is a chance to meet people. That and plenty of money."

Once he read the letter Jacob immediately arranged for Marie to complete her studies at Columbia College. Most of the girls here were from other towns in the state and they had no prejudice against Marie; but, though she was always pleasant and agreeable, she held herself aloof and, despite the hubbub of life in a girls' school, she was solitary. For at Madame Togno's Marie had learned that it was no good for her to swap family tales and secrets with the other girls. She was not their match on that score. However, at Madame Togno's she *had* learned that she was the prettiest girl and that though they might snicker at the gaudy coach, the ultra-stylish, too grown-up clothes she wore, her mama's cigar-smoking, the Newberry tragedy and the other ugly things, the girls all wished they looked as she did and had the seat on a horse that she did and danced as she did and that the boys stared at them when *they* passed by the way they did at her.

But often Marie's heart was heavy. Amelia and Jacob were so rude to each other. They had become tyrants and enemies. As a matter of fact Amelia had changed in her attitude to all of the family from the summer day she had taken Marie to Madame Togno's. Soon after that was when she "got in" with the card-playing set, mostly drummers or people from the North who were working on the new State House. After Lincoln's election she changed even more. Jacob, who was growing afraid of her, tried by devious ways, such as persuading Marie to intervene, to urge Amelia to live more quietly and more respectably within their means. She just gambled more and more recklessly and bought more expensive clothes for herself and Marie.

Following the Secession of South Carolina from the United States when war talk began to boil up, Marie lay awake and prayed every night that war would come. She was ready for gay adventure and excitement. A war was now, apparently, the only way she would be able to come by it.

And so war came and she was ready for her part in it.

> Mary Boozer was the most beautiful piece of flesh and
> blood my eyes ever beheld.
>
> *Colonel John S. Preston*

7

February the eleventh, 1861, was set aside as Celebration Day in Columbia in honor of the formation of the Southern Confederacy. At noon, the signal being given by the fire bell in the tower of the Town Hall, all the bells of the city began clanging at once. The Negro bell ringers were swinging on the ropes in unusual glee, for many reasons, oblivious of the bugles blowing all over Columbia.

All of the city poured onto Main Street for the great event. Here came the mayor, Dr. John Boatwright, and Governor Manning and Governor Means and Colonel John S. Preston, in new gray uniforms with crimson sashes, brushing shoulders with shopkeepers from Butcher's Town and hard-eyed traders from Cotton Town and even Dutch Rose, who had brought her fancy girls out from the Holy Land to see what was going on!

The nuns with their students watched from the Convent garden on the corner of Blanding and Main Street. Young ladies in velvet and merino hoop skirts, their hair arranged in mesh nets, defied the sharp winter air and tripped over the paving stones in soft kid slippers, trying to follow or avoid the massing soldiers. Lawyers, legislators, judges, Negro barbers and serving men, Irish stonecutters working on the new State House, and children were everywhere in the mounting excitement, pushing their way to see the parade of the newly formed Confederate companies en route to Charleston to be on hand if an affair should develop following President Lincoln's cleverly conceived irritant—the sending of Yankee ships to provision Fort Sumter.

They were coming—Captain Wade Hampton's Dragoons, though he himself was in Mississippi and not leading them; the Columbia Grays; the Old Richland Guard; the Governor's Guards; the Congaree Mounted Riflemen; the Fairfield Fencibles; and the Butler Guards from Greenville: and after days of preparation Columbia was ready to give them her fervent blessing. The troops, hastily organized, were not all fully uniformed but who knew the difference? They had drilled, marched, wheeled, until each one knew his part if not with Prussian precision, at least with fanatic enthusiasm and undisciplined energy.

The Bonnie Blue Flag waved from hotels and taverns and stores and offices along Main Street and the house fronts were garlanded with smilax and native pine. Bands of brass instruments played by uniformed Negro musicians headed each regiment that was taking part in the presentation of the flags. The excitement was firing. Horsemen cantered to and fro along the sidewalks and through the crowd. Droves of little boys, Sandhill tackeys, yellow-skinned and leathery, nipped in and out crying their wares, "Want to buy any caged mocking birds, sassafrac, kindlin' wood torch?" Sandhill women, stumpy and strong and sandy-haired, held up bunches of pink trailing arbutus and narcissus tied with bits of straw; hucksters sold blue rosettes and palmetto cockades to put on hats and crimson ribbons to hang from ladies' shoulders; Daguerreans set up their cameras and snapped this happy face and that; merchants offered patriotic songs which had been hastily printed at Evan's and Cogswell's press: *The Bonnie Blue Flag, The Yellow Rose of Texas, Dixie's Land, The Secession March!*

The gentry of Columbia packed the decorated balconies. For this was not alone a celebration for the young and brave, but the culmination of their dreams as initiated by Saint John C. Calhoun and kept alive by the various lawyers, legislators and planters of the state.

To the common folk in the street, these aristocratic gatherings on the balconies to which the parading soldiers raised their swords, or touched their broad-brimmed hats and peaked caps, were the biggest part of the show and none more so than the group on the balcony of Jacob Feaster's house.

Jacob Feaster, marching with the Fairfield Fencibles, just behind Captain James Rion, lifted his hat and bowed slightly to his wife and called, "You look lovely, Marie!"

Marie and Jay waved and threw kisses at him. Evie, hurt at Jacob's overlooking her, made a hideous grimace at his departing back. Amelia was speculatively appraising the elegant young cavalrymen with the cold eyes of an expert making an inventory and didn't notice Jacob or Evie.

As the Fencibles turned onto Sumter Street and the Butler Guards approached and came to a halt and presented arms, the one who caught all eyes was Marie, standing at the edge of the balcony holding a fringed flag with a crimson border and a star in the center. She had on a Confederate-gray riding skirt with the long train looped up on her hip and a tight short jacket lavishly ornamented with flashing gilt buttons and with masses of gold fringed epaulets on her shoulders. On her head she wore a gray cavalry officer's hat with a yellow plume that was indistinguishable from the waterfall of yellow hair that cascaded down her back. And her eyes, taking on the color of her hat and dress, were as gray and exciting as the uniforms.

An officer on a high-stepping sorrel mare reined in his impatient mount and glanced excitedly at the Feaster balcony overhead, then back at his captain who motioned him to ride forward.

Marie shrieked, "Willie C.! You angel! Wherever did you come from?"

Marie leaned forward, waving the flag wildly. Willie C.! The boy with whom she had run away to Greenville when she was ten; who had kissed her so deliciously one long ago day under a gold-shadowed tulip tree! Four years older than she, he couldn't be more than eighteen now, and he was divinely handsome. He had short tightly curled brown hair, and his complexion was deeply tanned and his narrow face almost too classically featured. But his wide-apart faun-like eyes were lively and his ecstatic smile was utterly charming. His muscular body moved powerfully with every restless step of his fine-boned horse. Sparkling, she lifted the flag—the horns blared wildly "Hurrah! Hurrah! For Southern Rights Hurrah!" The crowd yelled, rather than sang the anthem. Many of them cried, "Marie—Marie!" instead of Hurrah!

She bent over the banisters to present the flag to Willie and as he reached up to take it, she was so intent on the way he was looking up at her that she whacked him right between the eyes with the staff.

The crowd roared. Willie fought to gain conrtol of his maddened mare and struck this way and that with the flag as the whole regiment scattered and then came together with wild whoops as Marie's merry laugh rang out and she impetuously threw her lacy handkerchief and her white kid gloves and pine branches and twirls of smilax into their midst.

All through the day flags were presented and addresses made and parades marched and at three o'clock a great picnic took place in the park at which Captain Casson of the Governor's Guards made an impassioned speech to his company telling them that the city expected them to "go forth and extinguish themselves."

In the late afternoon everybody gathered in front of the South Carolina College Hall for the finale: Mr. F. W. McMaster presenting to the Columbia Grays a white satin flag with gold stars and a gilt border and fringe with the head of the staff in the form of a palmetto tree. Marie, having tossed a blue velvet cape bordered with swan's-down over her gray riding habit was watching the ceremony from the "showbox." Amelia in a black velours hoop skirt and sealskin mantle was sitting beside her. From the Arsenal came a salvo of artillery fire. Cannons boomed, rifles rattled, fireworks shot up. Mr. McMaster spoke movingly but long. Marie kept seeking the crowd for Willie but his outfit had marched away somewhere.

Colonel Preston came riding by the old red oak under which the "showbox" stood among a crowd of fashionable equipages. He stopped beside the sleek, exquisitely balanced, light coach of the Elmores. Watching him.

Marie thought: he is comparing that coach with ours. It is like comparing a thoroughbred race horse with a heavy but showy circus horse. Oh, I wish that was our coach!

She folded back the glass windows and waved her gloves at Colonel Preston. He, always alert to the glance of a beautiful female, whatever her age, made his white stallion curvet and prance dashingly away from Grace Elmore and her mother.

The sun was setting in the darkling sky. As the Town Hall clock struck six, barrels of pitch that had been placed on every street corner were lighted to make bonfires; simultaneously all the public buildings and offices and dwellings and the whole State House were illuminated and a fiery prophetic glow enveloped the excited, happy city.

Amelia was ordering Stobo to fasten up the horses' heads and drive home, when Buck Preston, riding a Kentucky-bred bay, paced up alongside the "showbox." Buck had on a black velvet riding costume banded in ermine. Her long neck curved forward and her dark hair lay in a glossy coil low under a tall black beaver hat. Rudely, she ignored Amelia's presence and said with freezing dignity, "Marie, will you come for a little supper at our house tonight? My brother Willie has suggested that since Willie C. is invited, you might like to join us in our farewell party for the boys. I'll tell Willie C. to call for you at seven."

Before Marie could answer, Buck struck her horse hard and he jumped away from the showy coach carrying Buck to the safety of the Governor's open barouche where the Governor's lady, the lovely Lucy Holcombe Pickens, was languishing in a nest of Russian sables given her by the Czar of Russia. Buck spoke a few words to the lady and when the fabulous Lucy turned her big blue eyes toward the "showbox" and encountered an even bigger, bluer, more beautiful pair of eyes, Amelia pinched Marie on her knee and exclaimed —"Hussy! You made it! Mama knew you would."

In the early darkness the streets and parks were still massed with celebrating people. New soldiers tipsy on peach and honey, a potent brandy of the district, careened down all the ways. Hordes of masked revelers, calling themselves the Invisibles, up to all sorts of tricks and deviltry, roamed, secure in their disguises. This was a gay, mad night and the gentry, if they ventured out, had to take their risks.

At eight o'clock the guests began arriving at the Preston mansion. Built by the architect Robert Mills in the early 1800's for Ainsley Hall, the property was sold to General Wade Hampton of Revolutionary fame in 1820, and upon his death it was inherited by his daughter, Caroline Martha, the wife of Colonel John Preston. The house was set on a high brick basement with a broad, marble-tiled piazza flanking its entire front. At either end as well as in the middle of the piazza were marble steps leading into a garden, landscaped by a London artist, that covered a whole city square. The front door faced the middle steps and a driveway which entered from the street between massive iron gates. There were little Negro boys with torches everywhere and hundreds of wax candles in hurricane shades to light the drive.

Everyone of consequence was coming to the party: elderly couples in carriages, accompanied by their Negro maids and serving men with bundles of shawls and smelling salts and flagons of brandy; young officers on horseback; gallants bringing their girls in landaus and barouches.

The older gentlemen wore the tight breeches and swallow-tailed coats, the ruffled shirts and embroidered satin waistcoats and wide white cravats of the period. But the younger men were all in finely tailored gray uniforms with gilt buttons and gold braid and scarlet sashes.

The ladies reflected the same contrast of styles in their party costumes. Those older ones who still dreamed the dream of Calhoun's slave state as the perfect model for a republic came in elegant black or purple brocade and feathered hair ornaments, leaning on thin lacquered sticks, and quizzing the guests through lorgnettes on jeweled chains. All the young, however, wore exaggerated crinolines of pastel tulle and gauze and embroidered tissue cut shockingly low; their dainty feet sewed in satin slippers by their maids at the final enchanting minute before the mirror; and their hair hanging in heavy ringlets over bare sloping shoulders.

The wide, high-ceilinged hall was divided by a beautiful arch, beneath which a fine circular staircase climbed to the floor above. On either side of the hall were the east and west drawing rooms with tall French windows leading onto the piazzas and the gardens. Tonight the whole front of the house was thrown together making a magnificent ballroom.

Colonel and Mrs. Preston were standing in front of the white marble mantel, carved by Hiram Powers, in the east drawing room to receive their guests. Tall enough for her husband, Mrs. Preston was splendid in cream-colored velvet and point lace and diamonds.

The walls of the room, lit by a branchy crystal chandelier, were hung in tapestries and priceless paintings by great masters. Polished, satin-covered sofas from England, lacquered cabinets from Italy, dainty, gold-leaf chairs and tables from France had been pushed back to clear the floor for dancing.

In the hall, on each side of the front door, was a pair of long, black leather sofas holding an overflow of frothy girls and their beaux. At the far end of the hall, beside an antique Greek marble Venus in the crook of the stairs, Joe Randell, the popular free Negro musician, was standing with his orchestra. Joe was wearing a bottle-green dress coat lined with white silk, a yellow vest and pants, and a high, white silk hat. He was lifting his trumpet and signaling his men: Scipio, the slew-footed West Indian barber tuning up his fiddle; Catfish Dick Porter, the fisherman, with his silver flute; and pumpkin-colored John, a slave of Mr. Levi Sherman, trembling a Spanish tambourine.

Downstairs the dining room, dark with family portraits, was crowded with handsome Georgian and Adam furniture, and dozens of liveried Negroes, white-gloved, who presided at mahogany wine coolers of champagne and china punch bowls of eggnog and silver waiters piled with salads and game and oysters and ham and jellies and soufflés.

The first dance was a waltz and the next would be a cotillion. Everybody who had been invited was here except one couple. And then they came.

The cotillion had just been called; enough champagne and punch had been consumed to break down the stiffness of a provincial society unused to an army of vital, undisciplined soldiers. Suddenly there was an interruption in the rhythm of the voices in the room. The dancers continued the dignified movements of the cotillion, but not perfectly, for everybody was looking at the door. A girl was just arriving, pushing with her escort into the room through the crowd of stags lounging lazily near the doorway—a girl marked by her easy, rich, friendly laughter.

As she came toward Colonel and Mrs. Preston no one would have guessed that an hour ago she was raging in her bedroom declaring she would die before she would go where she knew she wasn't wanted or expected. She walked gracefully and gaily with more than a hint of abandon underlying the controlled delicacy of her steps. She wore white taffeta, cut low over her breast and trimmed in silver lace—endless flounces of silver lace holding her skirt out like a bell. Her skin was clear as satin, her cheeks pink with excitement and a fear of this moment. Her gold hair was done up in a Grecian knot and fine tendrils escaping made a halo around her face and on her neck. She knew she had outdressed the other girls her age but she never cared to go to a party looking like a girl who would rather not be stared at.

"Sah," called the Negro butler, Henry, from the door, "Cunnel Preston, Sah, Miss Marie Boozer and *hes*cort!"

Marie honored her hosts with a low curtsy and a whisper of *grandes dames* uncoiled like a hissing snake around the room. A fat lady sitting in front of a naked marble statue of Eve was waving a gigantic peacock feather fan with great dignity and saying loudly,

"And *everybody* knows what her mother is!"

Later Marie discovered the name of this lady. But

at that moment the lady was merely a hurting deep inside. Willie, too foolishly happy to have noticed or heard, gave Marie his arm and they turned and faced the room and young gentlemen swarmed like so many bees around Marie and Willie.

"The next waltz?"

"The Virginia reel?"

"The Spanish dance?"

"The grande marche?"

"The polka?"

The orchestra struck up a Strauss waltz and round and round Marie whirled with Willie, oblivious of everything except the sweet, swift music and the closeness of his heartbeats, the way his mouth looked, parted. Ah! she was grown up. She was in love. She was beloved. All her life must be like this!

Round and round she danced—light as a cloud, cool and vital as first spring. Nothing to worry about . . . nothing . . . nothing. Her mother had been right to make her come. The Prestons had been kind, even Buck and Mary; especially Mary. Everybody was looking at her and talking about her. *She* would have more supper plates fetched her and more glasses of syllabub and champagne offered than any girl there. She was completely happy. As happy as she would ever be in all her life!

During a reel she let Willie C. take her out onto the marble-tiled piazza. But against every Doric column leaned a lazy handsome boy in uniform. So Willie led her down a set of marble steps at the far end of the piazza into the dark garden.

As far as Marie could see there was nothing but black tree trunks and a maze of boxwood-bordered paths, lighted at intervals by torches. But when she and Willie finally neared the end of his chosen path, she saw a sparkle of illuminated water spraying from a magnificent marble fountain.

"Oh—Oh—how glorious!" she whispered.

"This fountain," Willie said, not knowing what to say, "came from Italy or maybe Athens."

Marie said, "I wonder how Italy smells, and Greece? As sweet as here?"

And Willie said, "You are smelling the torches warming the boxwood leaves. Do you like it?"

And the brilliant water and the black-green garden and everything seemed as unreal as a dream. An interlude of perfection, but bittersweet because when Willie went away—

She gazed at the fountain, the jetting pulse of the fountain beating on his intent, slightly flushed face. She felt a violent rising in her throat. His brown hair was blowing in the wind. Her fingers trembled to touch it.

"Your eyes," he cried, "show all the rainbow colors of the fountain!"

When he kissed her the first time she put up her hands and pushed him away and stared up at him in a sort of voluptuous astonishment.

And then he was kissing her and holding her tight, but respectfully, against him and all the while running his hand up and down her back over the silver flounces as if she were a ruffled white dove.

At the Feaster house Jacob was packing his necessaries in a canvas bag. Amelia, cigar in mouth, was studying how to get a card from the bottom of a pile without Jacob noticing. The gas lamps in the second floor parlor reflected glarily in a pair of portraits recently taken in oil by Washington Ladd. Jacob was looking very mild in his picture and Amelia, wearing a cap studded with white satin spikes, her black hair hanging in a loop over one shoulder looked far older than her thirty years warranted.

Jacob said, "Anybody who comes out of this war without being ruined in estate will be lucky."

"Pooh—I intend we shall double ours," Amelia said.

"Well, don't ask your friend Mr. Frazee for any advice while I'm away."

"Why do you say that?"

"It is definitely proved that he is an abolitionist. I, personally, think he is a paid spy as well. I saw you talking with him early this morning."

"I was talking to him about a new axle for the coach. He's merely a Northerner. Now they are saying all Northerners are abolitionists and spies."

"That's the point. You're a Northerner and if they see you two together you'll be tarred with the same stick and then, by God, you'll *be* ruined, whatever tricks you intend to play with my business."

"Oh, foot! You get so upset over trifles."

A very out-of-tune hand organ from across the way began to grind out a march. The music was fast as well as loud, with the harshness of violence—hammers of sound beating toward an end without a trace of justice, or hint of gentleness.

Lifting her cigar, Amelia began to wave out the rhythm, oblivious of a growing uproar outside and a shrill, tortured screaming.

Jacob interrupted her absorption. He had walked onto the upstairs piazza. Jags of torchlight stabbed into the room through the parted claret draperies.

"Come here, Amelia."

The invisibles were turning onto Washington Street by illuminated Town Hall on the corner of Main. They wore sheets and peaked hoods and monkey suits and clown suits and all sorts of old-fashioned costumes. Those who were not masked had blacked their faces. The leaders were carrying a pine rail on their shoulders and straddling the pine rail was a ghoulish figure, black with tar and covered with goose feathers. The feathers parted and a round hole opened. This was a mouth seared and blistered from the hot tar. Feathers flickered and a howl blew forth.

The Invisibles' whooping drowned out the howl and the untuned hand organ. Jacob pulled Amelia back into the room.

"That," he said harshly, "was your friend, the estimable Mr. P. F. Frazee, the coachmaker."

"But," wailed Amelia, "he's a rich man. How dare they? How dare they?"

"They dare anything. Don't forget, Amelia, a civil war is in the making."

"Don't tell me what to do."

"Don't look at me that way."

"What way?"

"So glittery-eyed and strange."

Amelia shrugged and relit her cigar with a coal from

the open grate. Studying the tongs a minute before she replaced them on their hook she said coldly, "Don't forget to put in your calomel pills and your Dover powders."

Mrs. Feaster had a daughter who had been adopted
by her third husband, who had provided handsomely
for her on condition that she took his name. So she
was known as Miss Mary Boozer, and was considered
one of the most beautiful girls ever seen in the state.

James G. Gibbes,

PHILADELPHIA TIMES

8

Stobo woke Marie at noon the next day. He was in a
great good humor. "Wake up, Miss Marie! Make haste
and put on your clothes."

"What? Go away. It's the middle of the night. You
look exactly like a black Abraham Cohen. Are you
really a Hebrew?"

"Go on with you. It's just I'm so smart makes my
nose hooked. Come on now, get up."

Laughter and voices came up from the drawing
room. Evie ran in with a gilt paper cone of violets,
three boxes of bonbons and sugar plums and a pile
of lacy Valentines and threw them on the quilt. In
her hurry she'd loosed the ribbons from around the
stems of the violets and they spilled all over Marie's
face.

"You—Evie—knocking things all over Miss Marie,"
Stobo growled.

"What's happening?" Marie sat up, looking like a
very young bacchante with violets in her yellow curls
and covering the *broderie anglais* yoke of her linen
nightgown.

"Oh, there're dozens of soldiers downstairs. Mama
says don't stop to even eat your breakfast. How
funny—your eyes have turned the color of the violets!
There's lots more violets and candy, too." The eyes forgotten, Evie flew away to devour the candy.

"What is it, Stobo?" Marie began gathering up the

violets and pressing their cool sweetness into the hollow of her neck.

"Honey, I am the proudest nigger in Columbia. Now, tell me where to find your prettiest dress. I'll hook it up for you, too."

"You're crazy and I'm starved. Get me some breakfast."

"I got it right here—hot chocolate and biscuits and fig preserves. Butter your biscuit while it's hot."

"If you don't tell me, Stobo—"

Stobo buttered the biscuit and popped it into her mouth. "Old man Henry, the Preston's head nigger, come up to me in the market this morning before day. I knowed right off something important had happened. Henry took off his beaver and he said right there, where everybody could hear, 'Buh Stobo, how'd you like to play some poker with me and my wife tonight?' And, honey, that means Stobo has reached the pinnacle of the temple."

"These biscuits are hard as rocks. I'll eat some sugar plums. I don't understand a word you're saying."

"Yes, you do. Slaves occupy the same round on the society ladder as their owners. That old Henry kept talking, 'Your missy, Buh Stobo, was the belle of the ball at our house last night, the belle of the ball! Everybody in Columbia was admirating over her!'"

"Ah!" Marie stretched her arms and arched her neck.

"You like that, hey? You like being a belle? Then get up and put on the finest things you got. You got to work to stay a belle. Every round, you know, goes higher—higher! Where's your best dress?"

"In the wardrobe: a yellow challis. The one with all the black beads on the bodice. But what's going on, really?"

Jay flew in. His eyes round with excitement. "Huwwy, Mawie, or the men's gwine weave. And they been wet me wear his swords. One of them did. And Papa has gone off to war. But Mama says we got so many men we won't miss him. But we will, a wittle, won't we?"

"You going to get an attack of them wheezles from these here flowers, Jay. Didn't you cough for an hour after your pa left last night?" Stobo picked up the dark-haired boy child who had the sweet look of the Feasters, and went out, chuckling.

With trembling fingers Marie brushed her teeth and tied her strings and buttoned her buttons and fastened her garters. In the mirror she studied the too stylish yellow frock ornamented with too many jet beads. Yesterday Buck Preston had been terribly elegant in her stark black velvet riding dress. Marie opened the wardrobe and took out *her* black velvet riding habit. Yes—that would be just perfect. The train, looped up, showed off her slender hips and the jacket was tight enough to make her breasts appear to be pushing their way through the frog closing. And yet respectable! Now —the hat with the black plume, and chamois gloves. Boots? Where were her boots?

A few violets lay on the floor by the silver slippers she'd danced to shreds last night. She touched them with her bare toes and whispered to the radiant face looking at her in the dressing table mirror, "I hope Willie brought these. And oh, I hope he will kiss me again tonight!"

There was a roaring fire in the drawing room that shone on the mass of new Confederate uniforms with red and gold sashes and clanking, unscratched scabbards; and one young man with a regular army captain's insignia, his tight pants dusty and unpressed. He was telling Amelia a story of the previous night.

"Gus H—— rode his horse right through Nickerson's Hotel and into the barroom. Mrs. Feaster, you should have seen those long-haired senators flying around. They sent for me to come and punish Gus."

"And what did you do?" Amelia and the soldiers chorused.

"I took off my hat to the most important man I saw and I said, 'My gawd, Mr. Chesnut, suh, ain't Gus a splendid rider?' "

Marie's heart missed a beat. The captain was toughly handsome. Not refined handsome like Willie who was standing beside him. Then heads turned, sighs were audible and all the soldiers crowded round bowing and reaching for her hand to kiss and trying to press their flowers or Valentines or candy into her arms.

Stobo with his most superior Lowcountry air appeared with a tray of small glasses filled with Madeira and Hannah stumped behind him with a waiter of cheese straws and fried oysters. Evie and Jay opened all the boxes of candy to see if any was better than the rest. Amelia, holding Jay's cat in her lap, sat by the fire and her eyes glittered with pleasure. She was wearing a white lace cap and a navy-blue velours hoop skirt trimmed in bands of white silk braid. She looked very handsome and it was obvious that the young gentlemen had found her agreeable.

At that point Jay asked, "Which one is Mawie's sweetheart?"

"Yes—which one?" They all hung on her reply. Waiting for Marie to declare her tactics. After all these were war times. Wonderful times. Thrilling times. Maneuver was the order of the day.

Marie realized that this was a very important moment. One similar to the day so much had depended on whether or not Madame Togno accepted her in the school. She let her eyes travel from one rash, devil-may-care, proud, passionate face to another. She remembered what Stobo had said—"You got to work to stay a belle." She remembered the way the girls used to laugh behind her back at Amelia and her unladylike ways. Well—she'd better do as she always had—what she thought proper at this moment. She let her beautiful blue eyes, so soft yet so devilish, rest on each boy, in turn.

"Why can't I have dozens of sweethearts, Jay-bird? Oh—I'm so glad you all came by this morning. Wasn't the party last night wonderful? I can't begin to decide which dance I liked the best. All of them were so-o-o lovely. Let's go and jump our horses over the marble blocks piled up at the new State House. All of us." That Marie should include them all was perfectly natural and unaffected, as was everything she did.

The regular army captain was opening the French doors leading onto the balcony. Jay's mocking bird began trilling as the warm sunny air blew through his cage.

The captain said, "Here come Willie Preston and that

enormous Preston Hampton. All dressed up like city dandies. Preston must have just returned from the races in Charleston. Let's go and roll him."

Everybody trooped down into the yard where Preston Hampton, fifteen years old and handsomer than his father, was dismounting from an Irish hunter. He was bringing a bunch of pink and white Roman hyacinths tied with a pink ribbon to Marie

The ones in uniform descended on him with a whoop, teasing him about wearing fine French calf pumps and pale-yellow gloves to come acourting. He took it good-naturedly, even when they rolled him in the sandy street and ruined his gloves. But when the regular army captain deliberately stepped on the bouquet of hyacinths, Preston jumped up and with a brutal blow against the captain's head sent him sprawling in the dirt and everybody was laughing at *him* and rolling *him* in the dirt. Julian Selby and Henry Timrod came running from the *Daily Carolinian* office to get the story first hand.

Then all at once Marie was in the noisy, unruly group. Picking up the watery, bruised blossoms and pinning them on her lapel with a diamond horseshoe pin she cried, "Preston Hampton! How sweet of you to bring me hyacinths. They are my very favorite flower. We missed you last night. Willie kept saying you were on your way home from Charleston and I kept watching the door for you, so we could have a waltz. Like we used to in dancing school. Here—let me wipe a speck of dirt off your nose. No—you don't look disheveled at all. They're all jealous because you look so grand. Let's make haste and mount and ride away from them. All by ourselves. Oh, thank you, Willie Preston, I'll just step on your knee. Hurry, Preston—"

She was up on Tulip and giving him his cue and he was walking on his hind feet, his eyes rolling, his front feet pawing the air. Marie laughed delightedly, impudently, and waved good-by to her company. And the new, shiny soldier boys watched and thought: how daring she is; and beautiful; and nice; and above all terribly, scandalously exciting!

The war is making us all tenderly sentimental. No casualties yet, no real mourning, nobody hurt; so it is all parade fuss and fine feathers. There is no imagination here to forestall woe, and only the excitement and wild awakening from everyday life is felt.

> *Mary Boykin Chesnut*, Diary from Dixie,
> February 1861

9

When Willie's regiment took the train for Charleston the next week, all the young girls of the town were at the station with coffee and fried chicken and beaten biscuits and tea cakes for the soldiers who were getting on the train and also for the through passengers who jumped out of the cars to snatch a cake or a chicken leg from their baskets. Where many of Marie's experiences with some of these girls at Madame Togno's had been like bad dreams, this was a full-awake happy hour—to walk along the cars on Willie C's arm and see every soldier turn and stare at her. She was wearing her blue velvet cape trimmed in swan's-down over a blue hoop skirt and a leghorn hat dripping with white plumes. She had wondered, that day after the Prestons' ball, how she would get along in the world of high society, but even the most dour admitted that she looked truly aristocratic. That she behaved like an aristocrat. Oh well—a rather noisy aristocrat, to be sure. But that only made her more attractive.

"Marie," Willie said as they faced each other on coming to his car, "when will you be engaged to me?"

"When I am sixteen, surely. But I will be your girl now, Willie. Do you think it will be all right for you to kiss me good-by in front of all the people? Oh, I do like to kiss you very much."

In answer he grabbed her and kissed her and a hot

thrill trembled inside of her, as if a prophetic candle had been lit.

All the Togno school girls were watching—Ida Desassure, Grace Elmore, Isabella Martin, Buck and Mary Preston, Natalie Heyward, Sally Goodwyn, Kate Withers, and Lizzie Hamilton. But this time they did not whisper about Marie. They were indulgent to her. She was too formidable an opponent to be bested. So now, at last, they would accept her as one of them. Besides this was war; or almost war. It was quite respectable to kiss one's sweetheart good-by before he went away to be killed. Especially if it was a sweetheart from a respectable family.

As Willie reluctantly let Marie go and boarded the train, another train, from the West, pulled in and there was almost a riot in the station. Wade Hampton was alighting onto the platform. Grand as a lion, with piercing gray-blue eyes and much black hair and many whiskers he waved his enormous gray beaver hat and boomed: "My friends, I have good news for you. In Montgomery, day before yesterday, Mr. Jefferson Davis gave me permission personally to raise and equip a Legion. I hope many of you boys will transfer to my command—"

His vitality and enthusiasm was so infectious that even though this Secession, this Confederacy, this war had meant nothing but one continuous party and kiss after another Marie was moved and felt this man's dedication.

Then it came upon her suddenly that Willie was in the train that was moving slowly out of the shed and now she was alone and unprotected and there were the girls, still clumped together, watching her. She lifted her hand and waved at Willie as long as she could see him leaning out the train window, looking back at her. And now she must walk all the way down the tracks —alone—past those girls.

She straightened her back and lifted her chin. Nor did she betray by a single flick of an eyelash how frightened she was until she came up to them, and Wade Hampton himself had taken her hand. Even then his pleasant words, and the smiling faces of Madame Togno's girls, the distant shrilling of the train whistle, and the booming of hundreds of male voices all concentrated to make her feel shaky and unreal.

She only responded naturally when later, as she was about to let Stobo hand her into the "showbox," a positive-looking lady signaled her to wait a minute.

"I am Susannah Louisa McCord," the lady said, "I think you danced a polka with my son, Cheves, at the Prestons' ball. That *was* you in the silver flounces, wasn't it?"

"Yes, mam, I am Mary Boozer, Mr. David Boozer's daughter. From Newberry."

"Yes, I know all about you. I was standing near Mr. Hampton just now in the station, telling Cheves good-by, and wondered why you kept calling such an estimable gentleman 'Preston.' "

"He looked so terribly young and handsome!" Marie laughed her utterly gay, carefree laugh, showing her even white little teeth.

"Tonight I'll tell him what you said. He and his little wife, Mary, are dining with us. He'll puff up like a peacock when he learns that you really *took* him for Preston."

The next morning Wade Hampton sent a basket of partridges and ducks to the Feaster house with a note addressed to Mistress Boozer bidding her use her charm and influence to organize the young ladies in a "helping hand" group to support Mrs. McCord who was going to be in charge of the wounded. That is—if war and wounded actually came to South Carolina.

There was a girl in Columbia regarded as the prettiest girl in town, named Mary Boezer. She lived where the Courthouse now stands, in a very large house. She was wealthy in her own name and had one of the finest turnouts in the city, driving a pair of bob-tailed horses, which was the style then.

J. F. Williams,
Columbia Old and New

10

A year later, on February the twentieth, 1862, Amelia was sitting by the fire after supper, drinking a glass of brandy and smoking a very tiny new-style cigar just arrived through the blockade from Cuba. She was reading the New York *Herald*. Marie was studying her geography lesson. Suddenly Amelia threw the paper on the floor. "Hah—President Lincoln has come to his senses at last and ordered a general Union offensive in the West to begin on February twenty-second. That's the way *he* plans to celebrate Jeff Davis's Inauguration as President of the Confederacy!"

"Why, Mama," Marie cried, "you act pleased."

"Roanoke taken. Fort Henry on the Tennessee captured. Fourteen thousand Confederates taken prisoner by General Grant after retreating to Fort Donelson. That means the Mississippi River is vulnerable and after that, New Orleans will be easy. And then, my pretty poppet, everybody who has made their millions in cotton will be paupers. Your fine new friends— the Prestons, the Hamptons, the Chesnuts, the Taylors —everybody."

"What about my cotton? Haven't I got a lot of cotton?"

"Yes, but it's safe in a warehouse here in Columbia so we don't have to sell it on today's market of five cents a pound, thank the Lord! Or rather thank your precious Papa Feaster for that. And speaking of that gentle gentleman—I've let him persuade me to turn our money into Confederate bonds. And most of yours, too. What a fool I've been! Why, the Confederacy hasn't a chance to win now that Lincoln has come to his senses. Tomorrow I shall change every bond and bill back into bright solid gold."

"But, Mama, we lost the *Merrimac* at Hampton Roads. What would happen if everybody started hoarding gold?"

"If I tried to explain, you are too young to understand. And besides being young you never bother to read the newspapers."

"Don't you change any of *my* money away from Confederate bonds and ruin *me* in this town. If you do, I'll write Mr. Pope in Newberry and tell him on you and then you won't get another cent of your share of Big Dave's estate." Marie was clearly horrified. She jumped up from the chair and ran upstairs into her bedroom and flung herself down on top of the eiderdown covering her four poster bed.

From experience she knew that Amelia was either planning to do something or *had* done something. But what? What, this time? The past year Amelia had seemed more like other people than Marie had ever known her to be. She had even gone up to visit Jacob in camp near Richmond when word came that he was ill with a running off of the bowels. Amelia had been impressed with his fine friends among the officers. And she had written regularly to him after she came home. She even went to Trinity Church with the children occasionally. She had been, or appeared to have been, happy over the Confederate victory at Bull Run in the summer. She had, with the other women, taken baskets of food regularly to the soldiers coming and going on the railroad cars. She had spent hours ministering to the wounded Confederates at the Wayside Hospital, set up at the railroad crossing on Gervais Street. She had encouraged Marie to work with Mrs. McCord at the hospital; first at the Fairgrounds, now in the South Caroline College buildings. She had entered into the planning of a Gunboat Fair to be held in April as enthusiastically as that odd Mrs. Chesnut and Mrs. Cohen and Mrs. McCord. But now she was different again. From far away Marie heard an echo, *"Who did you and Big Dave see in the town?"*

"Evie," Marie said, going into the little children's nursery, "has anything happened to Mama today? She's acting mighty strange tonight."

Evie, who was smarter than she was pretty, was cutting out hearts from a sheet of red paper and pasting them on a square of paper lace. Without looking up, Evie said, "Well, there was a man out in the cookhouse. A white man in a dirty blue uniform. Mama gave him a whole pumpkin pie and a glass of peach and honey. He smelled real sour and stale and he talked sort of like Mama. You know water-r-r-r and sugar-r-r-r."

"Is he out there now?"

"No. Stobo drove him off in the wagon just after sundown. I didn't notice, but Jay said he saw the man get in the wagon and then Stobo covered him over with a rug and some straw. Stobo was real mad with Mama but he's more scared of her than a whipping so he went all right. Jay got so excited he wheezed until he almost died. You know, I think Mama is a spy. A Yankee spy."

Evie picked up a little blue paper cupid and fixed it in the center of the Valentine. "You needn't look at this so hard," she said, " 'taint for you and don't say 'It's after Valentine's Day.' I know it is."

Marie turned and ran downstairs.

Amelia was standing in front of the long gold-leaf pier glass beside the mantel. She was holding a lighted candlelabra face-level. Catching sight of Marie's questioning, widening eyes behind her in the mirror, she said softly, "I haven't a single gray hair! Black and shiny as a raven's wing! And my waist is as small as it was when you were born. I'm still beautiful. I have plenty of time to make a new life. I can still expect happiness and a rich husband if—"

"I play my cards carefully?" Marie mimicked Amelia's tone sarcastically.

Amelia turned in astonishment and faced Marie.

"Are you trying to be funny? What's there to be funny about? You know I've never liked Columbia. Suppose Jacob dies or is killed in battle? If I keep our money in gold we'll have plenty to spend a summer at a fashionable place like Newport or Southampton and meet fabulous people. I don't have any friends in Columbia. Why should I stay here if anything happens to Jacob?"

"Mama—you are making plans," Marie said with shocked sternness.

Amelia kept still, continuing to scrutinize her face admiringly in the dim mirror. The candlelight shone on her alabaster skin, her intelligent forehead and large brilliant eyes. The rest of her face was in shadow: the tight heart-shaped mouth, the too strong jaw.

"Plans," she exulted, "exciting plans."

"I don't want to hear about them. I came back down to ask about the man Stobo took away in the wagon this evening," Marie stammered nervously, "Evie and Jay say—"

"Evie has always been a liar and she puts outrageous ideas in Jay's foolish head. Evie tries to compensate for not being so pretty as you and I by pretending to know everything. It was only a poor beggar, half starved and sick. I rented a wagon from Mr. Carroll's stable and had Stobo take him down to the Wayside Hospital. For heaven's sake, don't you start prying and sneaking like Evie. There's always been such a great difference in my feelings for you compared to the others. I guess I'm an unnatural mother. I often feel as if you were my only child. Go in my bedroom and look in the box on the chest."

"You are trying to put me off. Please tell me the truth about the man Stobo took away."

"Do you really want me to? Wouldn't you rather not be involved? If you know the truth won't you have to go to the mayor and say, 'My Mama is thus and so—'; won't you have to write and say, 'Dear Papa Feaster, desert your regiment and come home at once?' Won't you have to tell Willie C.—'I can't be engaged to you because my Mama is a—' "

"Well, are you?"

Amelia laughed. "No. No. No, you ninny! As I

said—the man was nobody. And if it disturbs you to hear me say I think I am still a handsome woman and if I *should* find myself a widow I might—Oh—what's the use? You are so impetuous and uncontrolled. Run and open your present. I saw it in Mrs. Smith's window and couldn't resist it."

Taking a candle from the mantel, Marie went into the dark room that opened off from the living room. A low oak fire was burning and gave a soft flickering light. Marie put down the candlestick, opened the pink box on the chest, and unfolded the crackly thin paper. With trembling fingers she tied the strings of a beige straw bonnet with a wreath of crimson roses. She looked around for a hand glass. There wasn't one on the dressing table. Moving the pink box she opened the chest in which Amelia was wont to hide everything from a Christmas cake to Jay's stick horse.

Amelia had followed her into the bedroom. She still held the branched candelabra. Candlelight filled the room now. Marie made her face tight so as not to betray to Amelia the bewilderment she felt—the fear of the future. For the chest was packed for a journey; neatly and completely packed. Rows of her, Marie's, finely worked nightgowns, *her* boots, *her* gaiters, *her* best peignor, *her* traveling dresses, *her* fur tippet, *her* silver drinking cup, and the silver brushes she was keeping for her honeymoon!

Carefully—carelessly Marie dropped the chest lid and said, "This is a lovely bonnet. I'll keep it for Easter. Willie writes he will be home for Easter. Oh—and I'm sure he will want us to be engaged. Do I have to wait until I am sixteen?"

"Why? You'll be sixteen next December. What's an engagement? Every girl is engaged these days. But nobody expects her to take it seriously or make a to-do about it."

Marie laughed. Her awful suspicions and anxiety lessened a little. Perhaps nothing terrible was going to happen. Perhaps everything would be all right. Then she felt her chest constrict and a rush of tears burn her eyes. But she blinked hard and stood very still while her heart beat very fast. She mustn't cry in front of

Amelia. She mustn't cry. Weakness in others always made Amelia cruel. Oh, if Papa Feaster would just come home for a little while. Or if she and Willie could get married at Easter and not merely be engaged.

Amelia untied the bonnet ribbons gently, affectionately, as if Marie were a little child. She said, "Don't be upset about the chest being packed with your things. I have boxes packed for Evie and Jay also."

"And you?"

"Oh, I packed mine first, naturally. It's a precaution in war times. Who can tell whether the fighting will be confined to Virginia. Suppose it comes here—to Columbia?" She sounded indifferent, meaningless. Whatever came her decision had been made.

Marie smiled through her tears and said lightly, "If fighting comes to Columbia I suppose I'll join the cavalry and fight too."

"The Hampton Legion would dote on that. I'm so happy you are pleased with the bonnet. I love to buy you pretty clothes. Go to bed now. You look tired."

Amelia watched Marie run up the circular stairs. She ran so lightly and easily. She was such a pretty child but so credulous. Always being moved by the sentimental. So romantic. So loyal to the Confederacy, to Jacob Feaster, to Willie, to *her*—Amelia decided not to hide things from her so rigidly. She thought that would make it easier in the end.

When news got around that a Yankee prisoner had escaped from the jail opposite Madame Togno's school, the public was in an uproar. You would have thought a gorilla had been loosed in the tree-shaded gardens. In the *Daily Carolinian* Dr. Gibbes printed a harsh criticism of Colonel Preston's lenient conduct to Yankee prisoners. Particularly the way he allowed them to walk in his boxwood gardens on Sundays and even come into his house and look at his art treasures.

Endless days followed with Marie living in terror that somebody would come up to her and say—oh casually—that *they* knew who had spirited the Yankee fellow away.

However, everybody continued to be the same except

Stobo. His hands twitched nervously and he talked to himself constantly. But one morning in March when he was driving Marie to the college in the small buggy he said sadly, "You know about the man last month?"

"Yes, Evie told me. Did you really take him away?"

Stobo nodded and a few tears ran down his cheeks. "I didn't dare defy Miss Amelia. I have dreamed about a half-a-head man too many nights lately. I'm sure Mr. Dave is trying to warn me to be careful. But the worst thing is—Henry knows."

"You don't mean Colonel Preston's Henry?"

Stobo nodded miserably. Tiny beads of perspiration dampened his temples, he was ashy pale.

"Then I'll never be invited to another ball in this town." Marie, too, looked as if she had seen a ghost.

"No. He won't tell on you. That ain't the way we colored folks do. But he hasn't and won't invite me to any more card games at his quarters. I have clumb down the ladder to where my owner has descended by her wicked ways."

"But I'm your owner, not Mama!"

"Jesus Christ, so you are! Soon as you get to the school I'll trot over and tell Buh Henry. He'll fix things for you, too."

"Oh—I'll be all right." Marie patted Stobo's arm as he handed her out of the buggy.

Marie was across the street chatting with Mrs. McCord, who had stopped her barouche to invite Marie to drive home with her, that afternoon when Stobo returned. The beatific smile on his face assured Marie that his place on the "ladder" had gone up again.

"So you're going to a card party tonight?" she laughed.

"Yes, honey. That is, if you'll be so kind as to write poor old Stobo a pass to stay out until nine o'clock. And we'll know," Stobo said mysteriously, "about you as soon as we get home. A fancy-looking letter is there from Mrs. McMahan's boardinghouse."

Amelia was sitting at the tall Hepplewhite secretary Jacob had bought when they first came to Columbia. She heard Marie's running steps and without a word, held up to her a letter with strong thin handwriting. A log in the fireplace burned in half and fell crackling off the iron firedogs so Amelia didn't notice Marie's quick, raspy breathing. She continued to make notes in an account book while Marie tore open the letter.

"Stobo!" Marie screamed, running out into the hall. "Listen!"

Dear Mistress Boozer,

    I having been put in charge of the restaurant at the Gunboat Fair planned for the middle of April to be held in the Athenaeum Hall insist that the prettiest girls in Columbia be my waitresses. The Preston girls have agreed and Isabella Martin and Grace Elmore. Now if you and Kate Withers will also oblige I believe we will make bushels of money. Please come and see me at Mrs. McMahan's at the tea hour tomorrow if you will do this favor for our cause. We are also planning a raffle. I am giving a string of pearls and Mary Witherspoon a silver teapot. If you have anything similar you will part with, bring it with you when you come tomorrow.

    I understand you like to read French novels. I have a shocker, *La Cousine Bette* which I will lend you if you are fluent enough in French. But—there—I know you are. I hear nice things of you from every side.

                    A bientôt,
                    Mary Boykin Chesnut.

"Well, well," Stobo chuckled, "well, well. I'll just run out to the cookhouse and tell old Hannah and Cary and Sam and Rachel."

Amelia came into the hall. She was frowning ever so slightly. "What in the world is all this commotion about?"

"The Gunboat Fair. Mrs. Chesnut has asked me to be a waitress. And I am to go to tea at McMahan's tomorrow afternoon and take something beautiful to raffle off."

"Such as?"

"Let's see—what is the prettiest thing I have? What will impress Mrs. Chesnut and Mrs. McCord and the girls? Oh—oh—I know—the new hat with the red roses!"

"My Easter present to you?"

"But Mama—I said it was my prettiest possession. So you know I adore it!"

"No. You adore Mrs. Chesnut and Mrs. McCord."

"And the hat! And you! And Papa Feaster and Jay and—yes—even Evie today!"

It was plain from her happy face that had Amelia entered into her joy and triumph Marie *would* have adored her. But sharing had little meaning for Amelia and what's more she had no intention of letting Marie slip away from her. She said nothing.

Marie stood still for a moment, smiled a little guiltily and ran to get the bonnet.

Mrs. Feaster championed the Union cause, and showed her loyalty by acts of kindness to the Federal officers and soldiers taken prisoners to Columbia. She carried them food and clothing and secretly helped them to escape whenever an opportunity offered.

SAN FRANCISCO CHRONICLE

11

From that time Amelia did not try to spare Marie's feelings but went openly to visit Yankee prisoners in the Jail, the Lunatic Asylum and Camp Sorghum, on the Congaree River, just outside the town. Marie pretended not to know about these expeditions though they were public enough. For with the "showbox" piled high with food and brandy and other comforts, Amelia never got away from the Washington Street house without at least one employee from the *Daily Carolinian* running out and taking notes, a crowd of children and Negroes gathering around, Jay wheezing asthmatically and throwing pebbles at Stobo from the upstairs piazza, and Evie running after the coach, shrieking "You forgot last month's New York *Herald!* You forgot—"

Amelia never having been accepted in Columbia, saw no reason why anybody should be concerned that now she visited homesick boys in blue rather than homesick boys in gray.

And strangely, almost contrarily, it seemed, Marie continued to be included in the goings on about town more often than before. Mrs. McCord may have had something to do with this, she being so full of praise for the way Marie behaved in her hospital. The other girls came to help at the hospital only at first, and then in off-shoulder muslins displaying their bare shoulders and soft throats, and fainted at the first whiff of putrefaction and the sight of blood. But Marie heeded Mrs.

McCord's advice that "a lady who is also a beauty had better leave her beauty with her cloak and hat at the hospital door." She wore a mask over her soft red mouth. She tucked her yellow hair under a coarse, blue denim turban that made her eyes as mysterious and deep as sapphires. She hid her beautiful body in a rough-dried, homespun gown and if occasionally, to comfort a dying boy or soothe a feverish one, she removed her mask and sang *Lorena* or *The Yellow Rose of Texas* or maybe kissed him a little, no one ever knew about it.

Easter of 1862 passed and still Willie did not come. His letters were long and serious, telling of going into the valley with Stonewall Jackson; of the Battle of Seven Pines; of Robert E. Lee being given command of the Army of Northern Virginia; of the sad Seven Days and General J. E. B. Stuart; and then of being slightly wounded at Malvern Hill on the first of July.

On the morning of the twelfth of August, when she came inside the college gates, Marie stopped a minute to chat with Emma LeConte about Professor LeConte's new powder plant. Emma walked a ways with her under the great elms where soldiers were lying on cots and blankets in all stages of convalescence.

Mrs. McCord was waiting for Marie at the door of the first college building.

"Come quickly, Marie, and put on your hospital gown. A train full of wounded arrived in the middle of the night. Lord, what a confusion!"

Marie followed Mrs. McCord into a tiny room where two of the paid professional nurses were drinking coffee. "I think they steal the real coffee from the patients and give the poor lambs a substitute," Mrs. McCord whispered. "But hurry now. Let me tie your mask. What a surprise this is going to be!" They came to the long corridor filled with cots and unwashed, moaning soldiers. "See that screen at the far end?"

"Yes. That means a dying soldier. Please, Mrs. McCord, let me help with some of these. It's so hot I might get sick."

"Marie! I've told everybody you are the only one of the girls I've never seen flinch away. Oh well—"

But Marie was already halfway down the line of wounded. At the screen she hesitated a minute. There was a terrible smell nearby. He must be rotten with gangrene. She pressed her lips together under her mask, straightened her back and stepped hesitantly around the screen.

She almost didn't recognize him, he was so thin and pale. But he was fresh shaven and washed and in a clean nightshirt and he had two arms and two legs and the bandage that went around his throat and onto his chest was clean, too, and he smelled of pine soap.

"Oh, Willie—"

He turned and stared at her. That voice! No one else ever had that husky voice that went right down inside a man and started him *being* a man just hearing it. He held out a shaking hand.

"Willie," Marie gave a crow of pure delight—"My darling Willie—"

This time he struggled to sit up. She tore the mask from her mouth.

"My Lord—Marie!"

"Does it hurt much, Willie, does it? Does it hurt to kiss me, Willie?"

She leaned over him and he clung to her desperately. "I thought I'd never get home. Never. Oh—I've dreamed of this so much."

Her mouth was seeking. "Willie—Willie—" she murmured kissing him on his forehead, his ear, his mouth—

Until the screen was jerked aside. Willie turned brick pink. But she wasn't embarrassed. She laid him down and pulled the mask back up from under her chin over her mouth. There were Dr. Trezevant and Dr. Boatwright and Mrs. McCord, smiling happily.

"Oh—I've already tended this one," Dr. Trezevant said. "He's going to be all right. He stopped a burst of grapeshot with his gullet but voice box and windpipe are intact. He has a hole in his chest, but that'll close. That is—*if* his heart hasn't already jumped out through it. Easy with him, nurse, and lots of good food and you'll have him ready to go back to Virginia with old Matt Butler before you can say Jack Robinson."

It was a hot noon in late September when Willie told Marie good-by before returning to his cavalry unit in Virginia.

They sat on the first-floor piazza in dense shade. Crepe myrtles in thick bloom, dark vines and climbing roses closed them in. It was a living wall, green and sweet. Marie had on a soft mull muslin all fluffy and fluted.

"Why is it you always look so much prettier and *newer* and more unpredictable than the other girls?" Willie moved closer to Marie, sitting beside him on the joggling board. He put his arm around her waist and felt with trembling fingers for the rhythm of her heart, cupping her round breast as if he wanted his hand to keep the shape of it so he could remember and recapture it on the long cold nights when he would be far away from such delicious comfort.

"Mama buys me more new clothes than other girls' mamas, I reckon," Marie said putting up her lips and pressing them on the tip of the still livid scar under Willie's chin.

"Where does Mrs. Feaster get so much cash money?" Willie's forehead wrinkled worriedly. Marie knew that this worry came from his parents. She knew, too, that they had given their consent to Willie being engaged to her but had persuaded him not to marry her until the *next* time he came home on leave.

"Oh—I don't know. Perhaps it's *my* money. My adopted father left me lots of money. I thought you knew. You mustn't blame me for anything you hear about Mama. She's self-conscious about being from Philadelphia. She feels people's hostility though she makes believe she doesn't care."

"Are they ever hostile to you?"

Should she say—General Preston pretended not to see me yesterday at the library in the Athenaeum Hall? And Mrs. Elmore is having a supper party for Grace tomorrow night but I am not invited. And I know Mama has been helping prisoners escape from Camp Sorghum and the Lunatic Asylum. We feed lots of filthy, wild-looking men in our cookhouse and the Columbia people suspect. But hostile to me?

"No. Not yet. But if the war goes on forever and people grow poorer and more boys get killed, they probably will be."

"If they are, you come and join me and we'll get married. I couldn't stand for you to be hurt."

"Then hold me closer, Willie, so I'm sure everything is all right and that nothing Mama does will ever come between us."

Two years later Marie was still in the good graces of most Columbia people. Only with her mother was she strained and ill at ease. Amelia followed the progress of the war with a fanatic absorption. During 1863 as Sherman wheeled through Mississippi destroying the face of the land and disrupting the lines of communication, Amelia clamped a tiny cigar between her teeth and hummed *Yankee Doodle* gaily, making a pin trail of destruction across the South on a large map hung on the wall of the upstairs parlor.

Once Jay took the pins out of the map and she whipped him so severely that he almost choked to death from the worst attack of asthma he'd ever had.

In March 1864 when U. S. Grant was made general in chief of all the Federal forces, and was replaced by Sherman as Commander of the Military Division of Mississippi, Amelia waltzed around the upstairs piazza waving a bottle of champagne as if already she heard the bugles of the Grand Army blow in the distance.

With the spring, Amelia gleefully moved her brass-headed pins across the hard mountains of Georgia as Sherman triumphantly outflanked Joe Johnston out of every position he held. In June when the trail of pins reached Atlanta, she bought a paper of pins with dull, black heads and spread a whole blob of them over the spot where a lovely city had once stood.

Gloating, she read and reread in the papers the series of indiscreet speeches orated by President Jefferson Davis in Georgia, from which General Sherman learned exactly where and how General Hood was planning to checkmate him with an enormous force. After that it was difficult for Amelia's pins to keep up with the erratic course of Sherman's troops but by

November the twelfth she stuck him back in Atlanta and, with an airy check-off of a crayon, indicated Hood marching the Confederates away from Sherman toward Tennessee.

That night Amelia celebrated by drinking a whole bottle of brandy, and Marie and Stobo had to send for a doctor to quiet her loud laughing and shouting. And even after an emetic and a sedative she insisted on showing the dumb-founded doctor her map and explaining exactly how, with the parting of these two main armies, Sherman could now march to the sea as fast as he willed.

Mrs. Feaster, (the mother of the too famous beauty, Boozer) according to Captain James, has left her husband.

Mary Boykin Chesnut, Diary from Dixie, Autumn 1864

12

Marie woke at dawn. Not wanting to see Amelia before she left for the hospital, she dressed quickly in a cool calico, flung a thin wool shawl over her shoulders and crept down to the dining room. There was no one there. The room was dark and gloomy and smelled of summer mold and autumn smoke. Outside, Sam, the yard man, was burning leaves and singing a sad song. It was a beautiful still morning such as often comes to South Carolina in early November; warm as first summer with a soft bluish haze over the brilliant gold and red and russet of the dogwoods and oaks, the yellow of the Pride of India, the Judas, the tulip trees, the climbing vines—grape and clematis. Marie walked to the corner where the market was in full cry in the open arcade under the Town Hall.

Here until about eight o'clock Negroes from the plantations sold the freshest eggs, butter, cream; the fattest hens and ducks and turkeys; the largest walnuts and pecans; the cleanest venison and pork; the greenest turnip tops; the tiniest peas; the orangest pumpkins. All the fancy house servants were there in livery and high silk hats followed by pickaninnies with great baskets to carry away what the "boss" selected for his "Massa's" dinner table. Trading, screeching, cackling, joking, threatening was going in great good humor. There were no ladies present. Except Marie. And she was so pretty and smiled so gaily that they did not resent her. Besides she was just passing through.

Stopping only long enough to buy a burst pomegranate from an ashy-faced crone, she walked quickly out onto Main Street. Up the street some of the Convent girls were picking lavender and rose chrysanthemums planted along the Convent wall. In the middle of the street a group of raggedy Sandhill boys were switching a yearling bullock pulling a cart loaded with kindling wood. At the far end of Main Street the sun was showing rosy and gold on the gleaming marble columns of the rising new State House.

As she made her way over to and down Sumter Street, the tall white dwelling houses all looked taller than usual in the hazy air but as the sun struck fuller on the gold-leaved trees the whole town seemed to be struggling to wake up. The street was heavy with the scent of cook fires and brush piles burning pungently. Behind the big houses the slave cabins crouched, the eyes and the ears of their inmates as closed as their shutters against the white world around them.

What were the Negro slaves really thinking, Marie wondered, picking out and sucking the juicy scarlet seeds, now that they knew Sherman's men were marching their way? Not once during the past four years had Stobo ever let her suspect that he even knew a war was going on, much less that one was being fought to set him free. He was like those slave cabins—close to her, yet as shut away from her as they were from the big white houses.

As she passed the wrought iron fence railings, she thought that during the past four years she had seen a flag-draped casket in almost every one of the dim, high-ceilinged parlors of those houses. Many of the occupants of those caskets had been her sweethearts, for as she grew up scores besides Willie C. had been in love with her. She had the kind of appeal men fell in love with at first sight. But it seemed almost as if an evil force had been at work to destroy her sweethearts, so many had been killed or died of fevers or dysentery. She had wept over every one of them, but her tears were like spring rain and when another lighthearted boy had come to take her dancing or riding in the park or walking in the moonlight, she was always ready to laugh and flirt with him too. And then *he* would ride away and she would watch, almost morbidly, to see how soon *his* name would be posted on the casualty list on the bulletin board.

Only Willie now, of all her beaux, was strong and well and persistent despite campaigns and wounds and marches and retreats and more retreats. Oh—and Preston Hampton—he was still the beautiful, charmed charmer in a plumed hat and a cavalry uniform and—the sun came out full now. A sudden puff of wind sent leaves flying about like whirls of gold butterflies. Oh—there were dozens more beaux she could think of if she tried!

She was passing the little house where the Chesnuts were living. With mules hitched to it, Mrs. McCord's barouche was in front of the house. Mrs. McCord had turned in her sorrels the last time the government called desperately for horses. Mrs. Chesnut's ponies, however, were still munching good oats in a little shed by the front piazza. Marie went over and patted their foreheads and called to Molly, the cook, who was watching her through the dining room window.

"Will you ask Mrs. McCord if I can ride to the hospital with her?"

Mrs. Chesnut, too, had evidently been peeping at Marie through the lace curtains of the dining room.

"Come in," she called tartly, "before those devilish VMI boys, camped over in the park, catch a sight of you without a bonnet and come whooping like Indians, all over my asters."

"I'll just wait outside."

"No, come in and protect me from the wrath of Susannah Louisa McCord. She's trying to *make* me give up my dear little ponies. I think her mules would be far more useful to the Cause than my delicate darlings. Take my side and I'll treat you to some *café-au-lait*. Lawrence just brought a bag of coffee beans and three jugfuls of clotted cream from the Prestons'."

Marie had not been at the hospital an hour when one of the paid white orderlies came and told her to go immediately to Mrs. McCord's office. Marie was bending over a poor boy whose lower jaw and part of his tongue had been shot away. She was trying to help him swallow some gruel, spooning the hot creamy substance down into his throat.

"In a minute," she said, "when I am finished here."

"It's your mother come for you. Lordy—what a elegant buggy you rich folks ride in. I can't imagine what you slave in this pest house fuh."

Marie bent over the boy she was feeding. Tears were in his eyes. He made pitiful little crying sort of noises and the gruel spilled back out of his wounded mouth.

"I'll come when I'm finished," she said to the orderly. "Now get away from here or I'll take a shotgun and blow *your* jaw off."

It was almost an hour before she entered Mrs. McCord's office. Blood and gruel were splattered all over her home-spun gown. Her hair was tousled and she was sweating strongly.

"Great Lord!" Amelia cried, "and to think you were so ill last night. Poor little one! I'm shocked, Mrs. McCord, to think you would allow this frail child to be used in such a way. Honey, I want you to come home with me." Amelia rose. She had never looked handsomer nor less as if she had been on an outrageous drunk the night before.

Mrs. McCord did not rise. She said wearily to Marie, "Go along, my dear. I've just had word that Preston Hampton was killed at some obscure mill in Virginia day before yesterday. I can't stand any more today. No—don't try and comfort me. Since Cheves was killed, I work, not weep. It is my way. I wish I could comfort you. You have to go with your mother. I understand your predicament. You know I realize that you have no choice but to obey her. We can't have a scene. Go as you are. Come back tomorrow, though."

"Well," Amelia said, putting on her most injured expression as soon as they were in the "showbox," "*She's* certainly no lady. The rudest woman I've ever seen. She talked to you as if I wasn't present. How fortunate I finally had the wit to come and put an end to *this* nonsense."

"Oh—Mama, you didn't tell Mrs. McCord I wouldn't be back! They need me so—Oh, Mama—"

"You're needed elsewhere more. As soon as you get a bath and into some decent clothes, I'm going to rid your silly head of thinking of Confederates are without reproach. Mrs. McCord has been pouring her fairy tales into you long enough. I'll show you how the Confederates *really* operate."

A sharp north wind had risen after the warmth of the early morning. The steel-blue sky looked tight like stretched silk. There was not a softening cloud anywhere. Marie shivered in her green plaid Delain skirt and jacket. Her feet in black glove-kid Congress gaiters were cold as ice. As the great pines along the Congaree soughed and roared with a sound of rushing waters, she had to bite her tongue to keep her teeth from chattering.

There was a large buffalo rug on the floor of the coach, and on the seat, baskets containing roasted meat: venison, legs of lamb, a turkey, several hens, hams. At her feet was a bundle of flannel shirts and good shoes that Marie knew Mrs. McCord would have bargained her soul to possess to put on the convalescing Confederate soldiers who wandered under the elms practically barefoot in homespun shirts and old dress suits—swallow-tailed coats and chamois-colored pants —donated by the citizens of the town.

Her eyes closed against the afternoon sun, Marie leaned her head against the gaudy, sky-blue upholstery. She was thinking: I wouldn't be here if Mama hadn't taunted me with being *afraid* of the Yankee prisoners. Dared me to prove I was as brave as she to go alone among them. Oh, why do I *always* play into her hand?

"Miss Marie—Miss Marie—you sleep?"

"No! Where are we?"

"I'll show you the gate."

The officer's prison at Columbia was located on the west banks of the Congaree River on a sandy bluff known as Mayrant's Hill. It consisted of a conglomeration of huts formed of loose logs, their sides daubed with earth, dugouts covered with boards and earth, and piles of brush. No chimneys. No signs of fire—cooking or warming fire.

His beady black eyes hooded, Stobo acted as casual as if he were handing her out at Trinity Church on Easter Sunday among the best people of the town.

"What am I supposed to do?"

"Somebody will meet you at the gate. They are expecting this vehicle. You won't wait long. We never do."

She went up to the paling fence and the wooden gate was opened as at a signal. A guard in gray frowned at Marie.

"Who are you—one of Dutch Rose's girls?"

"Who were you expecting?"

"Mrs. Feaster."

"I am her daughter. To whom do I give these things?"

"Well—I'm danged! Tell the nigger to bring 'um in and put 'um down—they'll come runnin' fast enough. There—Just look at 'um."

From the caves dug in the earth, from the few walled huts, from under the piles of brush a mass of dirty, unshaven-ragged, skinny, hollow-eyed men came stumbling and jabbering toward Marie. But it was the baskets they grabbed—not her hand. It was the shirts and shoes they stared at—not her eyes.

One, a little less desperate-looking than the rest, but with a baked chicken safely stowed in the crook of his left elbow said, "Did Mrs. Feaster send you?"

Marie nodded her head.

"Come this way to where the sickest are holed up. Under the big pine tree. You'd better hang onto those shirts for them. They need them more than we. We can at least run around and keep warm when winter comes. They—"

He led her into a windowless, floorless hut. On a patch of pine needles that must have drifted from the tree and been carefully collected, lay a skeleton of a man with fever-burned eyes glaring at Marie and Stobo, who had followed her closely.

"That," said the man with the chicken under his

arm, "is what's left of the heroic Major Reynolds. Behind the Major I have managed to loosen two boards of the hut. When you leave here you will tell your nigger to drive that fancy buggy of yours to a place in the outside fence exactly opposite this hut. Mark it by the pine tree. He will then—don't look so shocked—open two of the fence palings from the bottom and you—yes—you look strong enough—hell, you're stronger than the best one of us—you'll help lift Major Reynolds through the hole and into the coach while the nigger nails back the palings and then—off you go. It should have been me. But the Major won't last unless he gets a doctor's care."

From outside the hut came a weak rendition of *Yankee Doodle* on a jew's-harp.

"Quick—the guard. Get moving. And, Miss, you're a real sight to us. Bless you for coming."

As a sleepwalker moves, rigidly, but straight to his destination, Marie preceded Stobo back to the gate, nodded good-by to the guard, climbed stiffly into the coach and watched the fence closely as Stobo trotted the sorrels slowly to the spot where the tall pine tree towered above the pathetic line of little roofs that marked the most luxurious quarters in Camp Sorghum.

"I hate being called nigger," Stobo said crossly as he stopped the horses and climbed down off the box. He prized loose two boards and then signaled Marie to get out and wait. He disappeared through the loose boards. In a few seconds he was backing out, doubled over, and dragging a limp human body in the dirt after him. Marie took the bare skeletal feet, Stobo the shoulders. He was in the coach. He was wrapped in the buffalo robe. He must have recently vomited. The smell of him was loathsome. The touch of him like coming death.

"I'm going to drive. I'm not going to get in there with him." In frantic haste Marie was climbing up onto the box as Stobo knocked the palings back into place.

"You can't. They'll suspect. Get down this minute. Miss Amelia'll kill both of us. She's out with you anyway. Make haste. Listen. Oh—Gawd Jesus—get down—"

Everything had gone unreal and jangly as the untuned harp: the jew's-harp inside the fence, just inside, playing *Yankee Doodle*. Frantically—warningly. In the distance General Preston on his big white stallion and several officers in Confederate uniforms; overhead the pines blowing up a gale; summer ending suddenly; winter coming in an afternoon.

And now Marie was inside the coach and the horrible, matted, lousy head was in her lap and—yes—he had vomited again.

It was the dusking when they reached home. Evie was sitting on the banisters of the side piazza. She was wrapped in her winter cloak and her face was half hidden under a knit tam-o'-shanter. Holding a lighted lantern she waved it in Stobo's eyes as the horses trotted past her.

"Mama says take him up to Jay's room," she yelled.

Marie remained in the coach until Stobo got back with Sam. Then she jumped out and fled past Evie through the French doors, into the dining room. Jogging along beside her Evie was talking constantly. What was she saying? Papa Feaster had come home?

So *that* was why Amelia had sent *her* today to bring that—that—creature here! Knowing what it would mean to Papa Feaster to discover that his family was helping a Yankee prisoner to escape—knowing it would make him—

"Listen to them," Evie said, tearing at her thumbnail with her sharp teeth.

Marie stood still. From the drawing room above came the sound of violent quarreling.

"They've been fussing all afternoon. Papa got here at dinnertime. Mama knew Papa was coming yesterday or today on furlough. But she didn't tell anybody. Not even Hannah or Rachel. There was a tipsy cake but Mama wouldn't let Cary pass it. We just had fatback and collards for dinner. Cary cried and told Papa she was sorry. Mama hit her with the fly switch. Tell me—can I go to the prison and help in the escape next time?"

"Next time—" Marie heard herself saying. "It was

terrifying. Horrible." She ran into the staircase room and started up the stairs. Stobo and Sam had lifted the half-dead prisoner and were carrying him ahead of her up the stairs. His greenish-gray face hung back from his shoulders, his mouth open. He was unconscious. Stobo looked down at Marie helplessly as if to say—No more card games with Henry in the Prestons' quarters. Not ever any more.

Jacob and Amelia were in the upstairs hall. The gas chandelier made the hall very bright. Jacob was white and sick-looking with anger.

"It will be the end," he shouted to Amelia, "if you allow them to bring that prisoner into this house. This time I'll leave you and never come back. But I won't divorce you. You'll not have the opportunity of marrying a rich Yankee as long as *I* live. Stobo, take this man back to Camp Sorghum."

"Put him in Jay's room," Amelia said to Stobo. "At once!"

"Papa Feaster—" Marie cried. "I think he is either dying or dead. He is gurgling."

Jacob looked around him at the scared faces. Marie, Jay, Evie, Stobo, Sam, and Rachel and Cary who had come from the kitchen. Outside, on the corner, the bell in the tower of the Town Hall began a ponderous tolling.

"That," said Jacob Feaster in a suddenly weary, lifeless voice, "is to announce to the city the death of Preston Hampton. I saw the boy die in his father's arms. I helped load him on a wagon and rode alongside the wagon off the battlefield. I saw General Hampton return and continue to personally direct the fire against the enemy. I took a train out of Richmond the next day for my first leave in three years—"

"You don't touch me a bit, Jacob Feaster."

Marie saw with dismay, then alarm, the blackness of Amelia's fury, her tightly clenched fists. Jacob saw it too.

He seemed to get smaller and thinner and weaker before their very eyes.

Marie ran to throw her arms around him. "Oh, Papa Feaster," she sobbed. But he pushed her away and picked up Jay, who buried his head in his father's neck and clung to him whimpering.

Marie was truly frightened now. Despairingly she looked from Amelia to Jacob. "Please don't go away from us, Papa Feaster. We need you. Jay and Evie need you. And I—I need you most of all."

Jacob said to Marie, "No. I'm a poor man now. My estate is ruined. You and Amelia don't need me any more. I will take Jay and Evie to Feasterville with me. But you—with your face like an angel in heaven. If I hadn't seen you bring him yourself in the coach, I wouldn't have believed you would have betrayed me. I wouldn't have believed——" his voice broke.

Evie moved over by Amelia. "Mama, I want to stay with you and Marie. I don't want to go and live in the country." She bit her nail and swayed slowly back and forth.

"Go or stay," Amelia said indifferently. "But," she looked full at Jacob again, "you must leave Jay with me until the war is over. I'm the only one who understands his asthma attacks."

"No, Papa! No, Papa!" Jay screamed, clutching Jacob tighter around the neck. "I want to go with you. And I want Marie to go. Mama made her get that man today. I heard Mama. Mama is a spy. But Marie ain't. Marie never went before. Please take Marie with us instead of Evie."

Jacob shook his head. Tears streamed down his cheeks. "No, son, Marie wouldn't be happy with my family, and in the end she would leave us. Evie, go upstairs and help Hannah finish packing your clothes."

"You don't have to Evie," Amelia said. "I would like to have you stay with me."

Jacob and Amelia looked at each other. It was a long look in which they declared all the loathing they felt for each other and hadn't managed to finish saying during the afternoon. "You had better come with Jay and me, Evie," Jacob said at last.

Evie shook her head and managed to squeeze out a couple of tears. "Perhaps I will come and visit you all at Christmas. To get my presents." She went over and pinched Jay on the leg. "I'll feed your cat, Bubber," she said.

"All right." He kicked her on the neck.

At this moment Stobo came down the stairs. Jacob spoke to him sharply. "Has Hannah finished packing Jay's clothes?"

"Yes, sir. Everything."

"Then fetch them and come back and get my portrait and Jay's bird cage. Put everything in the coach. I want you to drive us to Feasterville, no to Winnsboro to my sister, tonight."

After they were gone, there was a great silence in the house. Only the taffeta flounces of Amelia's black dress rustling as she paced to and fro in the parlor, sticking the pins back in the map very precisely. Evie was crawling around on the floor picking up the map pins that Jacob had thrown every which way about the room.

Her eyes red from weeping, Marie came in and faced her mother. "I want you to understand that I will never go back to Camp Sorghum again. Never. I can't. I won't."

Amelia said, "Go wash your face. God in heaven, what's the matter with you now?"

Evie giggled and put a pin in her mouth. They could hear the man upstairs sobbing.

"If I tell Mrs. McCord about that man, *you'll* be put in prison yourself."

Amelia looked searchingly at Marie. "You won't tell. I'm your mother. You'd share the family disgrace."

Marie shrugged her shoulders with the same indifferent gesture Amelia so often used. Amelia relaxed and reached out and traced the perfect oval of Marie's stubborn chin with her forefinger. "My own child! Do as you like about helping the poor prisoners. You know I won't force you to go back to Camp Sorghum. But I wish you'd please *me* by not going to that dreadful hospital any more."

Marie laughed a sharp, angry laugh. "What difference can it possibly make to you whether I continue to help Mrs. McCord at the hospital?"

Amelia called Evie to light a cigar and get it going before bringing it to her. Then she said, "Why, Marie, I suppose your mama is just a wee bit jealous of Mrs. McCord. You are too obvious in your infatuation for her. Oh—and about my drinking a drop too much last night. An accident I assure you. It was those oysters I ate. What with no ice and the disrupted train schedules and—my dear child, how flushed you look. I know you've got a fever. You must have caught a perish from one of those sick soldiers. I'll tell Rachel to make us a nice tea. The kind we used to have when just the two of us were together—with burned sugar cookies and orange instead of lemon in our tea. I bought some lovely tea today. A flower tea—rare and quite expensive."

Marie realized that a great effort was being put forth now to charm her. What an actor Amelia was, she thought, and felt strangely tired.

"I'm going to bed. I plan to be at the hospital very early in the morning. You and Evie drink the tea."

"I hate tea. I hate tea," Evie chanted.

Amelia raised one of the map pins. "Before you go to bed, please check and see if Hannah remembered to pack Jay's wool undershirts. He might catch a cold without them."

"Yes, Mama," Marie said, willing herself to speak cheerfully.

Tomorrow she must get up at first day and go to Mr. Learmount's gardens and buy a bunch of Roman hyacinths. If Mr. Learmount didn't have any, Oqui Adair, the Chinese gardener at the Asylum would give her some. After the funeral, after the people had gone away, she would slip into Trinity churchyard and lay the hyacinths on Preston Hampton's grave. Dear God, she prayed, don't let Willie come home draped in a flag. He is the only one left now for me to love.

"Don't you know the Boozer's engagement to Willie
C. is just broken off because she stole his watch, and
some money he had in his pocket, and he found her
out and made her give it back to him?" "I do not
believe all that! ... Not a word, Isabella!"

Mary Boykin Chesnut,
Diary from Dixie,
December 1864

13

Sherman presented Savannah to President Lincoln for
a Christmas present.

And in Columbia, the legislature debated States
Rights and the encroachment of the Confederate government and discussed the probability of South Carolina seceding from the Confederacy. The hotels and
boardinghouses and private houses ran over with refugees from the Lowcountry and from Georgia.

No one doubted that this capital city would be defended with the concentrated strength of the Confederacy especially as all the banks of Charleston and most
of those of the interior towns had removed here; and in
addition to their ordinary assets were crowded with
immense special deposits in the way of boxes of gold
coins, valuable papers, title deeds, bonds, etc., belonging to their customers and friends, many of whom were
refugees who had entrusted everything to the banks for
safekeeping. The Treasury printing works were here.
And the army of Lee and the safety of Richmond were
dependent on the several railroads that connected here.
Here, too, had been sent for safekeeping the accumula-
tions of successive generations of rich planters' wealth
in silver, jewelry, works of art, libraries and collections. Even the bells of Charleston's St. Michael's were
lying in careful crates in the basement of the old State
House. Warehouses bulged with cases and casks of wine

and brandies. Storehouses were jammed with cotton and Persian carpets and priceless furniture sent in carloads to be safe from Sherman's march which was supposed to bypass the out-of-the-way-to-the-sea-city of Columbia.

That Christmas of 1864 found Columbia the gayest city in the Confederacy with troopless generals and horseless cavalrymen and shoeless infantrymen galore and scads of pretty girls refugeeing from the great plantations of the Lowcountry.

Along with the flower of Wade Hampton's cavalry, Willie C. was in Columbia seeking a mount.

Marie gave him Tulip for a Christmas present and came to Nickerson's Hotel in the "showbox" to pick *him* up to go to the Christmas Ball being held that night in the decorated Athenaeum Hall.

"What a farce!" Willie scolded, and as the clumsy coach careened through the heavily wooded park, it being too early for the dancing to begin, he pleaded with Marie to turn in the sorrels to help mount Hampton's men. "As for this silver and glass coach, it is too absurdly vulgar for anything. If I didn't love you so I wouldn't be seen dead in it. And if you aren't willing to give up the horses—heaven help you when Sherman does come."

Marie snuggled closer inside Willie's muscular arms. He smoothed out the ruffles of her dress and felt underneath for her knee. It was the same silver-flounced taffeta she had worn four years ago at the Prestons' ball, its only addition a sky-blue sash. Amelia had bought her from some mysterious source, a new pink velvet made in Paris, but Marie had had sense enough not to wear it and make a spectacle of herself. Major Reynolds had complimented her on her decision. He was a nice man and since he'd begun to fill out, quite good-looking.

"I said—will you give up the horses?"

"Of course, Willie. Oh—don't pinch so hard! I wanted to turn the sorrels in ages ago. But Mama says so long as the Governor still keeps his and the Izards and the Elmores and the Chesnuts and the Prestons and—"

"Just promise me you will."

"I promise. And while we are where it is so dark— kiss me, Willie!"

Joe Randell's trumpet drowned out the fiddles and the tambourine. Marie was clutching Willie's arm.

> We are a band of brothers
> And native to the soil
> Fighting for the property
> We gained by honest toil
> And when our rights were threatened
> The cry rose near and far . . .

The song. The song of South Carolina, song that had started the war in the first place. The song they had played when Marie stood on the balcony and whacked Willie in the face with the flag and tossed her gloves and handkerchief and the swags of greenery to the boys marching away to defend their state; the state which now couldn't raise enough horses for them to ride out to stop Sherman's army.

> Hurrah for the Bonnie Blue Flag
> That bears a single star!

Old silk dresses swished, soleless shoes scraped, everybody whirled and turned as Joe Randell's silvertoned horn told them about why they had fired on Fort Sumter and why they had bound their lover's and son's and husband's sashes with unshaking hands and why they had stood so proudly beside flag-covered coffins and why they were wearing their old dresses and their shabby uniforms tonight with as much élan as if they were court-fresh and crisp. Then there came a sudden silence as the horn ended on a high note pure as heaven. Everyone was thinking that now the time was near, that this might be their last dance together, that these few young men who were left were getting ready to mount whatever horses could be found and ride away to stop Sherman—to stop the war, some of them forever. Marie felt a chill down her spine, tears bright in her eyes; a sublime excitement and sadness that was like the final note of the trumpet.

Young men and girls were leaving the hall and most of them saying good-by on the steps, quietly, but Marie clung to Willie and pressed close to him and smiled into his suddenly desperate smile.

"Marie—"

"Come—take me home. Quickly—before Stobo sees us and brings up that awful coach. I have a terrible feeling that you may go away and never—that we won't ever—"

They ran out into the night trembling against each other, not caring who saw—or what anybody thought. Up in the ballroom the candles still burned and there was shouting as the trumpet played the song again. It followed Marie and Willie all the way down the block to the Feaster house where a lantern was burning on the front steps. The hall had a single candle. Willie pulled off his coat and Marie took it and put it on the newel post of the stairs in the staircase room. "Let's go in the dining room. It's dark in there. Oh, come in with me, Willie, come in!"

The next morning Amelia woke Marie early.

"Here is a note for you."

"Oh—from Willie—"

Marie sat up and snatched open the cheap Confederate envelope.

Dear Mistress Boozer:

My watch and my money were in my coat that you hung in the staircase room last night. It is my father's watch and all my money. If you did this for a joke, please return them at once. I am very broken up.

So until you return my property, I remain ever your trusted servant.

Willie C.

"Did anybody come downstairs last night after Willie and I returned from the dance?"

"Yes. I did."

"Then you took his watch and money out of his coat?"

"Yes."

"Why? Why?" Marie started to cry—then began to kick the covers off, savagely—furiously—

"You hussy! You haven't got on a nightgown! You know Willie C. is a pauper. I wouldn't let you marry him for anything in the world. It would kill me. Why, with your looks—Lord! I never imagined such a beautiful body as yours—and if you don't play the fool—"

"I love Willie. I adore him. We're engaged. Don't you come near me or I'll bite you. Bring me the watch this minute and every penny of the money. Last night was the most wonderful—"

"Foot! You'll have a thousand more wonderful nights. A few hot kisses—Fiddle! Real love-making is much more than that."

Amelia laughed cruelly. Marie, quick as a cat, went up to her and gave her a terrible blow with both fists, in the stomach.

For an instant Amelia wavered, and then she drew herself up and said superciliously, "Put on your clothes. Then go and plead with Wee Willie to marry you and forgive you for being a thief. But the watch? It's far away from here and the Confederate money—trash. Burned as trash should be destroyed. I can't help your being a ninny. But I can keep you from acting one. A daughter of mine, whining to be poor and live in a cottage!"

Amelia succeeded in her scheme. The idealistic young Willie was furious with Marie. He broke their engagement and behaved like a martyr. Marie wrote to him over and over and tried in every way she knew to make him see her and allow her to explain.

The morning Stobo brought back Tulip and informed her that Mr. Willie said it was no use for her to keep sending letters to him as he was going to Greenville, she sat through the day on the joggling board out on the piazza though it was sleeting hard. She didn't go inside until it was quite dark and she heard the train for Greenville blow fainter and fainter and farther away.

Your fine Foreign Legion gave the first half of the afternoon to her yesterday, as I saw from my window; and then when Boozer drove off, they sauntered up to my party!

Mary Boykin Chesnut,
Diary from Dixie,
January 1865

14

In January, Sherman gave out with detailed ostentation, especially among the Confederates, that he was headed for Charleston or Augusta. But he had already decided not to bother with either except to keep them wildly fearful and thus make them retain for their protection vital military forces which might come together on his front and make his crossing of some of the great rivers that crossed his direct route more difficult and bloody.

Amelia was confused on the evening of January the seventeenth.

"Now where in the devil," she said pleasantly to Major Reynolds who was drinking a glass of peach and honey and playing piquet with her, "is Sherman headed? He's left Beaufort."

"He's almost here." Major Reynolds dropped the cards on the table. His voice was a hoarse whisper. "Sometimes when I can't sleep at night I fancy he is already here. I can hear the troops marching. And I can see them in the streets bludgeoning the people with their musket butts. I can hear the children screaming —smell the fur of animals burning. It feels as if I were killing and burning. The whole army hates South Carolina for being responsible for this war. I can feel them hating all the way from Beaufort here—right inside my head I can feel it. They think he's headed for Charleston. Fools! Important as Charleston is to them,

Branchville, where the railroads from Columbia, Augusta and Charleston join is far more vital. These people make me laugh—laugh—I tell you. Scream with laughing—" There were just two noises in the room, the cat purring and Major Reynolds' loud laughing.

"So you think Sherman is rapidly approaching Columbia?"

"He's almost here." Major Reynolds picked up his cards. "I think we'd both better pack up and be ready. But—Miss Marie—"

"She'll be in the game when the chips are down."

"You can't be sure. Yesterday I blacked my face and took the mule and wagon and followed her. Stobo drove her first to Mrs. McCord's for tea and then to Mrs. Chesnut's for tea and then she went and watched those new Virginia boys they call the Foreign Legion parade for the last time before they leave for Virginia. They broke ranks and clustered about her coach like flies around wet sugar."

"It *is* a puzzle. I thought when Willie accused her of stealing his watch and broke his engagement, people would turn against *her* and make her as eager to leave Columbia as I am."

"So long as she has champions like Mrs. McCord and Mrs. Chesnut and is so ravishing to look at and so friendly and laughs so easily and such shoals of men follow after her—"

"Watch out, Major—you too?"

"Who could help coming under her spell? Where is she tonight?"

"At the Soldiers' Bazaar at the State House. Marie says it's the most extravagant entertainment that's been held in Columbia during the entire war. I'd like to go—just to gloat."

"Your turn will come soon. As will mine. General Sherman, prepared to meet resistance at every river crossing and forest road has progressed unopposed, so far, through South Carolina."

"I thought General Wheeler was still playing the gadfly."

"He is—but the civilians hate him with his 'live-off-the-country' tactics about as much as they do us."

Amelia chuckled. "And here in Columbia, General Wade Hampton with his extraordinary powers, granted by General Lee, to raise men, money, and horses has only two small divisions of cavalry between himself and General Butler. Oh—it is a fine set of circumstances. Where have you been all day?"

"Oh—around and about. Selecting dwellings for our generals to occupy as headquarters."

Major Reynolds busied himself shuffling the cards, and Amelia asked him if he saw Marie before she left the house earlier in the evening? "She wore a new dress. One of two I ordered from Paris a year ago—a gold taffeta shot with green threads and a bonnet with gold feathers about the brim. I've never seen her look more bewitching. Sly little minx! When she spent the morning primping and brushing her hair and buffing her fingernails I knew she was up to something."

"She had promised to walk through the Preston gardens with me this afternoon and show me the rare Chinese parasol tree there. I waited for her by the fountain for two hours in the cold and she never came."

"She must have forgotten in her excitement. She thinks she's kept it secret from me, but I found out from Hannah that Willie C. returned to Columbia yesterday. His little spell of pouting has given way to one of longing. He tipped Stobo a dollar to deliver a note from him to Marie, inviting her to take him driving in our coach after dinner today."

"Presumptuous scoundrel! Did she?"

"That's where she was all afternoon. Out in the country with Willie who has forgiven her and is more in love with her than ever."

"If you knew Willie was back in Columbia, why did you let her go out at all this afternoon? Do you suppose she's with him now?"

Amelia shrugged her shoulders. "She's peddling kisses at the bazaar for Mrs. McCord's hospital fund. And as for letting her go out this afternoon—I learned long ago to handle Marie on a loose rein. She is such a wild heart she has to be fooled into the bridle, not forced."

"Did you get me a new Confederate uniform today?"

"Yes—it's in the wardrobe in your room."

"I'll put it on and start immediately for the bazaar. Several of us plan to circulate through the crowds and learn what's going on. I understand at least eight Confederate generals will be there. Wouldn't you think with Sherman just down the road—!"

The Boozer is a beauty, that none can deny and they say she is a good girl.

> Mary Boykin Chesnut,
> Diary from Dixie,
> January 1865

15

In its whole existence the old State House had never been so gala! Illuminated from top to bottom it glowed like a fine jewel in its columned, oak-crowned setting. Upstairs, in the Hall of Representatives, in front of the entrance, the Speaker's desk was canopied with gray moss. Garlands of smilax and twiney vines decorated the white pillars holding up the canopy and from among these glossy greens gleamed in gold letters:

A tribute to our sick and wounded soldiers

The whole building was a park of living green with pine trees and bamboo in tubs everywhere and swags and garlands of smilax and pine and myrtle and laurel. And the smell! Candle wax, resiny forest greens, French perfume on pretty girls selling chocolate and burned sugar and rum and brandy and sherry cobblers, and charlottes and fondants and cakes and puddings.

Each booth represented a Confederate state and the ladies had vied with each other as to which was the most exotic. The portières from their parlors made tents of oriental splendor: red and pink and gold and bronze velvet and silk damask and real lace curtains surmounted by the shield of the state represented.

On one counter the wonders of the world were piled. Or so it seemed to the people here who had been cut off from luxury for so long. Things that had come from Europe through the blockade—silks and linens and flannels and riding boots and Paris bonnets and French corsets and the latest style hoops for skirts. They couldn't buy these rarities for they hadn't any real money any more. But it heartened them to know that such things still existed. One booth was full of imported wax dolls in court costumes, any of which was selling for more than a live Negro baby. There was a doll house made by Dr. Julian Chisholm complete with exquisite miniature furniture. Most booths were jammed with treasures donated from homes: paintings, silver pitchers, cups and bowls, finger rings and bracelets, necklaces of pearl and emerald and rose diamond and garnet; Persian rugs; fifty-year-old brandy and Madeira and port; horns of popcorn; grab bags of wrapped tricks and foolishness. Oh—it was a Belshazzar feast to be sure and this night was the high point—the climax before the curtain came down.

There was General Joe Johnston, second only to General Lee, buying a bottle of French perfume for his wife; and Lieutenant-General Wade Hampton saying that if Sherman came here he was planning to fight from street to street and house to house to defend the city; and Brigadier General Matthew Butler of Edgefield, handsome as a god, hopping about on his wooden leg with Isabella Martin, to one of Joe Randell's lively country tunes; and the fiery-eyed, harsh-faced General Hood back from Tennessee, looking love at Buck Preston in a swan-white crinoline, and telling everybody his wedding clothes were here in Columbia—it only remained for Mistress Buck to set the day; and General Preston frowning on his prospective son-in-law who seemed unable to manipulate his artificial limb and rested too heavily on Mistress Buck's snowy arm; and the pretty little General Beauregard bragging about being in command here and how he was planning to cook General Sherman's goose; and General Lovell and General Winder and Governor Manning deep in criticism of Jeff Davis; and General Chesnut coming up and saying—"Now gentlemen, not here and now!"

And in the raffle, Willie C. being outbid by one thousand dollars in Confederate currency for a kiss from Marie Boozer by Major Reynolds disguised in a brand-new Confederate uniform when all at once the hall exploded in a giant whisper that was so loud the two belligerents got still and everybody looked around —"Sherman is at Branchville. The railroad to Charleston has been destroyed!" And then all the generals began leaving in haste and General Hood, shielded by Buck from the pushing crowd, was saying, "I asked to be sent across the Mississippi, to bring all the troops from there. It is still possible for the state to be saved—"

To tease Willie, Marie hurriedly left her place in the raffle tent and grabbed Major Reynolds' arm and ran toward the door leading into the long corridor. Close behind, Willie tried to intercept them in the House of Representatives but Marie hid behind the blue-velvet tent labeled *North Carolina*. Not till Willie disappeared, hunting her in the red-damask *Arkansas,* did she remember that she still had the bag of money she'd made from her kisses. She must take it back. Major Reynolds must take it back for her. He was hardly out of sight on his way back to her raffle booth with the money bag before Willie came charging out of *Arkansas* and Marie, laughing merrily, ran from behind *North Carolina* straight into his arms.

Yet, it is but fair to say that Marie Boozer's conduct in society here was irreproachable up to the time of her exit with Sherman's army.

Yates Snowden

16

Between the moment when the words were whispered at the bazaar "Sherman is at Branchville" and the triumphal entry of the Union troops into Columbia, much happened to the people who did not realize, until they heard the cannons across the Congaree, that total war was upon them. The end of a way of life had come and none were less prepared for it than the citizens of that city.

On Sunday, February the twelfth, 1865, they dressed in their now shabby best and went to church as was their custom. If the pews were somewhat overcrowded, why, one must welcome the less fortunate who had had the ill luck to dwell in Sherman's path. And if the streets up and down which they promenaded after the long sermons were filled with more people than usual, no doubt it was in token of the fourth anniversary of their celebration in honor of the formation of the Southern Confederacy!

Willie C., who had supper with Marie and a group of young people at Mrs. McCord's that night, reported that at first dark Main Street was milling with wagons and carriages and hysterical people from Orangeburg and Lexington. But, he added, the generals had dined with the Chesnuts at three o'clock and after sixty-year-old Madeira from Mulberry followed by roast turkey and steamed rice they put their war-hard fingers on an enormous map spread on the dining room table and pointed to where Sherman planned to branch off from Orangeburg and set out for Charleston. One said that in a spot of dense swamp, a narrow defile, an impenetrable thicket, with his eight hundred cavalrymen in partisan fighting he could stop three thousand. Another said—"But Sherman is coming with fifty thousand." Another—"I'm off for Charleston this evening by train, at General Lee's special order, to request Hardee and Cheatham to send troops here at once." Another complained bitterly that if General Lee hadn't been jealous of him and delayed until late January giving him command of the cavalry to oppose Sherman—What cavalry? another laughed bitterly. All had a safe plan to stop Sherman if—

Then the generals mounted their superb horses and all rode out to watch Governor Magrath review the reserves on parade.

"I never heard so many grand solutions of the fix we're in," Willie said.

"It's preposterous to even suggest that Sherman is coming here," one of the Charleston girls refugeeing with Mrs. McCord exclaimed. "Why not say he's going to Paramaribo? One is about as likely as the other."

Heartily they all agreed—with the exception of Marie who remained silent, picking at a plate of chicken salad and eggs stuffed with anchovies and merely sipping at a glass of iced champagne.

Because Marie knew that Sherman was coming to Columbia. She had studied Amelia's map carefully just this afternoon. Every time Sherman feinted as if he might be turning toward Charleston it was only with a wing or a flank. Columbia was where he was headed. She had tried to show Willie Amelia's map and to tell him as much as she dared without getting Amelia into serious trouble. But he refused to take her fears and forebodings seriously. "You're too pretty to think so much, sweetheart," he'd say. "I wasted a whole month sulking in Greenville. Come let me make love to you. That's what you want to do too, isn't it? Next to winning the war I would rather kiss you than anything in the world."

Tonight Marie was trying to win her own private war. The time had come when she would have to take a stand. Either she must reconcile herself to leaving Columbia with Amelia when Sherman moved on from here; or she must marry Willie *before* Sherman came and, as Mrs. Willie C., be securely one of this group around Mrs. McCord's supper table.

They were accepting her as one of them tonight. But how were they going to feel about her when Sherman arrived and Amelia was proclaimed with trumpets by the Yankees as their Columbia heroine—the savior of their horribly treated prisoners of war at Sorghum and the Lunatic Asylum? How would they react this instant if she put down her heavy silver fork and calmly told them that a trunk, full of her prettiest clothes, was in the upstairs hall at home beside Evie's trunk and Amelia's three trunks and that the "showbox" was packed with enough food and blankets and linen for a long hard drive? Or if she announced that the night before, two Union cavalrymen, in gray cloaks, had ridden boldly the length of Main Street, with the smoke of homes burned in Orangeburg still blackening their faces?

Perhaps Peter Trezevant or Julius Pringle or Albert Elmore would laugh and say—how you always amuse us, Marie, with your fancies! Or they might say, as Willie had said last night, when she whispered to him that those same two horsemen, at that very moment, were gobbling a steak and kidney pie in the Feaster kitchen—"Oh—the LeContes have a mysterious visitor, too!"

She looked up. Willie was watching her hotly. She hooded her eyes invitingly and he hurriedly finished telling the girls that tomorrow Hampton's men were supposed to put on their dress uniforms and parade to bolster the civilians' morale. Mrs. McCord said, "Willie, go over and open another bottle of champagne. We are too quiet. We need popping corks to liven us up."

No—she must keep her counsel. These people were only human. They would either mock her or shun her if she cried out, Cassandralike, that fire and sudden death were at hand.

She must listen and pretend to be interested in their conversation, twist a gold curl around a finger and let her eyes linger on Willie's lithe body leaning indolently against the Sheraton sideboard. Listen—

"The Martins left Friday—for North Carolina. They were afraid Isabella might be—"

"Oh no—the Yankees don't do *that*—at least not to white girls. At least that's what Papa says General Wheeler says."

"Pooh! Wheeler's Cavalry are worse than Yankees. Aunt Cissy said that in Georgia Wheeler rode by and stole every chicken in the yard and killed her best pig and barbecued it right there in her rose garden. Then the Yankees came and were as polite as they could be."

"And did the Yankees not burn her house?"

"Oh—they burned her house and chopped down all the boxwood bushes but Aunt Cissy said the Yankee officer—"

"Your Aunt Cissy is a fool!"

"Why, Mrs. McCord—"

"Go and cry in your room. If Mrs. Chesnut leaves the town tomorrow, as she will if Sherman comes any nearer, I am going to send you Charleston girls away with her. Every one of you."

"Then you believe the Yankees *do*—to white girls too!"

"No. I have just got weary of you silly creatures. Who would like to hear some pretty music?"

Mrs. McCord rose and, going over to a side table, turned the key of an intricate German music box and the heart-tearing falsetto strains of a Strauss waltz as quickening as a march and shattering as a farewell— the theme of these past four years—tinkled out.

Mrs. McCord, a glass of champagne in her hand, was calling the boys to roll back the carpets and finish the champagne so there'd be none left for the Yankees if they came.

And Willie was bending over Marie and whispering in her ear—"Marie, let's elope tonight. Before Sherman comes—"

"Yes—this minute!"

He must have been reading her mind!

"Oh Lord, I forgot! I'm on duty at midnight. In the morning?" he whispered pleadingly.

"Early in the morning." She spoke aloud and with a rush of urgency in her voice.

And now she had risen and was in Willie's arms and waltzing down Mrs. McCord's hall and Willie's heart was beating hard against her throat and he was saying—

"I'll be there at ten on Tulip. Can you ride one of the sorrels? I'll have everything arranged for Mr. Shand to marry us the minute we arrive at his house. I won't have more than an hour off duty before the parade. Will you mind hurrying?"

"No. We have a whole lifetime ahead of us."

She hardly slept that night because she was so apprehensive. Apprehensive about a thing that was about to happen and that she would not be able to do anything to prevent happening. Willie, she whispered, over and over, why ever didn't we go on and get married last night instead of waltzing that last time?

Yes, why? For Willie couldn't come for her the next day because all the reserves were called up and even the silliest could not overlook the riding out of town of a grim-faced General Hampton and a tight-lipped General Butler at the head of all the mounted men available; or the hastening crowds on Main Street; the hordes of Negroes trailing in from the country, ominously quiet, in dirty but fine ball gowns and swallow-tailed coats stolen from closets in burning houses; the wagonloads of household goods and fire-frightened women and children; the jammed hotels and taverns.

On Tuesday the town panicked. The Yankees were reported to be but six miles away across the river and early that afternoon heavy firing was heard about Congaree Creek.

"Are they ours or theirs?" Marie crossed to the black marble mantel in the drawing room and carefully moved the hands of the gilt clock back a few minutes.

"Ours, I trust," Amelia said.

Evie, holding Jay's cat in her arms, was looking out of the French windows. "Mama means by 'ours' the Yankees. What did you mean, Marie?"

"You know I meant the Confederates."

"I thought they had all left town," laughed Amelia.

"Marie and Mama!" Evie said scornfully. "Always picking at each other! Hey—Marie—come and look at your beloved Mrs. Chesnut. Scat—cat!"

Marie followed the cat through the French windows onto the upstairs piazza. Taking the carriage around the corner by the Town Hall on two wheels the bob-tailed Mulberry hackneys were extending themselves in a run. Mrs. Chesnut, her head swathed in blonde veiling, a handkerchief pressed against her mouth was white as a ghost. General Chesnut had his arm around her shoulders and a one-eyed yellow woman, sitting on the seat across from them, was gesticulating wildly in the direction of the capital.

"I'm going out," Marie said. "I'll ride one of the sorrels down to the depot and see the excitement."

Superb horsewoman that she was, Marie could barely control the sorrel when she came to Main Street. The turmoil, the shock, the rush, the complete disorder, was terrible. It looked as if everybody in the city was flying away simultaneously, without any plan of flight, bearing with them their families, their household treasures, their trunks, their jewels, their puppy dogs and baby dolls.

When Marie reached the Charlotte depot, she had to run the gauntlet of Wheeler's Cavalry encamped around the depot. They called to her and commented on her hair, her eyes, her seat, her teeth, and made smacking noises with their mouths. It was infuriating. A Sandhill boy with a cart full of kindling wood came to her rescue and offered to hold her horse while she went inside.

The whole depot was a heaving sea of luggage as wave after wave toppled over or was jerked off, or dragged, or, as whistles blew, just left in the maelstrom.

A short fat man with a box so heavy that six Negro men were staggering under its weight brushed past her almost knocking her down. One of the Negroes moved aside for her and the fat man rushed at him, cursing, and beat him furiously over the head with a silver-handled umbrella.

A prominent lady whose husband had gotten a seat for her in a boxcar provided she fetched no luggage strode by wearing several dresses, two cloaks, many pair of stockings and two feathered hats. Marie followed in her trail out under the shed where the cars for Charlotte were standing. The lady vanished and now Marie fought a solid mass of hysterical people to walk curiously up and down the platform.

There was General Chesnut talking to Mrs. Chesnut through a train window. And there were General and Mrs. Johnston, safely aboard the train, and there was the immensely fat Mrs. Izard—she who had said, "But everyone knows what *her* mother is"—demanding to be picked up and pushed through an open window since the doors were jammed. And three Negro men were picking her up—she of the great dignity screaming to them to hurry—hurry! And they were poking her through the window where she stuck half-in, half-out. And everybody was shouting with laughter and Mrs. Izard was screeching and General Chesnut took hold of her feet and Marie went up and helped him and finally the tiny, tiny little feet disappeared through the window into a mass of gray Balmoral petticoats and pink flesh. Oh—and there went Christopher Hampton trying to make a way for his sisters to get onto the cars. And Mr. Walker, struggling along under a load of his rare and precious books. And now here came the Middletons and the Ben Rutledges of Charleston with their Negro house servants loaded down with boxes and baskets, flying like swallows to another roosting place.

But Marie had seen enough. She forced her way out with more difficulty than she had pushed her way in. Well—at least the Prestons weren't aboard nor Mrs. McCord. The little towheaded boy who had hung manfully onto the irritated sorrel almost kissed her boots when she gave him a dollar in United States currency. He kept waving and shouting at her as long as he could see her in the turmoil of maddened people.

Back onto Main Street and to pull over by a magnolia tree in front of Wearn and Hix, the photographers. Her horse was fighting the bit and bucking. Foam from his neck flecked back onto her riding jacket. Some splashed on her cheek. Or was that a tear? She daren't loose her hold lest the sorrel bolt. And then she would run right into them. The Prestons in their traveling clothes in the open landau for all the cold wind: General Preston in a black, fur-collared cape over a brown broadcloth frock coat and fawn trousers; Mrs. Preston, trembling with her sorrow and fear; and Mistress Buck immobile as if carved of white stone looking straight ahead of her as if the street were empty of the seething crowd and this was an ordinary afternoon drive across the river. Behind the landau strung six wagons, loaded with Preston treasure and servants, pulled by sturdy mules.

The sorrel tried to rear. But he had met his match in Marie. Balancing on her stirrup foot she leaned forward and cracked him hard between the ears with a chamois-covered fist. Anyone hearing her swearing would have nodded their heads and said, "Ah—I told you so. Rough—like her mother. Hard and rough."

She galloped the sorrel in and out and up and down Main Street and over to Sumter and up and down Sumter and people forgot for a moment why they were running and indulged in admiration and envy and delight for the amazing exhibition of horsemanship.

She didn't let the sorrel slow down until he was trembling and blowing like a bellows. By then she was near the South Carolina College. She pulled him over to a hitching post just across the street from the college. Mrs. McCord, bundled in an Inverness cape, was sitting on the piazza of her house. She had been weeping. She was still weeping but not making any sound. Marie went and sat in a chair. For a time neither spoke.

"I just passed the Prestons leaving town." Marie was clearly horrified.

"He had to go. Having been in charge of the Yankee prisoners here and responsible for their treatment he'd be the first one shot by the Yankees if he remained. They're on their way to England. He has millions banked there. Don't blame him or Mrs. Preston. I went to them this morning and helped persuade them to get away at once. I feel devastated over Buck. She'll

never marry General Hood now. Her mother has at
least won there."

"Did your girls go?"

"No. I sent them upstairs and took away the staircase
so they couldn't."

"You aren't going?"

"No. More wounded will begin arriving any time
now. What about you? Your mother is in terrible danger if Sherman *doesn't come*. By now people are aware
she has helped hundreds of prisoners to escape. They
will hang her if she remains after Sherman leaves—that
is if he comes and goes."

"Don't worry—she's not planning to stay in Columbia."

"But what about you? Do you want to move in with
my girls? Could you?"

Marie reached out and clasped Mrs. McCord's
hand, "Willie and I are going to be married right
away. We were planning to yesterday but he had to go
with General Butler to skirmish and try and turn Sherman from here. But, Mrs. McCord, General Butler
can't. Not with eight hundred men!"

Suddenly the fire alarm in the Town Hall tower
sounded. Over to the right a rosy glow blazed up in the
chill February dusk.

"That must be the Saluda factory. First blood. I feel
quite a hundred years old and very weary. Come inside
and let's drink the best bottle of wine in the house."

Marie shook her head. "I'd better get back home.
The crowds are growing more and more unruly. Good-
by, Mrs. McCord."

"Good-by, Marie."

Mrs. McCord smiled. Marie wanted to throw her
arms around Mrs. McCord and cry. But when she
mounted the sorrel, still heaving from his running, she
made him buck a few times and waved gaily. She had
a feeling that this was the last she would ever see of the
gallant Susannah Louisa McCord. She turned quickly
and galloped off.

17

On Wednesday the cannonade and musketry began to sound distinctly above the roar of the tumultuous town. Wagonloads of wounded rattled through the college gates in a cold drizzling rain. The city was placed under martial law and all trains and conveyances put to the task of getting out government stores, records and personnel.

On Thursday the governor with his suite and a train full of officials departed in the rain. To the dismay of the state, General Beauregard was put in command of all the Confederate troops in South Carolina. And a dismal depression settled over the streets and shuttered dwellings of Columbia. Crowds still swirled about, but hope had vanished, and from the second-story piazzas the Union troops could be seen drawn up on the hilltops across the Congaree.

Thursday night the stars came out and a north wind blew hard and cold. Hampton and Butler rode slowly back into the town. Shortly after the big bridge across the Congaree was seen to be in flames and it burned very slowly throughout the night. Just at midnight the mayor and some of the councilmen waited on General Hampton in the wide hall of the Preston mansion where he and General Butler had set up their headquarters.

Worn-out men in gray were sleeping on the floors,

112

on the leather sofas, up and down the wide stairs, against the statueless pedestal at the far end of the hall. The marble Venus had been taken down and packed in a box in the cellar. Some of the men had unpacked the lady and spread the straw of her bed on the floor for pillows.

Henry bade the mayor and the aldermen sit on a marble bench pulled in from the piazza and brought them mellow old sherry. As the clock struck one, Wade Hampton opened the swinging doors to the east drawing room and called them in.

"Gentlemen," he was standing like a gray rock in front of the white marble mantel. "I have this minute dispatched Lieutenant Colonel Joseph Waring with a group of men, just in from Charleston, to get sabers and halters and saddles. But you must provide them with horses. Tonight. It is essential. We are in desperate circumstances. And if we stand and defend the city, as I plan to do—"

Mayor Goodwyn sat down hard on a delicate, French gilt chair. He said hesitantly, "You've got to move out, Wade. We've come here from the United States Hotel where we've had a conference with General Beauregard. He says that Hardee has again refused to move troops up from Charleston. And Cheatham hasn't arrived from Augusta. The state government has fled. Beauregard insists the city officials are now responsible for Columbia. That means you *can't* fight in the streets because *we* can't evacuate the twenty thousand women and old men and children and Negroes left in town. They are the ones you'd kill. Here read this letter. It's dated as of Friday. I wrote it in Beauregard's suite."

Wade Hampton looked over at the portrait of his grandfather, the doughty old Whig general. What course would he have followed? Would he have gone to the United States Hotel and given Beauregard a horsewhipping? Would he have forced a house-to-house fight in his beloved town? Would he have led eight hundred horsemen against sixty thousand? Shaking his head constantly, Hampton read:

MAYOR'S OFFICE

COLUMBIA, S. C.   February 17, 1865

To

MAJOR GENERAL SHERMAN:

The Confederate forces having evacuated Columbia, I deem it my duty, as Mayor and representative of the city to ask for its citizens the treatment accorded by the usages of civilized warfare. I therefore respectfully request that you will send a sufficient guard in advance of the army to maintain order in the city and protect the persons and property of the citizens.

Very respectfully, your obedient servant,

T. J. Goodwyn

MAYOR

"How are you going about delivering this?"

"First I plan to display the white flag from the tower of our Town Hall."

"If you do, I will personally climb up the tower and tear it down."

"Surrender of Columbia is inevitable, Wade. I hate it as much as you. Don't try a suicidal stand."

"I promise nothing. When do you propose to start out?"

"At nine o'clock tomorrow—no *this* morning. I'll take a deputation from the City Council and drive in a carriage bearing a white flag. We'll cross at the Broad River bridge."

"My men will be drawn up in battle formation in front of this mansion until we hear that you have made a contact and given him the letter—"

"What about burning the cotton stored in town—to keep the Yankees from getting ahold of it?"

"The cotton is not to be burned; the wind is too high; it might catch something and give Sherman an excuse for burning the town and blaming it on us."

Marie knew Willie was back in Columbia. She lay down on her bed fully dressed and listened to the wild west wind howling through the night. She left a fire going and for a long time the redness of it glowed in the room. She wondered if the town would be shelled again the next day. Several times she rose and went to her window thinking she would go and seek Willie. But disorder still reigned in the streets and with her flair for attracting attention in broad daylight—no—she would wait until the dawn. At last she fell into a heavy sleep. At six o'clock she was awakened by a terrific explosion. Several bricks tumbled from the chimney and clattered into the fireplace. The house had been hit!

She sat up. No, the house was still standing. A barrage of cannon sounded from across the river. The wind was almost a gale. It was quite dark but someone was in the room. Major Reynolds! She knew it was Major Reynolds. How his eyes narrowed and his cheeks reddened whenever they were alone together! She was about to call "Mama!" when Stobo spoke.

"I'm trying to get a fire going. Here's a coal with some spunk left in it. Why, you're all dressed." He was whispering. As the fat pine blazed, Marie threw off the down comforter, got up and began combing and arranging her hair.

"Mr. Willie sent word by General Preston's old Henry's boy, Jasbo. He wants you to come straightaway to the Preston mansion and bring both the sorrels, saddled. He's waiting by the front gate for you. Tulip rore up with him in the middle of the fight yesterday and got a full charge in his belly. Mister Willie must have given poor Tulip the signal you taught him when a crowd of hot-eyed men got gathering around. Sit a minute and warm your toes before I put your boots on you. Eat something. I brought you a partridge and some cold batter cakes. Take it with you then. I know Mister Willie's hungry."

The two crept down the stairs and out the back door to the stables. Day was beginning to break murkily. The air was full of frost and smoke. Marie was trembling all over. Feeling ill and weak, she rested her head a minute against the sorrel's warm, satiny side.

Stobo gave a final cinch to the girths, a last polish with his hand to the red-gold flanks. "I'm going to miss these gentlemen," he grumbled.

"We'd better worry over what Mama is going to do when she finds out they've been spirited away. She'll probably hitch you and Hannah to the 'showbox.' "

"Big old fat Hannah fill the whole shafts. Probably you and me."

Giggling like conspirators, Stobo and Marie spent five minutes deciding how she was going to ride astride in a skirt. Then Stobo unlooped the skirt, held up the train, and showed her how Africans made breeches out of a triangle of cloth.

It was cold riding through the streets, still full of people. Mostly Negroes now. At the corner, the open market under the Town Hall was deserted except for one old Negro woman with a basket of stolen silver teapots to sell. In front of the Town Hall, on Main Street, hundreds of bales of cotton had been piled up. Most of them had been torn open and shreds of cotton were blowing out in the wind and hanging like snow on the soughing pines and cedars. In some parts of Main Street corn and flour and sugar covered the ground. Wheeler's cavalry had galloped down the street earlier and broken into and plundered most of the stores. They had gone out of town toward the Broad River bridge. A continuous firing indicated they were still skirmishing. Negroes and white people with sacks and baskets were scooping up the precious food. The storehouse of the South Carolina Railroad was blown up and hundreds who were robbing it were killed in the explosion.

The gas lamps atop the gateposts of the Preston mansion were still burning. In the pale morning light Willie was propped up, lazily handsome, against one of the posts. As the sorrel trotted into the driveway Marie saw a mass of horses as if for a ball. She thought of her first ball here: the silver dress she'd worn—her first kiss by the illuminated fountain—the love in Willie's eyes.

Now as he lifted her down the love was still in his eyes but he blushed as she brazenly undid the triangle and looped the rumpled skirt rakishly on her hip.

"Your skirt looks as if you'd slept in it."

"I have. Waiting for you. Is Mr. Shand going to marry us *this* early?"

Willie was not being lazy now. He called to a tired-looking officer, holding a saber and a halter, nodding on a bench under a magnolia. "Colonel Waring, here is the mount I promised you. I don't think he's accustomed to a saddle but by night he'll be so worn out from running he won't care."

"But I thought we were going to elope," Marie cried. "Mama is definitely planning to leave Columbia with General Sherman when he rides away. She will insist on taking me with her if you and I aren't married. You'll never find me. Oh Willie—"

Willie answered harshly, "Listen to me carefully. It's true we may never find each other again. If we don't, my life will be ruined far more than yours. But this is what you are to do—General Hampton plans to follow Sherman—slightly to one side until enough troops make connection with us so we *can* meet him with a chance to win. If your mother does wangle a way to leave here with Sherman's troops, and takes you with her, be ready to escape the instant I send you word. Couriers will be back and forth between them and us at all times. I'll know where you are. I'm on scout duty most of the time. I'll come and fetch you. Believe me, my darling—"

A bugle blew. "Fall in! Fall in!"

"Oh, Marie—don't mind so much." He tore himself away from Marie and turned to Stobo, "Make her be a good girl," he cried hoarsely.

Stobo looked sadly at Willie. "I'll try. Take care yourself, Mister Willie."

Whereupon Willie swung up on the sorrel.

"Don't hold him so tight," Marie called crossly as the aggravated sorrel bucked out of the driveway into the street.

Old Henry, in his ambassadorial frock coat and white gloves, was standing on the marble-tiled piazza, protecting his ears with his hands against the wind that was rattling the bare trees like a thousand skeletons in the great garden. Now Henry was waving at General

Hampton who was coming up the boxwood-bordered walk from the direction of the fountain to join his men lining up in the street in front of the mansion in battle formation.

Marie and Stobo sat in the bench on which Colonel Waring had nodded earlier. The sound of musket fire continued from the direction of the Broad River bridge. She ate the cold batter cakes and the partridge and began to feel less nauseated and sad. About nine o'clock a horseman arrived and reported to General Hampton that the mayor and his deputation had ridden out in a carriage carrying a white flag toward the Broad River bridge road.

Hampton touched his hat with a gauntleted hand but made no sign. His and Butler's men remained drawn up in battle formation in the street. Marie knew Willie wished she would go away and not witness this retreat.

A great mass of people waited on the sidewalks. She didn't see any familiar faces. Her friends had all fled or shut themselves up in their freezing houses. Ominous mutterings of the crowd carried over to Marie.

"What are they saying, Stobo?"

"They want General Hampton to charge the Yankees."

At ten o'clock some of Wheeler's cavalry galloped up. One of the horsemen saluted Hampton and pointed in the direction of the old State House. Marie stood up on the bench so she could see better. From its eminence, the roof of the building showed through the bare, branched oaks. A hard sun was shining bright. The increasing high wind tossed the branches of the oaks about the State House this way and that as if they were great arms beseeching heaven to come down and shrivel up the Stars and Stripes that were running —running—running up over the proud old State House.

"General Hampton, sir, the mayor surrendered the city to Colonel Stone of the Iowa brigade three miles out of town. As you see—they have now entered the city. Colonel Stone has assured the mayor of the safety of the citizens and of protection of their property, while the city is under his command. Provided there are no Confederate troops left—"

General Hampton saluted Wheeler's courier curtly. He lifted his hand toward General Butler and leaning forward put his big horse into a gallop. With no word —no echo of the famous Rebel yell—his men wheeled their horses. The hooves made dry, bitter, crushed sounds as they retreated farther and farther away toward the Winnsboro road.

Hannah appeared. "Miz 'Melia want to know where de debbil you is. She 'lowed as how I'd find you mooning around dis mention. She say git ober to Main Street quick and watch her triumph march. Glory be! Hah! Hah!" Hannah shuffled her fat feet back and forth rhythmically on the gravel of the driveway. "Whut Miz 'Melia done oberlook is dat dis nigguh is now free—free—free till she's fool."

"You ain't fooling! You the biggest fool in this town." Stobo beckoned Marie to come along.

Hannah waddled off toward Main Street, stopping every now and then and throwing her arms up in the air and jumping around and around shaking like a pudding, and yelling—"I'se free—free—free till I'se fool! I'se gonna go to de white folks school."

All of a sudden, Marie heard drums and horns. Bands were coming playing *Hail Columbia* and *Yankee Doodle*. Ominously the people surged around her. She was walled in by hostile, desperate citizens. She walked very, very fast.

"Her mother—" they were muttering again, "her mother—"

On reaching the corner of Main Street and Blanding, Marie saw a skein of women and children running crazily in front of the smart-stepping column of hateful blue uniforms. Other kinds of women crowded the balconies waving banners and handkerchiefs. Negroes were jammed along the street cheering, singing, holding out stolen silver cups of wine and whiskey to the Union soldiers or drinking it themselves. Ringing cheers and shouts echoed from all sides mingled with the martial music.

To escape the pack that seethed around her, Marie made a quick move, leaving Stobo, open-mouthed on the corner, and ran, zigzag, with other terrified women who were fleeing to the shelter of the Ursuline Convent. But when she came to the Town Hall, Marie decided to stop and see from what she had been fleeing. The mayor's carriage, surmounted now by the United States flag, carrying the mayor and Colonel Stone came first. Then the Iowans—the Western men, the ones less prejudiced against the white Southerners—to make a good impression on the city. Then—yes—she might have known—ragged, unkempt, wild-eyed prisoners freed two days before from Camp Sorghum and this day from the Lunatic Asylum and the Jail—prostrating themselves and screeching and howling—"Our Lady of Mercy—Our Blessed Lady of Mercy—" around the black buggy drawn by a flop-eared mule and driven by Major Reynolds. And she was standing up in the buggy. Amelia, dressed in a fine black velours, ornamented with ermine frogs, that had come through the blockade, and a tiny Paris bonnet of black silk with a wreath of green feathers around the brim and green ribbons tied in a soft bow under the hard, too sharp jaw. Amelia, waving and bowing and being the heroine of Sherman's men who were marching, blue wave on blue wave, down the long Main Street.

Wearily Marie trudged through the now busy market arcade. Amelia had not seen her, thank goodness.

More troops were coming now. From far down—as far as the new State House she could see them stretched like some writhing blue serpent through the doomed city. Howard's, Logan's, Kilpatrick's, Sherman's! Guards were being stationed along the ways to hold back the crowds of Negroes that were swarming out from their cabins in back of the big houses to join the ones along the street. For Sherman was come indeed! Glory Hallelujah! They were free!

When Marie got to the high steps leading up to the first story of her home, Hannah was sitting on the joggling board; joggling up and down and humming happily.

"What are you doing out here on the front porch?"

Marie said sharply. All the bitterness of the day rising in her chest like gall.

"Joggling. I'se allus wanted jest to set and joggle out hyar on de front po'ch all de live long day. Jest set and joggle and watch de folks pass. And here I sets and here I stays."

"All right. But Mama's going to wear you out and you know it."

"Oh—no, she ain't. Not so long as dey keeps hollering about her being de bressed vuhgun. Hee—hee! Dat's de bes' joke I ever did hyar."

Stobo was turning in the gate. He would fix Hannah. A Yankee soldier was running toward them. Marie could see that, as they reached the Town Hall, all the soldiers were breaking ranks and scattering up and down the streets—in and out of stores and houses.

"Wait a minute, nigger!" the soldier called.

Stobo looked up in disbelief. Marie came back down the steps and stood beside him.

"What time is it, nigger?"

Stobo's bright Hebraic eyes narrowed and his hooked nose trembled at the tip. With a flourish he took out a big silver watch that Marie had given him one Christmas before the war.

"Now—now—that's much too fine a watch for a nigger. I'd just better put it in safekeeping for you. Safe from these here Rebels."

The soldier had been drinking. He snatched the watch from Stobo's cold fingers and held it to his ear. "Half past eleven! And you, miss—now—I wonder what you've got his under that pretty riding skirt?"

He squatted down and lifted her skirt and ran his hand up her leg to feel in her garter for money or jewelry.

As hard as she could Marie drew back her foot and kicked his face, bloodying his nose and knocking out his front tooth.

Cursing, the soldier jumped up and grabbed her arm and twisted it behind her. He would have broken her wrist if Amelia and Major Reynolds hadn't come driving past. Seeing a Union major advancing on him with a buggy whip, the half-drunk private let go of Marie's arm and cut across the street toward the now empty *Daily Carolinian* office, yelling back at them, "Just wait till tonight and you'll see hell."

"Major, they scared us near to death," Stobo sobbed. "And I just hate to be called 'nigger' specially by a Yankee."

Major Reynolds said, "I'll station guards at this house at once. Western men. Marie—why don't you go inside and change your clothes? Mrs. Feaster, are you coming in?"

"No. I want to wait and greet General Sherman. He's just behind General Logan's men. You promised to introduce me. Marie—look in your wardrobe —there's a new traveling outfit—"

Damn you. Damn both of you! Marie thought furiously and fled. Fled up to her empty bedroom. Sat down on the unmade bed. Listened to the growing disorder outside. And wept.

While the city was on fire and the house Mrs. Feaster occupied was burning, General Sherman passed by. She called his attention not only to her house, then burning, but showed him a large storehouse at the opposite corner, then burning, which she told him was her husband's, and that it had been filled with flour, bacon, tobacco and cotton, the truth being it was a government storehouse in which her husband had been employed.

Colonel James G. Gibbes,
Who Burnt Columbia?

18

Marie cried for a few minutes then fell asleep. Waking, she pulled the bell rope. Sam, in a wool stub jacket and a knit cap, came puffing up the three flights of stairs.

"Where is Stobo?"

"Gone with Miss 'Melia and the trunks. In a wagon."

"And Hannah?"

"Joggling."

"Are you going to run away and be free?"

"Nome. I'm goin' back to Newber'. I never did like Columbia and I don't like them Yankees and I don't like the way they's stealing and running their hands in and outa women's titties huntin' money. They robs from po' colored folks even more'n they does from whites. And what they does to the pretty mulatto girls is a pure sin. I'se been follering them ever since they broke the line and come swarmin' like locusts."

"What about Cary and Rachel?"

"They'se goin' to stay with you till you go off with your ma, then they'se coming back to Newber' with me. Rachel's got a good dinner cooked: fried chicken and rice and turnip greens. She says it's three o'clock and time for you girls to eat."

"Will you fetch me some hot water and the tub so I can bathe first? I'll hurry."

She had just stepped from the tub when a shot rang out in the front yard. She pulled a blue wool wrapper around her damp body and went and opened the window. A Yankee bummer had blown the head off Jay's yellow tomcat which had been walking along the iron fence. Evie was picking up the hank of fur and screaming childish curses at the ragged, smoke-blackened man. He threw a silver cup of brandy at her. A captain in a smart blue uniform passed and ordered the bummer on his way. The captain put his arm around Evie and she cried on his shoulder and then the captain helped her bury the cat in one of Amelia's cigar boxes. After they'd put some narcissus and breath-of-spring on the little mound the captain began prodding the flower beds with his sword, hunting buried silver, but the guard at the front door told him General Sherman had left orders about this place. The captain whistled off toward Mr. Mordecai's big brick house on the corner. Marie heard the guard begging Evie to come in the house.

"I won't. I won't. Won't. Won't."

From the joggling board Hannah laughed raucously, "You tell 'um, Evie. You looks jest lak dat black witch ob a Ma ob your'n. Why'nt you put a spell on dis gyard lak yo' Ma could do wid her leetle least finger?"

"Aka-Baka! Drop dead!" Evie said to the guard.

In answer the guard poked Evie in the leg with his bayonet and, screeching as if her leg had been severed, Evie ran into the house and up the closed stairs to the big hall. Major Reynolds came out from the drawing room and grabbed Evie by the arm.

"I was watching from the piazza. Why do you always have to be such a show-off?"

Still in her wrapper, Marie came down the curving stairs slowly, sinuously, with the utmost effect. She stretched, she yawned. At the foot of the stairs, Major Reynolds watched her. Marie was accustomed to the look in his eyes. Men always got it when she made the slightest effort. She trailed on down the steps. "You seem upset, Major?"

Major Reynolds loosed Evie who began biting her thumbnail.

"You've gotten mighty bossy all of a sudden," Evie said to Major Reynolds, trudging past Marie up the stairs to wash the cat's blood off her hands.

Major Reynolds turned to Marie and said excitedly, "I *am* upset. No one knows the exact hour the signal will be given to fire the town. Promise me you will be ready to leave this house at a minute's notice. This whole section is doomed. I will send you word where to go from here. Possibly the convent. The Mother Superior educated General Sherman's daughter, Minnie, in the Middle West. He has promised her the convent will be spared. Besides most of the pupils are from the North. In the meantime, keep Evie with you every second. Neither of you must put a foot outside the front door."

Marie stared at him, her blue eyes round with astonishment. "You sound as if we might be in actual danger." She leaned against the newel post gurgling with merriment. "These soldiers won't hurt me. They aren't going to hurt anybody. The city has surrendered."

Major Reynolds took Marie by her shoulders and shook her hard. He said savagely, hysterically, "Your mother left word for you. She's gone to get two horses General Sherman has promised her to pull the coach. Did you know someone spirited the sorrels away last night? I waited here until you woke to tell you that I am in command of the army of refugees that will accompany General Sherman north from here tomorrow—or the next day at the latest. I had to make sure you would be where I could find you after the fire. Yes—the convent. I will come and fetch you from the convent."

Marie watched Major Reynolds falling apart, fascinated, revolted; a queer religious smile was on his lips, making his dark face rather beautiful in a cruel and dedicated way.

"Major Reynolds," Marie said, "Major Reynolds." She pulled her wrapper tight around her. She was not afraid of him, but the sight of him hating there made her sick. "Major Reynolds, why don't you go and join Mama at headquarters?"

He turned on her fiercely. "You want me to go so you can let your sweetheart in. I saw General Hampton and some of his men, I'm sure Willie C. was among them, disguised in blue capes, in front of the Town Hall not an hour ago. Spying on me. Waiting to come here and get you."

"You'd better hush, Major Reynolds," Marie said, "you'd better go lie down somewhere."

He leaned very close to her. "Come with me onto the piazza and look in the direction of the Camden road. You will see a great cloud of smoke. It will be your idol's, Wade Hampton's, home burning. A special order! By sundown the whole of Millwood plantation will not be fit for crows. Just for vultures. Not a living thing will be left. Not even an unfeathered squab in the cote. The order read: 'Lead away the brood mares'—after all they're the finest stock in America—'slit the throats of the foals and the blood colts. Destroy—' "

There was something sensual and horrible the way he was blurting out his words. His lips opened in a peculiar way. There were red blotches on his blue-bearded cheeks. He was showing the whites of his eyes, just like a horse does, when you are going to whip him.

Marie's heart began beating very quickly. "Damn you! Standing there telling me things like that."

"It's just too bad, isn't it?" Major Reynolds said. "A nasty man like me coming and throwing mud on your heroes. But if you'd been kept prisoner for three years by Wade Hampton's uncle; if you'd lived under conditions worse than a dog; if you'd had bloodhounds slavering after you—"

Marie's startled cry shocked him into silence. He reached out for her but she pulled up her wrapper and flew up the stairs in a rush of bare feet, yelling, "Rachel —Sam—Hannah—Evie!"

At seven o'clock Marie and Evie were on the upstairs piazza. Marie had thrown a large, blue wool circular around her shoulders and Evie was buttoned in her heaviest cloak. They were listening to the high wind and watching the thousands of shouting, singing, cursing soldiers led by Negroes with torches and light-wood knots staggering up and down the streets carrying huge silver waiters and candelabra, quart cups of watches, sacks of gold coins and silver spoons and tatters of portraits by Sully and Peale and Inman. Some wore plumed ladies' hats and many small ones capered about in gauze crinolines and swan's-down *sortir-de-bals* and carried lace parasols like banners over their heads. Suddenly three rockets went up at different parts of the town and simultaneously fires in strategic points blazed up in a roar from timbers saturated with turpentine.

"We'd better go straight to the convent," Marie said.

"But what about Mama?"

"Sam says she's dining with the generals at the Preston mansion. She's the Queen of the Union Army."

"Well, I wish I was with her and not with you."

"So do I."

Hand in hand, they came through the French doors back into the drawing room. It had filled up with dirty bummers and men in blue uniforms. Their guard, completely sober, was beating in the glass cases of the wax flowers on the mantel with his pistol; another was pushing the gilt clock into a crokersack bulging with other treasures; another had just cut Amelia's portrait into three pieces; another was lying on the sofa crying because there "warn't a pianner for him to dance on and they'd promised him *he* could tear the strings out of the next one!" The gold-leaf pier glass went in a shatter of shining slivers. No one paid any attention to Evie or Marie. What was a pretty girl compared to all this loot? The bummers were methodical in their work of pillage and destruction. When they'd wrecked the room thoroughly, a new contingent rushed in carrying pots of combustibles and cotton balls soaked in turpentine which they placed in the corners. Then a giant Negro man holding a flaming pine torch in one hand and a bull whip in the other spun about the room touching the torch to the velvet draperies.

Marie started running. With a wail, Evie took off after her. "Wait for me."

The man who wanted to dance on the piano had passed out and fire was already licking at the sofa on which he lay unconscious. No one cared.

Evie said, "There's that captain who buried Jay's cat standing in the front door."

"We can't bother with him now. Come on."

Marie pulled Evie through the door, down the dark front steps. Evie stumbled. Marie swore at her impatiently. They could hear the joggling board creaking up and down, up and down, and Hannah mumbling. The girls ran into the street. Everywhere it was getting bright as day. They came to the arcade under the Town Hall. Behind them the whole of Washington Street was beginning to take fire. A clump of men were gathered on the corner. Marie stopped a minute. Then she saw Sam lying dead, warm and bleeding, on the sidewalk. A general near six feet high but so spare he seemed taller, with lean and muscular cheeks marked with deep gashes and covered with a short grizzly beard of a sandy color, was chewing on a cigar and poking Sam's head to the side with his boot. His light eyes bounded like a ball from one to another of the Union soldiers.

"What does this mean, boys?" he said jerkily, his features twitching nervously as if he were suffering.

An officer replied coolly, "General Sherman, this damned black rascal gave us his impudence and we shot him."

"Well, bury him at once! Get him out of sight."

General Sherman turned away and began talking to his companion. Marie and Evie clung to each other and shrank back against the shadows of the arcade as a brilliant-eyed, young-looking Amelia put her arm through General Sherman's and said gaily, "It's just a few steps from here. There—that house beginning to burn on your far left—the one with the wrought iron railing around the roof."

I trust I shall never witness such a scene again—drunken soldiers, rushing from house to house, emptying them of their valuables, and then firing them; negroes carrying off piles of booty and grinning at the good chance, and exulting, like so many demons; officers and men revelling on the wines and liquors, until the burning houses buried them in their drunken orgies.

> *Capt. David P. Conyngham,*
> War Correspondent for the NEW YORK HERALD,
> Sherman's March through the South, 1865

19

Aided by the gale-force northwest wind and thousands of soldiers and escaped prisoners and Negroes armed with pots of kerosene, cotton balls soaked in turpentine and great packs of matches, the fire was breaking forth in every direction. Inside the convent under the vaulted roof serenity still existed. Still the terror of the night sifted through the solid walls. The scores of women and little girls and the white-faced nuns could hear the roar of the flames as of a great wind over a seething ocean far, far away. Marie put her arm around Evie's shoulder.

"Are you afraid?"

"No. And don't try to comfort me. I'm not going to cry any more. It was just because of the cat."

Evie had burst into tears as soon as the grandly beautiful Mother Superior had said, "Come inside, my children." and Marie had squeezed Evie's hand tight without having any idea what had upset her.

Evie stopped weeping the minute she saw the Huger girl from Charleston and Sara Aldrich from Barnwell and Belle Cohen of Columbia, and pulled her hand away from Marie's. Belle Cohen said to Evie, "What did you come to the convent for—your mother's a Yankee."

"Well, yours is a Jew so that makes us even. What's all that mumbling?"

"It's the nuns coming from the chapel saying their beads. They've just taken the sacrament so the gold altar things can be saved by Father McNeal. They cried all during the time Father O'Connell gave them the blessing."

Marie leaned down and whispered to Evie, "I'm going back and talk to Mama. I know she's still at our house—or nearby."

Evie got rigid and clutched at Marie's arm. "Take me with you."

"No. You stay here and I'll return as soon as I've let Mama know where we are."

"She knows where we are. You're going to look for Willie and run off. Major Reynolds said—"

Marie freed her arm from Evie, trembling beside Belle Cohen, with a forlorn look of being left in her eyes and an acceptance that Marie was going to let her down—go away and never, never come back for her.

Marie hurried away from the convent toward home. There was so much shouting and so many galloping horses and running people she could hardly cross Main Street, brightly lighted now with the spreading conflagration. At the edge of the iron fence of their house, withering narcissus were silhouetted against the illuminated basement. Several figures stood in front of the narcissus. They were dragging a heavy, dark object. Oh Lord, it's Hannah, Marie thought, and ran up to the group who shouted gleefully at the sight of her and dropped the thing they were dragging and reached out to open her cape and feel inside for—

"Git on!" Hannah howled. She was very drunk, leaning up against the banisters. The dark object the soldiers were dragging was the joggling board. "Thesh men shaving my house. Hyar—shet it right hyar, boys, on de aidge ob de gyarden. Hannah jesh gwine watch dish show all night long. Free till I'sh fool!"

Marie shook Hannah as hard as a hundred and ten

pounds could shake two hundred and fifty. "Have you seen Mama?"

"Sho—sho—her and ole Billy gone riding off in de Boozer."

"The Boozer?"

Hannah laughed and belched loudly, "Ain't you know dat's whut ebrybody in dish town call dat glash box you and—and—*She*—sasshays aroun' in?"

Marie looked up and saw that the Town Hall was being set on fire at the top of the tower. The small flame looked so close that she felt she could reach out and touch it. She picked up her skirts and began to run.

"Wait—wait—"

It was Major Reynolds.

"I followed you from the convent. Please go back there at once. General Sherman has promised the Mother Superior it will not be burned."

He was calm again. The demented look in his eyes had disappeared, soothed by the rising fires.

"I want to find Mama."

"She's gone to General Sherman's headquarters in the Blanton Duncan house on Gervais Street."

"And Stobo?"

"He drove her away in the coach. General Sherman gave her two ponies."

Marie slowed down and let him take her arm. "Let's walk around and watch what's going on."

"Always after excitement. But people will hate you. I beg you to return to the convent."

"Just let's walk a little. I'll be safe with you."

"You're trying to find Willie. But he and the others have left now, for good."

A feeling of hopeless loneliness and grief came over Marie. What could she do without Willie, here in this flaming city? How impotent a girl was all by herself. She moved closer to Major Reynolds to still her sickening despair.

Major Reynolds' cheeks were flushed, but his eyes remained calm and cold as they started down Main Street where the fire was now raging. Liquid light of the flames flowed over Marie and bathed her yellow hair in a sublime light. The color had drained from her lips but the leaping fire, like a living volcano, erupted through her body. She felt the flowing of it with an erotic wonder. Her eyes were as gold and red and blue as the fiery spectacle of this inflamed excitement and the licentiousness of this Saturnalia.

An officer joined her and Major Reynolds. It was Lieutenant Conyngham, the correspondent for the New York *Herald,* attached to General Sherman's staff. Marie walked between the two men. No one talked. The sounds of the fire leaped in and out of their ears along with screams and moans and cries of distress, and cheers and demonic laughter. Old men and women and children ran frantically hunting each other and home and somewhere to hide. The Union generals rode their horses here and there, attending little trage‑ dies; oblivious of great ones. Soldiers set fires and a few helped put them out. Soldiers tormented and tortured and yet some soldiers comforted and helped. The night was turned into bronzy day with a thousand scorching, glaring meteors and columns of suffocating clouds of smoke, a boiling aurora, and brimstone sounds of crackling blaze and crashing timbers and falling build‑ ings.

For four hours Marie walked the burning streets with the two men and then she asked them to leave her at the convent. And Major Reynolds and Lieutenant Con‑ yngham went their way; silent and sad the latter; com‑ pensated and at peace the former.

Evie was crouched on a bench by the door when Ma‑ rie, her hair wild as a nimbus of fire, her circular a mesh of singed burned places, her face smudged with soot, came into the sanctuary.

"Dominus vobiscum," Sister Ursula was saying, beckoning the girls, Protestant and Jew as well as Cath‑ olic, to come and kneel with her in a classroom near the little "altar of God," while she recited the rosary. All the other nuns were kneeling in the hall and telling their beads. Marie kept the blue circular wrapped tight around her so no one would see her new, mushroom‑ colored traveling dress, gay with brown silk frogs and smoked pearl buttons.

While they were still on their knees, there was a ter‑

rible battering in of the chapel door, reached by a stairway from the Main Street side. Drunken soldiers came piling over each other, the guards Sherman had sent leading the way, rushing for the sacred gold vessels of the host which Father McNeal had taken away earlier under his cassock. When the soldiers found the gold gone they threw torches up to the rafters and knocked over the plaster saints and crushed the feet of the baby Jesus and cut off the head of Mary with their bayonets.

"Get these damned women out of here," one of the soldiers yelled to the Mother Superior. "What do you think of God now? Is not Sherman greater?"

In answer the Mother Superior gave a few sharp commands to the girls and the nuns and, in a line, they marched out into the seething caldron of Main Street.

Father O'Connell, holding a crucifix high above his head, led the procession through the heaving, molten sea. There was not a cry, not a moan from any of the women or children though sparks and flying embers came down on them like burning snowflakes. For one small second as they emerged from the convent, even the drunken soldiers hushed, the horses stopped in mid-trot, the leaping tongues of fire froze. Then there was a great roar and the tower of the Town Hall thundered into the street and dozens of crushed soldiers were swallowed up in that immense pyre.

The great clock hung crazily on a rafter while it struck eleven times then disintegrated as if it had never existed.

Father O'Connell, lifting the cross higher, turned down Blanding Street leading his little band between a living wall of fire and solid sheets of flame: the majestic figure of the Mother Superior following where the crucifix led, the long line of stark, shocked faces of the little schoolgirls, the women, the trembling nuns. As they approached the church on the corner of Blanding and Assembly some officers galloped up. General Howard, his empty right sleeve pinned on his chest, reined in his horse and escorted Father O'Connell and the cross safely through the crackling, red, devouring inferno past packs of rioting Negroes and soldiers, the rest of the way to the church where they went inside and lay down for a few minutes, exhausted, in the pews.

But not for long. A Union soldier came crying, "They are going to blow up the church," and everybody ran out and hid among the graves and crouched on the cold tombs and wept under the scorching trees.

At 4 A.M., Marie was lying on a flat tomb wrapped in her circular watching the palpitating, fiery furnace that was the sky. The convent was in its last stages. She shuddered as the cross, showing clear and near as far-off things do in such brilliant flagration, toppled and disappeared. Shortly after, she saw Stobo, riding a mule, enter the cemetery. Without waking Evie who had fallen off her side of the tomb and was curled up in a clump of dead fern, she rose and met him beside an unstrung harp leaning against a monument.

"Your ma wants you."

"Where is she?"

"Headquarters."

"I'm too exhausted to walk there."

"Stand on that tombstone and I'll put this mule up close to it. Get on behind me. Just kick that harp out of your way."

The roaring and crashing had crescended. The fire had hold of the entire city now. The old State House was one grand arc of lambent flame. Soldiers were shooting at the Houdon statue of Washington and the iron palmetto tree monument, and the bells of Charleston's St. Michael's in the State House yard. The high, piercing "pings" of the bells tore through the black columns of smoke. Passing the South Carolina College, Marie saw the Commons opposite the gate packed with women and children shivering in the bitter night. The piazza of Mrs. McCord's house was full of Union officers. They were drinking her champagne and brandy and singing homesick songs, glutted with incendiarism.

Stobo did not respond when Marie told him about Sam and Hannah. Merely hunched up his shoulders and sighed deeply.

They came to the Preston mansion. The outer gateposts guarded by two soldiers held United States flags; another United States flag of immense size floated over the roof. Soldiers of all ranks squatted over the driveway spitting and coughing as wads of smoke from the burning house adjacent irritated their lungs and throats. As the mule passed them, they grabbed at Marie's ankles and made coarse jokes about her yellow hair and her riding pillion with a black man. The marble-tiled piazza was crowded with smoke-blackened bummers, drunk and quarreling. Stobo handed her down and told her to go in and ask for her mother.

Henry met her at the door. He seemed sad and very tired but the scorn in his eyes for her and everybody in this house was as withering as the fire. The great east drawing room was crowded with women arranging to go north with the enemy. The marble mantel had been written over and plans for marching drawn on the walls. In the corner the marble statue of Eve wore a blue forage cap and a black mustache. Officers came in and out with books and Dresden figures to take away with them.

Smoking a long cigar, Amelia was sitting in a gilt armchair at a marble-topped table. She was in charge of interviewing the women.

She nodded to Marie and motioned to her to come and pull up a chair beside her.

"Is Evie all right?"

"Yes. She is with the nuns in the churchyard."

"Excellent. Stobo will take you in the coach to fetch her soon after you hear the bugles blow. General Wood's men are standing at attention waiting for that signal to march in and put out all the fires on the instant."

"Why must I wait until then? Evie's cold and all alone."

"I don't want you out of this house now. These last two hours will be the worst. The soldiers are crazy with the wine they have drunk and the power they have felt as they cremated an entire city. Even the wind has been in their favor. Just so was it blowing the night you were born. I've never been so unhappy as

I was that night. I remember looking out at the dark streets and hearing the wind and hating every brick and lamppost and chimney of Columbia."

"I suppose you are happy now. Just as Major Reynolds is happy. Your grudges are certainly settled against Columbia. I bet you set the first fire yourself—or sent off one of the rockets."

Amelia shrugged and flicked the ash from her cigar. "So?"

"So— I loved Columbia. I suppose I loved you, too. I must have or I wouldn't feel so definitely that I don't love you any more."

"Tomorrow you will. You are tired and hungry. Go somewhere and comb your hair, then have something to eat. A buffet is set up on the sideboards in the dining room. You never saw such a collation. And the wines these Prestons had! No wonder you liked to come here to parties. Tell Henry to bring me another bottle of that fifty-year-old Madeira. I must keep my strength up for I have full power in granting permission to the families who want to leave with the army."

Marie went out. Lieutenant Conyngham was lying on one of the long leather sofas in the hall by the front door. He was writing on a thick tablet. He said wearily, "Why did you leave the convent?"

"Oh—it burned down hours ago."

"Where will the nuns go?"

"People in this town are kind. They'll be cared for someway."

"I realize now why General Sherman kept the brigades of Irish out of the city."

"Why?"

"They would have given assistance to the Roman Catholics."

"General Sherman knew all the time he was going to burn the convent, didn't he?"

"How do I know? You talk too much. Say—have you seen that antique Greek marble Venus in the basement? It must be worth at least thirty or forty thousand dollars. If I can get it properly crated—"

"It used to stand in the turn of the stairs."

"Over there?"

"Yes."

"Are you going back to see the nuns?"

"Yes, after the bugles blow."

"Tell the Superioress that when General Sherman comes to make peace with her at daybreak, as he plans to do, and offer her any house in the city to compensate for the burning of the convent, to request this house. I should hate terribly to see it destroyed and I've already heard General Logan give the order to fire it the minute he moves out."

"I wonder why?"

Conyngham chuckled, "General Preston referred to him publicly some years ago in Washington as 'that half-breed Logan.' It hit the mark!"

Inside the coach was like being back home. Marie nestled her cheek against the familiar sky-blue upholstery and rubbed her hand over the cool, crystal windows. She was leaning back as far as she could so that she wouldn't see any more than she had to of the desolation. For the whole city had disappeared as if by magic.

Her beautiful eyes reflected all the gray emptiness that they looked upon: the sun rising with a ghostly, pale glimmer through the dense smoke still hovering like a soul above its just expired corpse; the chimneys standing like tall, black tombstones; the fresh mounds of brick and charred timbers and rubble—graves that yesterday had been fine houses; the desolate mourners reclining on mattresses or piles of soggy cotton or just a bed of ashes—the wretched old men and women and children staring vacantly and grieving and hating—

The old State House was a length of shattered walls and a few chimneys; Sumter Street, where the finest houses had been, with only one house left, the brick house of Mr. Mordecai; Washington Street where *she* had lived—a pile of chimneys and bricks and a joggling board standing on top of some singed rags and fragments that must have been the crazed Hannah; the market, a ruined shell supported by crumbling arches, its spire fallen in and one of the clock's hands pointing like an accusing finger upward; Main Street—a mile

and a half of ashes with edges of rubble. At the far
end though, the rising new State House was catching a
pale sunbeam on a broken pediment and somewhere
on a houseless chimney a red bird was singing a morning song.

After trying to find Blanding Street and seeking for
some mark of the convent, Stobo finally turned the
ponies to the left.

A woman hunting for the place where her house had
stood recognized the showy coach and screamed and
cursed the occupant. The scream stabbed through Marie, a chill passed down her backbone to her toes. Her
heart started thudding in an indefinable anguish.

For that scream was a foretaste of her future. It
meant she could never come back here. Never. Never.
Just as she had never been able to return to Newberry.

For an instant she wondered if the sundial was
still telling the hours at the Boozer place? Whether
Judge O'Neall had built the high wall around and the
roof over his grave as Big Dave had willed. That must
have been to keep Amelia from ever looking at his
grave. Even in death he must have feared her. Marie
feared her too. She had proved so powerful. Her black
magic had always, in the end, worked.

Marie felt a choking in her chest as the memory
came to her of the way the back of Willie's neck had
looked, arched and vulnerable, as he leaned forward
in his saddle and disappeared down this very street
twenty-four hours earlier. Her anguish would only be
stilled when she and he came together again. And she
could be free of her mother forever.

When she gave Lieutenant Conyngham's message
about the Preston mansion to the Superioress, her voice
was strained and hoarse. But the beautiful lady was too
heartsick and too angry with a man who had broken
his word to notice Marie Boozer. Someone had brought
the unstrung harp onto the church porch. The Mother
Superior put her back against the harp so she would
keep herself erect and not let her shoulders droop. She
waved Marie away as General Sherman in a uniform
neither old nor new came riding up to the church door
and, not dismounting nor removing his hat, gruffly be-

gan explaining how the fire got beyond his control from buildings he had to burn, and blaming Mayor Goodwyn for not having sent the liquor from the warehouses out of the town and—"You can have any house left standing." He galloped off and reached his headquarters on Gervais Street a good while before the cumbersome "showbox" arrived there with Amelia Feaster's sleepy daughters.

PART THREE

MARCHING THROUGH THE CAROLINAS
FROM COLUMBIA, S.C.
TO FAYETTEVILLE, N.C.

February 20, 1865–March 14, 1865

Colonel Childs had news of the beautiful Boozer.
"She went off with flying colors." "No doubt," said
Isabella . . . and to me: "Your defense of Boozer
in Columbia was a mistake, you see!" The Boozer
talk was sotto voce, not for Colonel Childs to hear.

> *Mary Boykin Chesnut,* Diary from Dixie,
> March 1865

20

At five o'clock on Monday morning Amelia woke Marie and Evie. "Make haste and dress. Marching orders to the army were issued last night by Sherman for seven o'clock this morning. The bummers are already on the way ahead to forage for us. You and Evie go down and eat a hot breakfast and then take the coach to the Preston mansion. Stobo is waiting outside for you. I'll join you at the Prestons' as soon as I bathe and change into fresh clothes."

Marie looked up at her mother, taking out the pins and letting her long black hair slither down her back

like a thick, shiny snake. Amelia looked fresh and un-
tired as if she'd just stepped from a bath.

"Have you been up all night?"

"Yes. The Preston mansion is still jammed with
Union sympathizers who have been burned out, begging to be taken off. Major Reynolds is organizing a
special train for them and the thousands of Negroes
from here and the country. I got here about an hour
ago but stopped downstairs long enough to eat breakfast
with General Sherman. He's putting us in General
Howard's special care so we can be near his headquarters whenever we stop. Sherman likes to play cards. We
played all yesterday afternoon. I slightly soothed his
feelings which have been terribly hurt by the Columbia
ladies who have abused him outrageously to his face.
Mrs. Elmore even poked him in the back with an umbrella—a cotton one at that! Oh—you'll be happy to
know I've made a friend. A *real* lady, who is going
along with us—Mrs. Craft. She's taking her white
nurse and her three children to her sister in New York.
Her husband left her this morning. He's a snob,
though, all mixed up with those Middletons and Smiths
in Charleston and refused to be reasonable about her
or the children. Heigh—ho—have you girls stayed inside this room the entire time?"

"Marie was scared to go out. Scared some of her
fine friends might holler at her. She just lay here reading a book of poetry all day. Love poetry," Evie
growled, getting up and shaking out her starched pan-
taloons, "but I went out and walked and walked.
Somebody sure put a curse on this old town."

"Why do I always have to be deviled with Evie,"
Marie fumed. "I've been shut in here with her since
Saturday."

"You don't. She can come later with me."

"Just because Marie's older and prettier you always
pet her. I wouldn't go with her anyway," Evie said to
Amelia. "But what do you care? I bore her! That's
what she always says, 'Evie bores me . . .' " There was
a long silence and then sobs came.

Marie calmly finished buttoning her wide, divided,
linen drawers embroidered in yellow bees and stepped

into the brand-new Paris traveling dress. Evie *did* bore her. Let Amelia comfort her. Amelia was the one who'd messed up all their lives.

Marie kept her eyes closed as they drove through the ghostly streets. It was a warm pink dawn with spring in the air and mockingbirds becoming accustomed to charred rafters instead of branchy trees and singing their heads off. Thousands of soldiers were rushing about falling into ranks. At the entrance to the Preston mansion the whole of General Kilpatrick's cavalry were prancing and trotting about to their general's rapid fire curses about any and everything and everybody.

General Logan, mounted on a limping gray horse, was under the great magnolia tree motionless as a carved, dark-bronze image of an Indian chief. As Stobo piloted the coach into the driveway, Marie saw ambulances, buggies, wagons, carriages and every kind of vehicle put in requisition and all kinds of mules and horses in use. Each conveyance was heavy with feeble and old and eager men, women and children, flour, hominy, hams, candles, cook pots, and on the top, with tied legs, jerking heads and sad eyes—the turkeys, geese, chickens and hogs of Columbia that had somehow escaped the conflagration. The refugees were crowded together willing to undergo all the hardships and dangers of the campaign in order to escape the certain starvation that faced South Carolina and the infuriated hatred of the Southern soldiers and citizens. Men and women who, for some reason, were not able to join the train stood around weeping.

Since it was impossible to maneuver the clumsy coach into line, Marie climbed out and made her way to the piazza between the waiting carriages. Old Henry was directing the Preston Negroes, who had stayed behind, in moving out what furniture and treasure had been too heavy for the Union soldiers to take away with them, so that when the house was burned something would remain for his beloved master and mistress. Marie tried to speak to him but he purposely bumped into her and shoved her off the top step. Mortified, she returned to the coach. Stobo said crossly, "I

wish you'd of stayed away from Henry. Don't make
me have to knock him and get in bad with General
Howard. He's a peaceable man. You ought to know
better than anybody else that your goose is cooked in
this town. You got to start working all over somewhere else to be a belle. But don't look so unhappy.
If you'd open your eyes, you'd see that every man-jack
of a soldier is staring at you the same as if you was
Bathsheba. They is all talking about you, too."

"Oh, I see them. And they're all ugly. I'm unhappy
because this house has been a symbol to me and I hate
to see it burned."

"It's not going to be burned," a courtly, rather frail,
heavily bearded man, leading a grand horse, said
gently to Marie.

"But General Logan has ordered it to be burned.
Look at him sitting there waiting—"

"I know. Here—will you pin my empty sleeve onto
my jacket. Buttons, pins, and cutting meat are the only
things I haven't been able to master."

With deft fingers Marie arranged the officer's empty
right sleeve across his chest. She smiled up at him,
lowering her lashes. "They're ready to burn it this very
minute."

He shook his head, "General Sherman promised the
Mother Superior of the Convent any house standing
in Columbia so long as she was in possession when
the orders to forward march were given. Logan's over
there praying the bugle'll blow before the good lady
arrives. He's placed hundreds of pots of kerosene in
every room so if the bugles do sound first the mansion will go up like a skyrocket. A pretty house and the
garden is a jewel. A shame so many of the soldiers
wrecked the boxwood. Are you Mrs. Feaster's daughter?"

"Yes."

He bowed. "General Howard, mam. I am in special
charge of your carriage. Where is it? I'd like to look it
over since General Sherman wants you to move right
along with the cavalry."

Reaching the coach, Marie turned and looked
straight at General Howard. Her eyes were as deep

blue as his uniform. Her skin had a gold sheen reflected from the rising sun. Perched on her yellow hair was a swirl of blonde gauze veiling and her mushroom-colored traveling dress revealed and hid her curves with just the proper amount of voluptuous allure.

General Kilpatrick rode up on a spotted stallion. "By damn, that's a rare filly you've caught. God damn it, Howard, put her in my group. Old Billy's picked her mother. At least give me *mon droit* with the daughter!"

The garden, the magnolia tree, the ogling soldiers, the massed carriages began to spin, balls of light danced before Marie's eyes. She felt she was going to faint. She should have stayed with Evie and eaten breakfast. For Willie was in the garden. He was standing under the rare Chinese parasol tree in a blue cape. He was looking at her through the great heart-shaped leaves and his face was gray with fury. She knew he had heard Kilpatrick and his offensive insolence.

As from a great distance, General Howard's voice reached her. "Get on with you, Kil. This child is my personal responsibility. I'll have none of that. We've got enough confusion with these confounded thousands of refugees without you making more trouble."

"Now, Howard. Just because you're the most gentlemanly soldier in the army doesn't make a lady out of a—"

"Here, honey, sit down—put your head in your lap." Stobo had heard General Kilpatrick and seen Marie's face. She leaned over for a minute. The house stopped going around. Wavy lines grew straight again. There was no one under the Chinese parasol tree. And the piazza was filled with little girls and black-robed nuns; and in the front door smiling like a very pleased guardian angel, the Supeioress! And prostrating himself at her feet, black Henry Preston sobbing and yelling, "Thank Gawd, my lady, you is here—you is here! Oh, thank you, Gawd. Thank you very highly."

The bugles blew. Horses reared and plunged forward. Roosters crowed, pigs squealed, babies cried, soldiers sang, wheels creaked, cannons and caissons rumbled. Major Reynolds rode back and forth getting his train in order. Sherman's great army, swollen now, with the rufugees, to over a hundred thousand mouths to feed, was again on the march.

General Howard put his hand on the heavy glass window of the coach. "This coach won't do, Mrs. Feaster. General Sherman plans to march across South and North Carolina in a straight line disregarding roads except as they please his fancy. If it rains, we corduroy the way with saplings. Rivers have to be crossed, half the time on pontoon bridges, sometimes forded. This big heavy coach just won't make it."

Amelia tightened her little red heart-lips and her chin jutted out stubbornly. "This is February, General Howard. My children will perish of pneumonia if we don't have a closed vehicle."

"But not this one. You'll have to transfer to a baggage wagon. I'll find you something better along the route."

"Which way are we going, General?" Marie had a vestige of color back in her cheeks now and her eyes had begun to sparkle. Yes—she had seen Willie again. This time he was in the second-floor front window—in the east drawing room—the room where they had danced their first waltz together. He had blown her a kiss. When she had lifted her hand to wave at him Stobo had pretended to stumble and when she reached to catch him he had whispered, "No—no—don't wave. They watches everything."

But he *had* blown her a kiss and nodded at her. So he still loved her and she was going to find him. As soon as she could, she was going to find him.

General Howard said, "We are headed straight for Winnsboro. I am in a hurry to arrive there ahead of the bummers. It's a lovely little town. General Slocum and I don't want it to be burned. If one of us reaches there in time we may be able to save it. Madame—this coach cannot—"

The Winnsboro road! Willie had gone down the Winnsboro road last Friday. Hampton's cavalry must be camped in that direction. Willie would be going that way, too, this morning, with his information for Hampton that Sherman was quitting Columbia.

Marie's lips trembled in excitement. "Then let's get along, General. The Elmores live about a mile out of the town on the Winnsboro road. Mrs. Elmore has a stunning, closed carriage that is as swift as a race horse. You remember it, Mama? Mr. Elmore had it built especially for their trips to the Virginia Springs. We can leave 'the Boozer' there and take hers—"

"Good! Good!" General Howard was up and giving his brigade the signal to forward march! The heavy, painted coach creaked and bumped as the rather small hackneys strained to get the big wheels turning.

Marie sat back in the coach and looked out of the rear window. Willie was not in the window of the mansion now but across the piles of rubble that had been a city block she saw a lone horseman galloping on a familiar bobtailed sorrel. His blue cape flying out behind him revealing his gray trousers, he was headed in the general direction of Winnsboro.

Amelia was smiling and saying tenderly, "You always do what I want eventually. I knew you'd play the right cards when I called for them."

For years the Boozer glass coach remained in the Elmore carriage house, big as a boat cabin, and useless as any big thing which cannot fit to a small need.

Mrs. *Thomas Taylor*,
South Carolina Women in the Confederacy

21

General Logan reached the Elmore plantation ahead of them and took a fine, black Morgan mare, leaving his lame old gray in the stable in her place. A black Gordon setter, evidently the mare's stable mate, was leaping up to snap at General Logan's boots. "Easy —easy—come along with us, boy." General Logan leaned down and patted the dog and the dog licked his hand and loped after the pretty black mare.

General Howard had sent two cavalrymen ahead to fetch the Elmore carriage to meet them. They were waiting with it under an enormous red oak tree by the road. They had it loaded with hams and bacon and soft white wool blankets. Long and slim and sleek the carriage was. Thoroughbred in every spring and shaft and silver lamp.

Marie hid herself in a harass of horses while Stobo unhitched the puffing ponies and directed Horace and Billy, two of Mrs. Elmore's houseboys whom he knew well, to pull the "showbox" out of the road under the red oak. He helped Horace and Billy transfer the hams from the carriage to the coach but he craftily called up the cavalrymen before the Elmore Negroes had time to retrieve the blankets.

Mrs. Elmore came running out of her house. She had on a poke bonnet with a long crepe veil hanging to her shabby heels. She had been dressing to go into the town.

"That is my carriage and those are my best blankets," said Mrs. Elmore on reaching the red oak. "What are you ruffians doing with my things?"

"We want them for a good Union lady," said the older cavalryman.

"Then you do not want it for anyone you will find here," said Mrs. Elmore.

"Oh, yes, we've got *two* loyal ladies, and we've got to have a light carriage for them to go along with us," said the younger soldier.

"But that is *my* carriage," protested Mrs. Elmore, "and your loyal ladies have no business with it. If you have any Union ladies, you must have brought them with you."

"No, we didn't, they've been here in Columbia under your nose all the time."

Now the ponies were hitched and Mrs. Elmore said to the younger of the two men, "Young man, have you a mother?"

He looked at her saucily, but respectfully, and replied, "Yes, ma'am—a nice, sweet-looking old lady, just like you."

And Mrs. Elmore sat down on the ground and laughed and laughed and laughed.

"The carriage must go—it's General Howard's order, ma'am. I'm sorry—mighty sorry. But you can keep this fine glass coach and all the food inside of it. General Howard said for you to. So it ain't really putting you out too much. Good day, ma'am."

Marie and Amelia and Evie tried to slip into the carriage without Mrs. Elmore's seeing them. But Horace and Billy saw and they told Mrs. Elmore afterwards.

"Whey to put this here chariot at, Missy?" Horace asked Mrs. Elmore when that special regiment had passed on by.

"Oh—put the car of Venus in the carriage house, Horace," Mrs. Elmore sighed and got to her feet. "And they took our black mare?"

"Yes'm and black Mac went off following after her. 'Nyung Massa go' hate that awful when shootin' season come. Mac was the best ole bu'd dawg in Richland County."

Mary Boozer had two troops of Cavalry as her escort. Her wagons containing the household goods were put under the charge of an officer and detail. The march began. Officers before the carriage, officers behind and at each window, were in one continual struggle to be near her, to catch the sound of her voice or even a flitting smile.

HERALD & NEWS,
Newberry, S. C., August 6, 1909

22

They were off! And what a traveling! General Slocum was double-quicking from Newberry with the Fourteenth. General Howard was making all possible haste and General Pardee and a brigade of General Geary's division forcing themselves to the limit to reach the historic capital of Fairfield County, Winnsboro, ahead of the bummers and foragers and stragglers from the Grand Army, so there would be no repetition of the Columbia scene.

Mrs. Elmore's graceful, lean little carriage pulled by the high-stepping hackneys skimmed over the sandy clay road. This carriage had an immediate effect on Marie. She felt as if she had stepped from a dark, thick cocoon into a pair of wings. The heavy glass and silver and gilt coach with the clumsy wheels and all that it had signified was left behind forever. She was going ahead now to a new life swiftly, genteelly. Willie was always going to be proud of her. And how they would love each other!

Her bubbly laugh rang out like a silver trumpet and she constantly showed her pretty teeth smiling at the soldier boys in blue who trotted alongside paying her compliments or who came galloping up with offerings: a tiny, white French poodle with a hot, pink tongue, a yellow parrot crying, "Oh Miss Annie! Poor Miss

Annie!" finger rings set with garnets and emeralds and sapphires and rose diamonds, enamel watches to pin on her lapel, boxes of fondant, rose-point collars, *Venise* berthas, and ruffled parasols that they had intended to send the girls back home.

Marie took the little poodle in her lap and sat the yellow parrot on her shoulder and nibbled at a fondant and covered her fingers with the gaily colored rings. She forced Evie to get out and ride in Mrs. Craft's carriage because she teased the poodle. She made fun of Amelia sleeping soundly with her bonnet fallen on her nose. Impudently, but gaily, she sang *Dixie* and *The Bonnie Blue Flag* and she clapped her hands admiringly at the tricks the Cavalrymen made their fresh horses perform to impress her.

How Willie was going to laugh with her when she showed him all those outrageous presents. They would ride away together from Winnsboro, laughing and whispering, she pillion behind him. Or perhaps she and Stobo might manage to slip away with the carriage and the ponies during one of Amelia's card games with General Sherman. Then she could follow Willie respectably till the war's end.

Major Reynolds fetched Evie back to the carriage at first dark. He needed a shave and his light eyes were dull as stone.

"Mrs. Craft has no room for Evie to sleep in her vehicle," he said tersely.

Amelia sat up in bewilderment when the Major opened the carriage door. Seeing Evie she said, "Oh, you," and closed her eyes again.

Marie said to Major Reynolds, "Mama's been asleep all day. Making up for the past three nights, I reckon. She hasn't even smoked a cigar. When are we going to stop and eat? I've had nothing but candy since we left Columbia."

"We aren't going to stop tonight. You shouldn't be hungry—you've had the admiration of the entire army to feed on."

Remembering the wild way he had behaved the day of the burning, Marie smiled gently and said drowsily,

"Oh, that was all in fun. I've tried to be good-humored. But you know which side I am on."

"You'd better keep quiet about that. And don't try to run away from me along the march. Remember I watch you all the time. You mustn't forget that we are old friends. I saw you first."

"No, I won't forget. But I saw *you* first—at Camp Sorghum."

"I'll fetch you some ham sandwiches and coffee soon. There's a station set up ahead to feed us."

Marie nodded her head. A sense of sadness came over her all of a sudden. She let Evie hold the poodle and the parrot. The stars were out and a bright glow along the horizons told of blazing houses. All day she had been too excited by the attention of the soldiers to look around. A southwest wind was blowing. The night was soft and fresh with spring, cool but not cold. She unfolded one of Mrs. Elmore's white blankets and threw it across Amelia's knees and wrapped another around herself and Evie. Where was Willie tonight in the balmy dark? "Oh Willie—Willie—" she whispered, "I'm very near you tonight. Very near."

They reached Winnsboro early the next morning but the bummers and stragglers had got there first. There was noise enough as they approached the town but it was not the usual brass band that heralded their advance. It was swollen-teated cows bellowing as they were whipped savagely along the way, and it was geese gabbling and turkeys gobbling and pigs squealing.

Marie drew back the curtains in front of the carriage windows. In revulsion she peered out on a ragged army at their task. An army still drunk with the fire and whiskey and gold and pearls and silk of Columbia, they were shouting and cursing and pillaging and burning. Bonfires made of mounds of cured hams and bacon and wrung-neck turkeys decorated the street. Snowball fights, of flour and molasses pressed together, were going on everywhere. Horses were being fed sugar out of silk top hats. Hogs, bayoneted and then hung on quarters on the bayonets to bleed made crimson banners. Chickens, geese, and turkeys, knocked over the head, hung around the necks of big Negro men in garlands. Horses in foal were being beaten along, weak and trembling, or carelessly shot so that no rebel might save a thoroughbred foal.

The wool-hatted, smoke-begrimed bummers were running in and out of houses, beating music out of grand pianos with their musket butts, multiplying mirrors, knocking down Negroes or planters if a bee stung them, chasing little pet dogs that barked, and stabbing them with their butcher knives, jeering at terrified women and children, black and white, who cried when their lovely houses or tiny cottages were immolated.

With the entrance of the first column of the Grand Army, however, all the officers immediately turned their attention to stopping the fires and rounding up the drunken stragglers and renegades. Columbia had been enough for the present. This was too much. Six of the generals—Slocum, Howard, Williams, Geary, Pardee and Barnum worked side by side with their men, burning their whiskers and scorching their clothes to get the fires and the town under control of the army. Of the other two generals, General Kilpatrick had departed on a feint toward Chester to make General Hardee and General Cheatham think the Union army was headed toward Charlotte, and General Sherman had gone straight to a dwelling in Winnsboro picked out for his headquarters, without so much as a comment on the vindictive and wanton destruction of this fair place.

Stobo knew Winnsboro well. He remembered exactly how to reach the house where he had taken Jacob and Jay Feaster in November. To get there he drove through the northwest corner of the town, away from the general debacle. The house was near the Episcopal Church but when he neared the house he whipped up the ponies and drove on rapidly for a crowd of bummers had dragged the church organ into the street. One of them was playing *Yankee Doodle* on it. Others, wearing Mason's hats and crinoline petticoats and silk shawls were dancing a drunken jig. Propped up on end against a red-and-white, flowering camellia tree was a freshly exhumed coffin that had been split open with an ax so that its recently dead occupant, dressed in a torn Confederate uniform, might enjoy the reveling.

Evie yelled up at Stobo, "Stop—you've gone way past Auntie's house. I want to see Jay."

Marie put her face to the window, saw the corpse staring at her and cried, "Mama! Wake up, Mama!"

Amelia roused and asked thickly what was going on.

Evie said, "I want to go in Auntie's house. I may decide to stay with her and Papa. Jay is there. Don't—"

"Who? Who? Who? What? What? What?"

"Jay—your son—Jay—don't you want to see him too?"

"Marie, tell Stobo to stop this rambling and take us straight to General Sherman's headquarters. I must have a bath and some food immediately. Lord have mercy, I'm all cramped up. My back is killing me. What nonsense are you mumbling, Evie? Son? I have no son."

"How can you say such a hateful thing?" Marie's cheeks were flaming. "Stobo—stop at once."

The carriage slowed and Evie stumbled out. The little poodle hopped onto the ground and immediately squatted down to relieve herself. Marie jumped after Evie and Amelia called up in an angry voice to Stobo to get going and come back later for the girls.

Followed by the poodle, Marie and Evie went to Evie's auntie's house. There was no one there. One of the bummers saw them and started shooting at the poodle. Marie grabbed her up and she and Evie ran off in the direction in which Stobo had driven.

By this time General Geary had rounded up most of the bummers and stragglers and ordered them back to their respective commands—thus separating them and breaking up their mob violence. He put Brigadier General Pardee in charge of the town with orders to protect private property and cause guards whose "conversation was generally kind and indicated respect to be stationed throughout the town."

Hours later, Marie and Evie discovered Jay. They were walking past a large, handsome house with guards standing at attention all about the grounds. Rank-and-file soldiers were packed resentfully outside the fence but none dared cross the pickets. For this was the home of Mrs. Rion, whose father was a wealthy manufacturer in Pennsylvania, and these guards had been sent to Winnsboro by Sherman before Columbia was occupied so there would be no chance of an incident at this house. The sun filtering through the oak trees' great branches sparkled and winked on enormous piles of silver and china and Persian carpets and portraits and furniture. Droves of children, white and colored, played and frolicked over the lawn. Ladies, white and colored, sat about in wicker chairs or reclined in hammocks near their household treasures. All those who had been able had flocked to this sanctuary that looked, this warm winter day, like a great open-air market of precious goods.

Marie and Evie crowded up to the picket fence to stare curiously at the exhibition of beautiful things. Marie was still carrying the poodle. All at once Marie felt a tug at her skirt. She looked down. Inside the fence was Jay.

"Don't look so surprised. Do smile, Marie," he said. "I've missed you."

"I've missed you, too. Do you mind if I kiss you?" She leaned over the fence and kissed him hard. "Where is Papa Feaster?"

"He's back in Virginia with General Lee. Where are you going?"

So many eyes were on them now, so many of the children swooping to the fence, the little dog barking shrilly, Jay putting his hand in hers. "May I hold the little dog, Marie?"

Marie handed the dog over the fence.

"Where is my cat?" he asked Evie.

"Oh, he's dead. A Yankee shot him and another one helped me bury him in a cigar box of Mama's. You've gotten fat."

One of the soldiers said to Evie, "You shouldn't say 'Yankee' in that tone of voice. Ain't you one of us? Didn't I steal a fine carriage from a poor old lady for you to ride up North in?"

Jay started wheezing and coughing. He pushed the poodle back over the fence into Marie's hands.

"Go away," he said, then he began to cry. "I bet you all are with the Yankees. I don't love you. Not either of you. Nor Mama either."

"Jay," Marie called, "Jay-bird—"

But he was running over to a hammock where lay a sweet-faced lady, who resembled Jacob Feaster. Marie called again, "Jay—look—"

Hastily she dropped the little poodle inside the fence. "Call her, Jay. She's a present for you."

The sweet-faced lady was sitting up in the hammock and smoothing Jay's hair back from his forehead. She was pointing to the poodle. Evie waved at the lady but her aunt ignored her entirely. Jay ran forward and scooped up the poodle which began licking his tears and wagging her tail happily.

Evie bit her thumb and said crossly, "Now why'd you do that? I liked that puppy dog. Why didn't you give him the nasty old parrot?"

Marie said, "Parrot? I suppose—I don't know what I suppose." She broke off half afraid she might begin to cry herself then she turned away and went quickly down the street toward the burned heart of the town.

The refugees from Columbia who followed Sherman's army began to pass; among them I recognized Mary Boozer and her mother in a carriage, she in lively conversation with a gay looking officer riding by the carriage.

Mrs. *Poppenheim*,
The Women of the South in War Times

23

The next day the people of the devastated town gathered on the sidewalk and hissed and booed the army and the refugees marching away with bands playing and flags flying. The bummers and foragers mounted on their scraggy mules and castoff horses had gone on about twenty miles ahead in the direction of Camden to continue "living off the country" and providing food for Sherman's army. General Geary and General Hampton had met somewhere during the night and Hampton had given his word that any Federal soldiers left behind as safeguards after the main army departed from Fairfield County would be protected by his cavalry.

Major Reynolds rode as escort to Marie's carriage and she kept teasing him and laughing at him to convince him she hadn't a thought in her head at the moment except him. But where was Willie?

On the edge of town Stobo cracked his whip in the direction of a group of horsemen huddled under an oak on a little hilltop. Was Willie among them? In case he might be, Marie leaned out of the window and waved her gauzy hat. A bobtailed sorrel horse reared up high. Yes—there was Willie—scouting for Hampton. He'd seen her all right. He knew now she was in Mrs. Elmore's carriage.

Major Reynolds struck his horse hard and galloped toward the rear of the refugee train.

Amelia reached a strong hand and pulled Marie back inside the carriage.

"I recognized the horse which reared up in that grove. And the rider—he has a sourly familiar look about him, too. It would be pitiful for you to be the cause of his being shot."

Marie lowered her head and dragged the blonde gauze hat down over her eyes, tearing the soft net. "He won't be caught. Not Willie. I am going to leave this refugee train the very first chance I get. I told you that night of the fire sitting in the Prestons' drawing room that I hated you. You didn't believe me but I do—I do."

Was that choked sound her voice? Pulling the net inside her mouth she bit hard on it but suddenly she was weeping.

Amelia said Foot! and laughed and chatted along about the things they were going to do in Washington and New York with the money General Billy Sherman assured her his brother, Senator John Sherman, could collect for them from the U. S. Government. General Sherman had already written a statement and sent it to the Senator swearing he'd personally seen the Feaster property in Columbia burning.

"It wasn't *our* property. It was a rented house and—"

Marie sniffled a while longer into her hat. But it got all sticky and hot so she threw it out the window.

She watched the Confederates across a field about a mile to the left trotting in and out of thickets and jumping ditches and hedges. They knew they were safe from attack though every now and then a musket or a pistol would bang as some Union cavalryman took a pot shot at them. And certainly *they* weren't going to attack this succession of phalanxes. David's slingshot wasn't primed yet.

Marie kept her eyes on them away from Amelia who was staring fixedly at her, trying to put one of her wicked spells on her. She wondered why Willie had made no attempt in Winnsboro to contact her. With all the Negroes rambling back and forth it would have been easy for him to have sent a note to her through

Stobo or blacked his face and found her. Why had he not? Why?

Echo answered—you silly—because you were in General Sherman's headquarters all afternoon and night taking a hot bath and eating a Christmas dinner and drinking champagne and playing piquet with Major Reynolds and dancing reels with dozens of handsome officers. If Willie *had* come knocking at the door or peeping in your window—he'd have been shot like that poor Mr. Manigault had been who was standing in the coffin watching the mad carnival at the Episcopal Church yesterday. Tomorrow, she whispered to herself—tomorrow along the way. Tomorrow will be time enough. Tomorrow. Tomorrow.

Suddenly she willed herself to sit up straight and look into her mother's face. And she realized with a shock that Amelia had stopped trying to put a spell on her and was looking lovingly at her. Amelia *cared* about her. *Really* cared. And she didn't care. That made *her* the stronger. This was the first time she'd comprehended it. She *was* the stronger. She could feel an exultant power flowing into her thighs and down her arms and into the pupils of her eyes.

"Dear Mama," she purred in false sincerity, "how I do annoy you. But I don't mean to, Mama. And you needn't worry about me and Willie. I'll stay with you and Evie. I promise, Mama."

Evie said, "Well, my Lord, what's got into you?"

Marie mashed Evie's foot into the rug of the floor. Evie, noticing the hard blue glitter of her sister's eyes straightened out her foot and didn't wince though she was positive her little toe was broken entirely off.

"Oh, Evie, you know Mama and I never mean anything by our quarreling. We understand each other. Don't we, Mama?"

It was said that when passing Society Hill, Mrs. Feaster by mistake, loaded up and took off the family silver of the Witherspoons, a prominent family, at whose home she stopped and who had put their silver in her room for safety.

James G. Gibbes,
PHILADELPHIA TIMES,
September 20, 1880

24

And the smart little carriage bowled on and on at the head of the bizarre refugee train following in the rear of Sherman's army.

Though the white refugees had outnumbered the colored when the train assembled in Columbia, all through the Carolinas, on each side of the march, crowds of emancipated slaves flocked across the fields and joined in. Yellow girls, pillion behind bummers and foragers, galloping up on thoroughbred stock; house slaves and head slaves drove, arrogant in glee, in their former masters' coaches and carriages and wagons; field hands rode along on mules and safely stowed away behind them, in pockets or crokersacks attached to the blanket that covered the mule, were their woolly-headed, bright-eyed children, sometimes as many as fifteen in separate pockets. Often the refugee train outnumbered the army that fed them and itself off the countryside and it took a river to decimate their ranks.

The bridges having been burned by the Confederates, there was a scramble in crossing the pontoons the Federals laid, for the Negroes soon learned that the pontoons were always taken up before half of them had crossed and then they were left behind on the bank of the river, bewildered and lost and far from home. Too, they soon caught on to the fact that the ones next to the edges of the pontoons were often "accidentally" pushed into the water and the soldiers would make bets as to how long the patient-faced mule, with its floating pockets out of which peeped the now terrified black eyes, would stay afloat.

And around and about the rear of the march hovered the gray scouts and the gathering cavalry of Hampton and Butler and Wheeler and up ahead the troops of McLaws and Cheatham and Hardee and finally the army of General Joe Johnston who, too late, had been ordered by General Lee to supersede old "never-arrive" Beauregard in South and North Carolina.

Yes, this *was* a march! And if it should be safely accomplished, the Confederacy would be doomed for it would mean the utter destruction of the towns and the plantations—the homes, the saw mills, the cotton gins, the animals, the workers, the morale of the troops. And it would mean, also, the uniting of the Grand Army of the West with the Grand Army of the East in front of Richmond and General Lee.

The traveling through South Carolina and on to Fayetteville, North Carolina, seemed to Marie to last forever although it was only three weeks. But those three weeks changed her life forever. And she never, as long as she lived, forgot the people booing and hissing along the streets, nor the houses burning, nor the stench of the countless animals ruthlessly slaughtered and left lying by the roadsides, nor the occasional huddle of a shot Yankee bummer among a pile of rotting cows and pigs, nor sometimes a hung Confederate scout who had been caught sleeping in a tree, nor the smell of the thousands and thousands of sweaty Negroes.

In later life, she would look at a map of the Carolinas and it would bring back memories as vivid as this morning's roses, for each place they stopped represented a rendezvous with Willie or a defeat by or a victory over Amelia.

Every place stood out, a milestone.

First, Liberty Hall, where they bivouacked after crossing the Wateree at Peay's Ferry on February the twenty-third.

Stobo came to her, sitting on the piazza of a deserted

mansion with General Howard and Amelia and Major Reynolds. Panting, he dashed up with a large basket on his arm. "Mister Big Dave's sister is refuging here. I just seen her. She wants to talk to Miss Marie. She said she recollected Mr. Big Dave loved Miss Marie and so she is curious as to what kind of a young lady Miss Marie has growed to be."

Major Reynolds flashed a mean look at Stobo and said to Marie, "You're too tired. Why don't you go and lie down before supper?"

Marie was already halfway down the steps. "No. I won't. And, Mama, don't expect me right back. If she asks me to stay for supper, I will."

The flaming red sunset showed angry flecks in Amelia's eyes. She made a move to restrain Marie but General Howard said, "Let her go. You and Major Reynolds smother her. We can have a rubber of whist. Mrs. Craft will make a fourth."

Stobo had two mules waiting. He led the way through the lovely town, past the spacious church and the old academy, down to the river and along a trail winding through oak and gum trees and cane thickets. Several times Marie tried to question him, but he shook his head. Not until they heard an owl cry three times did he finally speak.

"We right at General Butler's scout camp at Fishing Creek."

General Butler had taken off his wooden leg and was lying on a couch of pine branches beside a cook fire. About ten of his cavalrymen were with him gathered around the fire getting ready to fill their bowls with a catfish stew that a blind Negro was stirring with a hickory stick.

They greeted Stobo as a long-time friend. Willie pulled Marie off the mule and carried her in his arms into the circle of light. She knew some of the men. Others she greeted gaily. Stobo grandly took the napkin off the basket and brought out dozens of white-flour biscuits, a boiled ham and three bottles of French brandy.

"That old mealymouth General Howard ain't going

to be able to give Miss Amelia no brandy tonight with her seegar," he laughed.

"Where'd you get that?" Marie asked

"The pretty mulatto in the kitchen gave them to me when I told her where you and me was headed."

"Will she tell Mama?"

"Not her. She hates Yankees. One of them reaped her last week. I'm going back right now and pleasure her with my company to make up for it. Mr. Willie says he'll bring you home."

It was a real feast—ham and biscuits and tin cups of brandy to go along with the bowls of greasy catfish stew. And the fire flickering kindly and the scouts around it; and the blind Negro picking a sweet lonesome guitar and they all singing:

> The years have gone but
> I am true, Lorena.

And suddenly she was blurting out to General Butler that Sherman and the left wing had not crossed at Peay's Ferry that day but farther up at Hanging Rock, and Kilpatrick had arrived and received orders to move at once with the cavalry to Lancaster so Hampton would think the army now was headed for Charlotte and hare off after him; and she knew, having heard General Howard say just before she left Liberty Hill, that really the army was to move in a straight line, the flanks somewhat separated, for Fayetteville, North Carolina. And oh, General Butler—can't I just stay with you all and not go back to Liberty Hill at all?

And the blind Negro danced a buck and wing and sang a hoedown song but General Butler said, no, she couldn't stay because General Howard would come after her and they weren't ready to meet him yet. But he swore that just before they reached Fayetteville or in Fayetteville he'd send Willie and enough cavalry to snatch her right from under old Sherman's nose in return for this information. And he'd taken a fancy to Kilpatrick's peculiar piebald stallion. Perhaps they could steal him at the same time. A bugle sounded and three more of the eerie owl calls.

"Take this enchanting minx back to her mother, Willie, we've got to break camp. That's Hampton's signal he's ready to ride. Besides it's fixing to rain. We'd better get across Lynches River tonight and leave the Grand Army to cope with the mud. We *must* reach Cheraw by the time old Hardee limps up from Charleston."

Marie helped Butler put his leg back on and he gallantly held his hands for her to step in to mount and bowed farewell to her with a true courtier's flourish.

A fog had gathered along the river bank and the stars had disappeared back into the sky. But there was plenty of illumination everywhere, from houses and whole tracts of woodland burning. Once she and Willie discovered two Yankee scouts in Confederate gray riding alongside them in the mist. Marie recognized a sergeant, one of General Howard's cleverest scouts, and Corporal Pike who had been at Camp Sorghum the day she'd rescued Major Reynolds.

"Out courting?" Corporal Pike asked.

"Yes."

"And I bet that's Major Reynolds hiding his eyes under that floppy hat?"

"Who else? You know he's my best beau, Corporal Pike."

Willie said, exactly in Major Reynold's fretful way, "Can't you see we want to be alone, Corporal?"

The scouts saluted and wheeled off.

"How lucky you put on that blue cape." She glanced over at him. Willie was looking at her with a strange expression in his eyes, almost as if he saw right through her into another person.

"What is it?" Marie asked.

"It's fortunate you told that bit about Kilpatrick not being with the right wing. They say he's got a beautiful woman traveling with him and sharing his comfortable couch. I've been devilish jealous ever since the encounter he had with you the day you left Columbia. I wasn't the only one heard it."

Marie pulled up under a magnolia tree. Her face was in the shadows. "Don't be jealous of me, Willie. And never of Kilpatrick. Major Reynolds says he's got a yellow *and* a white woman with him."

"They say he can seduce any woman he sets out to charm."

"Willie! I've never heard you talk so rough."

"This is a rough march."

She heeled the mule but Willie put out his hand and pulled her over against him, half off the oriental rug that served for her saddle. It was beginning to rain. Big drops fell on her upturned face.

"You're hurting me."

"But don't you like it?"

She laughed and let him pull her all the way onto his saddle. All against him. And there seemed a new hardness about him that she had not realized before. His eyes looked slanting and fiery in the misty light.

She whispered, "You should marry me tonight. I feel it. I have never loved you so much."

Suddenly he bent and kissed her on the lips very lightly. He said lazily into her mouth, "I'll marry you when I am ready. But take care that you don't make me too jealous."

She stroked his upper lip with her finger but he shook his head. "You don't realize how notorious you are. You and that carriage of Mrs. Elmore's. All Butler's scouts make a point of keeping up with you. You've caught hold of their fancy. It has been gossiped that Kilpatrick has bragged he'd have you if and when he decided to and be damned to General Howard and Major Reynolds playing like mother hens."

"You talk," she said, "as if you believed those things."

"I very nearly do."

"But not quite?"

"No, not quite."

She looked up at him again. The harshness in his eyes had disappeared. Nothing there now but desire and love and sadness. "I'll be waiting for you to fetch me."

He kissed her eyebrow, and the tip of her nose and the end of her chin, her throat, the place between her breasts—"The perfection of you," he choked, "the woman-perfection of you! What fool wouldn't be jealous?"

That night she was sick and let Amelia hold her head.

"Fish and brandy!" Amelia sniffed. "Just where did you go to be soaking wet when you got in? That falderal about Mr. Boozer's sister was the thinnest tale that jackass Stobo has made up yet. I'll tan his hide good for him if he took you to Butler's hideout."

"Oh—Mama—don't fuss. I went to a dance the Missouri regiment gave at the academy. There were lots of pretty Liberty Hill girls there and—"

"You didn't and you know it," Evie said from the far side of the big, puffy bed. "I heard the mulatto in the kitchen say—"

"Dry up!" Amelia said to Evie and tenderly sponged Marie's chilly forehead with some special violet cologne she found in a silver bottle on the marble-topped dresser.

They rode through Camden the next day. Rather what was left of the rich Revolutionary town. General Logan had sent Colonel Adams ahead the day before with special orders to "march through Camden." And here in the wide streets, arcaded with old oaks and cedars, Marie was aware that spring had arrived in a fountain of yellow and pale willow-green and that the well-executed effigy of the old Indian, King Haigler, atop the Mills-designed Market House, one of the few buildings left standing, looked oddly pleased that the people who had burned *his* council house, once standing on this very spot, had got their houses burned in turn.

Then there was a shoddy boardinghouse for two days while it rained and rained, the army stuck in the mud and General Howard corduroying roads and building a bridge, there being too many snags to pontoon across Lynches River.

Amelia fumed and grumbled because they had lost contact with General Sherman. So after crossing Lynche River, while Major Reynolds guided his band across Black Creek and past Sugar Loaf Mountain and through Kelly Town on the old stagecoach road to Society Hill, Amelia and Mrs. Craft with some scouts, detoured through Chesterfield Courthouse and paid an afternoon call on Sherman who was bivouacking inside the dingy courthouse itself.

She rejoined Marie and Evie that night at Howard's headquarters which was the Witherspoon house in Society Hill.

It had begun to rain again, but Amelia was now all smiles and high spirits. Marie braced herself to hear bad news. Amelia took off her bonnet and shawl and ran her fingers through her shiny hair. She was humming a harsh tune, *The Battle Hymn of the Republic.*

"There was a skirmish with Butler and some of Sherman's men just after we left Chesterfield. We had to stop the carriage and wait. It didn't last long. We watched them march the rebel prisoners they'd taken back to the courthouse. My, it was a nasty little town. Not nearly so nice as Society Hill. Oh—I thought I recognized Willie among the prisoners. Here—where are you going? It's pouring outside."

Rain fell hard on her head as Marie stood without moving in the shrub garden. Roman hyacinths and violets and tea olives were giving off a cool, wet fragrance. Major Reynolds came from the house and took her by the arm and made her come back inside to a warm fire. He stayed close to her all evening. She saw his light, cold eyes, his critical expression. "I want to go to bed," she said during their supper of fried ham and hominy grits and red gravy. Amusement flickered over Amelia's face. Marie felt her eyelashes sting and her lips quiver, but Amelia didn't notice that she was crying.

Tense and frightened, Marie lay huddled in a ball in a great big four-poster bed upstairs while Evie recounted with relish what the cook had said about old Mrs. Witherspoon having been murdered in this very bed at the beginning of the war by two of her Negro house slaves. She was a very rich lady—the old Mrs. Witherspoon—and she spoiled her house servants outrageously. One night the butler and the cook smothered

her with a pillow and she died and they put her in a
chest and later they heard a noise in the chest and she
had come back to life, so they took her out of the chest
and killed her all over again. And the only way they
found out who murdered her was one day in Mr.
Caleb Coker's store the butler took out a big gold
watch that Mr. Coker recognized as belonging to old
Mr. Witherspoon. Then detectives came from Charleston and found bloody handprints on the bedside table
and blood on the butler's clothes. And tonight old Mrs.
Witherspoon's ghost was due to come count her silver
that her son hid under this same bed this afternoon to
be safe from the Yankees. She counted it every Tuesday night.

Marie said, "How ridiculous to hide anything in *our*
room. What do they think *we* are?"

And Evie said, "Oh, everybody knows you're Willie
C.'s intended. He's sort of a relative of the Witherspoons. They visit each other every summer."

In the morning when they left Society Hill, Amelia
rode a ways in Mrs. Craft's carriage to plan the pleasant
things they were going to do in Cheraw, where, Sherman had told them, they would rest for a few days.

She and Evie alone in their carriage, Marie noticed a
strange box that had been put under the seat. She
peeped inside and there winking and twinkling evilly
at her was the handsomest set of table silver she'd ever
seen, every piece marked with a flowing script "W."

"What's this?" she asked Evie.

"That's our family silver to take to New York with
us so people will know we're real Southern aristocrats,"
Evie said. "Mama had it brought down while you
were walking in the garden with all those Illinois boys."

"Oh, Evie—whatever will the Witherspoons think of
me?"

"They'll think you stole the silver and tell Willie's
parents, which is exactly what Mama wants them to
do."

In Cheraw, General Sherman stayed with General
Blair in a large house that belonged to a blockade-
runner. The family remained, and so General Howard

and his charges occupied another white-columned house farther downtown. Howard was busy ordering a pontoon bridge to be laid across the Pee Dee so there was no one to halt the burning and robbing and looting of this town. The worst since Columbia. For in Cheraw, as in Columbia, were great warehouses filled with household treasures from the Lowcountry and an arsenal and much army ordnance. During the days there Marie was in despair wondering if Willie really had been captured. Or if it was just one of Amelia's tricks. She forced herself to go with a crowd of gay, fast-riding officers and watch General Logan shoot the prisoners he'd taken at Chesterfield, in reprisal for General Hampton's having shot seven bummers just before the Confederates crossed the bridge out of Cheraw over the Pee Dee River, and then burned it after them. She went over and examined the faces of every one of the very young and very old dead. But Willie was not one of them.

The next day General Blair gave a sumptuous lunch, it being rainy and chilly too. Sherman was in a good humor in his fidgety, nervous way. He had his generals all together again. Except Kilpatrick who was heading straight into North Carolina from Lancaster by Wadesboro and New Gilead so as to cover their trains from Hampton and Butler and Wheeler's cavalry. Cheraw was the last stop in South Carolina. The sand was running out now. Fast. Sherman laughed at Amelia's jokes and he ate roast goose and ham and sweet potatoes and drank glass after glass of wine.

"Damn! What fine Madeira, Blair. Where did you get it?"

General Blair said, "I found eight wagonloads of it here. I've sent a lot of it out to be distributed among the officers, it being such a cold and dreary day."

And General Sherman said, "Why, I think it's a lovely day." And he and Amelia and General Blair and Mrs. Craft sat down for an afternoon of whist and General Logan played sweetly on a violin he found in the parlor and Adjutant S. H. M. Byers, who had been one of the prisoners in the Lunatic Asylum in

Columbia, sang the poem he'd composed—*Sherman's March to the Sea*—over and over.

Marie was thinking of the shot Confederates and staring out of the window at the drizzly rain and the drunk soldiers, staggering along the muddy street, wearing Persian rugs for raincoats and brandishing French wine bottles and rattling quart cups of spoons and necklaces.

When Major Reynolds came and sat beside her on the window seat, she shrugged her shoulders at him and wouldn't answer and hoped he'd go into one of his fits. But he didn't. He just stroked her arm and fetched a cushion and put it under her feet and looked at her in a silly way that made her feel like she had worms all over her back and legs.

"Listen," he crooned in her ear, "just listen at Byers. It's like hearing an angel sing."

> Then cheer upon cheer for bold Sherman
> Went up from each valley and glen,
> And the bugles re-echoed the music
> That came from the lips of the men;
> For we knew that the stars in our banner
> More bright in their splendor would be,
> And that blessings from Northland would greet us,
> When Sherman marched down to the sea!

Through this state, through North Carolina this pageant passed along, as if some Oriental queen or princess were driving through her realms to receive the plaudits and worship of her blinded and infatuated subjects. The writer did not see all this himself, exactly, but while on a scout mission he got it all at first hand and saw enough to make him hold his breath.

The Sorceress of the Congaree,"
HERALD & NEWS *of Newberry, S. C.,*
August 6, 1909

25

They left Cheraw on March the sixth, crossed the pontoon over the Pee Dee River, and were soon in North Carolina. There was no line between the states, only a sign which read "fift 3 mils to Fatville."

Everybody was suddenly in a hurry—Sherman, because he'd learned, the last day in Cheraw, that his "special antagonist," General Joe Johnston, was waiting up ahead for him with his old command and, unlike Hardee and Beauregard, would not be misled by feints and false reports.

Amelia, because she was becoming broken down with the interminably jolting and bouncing, her back having hurt all the way from Winnsboro. And on top of that, Marie exuded a restlessness that made Amelia nervous. Surely not now—not after all the years of planning—surely God would not let anything happen to her plans now.

And Marie, well, she was in such a hurry to be with Willie she was wild. Fayetteville was so close. Not more than two or three days away—if good weather held. And though Amelia had been unusually gentle and pleasant, Marie had lived with her too long to underestimate her scheming power.

Two days out of Cheraw the little carriage was whizzing along over the slick, pine-needled road. Marie was alone in it, Amelia being back riding with Mrs. Craft, her coach having room to lie down on the seat. And Evie was still farther in the rear in a baggage wagon playing Indian with some English children named Hunt whose father, an engineer, had come to Columbia five years ago, to " 'eat the new State 'Ouse."

The air was thick with smoke from burning pine trees and the high March wind stung Marie's eyes. All at once the door of the carriage opened and a man jumped lightly inside.

"God damn—these seats are comfortable. I'll ride in here with you for a while. I've been waiting for an opportunity to get acquainted with you."

Marie just looked incredulously at Kilpatrick and gave no answer.

"Hell fire! Do you realize how exciting you are?"

At that she looked at him—the little wiry man with the brutal, bright eyes, searching yet sure of victory— the small, sensual mouth—the bold nose. He was so ugly she found him very attractive.

"Yes," she said slowly, "I know."

"And you will let me ride in your enchanting carriage? I was wounded in the thigh recently. Get damned sick of the saddle. Call me Kil—and you don't mind if I just put my head in your lap, do you? Didn't sleep a wink last night. Ah—soft as a damned swan's seat —soft as—"

He slept a long time, restlessly. Once Marie looked out of the back window and saw Kilpatrick's spotted stallion tied behind the carriage. A worn-out, captured Rebel private was tied alongside the stallion. She hoped none of Butler's scouts were lurking about. They would tell Willie that Kilpatrick was with her. And what if the Rebel prisoner escaped and told that Kilpatrick had been sleeping in her lap! She started to push Kilpatrick onto the floor. But what good would that do? He looked like a child sleeping with his lips apart. Go on sleeping, she whispered to Kilpatrick. You aren't to blame for the predicament I'm in. You know nothing of it. Nothing. She yawned and took a little nap herself.

Later they woke and prattled away flirtatiously, for what would she gain by not? And when Major Reynolds, tight-lipped and furious, put his head in and told Kilpatrick that General Sherman was hunting for him, she let Kilpatrick put his arm around her waist and squeeze her as hard as he liked. She even airily waved her hand out of the carriage at him as he mounted the spotted stallion—just to annoy Major Reynolds.

Major Reynolds refused to speak to her when she asked him where they were going to stop that night. But he remained by her carriage till they reached Laurel Hill. It was late afternoon and the army had already made camp.

She stumbled getting out of the carriage.

"I'm stiff as a board from sitting still all day. Is there a horse available for me to take a quick gallop before I settle down?"

He went away and soon returned with a fine mare which had been led away from a rich farm an hour or so earlier.

"You must let me ride horseback along with you tomorrow," Marie said to him. "I don't want another dull day like this one has been."

Immediately he was in a fine humor. "That's a good girl," he said, "will you take a walk with me tonight? After supper?"

"Let me rest tonight. I'll ride with you the whole way tomorrow."

"Very well. It wouldn't be possible anyway. I'm supposed, with Adjutant Byers, to make out a full report of the number of white and colored refugees left in the train for General Sherman. We might just possibly reach Fayetteville in a couple of days and he wants to get rid of them."

"Mama, too? Who'll he play double solitaire with?"

Major Reynolds laughed. His laughter was shrill, and he was shaking unnaturally. "I'll answer that with another question when we get to Fayetteville. I've already asked your mother." With that he rushed away and Marie felt a touch of pity for him.

The mare was fresh and she jumped sideways as Marie settled herself in the saddle.

"Which way you going?" Stobo asked as he rechecked the girth.

"Just up and down the road. I don't want to get lost. This pine forest is bewildering as a maze."

"We passed a friend of yours about a mile back by that log cabin in the huckleberry thick. Ride down this road past it and go to the well. Throw down the bucket and if they haven't rode to *their* camp, you'll make a connect."

She was away before he had finished speaking. Her hat blew off and the wind caught her hair and flew it behind her like a golden banner.

Willie was waiting. As she had been confident he would be. She handed him her reins and jumped down and before he could say a word she was telling him all about that dreadful Kilpatrick having forced his way into her carriage and he had been eating onions and Willie knew how she hated onions and he had made her let him put his head in her lap and had snored and looked just like a clown and oh—his breath had smelled horrible and he couldn't have bathed in weeks and—

"Stop it—I know all about it."

She quizzed him slyly a minute and saw that he didn't know all about it and that she must be looking unusually pretty for he had gone all sleepy-eyed and wasn't thinking of Kilpatrick any more than a monkey and he was kissing her very differently than he ever had before. Deeper and more thrilling. Demanding and giving. Or was she just learning how better? And if General Butler had not come riding by with his wooden leg jerking back and forth in the stirrup they might have—they *really* might have—because they both wanted to so terribly—

Back at camp, she looked curiously around the tent to which Stobo had taken her. Amelia must have helped loot a house and then directed the troops in loading a baggage wagon with this stuff. The camp cots were covered in linen sheets and soft, white wool blan-

kets. On a dainty Sheraton table on one side of the
tent was a leather-bound copy of John Donne's poetry,
a box of cigars and a crystal decanter of Spanish wine.
There was a Dresden mirror in the center of the table.
Marie studied her face in it. Her cheeks were red
and glowing from the gallop in the crisp air. Or from
Willie's kisses. Her hair, primitive in its tousled gold-
ness, caught sparks from the lighted candle. Even to
herself she had never looked lovelier. No wonder it
had not been difficult to persuade Willie that none of
the Kilpatrick episode had been her fault.

Deciding not to comb her hair she made her way to
the mess tent. Officers and orderlies were lounging and
riding about. They stared or called out to her and she
swung her hips as she walked over the slippery pine
needles. Inside the mess tent, lighted by six candles in
a massive Adam silver candelabra, probably from
the same house as the things in their tent, her mother
and General Sherman and General Howard and Mrs.
Craft were laughing and talking together over their
meal.

They greeted her indulgently and she sat down at
the rough camp table covered with a real Italian lace
cloth and ate out of flowered Worcester china plates
that would be broken up and thrown away in the
morning.

Amelia frowned at Marie's untidy hair but the two
generals pulled their mustaches and said Oh! and Ah!
and where have you been with dark coming on?

Marie lowered her lashes at General Howard and
poked General Sherman in the ribs with a heavy silver
fork. As she gobbled up a plate of stewed beef, hashed
potatoes, and broiled baby turkey, she wondered what
they'd say if she snapped her fingers at them and told
them that tomorrow night, or the next, she'd be safely
away from all of them in General Butler's camp and
they'd never see her again. Not ever.

"Here, have a little drink," Amelia said, handing
her a silver chalice, taken from the last Episcopal
church they'd passed. The chalice was full of Irish
whiskey and sugar. "You seem overexcited. It'll quiet

you." Marie put her tongue in it and then drained the whole cup without stopping.

"You'd better go to bed," Amelia said eyeing her suspiciously. "You act as if you had a fever."

"We've got a hard day's marching tomorrow," General Howard put in kindly.

"I'll see you next in Fayetteville," General Sherman said, twitching his cheek and lifting his eyebrows in a fantastic jerk. "May be the last time too."

"Why?" Marie asked carelessly. She was feeling very loose and easy. But not drunk. Not in the least.

"I have to rid the army of the refugees now. They've served their purpose in helping desolate the Carolinas. And big battles are not for little girls," he went on in his jerky dictatorial manner of speaking. "When we leave Fayetteville, we'll move straight to Goldsboro where my supplies are waiting. And, I imagine, old Joe Johnston and his ragged rebels."

"We're going to Wilmington on a boat from Fayetteville," Amelia said. "And then to Washington, where General Sherman's brother is going to look out for us. Then New York! The Union League Club has sent word to General Sherman by his brother, Senator John, who is a member, that the Club wishes to sponsor us and pay all our expenses. Loyal Southern ladies!"

"Lord but they must be rich. Why are they sponsoring *us?*"

General Sherman snapped his knees together and his eyebrows apart. "Because you vindicate their stand."

"What stand?" Mrs. Craft asked.

"The Union League Club was incorporated by a group of gentlemen from the very social Union Club who became enraged when Judah Benjamin, the Confederate Secretary of War and one of their Southern members, was allowed to resign instead of being expelled from the Union Club. But rather than disrupt their card games on account of their political peeve, they formed the Union League Club where they could air their Union-minded views as hotly as they chose."

"Are you a member of either?" Amelia handed

Marie a linen napkin and motioned her to wipe a dab of gravy from her chin.

"Both. So's my brother, the Senator. Honorary. So's President Lincoln and General Grant."

"Why do they want to sponsor us? You never answered me," Marie said crossly.

"Well, they've been up to a lot of abolitionist activity organizing colored regiments to fight in the South, encouraging colored men to run away and join the Union army, insisting on Negroes marching in parades and riding in railway cars, donating thousands to the Negroes who were mobbed in the New York City riots of '63—for which they have received frowns from several quarters. Now for the Union League Club to have you lovely ladies to exhibit as proof they *do* help white Southern loyalists as well as colored! It's a feather in their caps and they know it. What a crow they intend to have telling about all the prisoners you help escape and the vengeance the rebels wreaked on your fragile fortunes."

"Well," said Marie, yawning, "my foot! and fiddle! and good night!"

She wasn't too steady on her feet but she didn't hit the post going out. She could hear them laughing at her. Ha! Ha! Well the laugh was going to be on them —just wait—

She walked past the tent, one in a row of officers' tents, not recognizing it, dark having come and the whole scene having changed.

At some distance from the officers' tents the modest tents of the rank-and-file and company officers were arranged in streets. She rambled unsteadily along, curious and restless at the same time.

The men were collected in groups listening to long yarns beside the cook fire or formed into little parties playing cards, pitching and tossing. The cooks were busy around a huge tin cauldron containing ham and peas. Smaller vessels simmered near with chickens and squabs and ducklings.

"Come and play," they called; or "Come and eat"; or they whistled the way they felt, watching her swing past.

Deep dark had come now and over the rolling ground under the giant pines for miles, campfires glittered and sparkled like the lamps of a great city. "New York!" she said, out loud. "The Devil take New York!"

In the valleys below campfires also glowed and the noise of song and merriment floated all around her. Everything now was floating around her. Even her head had come loose from her neck. In many places the tall pines had been ignited and were roaring up in hundred-foot-high torches of flame which leaped from branch to branch and, feeding on the resinous trunks, seemed to be a thousand flaming pillars of fire.

She made her way through this crackling arched cathedral over to the far edge of the camp toward a concentration of smaller fires. The men crowded around these were gambling and shouting in the light like dark devils in a hellish orgy. The sentries walking up and down with their glittering rifles reflected the fire—dark angels adding to the sublimity of the scene.

And beyond every fire Negro minstrels were entertaining their saviors, capering about, jigging, cutting the buck, drinking peach brandy, falling down onto a pile of others. As she turned to go back up the hill, she saw one immensely tall Negro stand up. He opened his huge mouth and imitated a drum, then a piano, a fiddle—a chuck-wills-widow—a screech owl—an alligator—a Charleston lady—a bobwhite. And in between each different imitation he'd take a pull on a jug of peach brandy he was holding over his shoulder. Finally he fell down on a whole pile of Negroes who had preceded him in the limelight. Marie turned and started back into the burning circle of trees.

How long had it been since she had walked through the night of fire in Columbia? Forever? Was she still only eighteen years old? Or was she eighty? Could she and Willie ever come together again and live together as if there had never been these two nights of fire between them? One at the beginning and one at the end? But which was the beginning and which the end? The end of what?

Stobo found her wandering, utterly lost, in the circle

of crackling pine trees. Her hair was singed in several places and the lace collar of her dress torn off by briars and thorns. One shoe was gone and her big toe was bleeding. Gently he led her back to the tent and took off her dress and her shoes and bathed her feet and opened the blanket beside Evie and laid her down to sleep.

"Poor little thing," he whispered as he put out the guttering candle. "Poor pretty little thing."

"It is Marie Boozer! I know it is!"

"By Jove! Certain?"

"Yes! I tracked the wheels for hours today. No chance to mistake the wheel-marks of that victoria among these heavy wagon-trains. She is in his camp, and we will be sure to see her in the morning."

Then they all whispered "By Jove!" with great earnestness.

Edward L. Wells,
Hampton and His Cavalry

26

Torrential rains set in the next day. The way became a morass of mud and water and was almost impassable for the troops and the baggage and refugee trains. Every foot had to be corduroyed with fence rails and saplings. The dark rushing water of the Lumber River and its sucking swamps caused Sherman to write in his diary: "It was the damnedest marching I ever saw." Wagons and artillery were dragged along by mules aided by soldiers who literally put their hands to the wheels and forced them on. The drivers cracked their whips and shouted curses and oaths that could hardly be heard above the splashing and yelling and groaning and praying. Mules and Negroes drowned by the hundreds. Yet that night they still went on in the hellish glow of thousands of blazing pine trees.

There was an air of great excitement; for to the rear, to each side, and up ahead, thousands of Confederate cavalry were known to be riding rapidly. Would they attack? Tonight? Was this to be the night?

The little carriage made it easier than any of the other vehicles but as another night fell, on March ninth, Amelia was almost insensible with the pain in her back.

At General Howard's direction Stobo pulled in at

Solomon's Grove where Kilpatrick and his cavalry were camped. Marie urged Amelia to stay along with General Howard so they could get on to Fayetteville quicker, but Amelia was too ill to travel any farther that night.

So General Howard escorted them to the Charles Monroe dwelling, Kilpatrick's headquarters. He arranged with an orderly for Amelia and the girls to have lodging there for the night and told Stobo to make haste and follow him on the plank road leading to Fayetteville, on the morrow.

Marie detected a leer on the orderly's face and the minute they were in an upstairs room she grabbed the key to turn it in the lock.

The man laughed coarsely. "You needn't bother with that. The ginral has got the yellow girl to warm his back tonight. He's not studying about you."

Meanwhile Hampton, having learned where Kilpatrick had set up his headquarters, decided to make a call on him the morning of the next day. Hampton said to Butler, "If we can rout Kilpatrick, we'll open up the road to Fayetteville which the Federal camp blocks. We can join Hardee in Fayetteville by tomorrow night and be there waiting for 'them.' "

So around midnight, Butler took Willie C. and some scouts and reconnoitered the situation and discovered that Kilpatrick had carelessly posted no pickets to protect his rear. Willie rode almost up to the house without being noticed. Had he been aware, he would have detected the presence of the familiar carriage parked under a tree by the piazza, near the spotted stallion Butler had set his heart on. As it was, Willie did see the stallion through the rain but missed the telltale carriage.

Returning to camp they met a picket of about forty men. In the thick fog they took them prisoners without firing a shot. This picket was the detachment sent out by Kilpatrick to guard the road that night while he enjoyed his evening's dalliance.

Back in the Confederate camp, Hampton and

Wheeler and Butler swiftly outlined their strategy. Butler was to lead the attack at dawn, moving in when Wheeler's column came in view in the rear. Captain Bostick of Young's brigade was to personally capture Kilpatrick, and Willie was given orders to bring in the spotted stallion. Those two were instructed to rush straight for the house, where they knew Kilpatrick was sleeping, when Butler gave the word. Butler and his cavalry would be right on their heels and Hampton after them. Wheeler would dash out from the swamp to the rear.

Around 3 A.M., Willie and the other of Butler's scouts who were to attack the house came up and dismounted and felt their way cautiously down the road. The whole guard having been captured, there was no one about. For hours in the dark and the wet the scouts stayed there waiting. They did not light a fire nor a pipe. Occasionally they whispered together, wondering about the identity of the lady with Kilpatrick. Each man sat on the ground holding his bridle rein and stroking his horse's nose to keep him from whinnying. Confident Howard was on his way to Fayetteville, Willie huddled close to the bobtailed sorrel and planned how he was going to keep his rendezvous with Marie in that town. For he would get there first if they succeeded in surprising little Kil. He would be impatiently waiting. And this time he was going to keep her.

Just before daylight Butler and his cavalry moved in on a slow walk, joined the scouts, and proceeded to within a hundred yards of the silent house. Webs of mist shrouded their uniforms and soft mud muffled the sounds of hoofs. Quietly, quietly the gray ghosts were converging. Two little birds twittered crossly, but that was the only sound, except now and then a hare, startled, drumming with its back feet to warn the squirrels and coons that something fierce had penetrated their wet domain.

As soon as there was light, Butler placed his horse between Willie's bobtailed sorrel and the big bay of Captain Bostick. He was not carrying a weapon—only a lady's silver-headed riding crop. He removed his hat with a dripping, draggled plume still gallantly attached. He cried:

"Forward! Charge! Troops from Virginia, follow me!"

The strange apparition of a lovely woman in scanty nightdress on the field of battle brought one Confederate captain's horse to a fast halt, Southern chivalry rose to the occasion. Dismounting the cavalryman led the distressed one to the safety of a nearby ditch.

> John G. Barrett,
> Sherman's March through the Carolinas

27

Through her sleeping Marie heard Butler's shout. The rebel yell tore apart her dreaming; then pistols firing and men screaming and horses neighing and Stobo beating on the door and hollering—

"For God's sake, Miss Marie, run fast! Just like you is. Mister Willie has done come for you. But from the looks of things he can't wait long. I just seen him downstairs right by the piazza steps. He's leading a horse for you to ride."

"Marie—where are you going in your nightgown? Come back in this room at once. Oh, my back! Oh, my God! Evie, catch her—"

But Marie gathered up her trailing nightdress and, barefooted, rushed down the steps. The front door was locked. No, there was Stobo opening it for her. She made a leap to reach it. Just then a door off the hall was flung wide. A yellow female hand slid back around the panel and Kilpatrick, in his nightshirt and drawers, ran, barefooted and cursing, out of the room. Giggling, Marie pulled her nightgown tighter and tried to make it through the front door first. But somehow they reached it at the same time and burst out together in a melodramatic entrance.

"Willie," shouted Marie. "Here I am, Willie!"

He was right by the steps mounted on the bobtailed sorrel and leading Kilpatrick's startled spotted stallion.

Marie tripped down the steps and stood there amid a whizz of bullets, smiling. What mad excitement! What a wild, thrilling way for one's lover to snatch one away from the enemy.

But what was this? A crowd of Confederate cavalrymen suddenly halted, all goggling at her like struck-dumb people. Willie gave a groan and ducked his head. Marie went on smiling and dug her bare toes down in the muddy earth.

Captain Bostick galloped up and yelled, "What in the hell's going on here, Willie? Get the lead out of your pants. There goes Kilpatrick escaping under our very noses."

By now, Kilpatrick had gained the tree where some of the horses were still tied. He jumped up on a horse without a bridle or saddle and, with Captain Bostick close behind him, skedaddled toward the thick swamp in the rear. Once a Confederate headed him off and asked if he had seen the General, to which Kilpatrick replied, "There he goes on that black horse." Whereupon the Confederate pursued the figure pointed out to him.

It was as if a tornado was roaring through the camp. A stampede on foot was underway as the Federals waking in hysterical alarm were trampled by horses' hoofs under their flies, half-asleep, and not sure whether this bedlam was truly hell itself or just another nightmare battle. Horses ran them down, sabers clove their skulls and cut off their hands, they scattered this way and that toward the nearest infantry encampment to fetch help to the exploding camp.

Willie still did not move but kept staring at Marie, the stallion's lead line trembling in his hand. His face was as gray as his uniform. A Confederate horseman dashed up and said something pointing toward the swamp in the rear where Wheeler had now appeared. Willie waved him away impatiently. Marie hesitated now. Something was strange. Why did Willie look at her as if he were ill? Why were so many of the cavalrymen stealing sly looks at her even in the middle of shooting and stabbing? Why didn't he lift her up onto the horse and fly away with her?

A Federal crept up, and, sensing that something was wrong between the girl in the nightgown and the Confederate dummy, snatched the lead line away from Willie and jumped on the back of Kilpatrick's horse. Willie instinctively wheeled and galloped after the Federal and the two men fought, hand to hand, coming so close together that it looked as if they were caressing each other. And then two shots rang out simultaneously. The Federal rolled off the speckled stallion but as he fell on the horse's neck he shot once more and this time the bobtailed sorrel screamed and went down threshing his legs in a death agony.

Marie moved like a sleepwalker among the galloping horses and the swishing sabers and the running Federals to see about her horse—her dear old bobtailed sorrel coach horse. Willie had caught the stallion and he was walking forward, his eyes frozen on her face.

Marie's throat began to close up. Her hand fluttered toward him. "What's the matter?" she asked. "Have I done something wrong?"

"Damn you, Marie. Damn you." He wrenched open his tunic, dragged it off, and put it around her bare shoulders. He buttoned it savagely. Tears blinded Marie's eyes.

"Are we going now?"

He turned and half pushed, half threw her down into a drainage ditch. "Stay there. Not that it matters, but it wouldn't do any good for your head to get blown off."

Marie hardly recognized Willie's voice. It was so harsh and freezing cold, the voice of a stranger.

"I'll wait here for you," she said, frightened at his look, at his words.

"Wait in hell for all I care," came from the ashy mask with the ice eyes that had become Willie's face. "With Kilpatrick or the whole of Sherman's Grand Army."

She could not speak, she lay there looking up at him, the sad sky taking color from her weeping eyes.

Without even glancing at her again, Willie mounted the spotted stallion and kicked him so cruelly in the belly that the tough campaign animal reared up and

almost fell over backward. And then Willie was gone
away into the mist and smoke of battle, cursing and
shooting his pistol up into the sky as if he were so furious he even dared to take a shot at God.

And from the window of an upstairs bedroom of the
Monroe house two faces peered down on the debacle
in the grove. Evie—astonished and frightened. Amelia
bright-eyed and triumphant. Looking exultant as when,
without cheating, she won an exceptionally difficult
game of solitaire with most of the cards seemingly
stacked against her.

I ordered Captain Byers to get ready to carry dispatches to Washington. I also authorized General Howard to send by this opportunity some of the fugitives who had traveled with his army all the way from Columbia, among whom were Mrs. Feaster and her two beautiful daughters.

William Tecumseh Sherman,
MEMOIRS, Part II

28

The twelfth of March was a sweet, warm Sunday in Fayetteville. Early there was little sound except songbirds and church bells. Shortly after noon there was the shrill whistle of a steamboat coming nearer and nearer, and soon a continuous shouting, as Sherman and his generals and his men and the refugees realized that at long last here was a messenger from home with letters and newspapers and packages and news. For them it was like waking to a new life after being so long shut in their marching, away from the outer world.

A few minutes later there came through the cheering town to the cream-colored arsenal on the plateau where General Sherman had his headquarters, a large, florid seafaring man named Captain Ainsworth, bearing a mailbag and greetings from General Geary at Wilmington.

Sherman had a brief conference with Captain Ainsworth about the capacity of *The Davidson,* his ship, and that afternoon at 6 P.M., the chosen of the refugees boarded ship and headed back down the river for Wilmington.

There was a mail boat in convoy with two guns, the river banks being known to be occupied by Hampton and Butler's cavalry who had been the last to capitulate and evacuate Fayetteville.

Learning on the rail keeping our face turned from Lieutenant Conyngham, the New York *Herald* correspondent, who had seen her ignominiously climb out of the ditch at Solomon's Grove after the battle was over the day before yesterday, Marie fixed her eyes on the abandoned picket fires of the Confederates along the river banks. It was the edge of evening, with a full moon rising redly over the dark pine and cypress trees and casting a crimson glow like a stream of fire along the river. The evening star rode low and from the dark trees an owl was velvetly crooning to the strawberry moon. A solitary white heron with a reaching neck flew across the sky. Clear water-lapping sounds against the steady breast of the boat came to Marie and the happy voices of the refugees below.

He was over there on the bank. Willie, with a mask instead of a face, sitting by one of those winking little fires. Or was he running the spotted stallion in and out of the trees along the bank trying to get a good shot at the top deck of the boat hoping that she—

Captain Reiple and Lieutenants Curley and Jones of the Thirteenth Indiana Guard, armed with sevenshooters, her protectors from the enemy over there on the bank, came up and surrounded her.

"What a becoming dress you're wearing. I never saw so many ruffles."

"I hear you're going to stop in Washington for a while."

"Make it Wilmington. Our orders give us leave to stay there a day or two."

"There's a man with a guitar down below getting ready to play some dance tunes. Won't you come?"

"I do wish you'd take off your bonnet. The moonlight shines so nice on your yellow hair. I like the way you wind it in that low knot."

"Pity the Rebs stole your carriage back at Solomon's Grove. Such a pretty little carriage!"

"Can't we bring you something? You didn't eat a bite of supper? A chicken wing? A glass of wine?"

"Would you like a chair—that is if you won't come and dance?"

Promising she'd be down directly, Marie was again

alone on the deck, staring up at the darker and darker bank as the picket fires grew fewer and farther apart.

A chilly wind began to blow, but not hard. She could feel tendrils of hair fluttering around her eyebrows. She could feel the velvet of the owl's throat; the drumskin tightness of her heart; the sharpness of a tall pine tree scratching against the moon. But she couldn't feel her own emotion. From the ditch at Solomon's Grove she had watched Wade Hampton cleave a man's skull half in two with his saber. The two eyes had separated and each eye had looked very surprised but there had been no pain in them. Just shock that this separation had occurred. That now the man was even separate from himself. She could remember how Willie laughed and the lazy way he had of leaning his body against things, his upper lip reaching out for hers, trembling a little, when he kissed her. Yet she was aware of no feeling at all, no loss and no humiliation and no grief.

I will feel all those things gradually, she told herself. Someday what has happened will come to life in me and wrench and twist and beat the drumskin of my heart until it breaks.

"Marie!" Amelia had come up on the deck. She had on her navy-blue velours with the white soutache braid and a white egret feather toque on her black hair. The point of her cigar winked exactly like the last picket fire they'd passed a ways back. "Come down, child, and dance. Don't stay up here alone brooding over Willie C. Join the young officers and make an effort to be gay."

"Oh—I'll be gay all right. When I get to New York, I'm going to have so much fun you'll get on your knees and beg me to go back to brooding over Willie."

"Not I. Nor will I waste a tear on Major Reynolds. I bet he'll have a fit when he returns from Goldsboro tomorrow and finds you gone. You're the lucky one. By the time you've met several rich, handsome gentlemen you'll settle down, take your choice and—"

"I'll never love anybody but Willie."

"If he had loved you he would never have left you lying in a ditch like a common—"

"Mama—you know he saw me and Kilpatrick come running out of the house together in our night clothes. What else could he have thought?"

"Don't you hate him?"

"No. Only you."

"You don't mean that. You're just upset. Come closer. And I'll tell you something, though I wouldn't admit it before. Willie *was* an attractive boy. As a matter of fact, he was so attractive there were times I was afraid, even with the best of cards, I'd not win against him. And to think—I did—without even trying. It was sheer luck that General Howard guided us to Solomon's Grove. It gives me a strange feeling to win so easily."

"You really think you've won, Mama?" The numbness was going away. The drumskin was loosening, her heart was beginning to beat again and it hurt cruelly. She was coming alive and determination was flowing back. She took Amelia's arm and held it like a vise.

"Certainly I won," Amelia said.

Marie leaned closer staring hard into her mother's eyes. "Did you, Mama? Did you?"

"I'll tell the boys you'll be right down," said Amelia hoarsely. She jerked her arms loose and walked away, but it took her a long time to reach the door and she stumbled several times going down the ladder.

The moon was losing its redness. The owl was hushed. The banks on either side of the river were dark—dark.

Stobo was sitting on a mail sack just back of Marie. Had been there all the time. She didn't speak to him but she was glad he was there. His presence soothed her and gave her a sense of still belonging, in part, to the past, if not to the present. His being there made her think, just for a fleeting minute, that perhaps after the war Willie would miss her and find out where she was and come and insist that they belonged to each other. Inside the taut drumskin of her heart, however, she knew he would not. Willie had been brought up in too much tradition to accept any explanation for a situation like Solomon's Grove. His tradition gave him a peculiar ruthlessness. He could not forgive her for having made such a shameful display of herself. Nor was there any reason why he should.

Now she was doomed to a lonely life. She would always be pursued because she was too beautiful not to attract attention. But loved? Did one ever love but once? Truly love? Ah—where would she ever again find love? And if she did would it be the kind that lasted forever after?

The strains of the guitar below floated up through the water sounds and there was laughing and stamping and singing. If she remained up here—if she wept—Amelia would feel that she *had* won and that she, Marie, was soft. So she would not weep. She dared not. Besides, though for an instant she had felt herself coming alive when she faced Amelia down, she wasn't really alive at all. But she was beautiful. She would go below and show Amelia how easy it was. How very easy.

Her dancing that night in the stuffy little room on the gently rocking floor was wild and unrestrained. She even exhausted the big Western boys who had marched for six weeks without getting weary. She was flushed and animated and couldn't stop talking or moving.

By the time they left Wilmington on the steamer *Weybosset* en route for New York, Amelia had begun to relax and could get on about her planning and her business. The bruises on her arms where Marie had seized her that first night out from Fayetteville were fading. Her pretty love of a daughter was smiling quite naturally and being her usual impudent merry self with the officers. A little too impudent and merry perhaps but it would all come out the way she'd planned. The cards were there. The game awaited.

PART FOUR

NEW YORK

March 1865–March 1870

29

The steamer *Weybosset* carrying the remnants of the loyal-to-the-Union refugees who had left Columbia together on February the twentieth, arrived in New York from Wilmington, North Carolina, at noon on April the fourth. It was a sparkling, windy day and all the vessels in the harbor were decorated with flags of different nations. When the refugees disembarked it was to a celebration of horns blowing and flags waving.

"Is this for us?" Evie asked, twisting her thumbs nervously together.

But it wasn't. It was because Richmond had surrendered to General Grant the day before and the war was, in effect, won.

And what a day for Marie Boozer to ride for the first time through the streets of a city like New York!

From the Battery to Spuyten Duyvil Creek the whole town was a jubilee. Hundreds of cannons were booming in the parks and bands were playing everywhere. From the housetops floated the Stars and Stripes. *Old Hundred* and *Glory Hallelujah* were being sung by everybody. Church bells were pealing in a single carillon from Trinity to Harlem. All the public buildings were draped in bunting and hung with flags. The blue, red, and yellow white-topped omnibuses filled with flag-waving, hurrahing men and women clattered over the flinty paving stones. Carmen, in white canvas smocks, driving two-wheeled carts with a platform in front, standing with one foot on a shaft and one on the platform howled and whooped. Financial wizards from the warrens of Wall Street waved their stovepipe hats in the air and walked on the sidewalks with waiter girls from the concert saloons in low-cut bodices, very short skirts and bare legs encased in high tasseled boots strung with little brass bells. Irish politicians jigged on Fifth Avenue with silk-shawled matrons who had dashed out from their marble mansions when they heard the news. Elegant vehicles threaded in and out of the flowing rivers of people, expertly handled by liveried cockneys or, often, by their mustached owners. Negroes marched quietly, almost secretly, carrying signs up and down West Broadway.

Flags! Cannons! Church bells! Horses! People! It was the same sort of madness Secession had been in Columbia.

All the way from the dock through the rioting streets Marie wept without restraint. Amelia, calmer in public with Marie than she was, since Wilmington, alone with her, shrugged and tightened her mouth.

"Do control yourself, Marie. From the instant I deliver our letters from the Shermans and General Howard to the President of the Union League Club we are going to be on parade. Red eyes never became anyone. Oh look—there's Barnum's Museum! Evie—see all those flags on top of that long building? Marie—"

Marie who was wrenched with sorrow at the loss of

Richmond, sobbed, "Poor Willie—poor Mrs. Mc-Cord—"

"Didn't I tell you they'd come to a bad end suddenly? Poor is the proper word. Poor as church mice. If those Columbians had not walked in such stiff pride it would not have been necessary for General Sherman to have humbled them so. Why would those Southerners ever have thought their silly little flag had a chance to fly above the great flag of the United States?"

"You are becoming so pompous now that you're up North. I'll never fly the United States flag, I tell you. I will be a Southerner as long as I live."

Amelia looked somewhat less calm. Oh dear, she was thinking, don't let her act up now. Not today. Not here. She said, "We are beginning a new life here. We've got every chance to be somebodies in New York society. Dry up and use your head. You know you can't ever go back to Columbia. Not after riding away with General Sherman. Your name is mud there quite as much as mine. Why can't you take a middle course? I won't make you declare for the Union. But I do expect you to show me your loyalty and stop crying over the Confederacy. Will you be quiet? Look around you at the city. You're young. You have a mighty long life ahead of you."

"Yes," said Evie, "look all around, Marie. There's a cart man trying to flirt with you."

Amelia wanted to pop Marie's face. Sitting there, still strikingly lovely in spite of red eyes, and, whether she admitted it or not, eating up the excitement and patting her kid gaiters in time to *Glory Hallelujah* and, suddenly, waving her gloves boldly at the hot-eyed young man driving a cart of beer barrels as close as he dared to their hack's wheels.

Amelia snatched the gloves away from Marie and said harshly, "This is a city. A Northern city. You're behaving like a waiter girl. Thank heavens—we're here. Oh, it's like having all my dreams come true. Evie, this is the Astor House. No—no—that one with the four low columns—five stories high."

Evie said, "I wonder where the privy is. Is it five stories high too?"

Marie laughed through her tears, "Yes, and we can use a different one every week day."

Seeing Marie in better spirits made Amelia less wary. She forgave her for flirting with the common cart boy. She beamed on her. She must continue to impress on Marie how amazingly pretty she was and how much she counted on her to help make their fortunes in this new life.

The lobby at the Astor House was jammed with ladies and gentlemen drinking champagne and sparkling burgundy and toasting General Grant, General Sherman, President Lincoln, General Sheridan, Admiral Farragut, and General Robert E. Lee. Amelia registered as Mrs. Feaster, a widow, and daughters, late of Columbia, South Carolina. While she went up to inspect the suite Colonel Stetson, the manager, insisted she occupy after he understood that they were being sponsored by the Union League Club, Marie and Evie waited out on the portico for Stobo who was on the way from the dock with their luggage in two carts.

In front of the classic pink St. Paul's Church, next to the Astor House, a loud-mouthed Irishman was standing on a cracker barrel terminating a long speech.

"And, my friends—having returned from Washington on the cars this very day I personally heard Mr. Lincoln last night, announce the surrender of the Southern capital." Cheers and shouts and firecrackers exploded. "But, in his own immortal words, 'I will have naught to say in conclusion if you dribble it out of me!' "

"But what did he say in conclusion? What did he say?" yelled the crowd.

Marie and Evie inched through the people to hear the Irishman better. The noise all around was deafening. A brass band, passing by, hushed to listen to this gentleman from Tammany Hall who was running for something though nobody knew just what. From the Battery a big drum was beating, a cannon booming.

The Irishman made himself heard above the drum and the clatter of the street and the spirit of the crowd: "Mr. Lincoln said: 'I see you have a band—I propose now closing up by requesting you to play a certain piece of music or a tune. I thought *Dixie* one of the best tunes I ever heard—so let the band play *Dixie!*' "

The passing band in reply lifted their horns and the flute began—high and thrilling and fast and heart-breaking.

> Oh I wish I wuz in the land ob cotton
> Old times dere am not forgotten
> Look away, look away,
> Look away, Dixie's land!

The yelling and stamping rose to such a climax that the men taking the free lunch at the long bar at the Astor House and the carters in the street and the people from the lobby and the shopkeepers on Broadway came whooping toward the band blaring *Dixie*.

And suddenly a solitary woman was heard singing above all the orgiastic street noises and mob howling and it was like being in Paris when the Revolution was boiling at its highest and boiling over. And Amelia, standing in the pretty parlor of a suite on the third floor of the Astor House with Colonel Stetson, felt a cold hand scrape her tired back as that lone woman's wild singing penetrated the closed windows with a frighten-ing familiarity. She ran to the window, jerked it up and looked down, and sure enough there was Marie waving a small flag of the Stars and Bars (where had she kept it hidden on the voyage?) and she had pushed the big thick politician off the cracker barrel and was standing on it herself waving the Confederate flag and singing *Dixie* at the top of her strong lungs. And she looked so bold and valiant that the whole street was cheering and clapping and urging her to sing—sing—sing—

With the fury of fervent patriotism Marie sang every verse and at the end, as the drum ruffled off, she looked around at the crowd with the fierce eyes of a demon and waved the little Confederate flag as fero-ciously as if it were an avenging sword. Riffraff and respectable citizens alike shuddered and the ones in front moved back until there was only one person left very close to the box—a Union naval officer. As valiant

in his patriotism as she, he reached up and jerked
her down and she struck him in the face and left a
red scratch down his cheek. But he took the flag
roughly away from her and snapped it in half and flung
it into the crowd.

Then he turned and himself disappeared into the midst
of the goggling people who were avid for any kind of
new sensation and were wishing the girl would jump at
him again like the wild woman she appeared to be and
they'd have a good fight to excite them higher.

But at this point, a black man came through the
crowd and began speaking sharply to her. She made as
if to strike him but he shook his head and took her
firmly by the arm and struggled to make a way for her
through the mob that broke and divided for them to
squeeze through.

Marie lay in a big, cool bedroom all afternoon. She
slept restlessly and waked feeling that something terrible had happened to her. She heard Evie's voice in
the next room and Amelia's, then the voices of strange
men. Through the window, bars of sunset struck in.
Why had she slept so hard? Why had she kept dreaming of a man in a blue uniform—why had he hurt her?
What—

"Mama!"

Amelia and Evie rushed in together. Smothered her
with solicitude. They had on dreadful-looking old
clothes and worn-out shoes.

"Dear child—will you be able to get up and go with
us to the Union League Club celebration?"

Marie remembered everything. Go back to sleep, she
thought despairingly. Feeling nothing, loving nothing,
sleep—sleep.

"A whole delegation from the Union League Club
is in the parlor of our suite. Mr. George Bancroft and
Mr. Woolcott Gibbes—oh! he is a wag—and Mr.
Strong and Mr. Putnam, the publisher, and Mr. Franklin Delano and Mr. Horace Greeley. And they all
want to see you."

"Where is Stobo?"

"He has gone to Brooks Brothers to get himself a

suit of proper livery. Mr. Delano told him he could charge it to him."

"I didn't have any lunch," Marie remarked.

"There's a luscious tea in the parlor. A chicken salad and cakes and sandwiches and wine if you'd rather instead of tea. Won't you hurry? Put on these clothes. We mustn't seem prosperous."

"Yes," giggled Evie, "they want us to look very pitiful and noble for tonight."

"Will you be able to come? Three of us will make a better show than two."

"Yes, Mama. You and Evie go out. I promise to join you in ten minutes."

Marie got up and put on the disgusting shoes and the split, old, mauve taffeta dress for which Amelia had traded one of her good dresses to a less fortunate refugee on the *Weybosset*. She washed her face and brushed her hair until it shone.

Marie Boozer! Daughter of Amelia (Amelia what? She didn't even know her mother's maiden name) and who? Poor Peter Burton? Or some rake from Philadelphia whose mother had been a golden beauty and whom she resembled? Background? She had no background. And why wasn't Amelia angry with her because of her singing *Dixie* in the street? Everything cherished and valued suddenly seemed to belong irrevocably to the past—like Big Dave and Mrs. McCord and—yes—she must continue to think his name —Willie C.

This was a different Marie. Did she look it?

Her face was pale from the superb and awful grief that had engulfed her on the street. Around her eyes were dark shadows. Her mouth had a line at the corner. This line would deepen someday. She made her lips smile. There—now she recognized the girl in the mirror. She had, as yet, no deep familiarity with this new face but she appreciated the rarity of it. It was not the tender, volatile face that Mrs. McCord and Big Dave and Willie had adored. But it *was* a beautiful face and capable of ruthlessness. Well, even Willie had been ruthless. And so had the naval officer. And so would she, if it suited her. No more flag waving for lost causes. She laughed. Had the officer been handsome? The line disappeared from the corner of her mouth. Her eyes took on the purple and gold of the sunset outside the window. Powder hid the shadows under them. Rouge? No—the pallor was interesting —haunting.

She laced the disreputable bits of leather around her ankles and moving with a restrained but deliberate sensuousness, went into the parlor crying gaily, "My Law—I didn't know you were having a party, Mama! Is it all right if I come in in this old dress? It's the only one I could manage to sew the flounces back on—the other one has gone entirely to pieces."

When questioned recently about Mrs. Feaster, Mr. Thurlow Weed said he remembered the relief fund of $10,000 given her by members of the Union League Club. He added that he spoke to General Sherman, after the occurrence, and that the latter verified Mrs. Feaster's story.

SAN FRANCISCO CHRONICLE

30

By a bizarre set of events Marie was introduced, after a fashion, to the three men who were to play leading roles in her future life in that one day. Lloyd Phoenix, rich, debonair yachtsman, youthful naval hero of the *Monitor;* John S. Beecher, dedicated clubman, of both the Union and Union League Clubs, a shy, wealthy bachelor of forty odd; and a young attaché of the French Embassy in Washington, the small, sensitive but ardent, Count de Pourtalès.

The most impressive victory celebration in New York was at 8 P.M. in Union Square in front of the Union League Club house sponsored *by* the Union League Club with all its members in the stand or close to it. The fountain was lit and splashing beautifully. Bands were playing. The most fashionable people in the whole city seemed to have congregated in the oval on the green lawns and under the darking trees. From the Maison Dorée to a tree in the park, a rope had been stretched to which depended American flags and the great stand was hung overall with Chinese lanterns. The club houses around the Square, the Loyal League Club, the Union League and the Athenaeum were illuminated with festoons of Chinese lanterns and diminutive sperm candles in tin sconces.

At intervals rockets and Roman candles went up and off. In the flickering glow Marie and Amelia and Evie were standing with six carefully selected Negroes and the escaped prisoners from Andersonville and several whom Amelia had rescued from Camp Sorghum. The prisoners' worship of Amelia was obvious and Marie comprehended with amazement that Amelia was the cynosure of all eyes. *Amelia* was the one Mr. Wilcox and Mr. Stoner were lauding in their speeches. And *Amelia* was not wearing a sickly mauve-colored dress that destroyed *her* brightness, but a brilliant green brocade, terribly worn-out, naturally, but still eye-catching in the candle and gas and rocket light and going well with her satiny white skin and shiny black hair. Amelia had purposely made Marie wear the drab mauve. Amelia was looking ladylike and handsome. *Everybody* was staring at Amelia and *nobody* was staring at *her*. It was a new experience. One she must correct.

She twitched her left shoulder to make the puff sleeve fall slightly off and expose her bare upper arm. Someone coughed. Someone *was* looking at her now. A tall, dark man in a Navy uniform with a red scrape on his cheek. He had noticed her gesture and appreciated the pretty bare shoulder. There was no illusion in his gaze. He knew what she had been up to. He thought she was a bold, fast girl. Yes—it was the same naval officer who had jerked her from her pedestal this morning. She remembered now exactly how he'd looked. Hard and handsome. Marie jerked the sleeve back onto her shoulder and stood up very straight. She'd not look at *him* again and be made fun of. She never had liked mean men. As if she, too, adored her, Marie gazed up at Amelia.

Mr. Frederick Olmstead, he who had designed Central Park, was making a speech about Amelia. Then Mr. Marshall, the president of the Union League Club, spoke. First of the surrender and President Lincoln's *coup*—making sure that a Negro battalion was the first to enter Richmond. Just to show them. He spoke of the peace to come, the prosperity, now that States Rights had been annihilated. He gave credit to all who had helped Negroes escape and to the men from Andersonville. Then he took Amelia by the hand and led her to the front of the platform.

"This lady is the epitome of what Mr. Olmstead meant by loyalty. Look and you will see the marks of suffering on her and her two dear little girls."

Marie closed her eyes and tightened her mouth. Evie bit her thumbnail. The dark-eyed naval officer moved over and stood near them.

Marie was thinking: What if she jumped on the stand and pushed Mr. Jay and Mr. Marshall aside? It would be easier than the big Irishman this morning. And what if she told them that Amelia Feaster and her daughters had been carried in the little stolen carriage as gently as if it had been a palanquin of velvet across South *and* North Carolina? That they had drunk the finest *vins du pays* from the thinnest crystal goblets; eaten the fat of the farms and the forest off china plates: slept under downy white blankets—

"Shut up muttering, Marie," Evie butted her head back against Marie's mouth. "Mama is going to make a speech."

Mr. Marshall was bowing to Amelia. Mr. John Jay was handing her a bouquet of red roses. A rocket went up and in its glare Amelia's hair was as iridescent as a king-fisher's wing. She *was* handsome. And she was in her element, saying:

"The privilege was mine. The honor too. If, in any small way, such as giving up our home and our prestige in our community to aid the unfortunate men captured in their effort to help preserve our blessed Union, we too have helped the Cause, what we have lost has been little in comparison with the great happiness we have won. That you of the Union League Club have invited my children and me to be your guests until we can establish ourselves in this friendly city proves that our sacrifices have not been in vain and that true charity and love—true charity—" Her voice broke; sobs came. Poor tired dear! Poor worn-out thing!

Evie looked apprehensively at Marie as cheers and applause from the audience roared over them. Marie pulled Evie in comfortingly against her but two men grabbed them and pushed them up onto the stand beside their mother. And there Marie stood, stony-eyed and furious, as ladies and gentlemen poured up to thrust wads of bills and sacks of gold coins into Amelia's deep reticule. The poor, worn-out sack!

The naval officer was still staring at her. Well he *was* handsome. Not like Willie, but he carried his big body like an admiral and he was debonairly cruel looking in a highbred interesting way. His left eye drooped in a wink. What did she have to lose? Marie carefully closed her right eye and smiled ever so slightly. Oh —damn those women! All around her. Making it so he couldn't see her. And such gabbling! All about where to buy frocks and bonnets and shoes and shawls; where to attend church; when to come to tea—to supper. Would Amelia speak at their Club? The Episcopal auxiliary? The Ladies Aid?

A very young man, in an ultra-wasp waisted coat, had edged his way through the mass of female patriots. He had a beautiful face. His dark hair fell in curls on his forehead. He wore his clothes as easily as if they were his own skin. And he moved like a dancing master, quick, graceful, always going away.

"Pardon, Mamselle," he stuttered to Marie, "present to Madame thees *cadeau*—no—*cadeau* to Madame thees present. Pardon—Pardon—" He glided down the steps and ran through the people and the trees to the lighted fountain, his cape flowing from his shoulders like the wings of a bird. He paused beside the fountain and removed his beaver hat and fanned his flushed cheeks. A rocket burst over the fountain and Marie saw the naval officer approach the quick little Frenchman. They bowed and shook hands like old friends and the little Frenchman lifted his shoulders and his hands, as if he was telling some amazing tale. The naval officer nodded and looked her way and said something naughty and laughed and at the end he laughed very loud and saluted her and waved an imaginary flag in her direction. The Frenchman was laughing too and he blew her an airy appreciative kiss. But she shrugged and looked down and she was holding the little Frenchman's hundred dollar bill in her hand.

"Girls!" A pompous, middle-aged man was approaching Marie and Evie.

"Sir?"

"Your mother has gone over to the Union League Club house with Mr. Jay and Mr. William Blunt. I am John S. Beecher and she has accorded me the honor of escorting her daughters to the Club for a little supper we are giving in her honor."

The next night Amelia stood in front of the wardrobe in the bedroom and fingered a rich violet satin gown with a long train, fashioned, not in the wide, full-skirted mode, but long and narrow, showing every line of her tall, lithe body. Small purple ostrich tips outlined the Empire bust line and the low décolletage. Oh —she did so want to wear this dress tonight! This was her first grand party. To be truthful, her *first* real party.

The invitation had come this morning. Written in the Union Club at midnight of the past evening. She had been aware of the way he looked at her. Having had four husbands, should she not be aware when they had that certain gleam in their eyes?

John Beecher had written:

Dear Mrs. Feaster,

   I am entertaining at a little dinner at Delmonico's this evening and would deem it a rare privilege if you would join my friends: Mr. Ward McAllister, Mr. William R. Travers, Miss Fish, Mrs. Fanny Kemble Butler, and Mr. and Mrs. Pierre Lorillard Ronalds. Say that you will, brave Madame, and I will call for you at your hotel at six o'clock. With impatience I await your verdict.

                            Ever your obedient servant,
                            John S. Beecher

The luscious, new, violet satin bought from Madame Demorest's this morning, or the shoddy green she'd worn the previous evening?

There was a pack of cards on the marble-topped dresser. The cards would choose the dress. If she cut a red card, she'd wear the green—if a black card—the violet. She took up half the deck and without a tremor held the face card to the mirror. The Ace of Spades!

The violet dress slid smoothly over her body. She

looked queenly in it. Dividing her glossy hair she arranged it, raised over a purple velvet bandeau in front and confined behind with a cut jet comb. If only her skin weren't so dull! It was the flowing again and her back hurting. Ever since Mrs. Elmore's carriage had jolted her all out of place on the march. Ever since Big Dave Boozer had decided saving the baby was more important than—

What terrible thoughts! And just before a party too. And after the cards had been so kind. And—

She rubbed some paste rouge into her cheeks. Marie had come into the bedroom.

"Put some on your lips, too. That's a snaky dress. It shows how thin you've got."

"I couldn't decide on this or last night's green. But I am anxious to have Mr. Beecher like me. Do you think I'm too thin?"

"Not really. You look very grand. But you would be more in the role of poor pitiful refugee in the green. It became you too. Why do you want to impress Mr. Beecher? What an old maid he was, fussing over me last night as if I was about twelve years old."

"He's immensely wealthy. A tea and whiskey importer with offices on Front Street and a suite at the Clarendon Hotel *and* a member of the exclusive Union Club. I looked him up."

"Whatever for?"

Amelia shrugged and took a deep puff on the cigar.

"He knows you're married, doesn't he?"

"I registered here as a widow. I *am* a widow."

"Suppose Mr. Beecher finds out?"

"How could he?"

Now it was Marie who shrugged and said she was going to take Evie for a walk.

"Brandy's daguerrean gallery is open late. It's just beyond St. Paul's church. Why don't you both get your pictures taken?"

"Will you pay?"

"Certainly."

When the girls had left Amelia rinsed her mouth out with some water in which she had steeped cloves to take away the cigar odor. Then she rubbed some more rouge into her cheeks but the pink looked like a spot not a blooming. And inside she felt weak and chill. Damn Marie—spoiling her evening. Well, she'd not let her. She'd just not let her.

In December, 1865, when in New York, I received a note from Mrs. Feaster begging me to call and see her at the Astor House. On doing so I found her living in style, with a handsome suite of rooms and surrounded by a number of army officers. She was then working up her claim for loyalty and wanted me to give her a certificate as Mayor of Columbia that she was a widow. As I had seen Mr. Feaster but a few days previously in Columbia, I was not able to help her, but I heard that she recovered $10,000 for her loyalty—General Sherman having testified that he had witnessed the destruction of her property.

James G. Gibbes,
who burnt columbia? 1902

31

The choice of dresses proved, as the cards had indicated, proper. To compliment a dark lady's coloring. Mr. Beecher had ordered a centerpiece of Parma violets. And here was Amelia dressed in violet!

Mr. Beecher was pleased with his handsome Amelia, gowned in such exquisite taste. Her dinner conversation that night was keen and she described her adventures with Sherman's army with such wit and humor that his other guests remained long after midnight listening, fascinated, to this attractive lady who had been so persecuted.

It was one of John S. Beecher's most successful dinners at Delmonico's. Amelia obviously found him a delightful host. She told him so over and over. That pleased him, too, she being one of those rare women who *knew* and appreciated his serving gin cocktails with the caviar, Bass ale with the oysters. Amontillado Sherry with the green turtle soup, a Rauenthaler Berg, 1864, with the deviled marrow bones, Clos Vouguet with the roast canvasback ducks, Perrier Jouet with the mutton, and Napoleon brandy with the vanilla ice cream.

Throughout the summer and autumn there were other dinners, and carriage rides, and lunches and theater parties. Marie watched Mr. Beecher's timidly correct courtship of Amelia with scornful amusement at first, but more rueful as the months passed and it became evident that Amelia was falling in love or pretending to. And Marie could not discover a single reason to be satisfied. She knew she should get married —but to whom? She had no background, she did not know New York, she had antagonized the young ladies she'd met at the Union League Club by being too pretty and had frightened the young men by being too Southern.

On her nineteenth birthday in December of 1865, Marie grumbled to Amelia, "I am tired of our gypsy life. And of being swallowed up in our stupid refugee roles. I have tried to be gay with the dull gentlemen and the flashy army officers who come to see us. But I just don't like them. They're all too old."

"You may do as you please. I, however, intend to better *myself*. I've learned that my previous Mr. Beecher has purchased a lovely new brownstone mansion on Sixteenth Street near the corner of Fifth Avenue, the one he has been driving me by and making me exclaim over for the past there weeks."

"So?"

"So—this morning I had a note from him asking if he could call this afternoon at teatime; if we could be alone; if he could ask me a certain question."

"Mama—you wouldn't! Colonel Gibbes said when he was here yesterday—"

"Dry up!" Amelia looked furiously at Marie. "There's more—but for heaven's sake don't write Evie, she'll blab it all around—our money's gone."

"What?" Marie was dumbfounded. "The ten thousand Senator John Sherman got for you from the United States Congress *and* the ten thousand from the Union League Club? Are you crazy?"

"Eight months at the Astor House in this suite—

Evie at an expensive school in Connecticut. You and I have wardrobes fit for any entertainments. I've bought a few bibelots and speculated a bit. Twenty thousand doesn't last long in New York. And, this is what I was going to tell you a minute ago but your wild-eyed astonishment upset me, just before lunch the Honorable Thomas Murphy of the Union League Club, a friend of General Sherman, paid Colonel Stetson $2,000 to liquidate our board bill here in consequence of tales he has heard about us, from some of his prewar friends in Columbia. But our board is not all I owe Colonel Stetson. He's advanced me cash lately."

"And you think Colonel Stetson will—"

"He's going to demand his money and ask us to leave here I am sure. He flatly refused to see me when I went to complain about the fireplace smoking in the bedroom this morning."

"Oh—Mama—it's too horrible!"

Amelia picked up a cigar, grimaced as she bit off the tip, then smiled her tight little smile at Marie.

"No. We've had eight months of high living and I'll accept Mr. Beecher's proposal so fast this afternoon it'll make his head swim. Here—take this fifty-cent piece and go down and buy some violets for the tea table. I'll tell Mr. Beecher that Mr. Jay sent them. That will make him come to the point sooner."

Three o'clock struck. Amelia got up and handed Marie the soft sealskin capelet she'd bought her from Altman's for her birthday present.

A pulse was throbbing unnaturally fast in Amelia's throat. Marie noticed with some surprise that Amelia's throat had gone all crepy under the chin. Or was it the light from the window? And her wrist was sheer bone. How could Mr. Beecher think of marrying an old woman like Amelia? There were tiny wrinkles around Amelia's eyes and dark shadows under them, her lips were rouged a deep crimson. Her flawless skin was getting yellow, but her eyes were glittering in their old dangerous way. Yet, as on that day in Winnsboro, Marie managed to keep *her* eyes steady and finally Amelia turned away, saying crossly, "Go and do as I say. Buy

a bunch of violets and be sure they're fresh. Everything is in your interest."

When she came down into the lobby, Marie saw
Colonel Stetson talking to a group of men by the great
stove. They looked curiously at her. Mr. Stetson ignored
her "good afternoon," turning his back rudely. The
men's expressions hurt her so that she could not bear
it. But she tossed her head and slowed her steps and
walked as provocatively as she knew how out of the
front door and down the steps and then began to run up
and down the dark streets leading off Broadway. Below Bleecker, gay, glazing transparencies hung over
the entrances to the concert saloons, illuminating the
posters announcing the current entertainments. Waiter
girls just arriving at work looked curiously at Marie
running along the street as if someone were pursuing
her. "There's no one behind you," they called out to
her. But she only hurried faster and faster.

She felt disgraced, humiliated, guilty and deprived
of all hope of erasing her humiliation. What a wicked,
wicked woman Amelia was! Getting ready to marry
when she was already a married woman. Poor Papa
Feaster. Poor little Jay. Poor Evie—away at that cold,
unfriendly school. Poor Marie—poor Willie—poor Mr.
Beecher when he found out his wife was a bigamist. She
would tell Mr. Beecher. She must lift her head high in
this new shame and not permit Amelia to hold her
under her heel. She became aware of the faces of pas-
sers-by staring at her. She could feel the winter wind
burning her cheeks. They must be scarlet and her eyes
must have taken on all the brilliance of the blazing
transparencies. For everybody was admiring her, running, graceful and swift and afire with her shame because of Amelia, along the street. Where might she find
Mr. Beecher? At his club? Or at the house he had just
purchased for a bride?

She was near the St. Nicholas Hotel on Broadway
and Broome Street. In front of the hotel a flower lady
was sitting with her basket of hot-house blossoms
wrapped in paper cones against the cold, waiting for
the carriage trade that came with the dusk to this
fashionable spot. Enchanted by her determination to

free herself from the consequences of further humiliation by warning Mr. Beecher, she remembered the flowers she must buy for the tea table. In any event they would not be violets.

Mr. John S. Beecher invited her to accompany him
to the theatre and other places of amusement, and
finally made a proposal of marriage. . . .

SAN FRANCISCO CHRONICLE

32

John S. Beecher was a member of·an excellent New
England family. In his early forties, he had a long head
and a pointed nose and his hair was blond mixed with
gray. Being his best feature, he wore it long over his collar and in well-kept sideburns. His full, somewhat
drooping mustache was silky and gave him a lush,
sensuous expression, disguising his thin mouth and re-
ceding chin. His green eyes, deep set in prominent
bones and covered with thick, blond eyebrows were
small but shrewd. He wore padded, tapered coats
that hid his sloping shoulders and showed his narrow
hips to advantage.

Craving security and having had a fine education, he
easily maintained a personal relationship with the think-
ers and the wits in the Union Club and the Union League
Club. He had a horror of doing anything different or
being seen in the wrong company. Beneath his good-
mannered exterior he was hypersensitive and timid.

He had grown weary of living in an hotel. With the
expanding railroads too many strangers were coming to
New York and making noises in the hotel's halls at
night. Arrogant Southerners would start reappearing
again now, and Westerners too, no doubt; even Texans,
perish the thought. The five-block walk between the
brownstone mansion on Sixteenth Street, near the corner of Fifth, up the Avenue to and from the Union
Club each.day would give him the exact amount of
exercise his delicate body required.

It was *his* mansion. He had purchased it recently. He
would furnish it next week with treasures from his suite

at the Clarendon Hotel. He would move in. Then he would be married to Amelia Feaster. Thinking of his fat, safe, black-leather chair in the Fifth Avenue window of the Union Club, beside Mr. Schermerhorn's fat, black-leather chair, Mr. Beecher moaned a little, but to bolster up his morale, he let his gray, kid-gloved fingers close firmly around the brass key to the house. *His* key. *His* house.

He would go down to Clinton Place and tell Josie Woods the day before he married. But not a day earlier. Josie had valued his patronage, always keeping the choice girl for him whenever he sent a note in the morning telling her he intended to drop by her house after supper. Josie's house had been his sanctuary, as such places are for timid men. She would miss his lavish tips. He would miss her understanding. But after forty, a man needed a home. Particularly on cold, rainy nights when it was hazardous to go to the Club or to the theater or to Josie's house.

He heard a clock strike four. Time for tea! Time to be at the Astor House. And here he was—mooning in front of this house—wasting time—keeping her waiting —thinking of how it was going to be—

"Mr. Beecher—"

She had on a fawn-colored coat cap like an English dunstable with blond chantilly lace falling over her shoulder. Her sealskin capelet was close up to her chin, hiding the stubborn set of it, showing instead her soft young lips and even, little teeth as she smiled sweetly at him.

"Why, Marie—whatever are you doing out on the street alone? Come—I am on my way to the Astor House—I'll call a hack. We'll just walk over to the corner of Fifth. They're always plenty going up and down. Girls your age mustn't be seen on the streets in the dusk alone."

"Is this your house?"

"Why, yes. How did you know?"

"Mama told me. She said I'd probably find you here."

"Nothing wrong, I hope? I was on my way to ask her—"

"I'd like to see inside the house. Will you take me?" She lifted, then lowered her lashes at him. Her body swayed forward. She was wearing a perfume that smelled of young roses. She had a paper cone of yellow roses in her chamois-gloved hand. Her eyes were as soft and gray as the December sky overhead—with a hint of smoke in them—and fire. She was saying, "This is my birthday. Poor Mama was planning to have a party for me and who should come in at lunch time but Colonel Gibbes, the mayor of Columbia. He's still in our suite. He just won't go away. He's here in New York on business and came to see Mama and bring her news of Papa Feaster—"

"Papa *Who?*" Mr. Beecher was filled with a paroxysm of rage. Had he been hoodwinked by his woman, Amelia? Had he been on the verge of making a spectacle of himself? Had he been on the verge of—

"Mama sent me to tell you," Marie said, "she didn't think you'd particularly care to meet Colonel Gibbes, so not to come until five. Colonel Gibbes is a rabid Southerner and just hates Yankees."

"It was very good of you," Mr. Beecher said stiffly. "You know I thought—"

"Oh, you're angry! Did you think Mama was divorced? Lots of people do. But she's not. She and Papa Feaster had a quarrel during the war and Papa went away for a little while."

"It was my impression your mother was a widow."

"Oh no. Colonel Gibbes said he saw Papa Feaster in Columbia the day he left and he was fine."

"But—but—"

"Oh—I'm sure Mama never meant for you to think she was a widow. She has enjoyed being your friend and going to elegant places with you. She must have taken it for granted you knew she was married. She and Papa Feaster were happy until the middle of the war. Then she decided to be loyal to the Union and began helping the poor, pitiful Northern prisoners in Columbia and—"

"Have you had your tea?" Mr. Beecher had got a grip on himself. An icy lucidity was following his brief flare of anger.

He had told everybody at the Club about the house, about his plans to be married. He had not told them who, thank the Lord for that.

"Poor Mama has been through so much. She needs security badly. She values material comforts and she has great pride. She wants a home."

"So you would like to see inside my house?" Mr. Beecher took out the key and made a great fuss about cautioning Marie to walk carefully up the stone steps. The child had no idea what she had protected him from doing. From what disgrace she had saved him. The light in the hallway burned brightly as he turned up the gas. He looked at Marie hard. He coughed and took out his handkerchief and fumbled with it to keep his fingers from pinching her rosy cheek. Why, she was no child. She was a beautiful woman with wonderful eyes. Forgetting his usual timidity, he asked, "How old are you, Marie?"

"Nineteen. This is my nineteenth birthday." Marie watched him rubbing his hands together and coming closer. "Don't you think it's mighty chilly in here? By the time we get to the Astor House it will be five and Colonel Gibbes will have gone and Mama—"

Mr. Beecher reached in his pocket and took out a tin box, removed a glycerin lozenge and popped it into his mouth. "Slight cold," he said trying not to touch her throat. She clutched the roses and said well, it was time they went, wasn't it? Mama was expecting them.

He grew greatly daring and reached out for her hand, but she made her arm stiff and pulled her fingers away.

"Yes," Mr. Beecher said, "it's high time for tea. But let's not go to the Astor House. Let's go to Delmonico's and celebrate your birthday. Just you and I. With a bottle of champagne and some Russian caviar. Have you ever been to Delmonico's?"

"No," Marie stood very straight because she wanted to be sure she didn't act foolish. "But I'd like to go—very much."

Mr. Beecher leered joyfully. "Come then, I'll call a hack at once."

As she climbed ahead of him into the hack, Marie

raised her skirt and showed her ankle. Mr. Beecher stared. Then, throwing caution totally to the wind, he pinched her seat, and cringed, waiting for her to shriek in maidenly outrage.

But Marie only looked back at him with widened, beautiful eyes as if nothing had happened at all.

Mr. Beecher gulped and got in quickly and did not sit too close to her. Her stillness made him timid again. And when she did speak she said, "I can't believe I'm going to Delmonico's on my birthday. When I think of where I was last December—"

"Wherever you were, you pretty thing, I know you were the belle of the ball." He sounded silly, even to himself.

Marie winced. Why had he said that? It brought back in a rush all of the young hot sweetness and tenderness of the past December when she and Willie had been driven through the darkness of the park in the "showbox" to the Athenaeum Hall and Willie had put his hand on her knee and she had loved him so.

The hack stopped with a lurch. In the entrance to Delmonico's several gentlemen and ladies watched Mr. Beecher hand Marie out and gallantly give her his arm.

"This is a very exciting occasion for me," Mr. Beecher said formally.

All the way to the best table, Marie said not a word and when they sat facing each other she thought: he pinched me! What have I got myself into? Everybody is staring and wondering why I'm here with this old man. They think I'm fast. I can tell. But Mr. Beecher is fascinated. He's staring at me with that same infatuated expression Major Reynolds used to get. Well, it's only this once. I guess I can stand him for an hour. In this heavenly place I could stand almost anybody for a little while. It smells so good. And everybody is dressed up. Oh—and there goes the champagne pop! But I'll never try to be noble again. Lord in heaven, no!

It is amusing to a South Carolina octogenarian to recall that the shrewd Sherman, the Sacrosanct Howard, all of their new found New York friends were hoodwinked. . . .

A CHECKERED LIFE
by *"One Who Knows"*

33

Losing Beecher was a blow to Amelia's hopes, both financial and personal, but she still had a card up her sleeve. When, just before Colonel Gibbes returned to Columbia, he called to say good-by, she persuaded him to intercede on behalf of her and her daughters with Colonel Stetson. The interview lasted an hour. Colonel Gibbes gave such a touching account of the background of the beautiful Marie Boozer and such a glowing view of her prospects here in New York where she was being momentarily courted by a rich merchant, that Colonel Stetson promised to permit Mrs. Feaster to reside at the Astor House for another month provided she behaved herself and came up at the month's end with a rich son-in-law to settle all of her accounts.

The thought of the immediate future, the advice of Colonel Gibbes, the alarming and sudden dwindling of her physical strength, and her yearning for money —everything tightened Amelia's resolve not only to behave herself from now on but to see that Marie, having been responsible for *her* losing Beecher, compensated for her impulsive action by marrying him herself. After all, Marie was a very extraordinary woman and everybody knows that extraordinary women are not born for happiness.

And events played smoothly into Amelia's hand. His friends, who had seen John Beecher drinking champagne with Marie at Delmonico's that December afternoon, made a point of coming up to him at the

Union Club and wagging him about his young companion and what a sly fox he was, pretending to have been interested in the mother and all the time pinching the tender young bud.

Mr. Beecher preened himself and his ego soared. Happily, he went about making a fool of himself. From the instant that the idea entered his head that marriage with a nineteen-year-old beauty would be a feather in his cap, he erased any memory of ever having considered a match with her mother.

Three weeks after the tea party found him closeted with Amelia, relating in detail his unsuccessful attempt to persuade Marie to elope with him.

Another week and Mr. Beecher rushed in one noon and found Amelia playing solitaire. "Thank the Lord you are here. I must talk to you."

"Sit down and pour yourself a glass of port," said Amelia and coolly finished the game while Mr. Beecher fumed and frantically pleaded with Amelia to urge Marie to marry him. Why, wherever they appeared together she was a sensation, the talk of the town, the mystery beauty of the decade, the—

"When are you seeing her again?"

"We were going to the opera tonight but I have received a note from her refusing to accompany me."

"Call here for her at seven. She'll go."

"Suppose she won't?"

"She will. She's as bored with this miserable nomad life as I. She's nervous and confused. That's probably why she wrote the note. She was probably just indulging in self-pity. By seven she'll be dying to get out into the bright lights and hear gay music. Now—if we weren't so poor I'd take her to Madame Demorest's and buy her a new gown and you couldn't pay her not to attend the opera and show it off. She's a beauty. Beauty feeds on admiration or it withers. She's been cooped up here with me far too closely." Amelia sighed discreetly and picked up a small cigar.

"Go to Madame Demorest's. Have her send the bill to me. Anything you want. Just so long as Marie is pleased with it. If only *I* knew how to please her. If only—"

"Do stop running about the room and sit down and drink your port. Doesn't she act pleased with you when you take her out?"

"Not lately. Why if I even try to tweak her precious little ear, she jerks her head away." His voice shook and his mouth worked frantically. "She would be angry if she knew I was telling you this."

Amelia coughed and grimaced. She had swallowed a mouthful of cigar smoke to keep from laughing. "What can I do to help you, Mr. Beecher?"

Now—that was like the Amelia he had been drawn to in the beginning. Ladylike and sincere and thoughtful of his plight.

"Tell me things that I can do to make her happy to be with me."

Silence for a moment. Amelia put down her cigar and looked hard at her former suitor. He seemed older. She felt a physical antipathy to him. His face was drawn and his eyes had red rims from sleepless nights. There was the beginning of a cold sore at the corner of his mouth. Even his hair that he usually groomed with such care was sticking out in tufts over his ears. She said, "She's always had a liking for older men. I think in her mind she mixes up the words *father* with *sweetheart*. Don't be too enthusiastic over her tonight. Try being paternal. She's got a soft heart and adores being petted. My last two husbands could wind her around their little fingers by being gentle with her. Once she's got confidence in you the other things will follow naturally. Kisses and tweaks, things like that."

"Since you advise it, I will try," he murmured, seized her hand and covered it with wet little pecks and then went away, running down the hall as if he, too, were just nineteen.

When Marie returned to the hotel in the late afternoon she was immediately apprehensive. The excited glitter in Amelia's eyes presaged something unpleasant. As was customary between them, each stiffened against the other. But Amelia held the trump card and she knew it. She smiled derisively with her tiny rouged lips and said, "I've written Evie she must leave school and I've just come from police headquarters."

"Why?" Marie's voice trembled in spite of her determination not to be upset.

"Colonel Stetson is suing us for indebtedness. I was trying to discover to what lengths he can legally take steps against us. Our month of grace is up. You know he only agreed to let us stay another month. I'm desperate. I've pawned all our furs and good clothes and every valuable we have. Even the Witherspoon silver that I had counted on to prove we *were* aristocrats."

Marie's heart beat faster.

Amelia went on, "Colonel Stetson is a vindictive man and furious at our 'hoodwinking him,' as he expresses it. He says he is going to write Colonel Gibbes and demand payment of our debts from him since Colonel Gibbes had assured him we would, in this time, be able to settle."

"That would mean everybody in Columbia will know about our throwing away all that money and fooling the Union League Club and that we are—"

"Disgraced. We might as well face it. Not a door anywhere will be opened to us socially. We will probably be forced to go into domestic service. What else could we do?"

"Mama—" This was worse than anything Marie had expected. It was humiliation at its rawest. She tried to keep her chin from quivering.

Amelia half closed her eyes. She seemed bored and in pain and weary. "If only we hadn't let Beecher slip through our fingers! He was a good man and reasonably rich."

Marie looked at Amelia. Pretending to be so tired and such a martyr and so alone. But up to something. If not about Colonel Stetson and what he was going to do, about something.

"Is all this true, Mama?"

"Yes, Marie. All true. We must get out of the hotel by tomorrow and where will we go? This is the end for us; absolutely the end. There is no way out unless—"

Here it came. It always came eventually. How lucky that dusk was deepening and they could not see each other's faces.

"Mr. Beecher was here this morning."

"I might have known. Well, I won't."

"I told him you wouldn't. That's why I say this is the end. But somehow I had so hoped you would that I borrowed Stobo's last twenty dollars and bought you a new dress to wear. Just in case you softened and decided to save us from complete ostracism. You've always been such a proud girl. Won't you at least look at the dress?"

Touching the creamy lace bertha on the off-shoulder white velvet gown that Amelia held up for her to see, Marie said, "You never got this for twenty dollars. Stobo doesn't have twenty dollars."

"He's received lavish tips, working this past month as a baggage porter here. And he'd give you his soul any time. What was it he used to tell you back in Columbia—'you got to work to be a belle but you got to work harder to stay one!'"

Marie sighed, thinking—and Stobo used to say, too —"every round goes higher, higher"—well, every round since she'd left Columbia had gone lower, lower—

She yanked at the buttons of her cloak and flung it off. "Here, help me with these hooks. My hands are freezing. I'm sick to death of all these old clothes. Especially this hideous dress. I think I *will* change my mind and go to the opera with Mr. Beecher. Ah—just feel this velvet!"

Amelia touched her arm. "That's sweet of you, Marie. I knew you'd save the day for us."

"Us? Don't fool yourself. I'm doing this to save myself. I don't feel a spark of loyalty to you. I won't to Beecher either. And I hate opera!"

"Beecher will make a kind husband and a doting father."

Amelia went and lit the gaslights and for the first time saw Marie's tear-drowned eyes. "Husband!" She whispered, "Oh, if I'd only kept my mouth shut and he was going to be yours instead of mine!"

The bride discarded her part as a Southern refugee to
re-appear as one of the leaders of New York society.

SAN FRANCISCO CHRONICLE

34

Marie's marriage to Mr. Beecher was doomed from the
beginning. Everybody seemed aware of it but the
bridegroom who puffed out his chest and gave her
$150,000 for a wedding gift.

They were married on Christmas Day, had a three-
day honeymoon, in his suite at the Clarendon Hotel,
settled down on the fourth day, in the brownstone
mansion on Sixteenth Street, and were "at home" to
callers on New Year's Day of 1866.

On the morning they moved into the house Marie, in
a state of nervous prostration, refused to attend to
anything, locked herself in the big bedroom she was to
share with Mr. Beecher, and cried like a crazed soul
while packers unpacked, movers moved, servants were
hired and Amelia, to Mr. Beecher's unutterable relief,
agreed to live with them and take over the running of
the household.

At first Marie alternated between being bitter and
pathetic. For once the lamp was extinguished that first
night, and he was protected from seeing or being seen,
Mr. Beecher proved to be neither timid *nor* fatherlike.
Other nights with him didn't overwhelm her with the
same loathing. She just didn't care. Let him expend his
frenzy in whatever erratic manner he chose. She might
as well have been asleep, or watching a dull play.
And never in the future did she prize her lovely body
as inviolate. Nor did she feel that it in any way belonged to Mr. Beecher and each time she eluded or
humiliated him she repaid him for that first time. But
being Marie, she would not let Mr. Beecher make her
unhappy forever because he could not make her happy.

Nor would she allow Amelia to know what a great
anguish of soul and drought of body had been the
price of their present affluent security and impeccable
social position.

As for Mr. Beecher, he was blissfully unaware that
his marriage was imperfect. He was not sensitive
enough to have attempted to discover what pleased
Marie. Had he accomplished this, she would probably
have come to love him a little bit. But like most men
who remain unmarried too long and have spent their
necessary hours in the plush establishments of the Josie
Woods of the world, Mr. Beecher had no physical in-
tuition or liking for a woman. A tender and intimate
marriage was beyond his comprehension. The qualities
in a woman that commanded his esteem and love
were first: beauty, such as Marie had, that excited the
envy of women and the admiration of men; second:
the shrewd wit, the card-playing ability and housekeeping skill that were Amelia's special talents. He
was convinced he'd made a grand bargain and was the
happiest bridegroom in New York City.

At this time it was the custom in New York City
for the gentlemen of society to pay calls on New Year's
Day. The ladies stayed at home and received in their
parlors and served cakes, sandwiches, wine, tea, eggnog and punches between the accepted hours of 11
A.M. and 11 P.M. After 11 P.M. the gentlemen who
were unable, after sipping cups in too many parlors, to
discover their way home congregated on lower Fifth
Avenue where butlers and valets, sent by tolerant
spouses, found them and led them quietly to their beds.

On New Year's Day, 1866, the Beecher's brownstone
house on Sixteenth Street was jammed with gentlemen
callers, curious and benign. Amelia and Mr. Beecher
had done their utmost to have all, including Marie,
ready for this important inspection by New York society.

The new house was a deep, roomy, rather dark dwelling with a wide entrance hall, lighted by two bronze
torches holding gas bulbs on the newel posts of the
heavy oak stairs. The dark wainscoted walls were high

and old-fashioned sideboards and black tea chests on legs, enormous mirrors, tall silver candelabra, much delicate cut glass and marble figures were everywhere.

Stobo met the gentlemen at the door and bowed them into the parlor furnished in a brand-new set of carved Victorian furniture covered in red velvet made by John Henry Belter. The windows were swathed in heavy red velvet drapes and covered in lace curtains. A mulberry Brussels carpet blanketed the floor. The myriad side chairs had tapestry covers and there were two tilt tables in front of the bay window inlaid with mother-of-pearl. In the center of the room under a spreading crystal gas chandelier was a round, marble-topped table with a lamp of brass dripping with pendants and silk fringe. On either side of the double entrance doors were heavy, carved rosewood bookcases filled with leather-bound copies of Gibbon and Scott and Shakespeare and Donne. The white walls were decorated with a needlepoint picture of George Washington, a beadwork bellpull, a shell picture, a set of allegorical engravings and a picture of Evangeline. On the marble mantel were two alabaster fruit bowls, a reclining marble angel in a two-foot-long onyx shell, and a pair of Charles II silver wine cups.

Marie stood in front of the mantel beside Mr. Beecher to receive their callers. She was unusually pale and in the heavy surroundings appeared ethereal. Her yellow curls were done in a "waterfall" and she was wearing a pearl-colored, stiff silk gown trimmed with Undine green overlaid with tulle made by Mr. Worth of Paris and imported by A. T. Stewart's store. Diamond and emerald pendants hung in her ears and a matching necklace outlined her strong young throat. She held a bouquet of white wax camellias in a holder of green enamel on gilt studded with pearls with a mother-of-pearl handle. Mr. Beecher and Amelia had arranged her toilette carefully. Never, in New York, had society met such a purely beautiful, perfect-appearing bride.

Evie had been left at her school in Connecticut during this period, at Amelia's orders. And Amelia, in a sleek black velvet with a bustle and a train, presided grandly at the tea table where caviar, dainty bread and butter sandwiches and *petits fours* surrounded silver wine coolers of champagne and heavy silver trays of fine old Port and Madeira and brandy and coffee and tea.

As the hours passed, Marie felt the dull clouds of despair that had engulfed her during the week of her marriage draw apart. Why, the most elegant gentlemen in New York were flocking to meet her, greeting her with lively enthusiasm, listening attentively at her charming candor, marveling that the poor pitiful Southern refugee, driven ignominiously from South Carolina, could carry herself like a princess before them. Many, having heard Mr. Murphy's bit of gossip, had expected her to be bold and ordinary as her mother must have been to have done the things Mr. Murphy swore he had heard she had done back in South Carolina. Some were delighted that old Beecher had pulled off such a coup.

Aware of their interest, Marie's natural ebullience began to assert itself and she responded gaily even to those who expected she *would,* as they were sure all Southerners *did,* do something *outré* or countrified. The fathers and sons of the old Knickerbocker families came and the members of the exclusive Union Club and, naturally, all of the Union Leaguers, spouting platitudes about how the North and South had come together and the South should learn to be a part of the North and obesisant to the North as its liege lord and—

Suddenly there *he* was—in the doorway—he who had hushed her singing *Dixie* in the street and had winked at her as she stood on the Union League Club platform the night after Richmond fell. He was looking at her as if he were hoping she would commit a *faux pas.* He was hoping—he was gone.

The gentlemen she had admired driving their horses on Harlem Lane came in a group—Mr. Belmont, Mr. Bonner, Mr. Jerome—even that grizzly old Commodore Vanderbilt gruffly complimenting her on having outrun him one afternoon with a hired nag.

How stimulating and exciting life was getting to be!

In the afternoon the naval officer returned, pleasantly inebriated, and this time entered the parlor crying out, "I've come to call on my friend, good old Beecher! And meet his wife. Hear she is a stunner. Oh —there you are old Beecher—"

Mr. Beecher acknowledged Phoenix's greeting with a tight smile and a slight scowl on his thick eyebrows. He usually concealed his dislikes rather well, but when irritated he would forget and scowl, as now. He said stiffly to his bride, "My fellow Union Club member, Lieutenant Lloyd Phoenix, hero of the battle between the *Monitor* and the *Merrimac*."

Phoenix was an extraordinarily good-looking young gentleman of twenty-four or five, tall and strong with sleepy brown eyes, smooth brown hair, and a dainty brown mustache, waxed and turned up smartly at the ends. He had a black silk stovepipe hat in his hand and was wearing a winter frock coat of blue broadcloth with a notched rolled collar, the borders bound in velvet. His double-breasted waistcoat was of tan silk plush and velvet in a large pattern. His close-fitting trousers of a smooth fawn-colored wool were cut tight at the ankles showing his excellent legs. He looked expensively snobbish and appeared to be in a maliciously high good humor.

But he was the ultimate in polished manners and Marie could feel her heart begin to beat faster and she laughed and said, "I'm so happy to meet you, Lieutenant Phoenix. In Columbia, South Carolina, we raised ten thousand dollars at a Gunboat Fair for the *Merrimac* back in 1861."

"Aren't you ashamed to have been guilty of such treason, loyal Madame?"

"Oh—no—I'm a genuine Rebel. Mama is the 'loyal' one."

"Mrs. Beecher—please—" Mr. Beecher protested.

He hastily led Phoenix (what a strange name—she liked it very much) over to the table and poured him a goblet of brandy. Mr. Beecher was gesticulating at his matched sets of books. Phoenix did not listen so much as watch Marie over the rim of the goblet. Marie could not guess what he had thought of her. She tried to hear as he began commenting on the literary tastes of the Beechers.

Amelia rose from her chair and glided over to Marie. The tight dress she was wearing made her body seem skeletal. She patted Marie's curls with maternal tenderness and fluffed out the green tulle of her overskirt. She had noticed Marie's sudden excitement with Phoenix. She was saying, "Take care and keep your eyes down. Try and remember names. You are making an impression on these gentlemen; even the ones who listened to Colonel Stetson and Mr. Murphy. They'll tell their wives about you and you'll be invited everywhere. Oh—haven't we come a long way from Newberry?"

Marie whispered, "I have. You haven't changed a bit. And don't forget, *I* hold the purse strings now. You'd better not annoy me."

No one heard this little interchange of pleasantries but all at once there was a chilly stillness in the stuffy room. Stobo came in and put a scuttle of coal on the fire. It blazed up, but all in the room felt cold. Amelia looked at Marie, astonished at her vehemence. Her eyes filled with unaccustomed tears and she swallowed hard.

"I was only trying to be helpful. This dress is certainly becoming to you. And tell me, little princess, who is the handsome gentleman Mr. Beecher is so cleverly guiding out into the hall?"

"I didn't catch his name," Marie declared and tossed her curls as if they were a mane.

Phoenix was gone and more and more gentlemen came. Late that night Phoenix was there again, buoyant, and very drunk. He sang a little song *Le Sabre de Mon Père,* out in the hall. He tried to teach it to Stobo. Marie heard Stobo cackling and saying, "Thank you, sir, Mr. Phoenix. Thank you, *sir.*" Then Stobo was hinging *Le Sabre de Mon Père* too and Phoenix wandered into the Parlor. It was almost eleven. His fine, soft hair had gotten mussed but his ruffled shirt was still stiff, his satin tie flowing, his blue frock coat hugging his lithe body as if it had been poured into it.

"Farewell," he cried and bending over in a rubbery

bow, took Marie's hand, turned it over, and kissed it several times in the palm. "I'm off for a sail on the seven seas in my new schooner. I've paid a hundred calls today and seen every belle in this deadly town. What bores! So I keep returning to you. Can't stay away from you. Oh God, here comes that old maid, Beecher, and—well, there you are—there you are."

He wove out into the hall and he and Stobo sang again and the few men left sang with them. Just as the clock began to strike eleven, Phoenix put his head back in the door and stared strangely at Marie. Mr. Beecher was staring at her too. And Amelia. Marie shrugged and put the bouquet of wax flowers to her nose. She said to Mr. Beecher, "Next time I would prefer real flowers or even just fresh green leaves. At least they'd be *alive*. Gracious, I'm tired. I think I'll go straight upstairs to bed."

She waved at Mr. Beecher and Stobo who had come in with a basket to collect the bottles. "Sweet dreams!" Then she quickly left the parlor, her silk dress rustling like the winter wind. She had looked very vulnerable all of a sudden and her voice sounded sad, awakening discomfiting memories in Amelia of a girl and a boy youthfully sharing a peach under a tulip tree long ago in Greenville, South Carolina.

As they went upstairs, Amelia was thinking, well, I have won again despite this wretched backache. Next week I'll see a doctor. I can't afford to be ill. Not with all this money to enjoy. Marie thought she was pulling off such a clever trick by telling Beecher I was married. But she's the one who has to pay the piper. I have an elegant home, social position, a man to smoke and drink and play cards with and with whom I don't have to do *that*—

And Mr. Beecher carefully undressed by the coal fire in his dressing room, put on his flannel nightshirt and cap and tiptoed quietly into the cold, dark bedroom. He climbed into the high-backed, walnut double bed and decided, well, tonight I'll let the child sleep. How quietly she breathes. How sweet and young she smells. But—I'm rather tired from having been standing on my feet all day. And after all—every night for a week—heigh ho—what a fine life I have before me. She must have everything her pretty heart desires —everything—

And Marie made herself continue to breathe as if she were asleep and kept saying over and over, Willie, you must try and understand how I've missed you and forgive me for feeling all warm and soft when Phoenix kissed inside my hand and, dear God, please don't let nasty old Mr. Beecher do that tonight—not tonight— just for one night—

Mr. Beecher took his wife to the ladies' reception at
the Union Club and there in an evil moment. . . .

THE COUNTESS POURTALÈS,
by "Felix Old Boy"[1]

35

As soon as the novelty of being indulged beyond all
reason began to wear off, Marie took for granted her
inexhaustible personal bank account, her thoroughbred trotting and saddle horses, her elegant phaeton,
her fur coats, her silken dresses and undergarments,
her diamonds and pearls, her trips to Paris and London, her summers at Newport, the silly aimless people
she gathered about her, and went about flinging away a
big slice of her young life. If she had had children,
things might have turned out differently. She and Mr.
Beecher might have found a common interest in the
nursery.

As it was, she took no interest in Mr. Beecher's business or his club life. She refused to discuss politics
which enthralled him almost as much as cards. But
she was rabidly a Southerner and a democrat and
their views on this, as on other things, were funda-
mentally opposed.

She was coldly indifferent to her mother. She allowed Amelia full sway in running the Sixteenth Street
house but that was because housekeeping bored her
and she thought the house was hideous, always comparing it and Amelia with Mrs. McCord's house back
in Columbia and Mrs. McCord herself.

Except for Evie, of whom she grew increasing
fond, most of her friends were ladies and gentlemen of
the horsy set. But, oddly enough, she had a reputation

[1]Yates Snowden

for being good and everybody thought she was an ideal wife for Mr. Beecher.

Everyone except Amelia, that is. Amelia was too knowing a woman to be on the alert for signs of an illicit love affair. For she knew that Marie was unawakened emotionally in her marriage and that sooner or later the memory of Willie would fade and some hot-eyed tempter would appear on the horizon and, noticing the ripe fruit hanging on the tree, would merely have to flip the branch and down Marie would come. Or worse—Marie might take up something like women's suffrage or spiritualism or start going with Mr. Beecher's reverend cousin to visit the salon of Ada Clare and that kind of half-cracked, arty woman.

When, on the day following April Fool, 1868, after Mr. Beecher had gone to work, Marie came down for breakfast in a pink-and-white cashmere morning robe, her gold curls all rumpled from the fatigue of the previous night, her eyes shining, and said to Evie (who lived with them all the time now, having been "finished" in the fancy school) ". . . darling—he was divine—simply irresistible!" Amelia could see plainly that their easy life was destined to come to an end suddenly if something was not done.

But what could Amelia do? For the moment, merely hide, just outside the dining room portière and listen to Marie telling Evie about the ball she and Mr. Beecher had attended the night before celebrating the opening of the new Union League Club House in the Jerome mansion on Twenty-sixth Street and Madison Avenue.

"Well, there were over a thousand people there."

"Any famous ones?"

"Oh—General Grant, he was very drunk, and the Chinese Embassy—all of them wearing funny peaked hats, and that strange little Frenchman—the one who gave me the hundred dollar bill that night of the fall of Richmond three years ago—remember?"

Evie nodded her head. "You were going to buy me a becoming dress but you never did."

"I will today. Now where was I? The funny little Frenchman speaks Chinese and he was escorting the Chinese around. He kept staring at me. I suppose he recognized me but couldn't believe it was the same poor creature."

"I'm sorry I wasn't here to hook you up. What did you wear, Marie?"

"A dress with thirty-six flounces all of Valenciennes lace. Really—I did look my best."

"What color?"

"Madame Demorest called it 'moon on the lake.' "

"You mean your regular mushroom? The color you always wear?"

"All right. Be like Mama and I won't tell you about the divine man."

"But you must. Did you flirt with him?"

"Well, I was intending to flirt with the Count de Pourtalès who was supposed to be one of the honor guests. But, unfortunately, I took him to be the secretary for those Chinese and flirted outrageously with a tall, dashing Frenchman whom I took to be the Count and who turned out to *be* the secretary for those damned Chinese."

"You mean our funny little Frenchman is actually a nobleman?"

"Heir to one of the great houses of France, they say. He would be quite smitten with me if I so much as crooked my little finger at him. He even laughed, not very mirthfully mind you, but he did chuckle a little when I told him I thought he was a Chinaman's secretary. So I was kind and danced half a polka with him."

"And afterward?"

"Afterward I led the cotillion with Mr. G. W. Blunt who is the most heavenly dancer and I teased him about having had his picture in the paper thumbing his nose at Mr. Horace Greeley and Mr. Greeley doing his nose at Mr. Blunt."

"Why did he do that?"

"Mr. Blunt is the one who had the Union League Club put Mr. Greeley out of the Club for signing the bond to free Jefferson Davis. And to get even Mr. Gree-

ley had one of his cartoonists draw the picture of Mr.
Blunt and put it in his paper."

"And then what happened?"

"Then I danced the lanciers with Mr. Woolcott
Gibbes. He puffed and wheezed like a pug dog, and
while we were flying around who should appear but
Lloyd Phoenix, his hair all brushed and curled and I
danced a waltz with him. I said, 'Oh, I thought you
were in Athens' and he said, 'I was but your hya-
cinthine hair brought me home.' And I said, 'No, that
was another lady. My hair is yellow.' And he said, 'Can
you read too?' And then he stepped on one of my
flounces and tore it and we stopped dancing and he
knelt down and picked it up."

"Did he look at your legs?"

"Everybody near us did. They all stopped and stared.
And Phoenix took from his pocket a pocket *nécessaire*
and found a pair of scissors in it and cut off the flounce.
I held out my hand for the flounce and he pressed it
to his heart and put it in the pocket *nécessaire* and
Mr. Beecher saw him and was furious and made me
come home."

"Was that why Mr. B. slept in the company room?"
Evie's voice cracked, she was so excited.

"Of course. He was very upset and cried. But he has
forgiven me."

"How do you know?"

Marie held up a bottle of Phalon's *Flor de Mayo*
perfume. "A special messenger just brought this. The
card says 'This afternoon there is a ladies' reception at
the Union Club. Wear your prettiest dress and this
scent and forgive your adoring John S. Beecher.' "

"Why does that make you so shiny-looking? A lady
tea in that stuffy old Club? I thought you hated the
Union Club affairs."

"Ah—this time it will be different."

"Why?"

"Silly—Phoenix is a member. He will be there too."

The next time that Mr. Murphy saw Mrs. Beecher, she was standing on the private stand at Jerome Park, watching the races, in company with Mrs. Charles O'Connor, the great lawyer's wife, who was noted for her fondness of the society of the gay young ladies of the haut ton. . . .

SAN FRANCISCO CHRONICLE

36

From that April afternoon, Marie was a young woman running headlong into thralldom to the man who was to utterly ruin her reputation.

Certainly, Lloyd Phoenix's background was the best. Having graduated from Annapolis in 1861, so long as the fighting war went on, he was happy in active naval service. But after the war, he had a spell of the doldrums which his grandfather, Stephen Whitney, cured by buying him a schooner. Phoenix was an accomplished sailor. To him a boat, like a woman, that could not go to sea and weather a heavy gale was a mockery. His *Intrepid* was a staunch, seaworthy boat. When he had proved this—he set about procuring all the luxury and comfort available—as he would have in a woman—and his main cabin aboard was as lush and splendid as a queen's boudoir.

He adored the ladies—that being his nature. He had great physical beauty and courage; he hated to hurt a lady's feelings. There was, however, always this: he wanted no lady's love to follow or try to possess him. If he wooed and won a lady's favors he felt himself wrong the minute that the worship he had inspired made any demands on him. And when suddenly he realized that the time had come to be hard-hearted or to be bored, he invariably found it easier to be cruel.

Marie was utterly dazzled by Phoenix and his swift, carefree world. She was in love with him and she knew it. If she had loved Willie like this neither Amelia, nor the whole of Sherman's army, nor Willie's adamant Southern "traditions" could have kept her from marrying him. She was caught up in a fierce physical attraction that made her feel burning and mad when she and Phoenix came together. His glance, the touch of his hand, set her on fire. She was ready and willing to wreck her life for him in order to marry him, for never had she experienced such a wild and wonderful happiness.

She knew that he did not want her friendship. She knew very well what he wanted. And, Lord in heaven, she wanted it too. More than heaven. She listened with rapture to the words he murmured in her ear—"Your beauty goes beyond a mere perfection of feature and color. It is exciting—"

Exciting—there was a release and absolution in those words. She was convinced that Phoenix was her destiny. He was debonnaire. He was ardent. He was a gentleman. He had suggested—

The eighth of June, 1868, and Central Park was a foam of blue-green spruce, emerald pine, yellow-green elm and larch, pale-green oak and creeper, and moss-green rock. There were hares and toads and sometimes a fox. There were whippoorwills at dusk and pigeons in the dawn, boats skimming over the lakes and bands of Annual Meeting of the New York Jockey Club in Jerome Park.

Marie was getting ready for the day with no little trepidation for after the races she and Phoenix had agreed (the past Friday during intermission of a matinee performance of *A Flash of Lightning* at the Broadway Theater) to dine daringly alone together in a private parlor at Burnhams Hotel (the former Vanenhueval mansion) far out on Broadway and Seventy-ninth Street. She was to follow him, after the next to last race when he left Central Park, and cut away from Harlem Lane. That was all. And later she was to say to Mr. Beecher, "My carriage wheel came off and I stopped to get it fixed and Miss Fish came along and I went in her coach for dinner at the Belmonts." She knew that Phoenix intended for them to become lovers tonight. And she knew that she would and later, naturally, she would divorce Mr. Beecher and they would be married and live happily ever after. It was very simple.

While Amelia helped Evie into a double-breasted linen suit with brass buttons and pinned a white bowler on her black hair, the French maid arranged Marie's hair in a huge gold chignon and fastened a yellow straw hat with a diadem of wheat spears à la Cérès low across her forehead. .

Every few minutes Stobo called impatiently from the street, "Ain't you girls ready yet?" But Marie couldn't get her hat on to suit her. Finally Stobo flung open the door and said, "I got two boys holding on but them crazy horses of yours are fixing to run away, hitched up in that outlandish fashion you insisted on yesterday."

"Just let me look once in the long mirror."

Marie was wearing a white grosgrain with a maize-striped overskirt fringed around and raised up to the center of the back where the folds were stopped by a crimson rosette. Over this she had flung a tent-like yellow taffeta sultane.

Downstairs the Beecher barouche was hitched to two livery-stable horses and a strange cockney driver was standing, whip in hand, by the block, to help Evie in. Marie turned to Evie and said—"You don't mind driving alone, do you? We'll meet at the Clubhouse in Mrs. O'Connor's box and sit together at the track. Stobo has got to ride beside me up Fifth Avenue in case I get into trouble with these wild animals. Pick me up, Stobo. And don't knock my hat off."

Laughing, Stobo picked her up in his arms and sat her in the dogcart, handed her the reins, fixed her sultane so it wouldn't catch in the wheels, straightened her hat a little, mounted his horse and called—"Now you can turn 'em loose, boys!"

The gray and the bay, beautiful creatures, were hitched tandem——one behind the other!

With a shrill neighing and rearing and much rising and bumping of wheels, the little dogcart flew off. The bay leading, the gray caught step at once and, heeding the expert touch on their sensitive mouths, responding to its strength and power, both stepping high, but not rapidly, they moved spectacularly and gracefully onto Fifth Avenue, their lifted heads well drawn up by the check rein, giving them swan necks.

And there sat Marie Boozer Beecher, at twenty-two, in the full bloom of her beauty and physical appeal. And all around the male population of New York applauding and acclaiming her.

Forever, it seemed to Amelia, the cheers kept rising along Fifth Avenue as the bizarre tandem team made its way through the procession of vehicles en route to the races. Amelia could still picture Marie— her gold hair shining, her eyes glistening, the yellow sultane flapping out behind, the foolish little hat with the wheat spears bobbing up and down! Well, she'd always had crowd appeal. She'd always excited the rabble. But what was she up to? What reckless thing was in her mind?

Amelia sat in the parlor for two terrible hours, emaciated in her black taffeta dress, smoking one cigar after another and continually consulting her cards and her horoscope. From no source did comfort come. Still, she was positive that Marie had not yet capitulated. Or that Phoenix had not yet demanded. Or that no opportunity for being that alone had presented itself. Yet through the late spring Marie had grown more and more beautiful and more and more restless and ebullient. And now it was June—summer was here and with summer Marie and Phoenix—

Amelia decided to go at once to her astrologer, Dr. Broughton, on Canal Street—some new star might have come in their orbit—hers and Marie's. No. Better be more sensible. She threw down the cards and put on her bonnet and made her way up the Avenue to the Union Club to advise Mr. Beecher to discontinue staring out the window on Fifth Avenue, counting Negroes or white horses or one-eyed cats or whatever it was he and Mr. Schermerhorn made their wagers about every day, and betake himself at once to the Jerome Race Track and discover just who his young wife was trying to impress by driving that dangerous pair of horses in such an outrageous fashion.

Meanwhile upward of four thousand vehicles were crowding through Central Park toward Jerome Park. The slanting sunshine fell on the drifting jumble of equipages, like a writhing serpent of many colors. Singles, drays, jaunty carts, doubles or four-in-hands, hansoms, buggies, sulkies, chaises, carryalls, phaetons, barouches, coaches moving at a walk, a trot, an amble or a gallop.

Going loose and easy, Marie passed Mr. Lorillard's gray and bay team; Mr. J. B. Fellows with four matched bays; Mr. Belmont driving his blacks; a barouche filled with a delegation from the sixth ward—rough Irishmen who knew more about the horses than any of these fancy ones calling after her "there's one knows a hawk from a handsaw"; a whole school of carriages, sleek, well-curried carriages of the new rich with splendidly gotten up coachmen and footmen in liveries of green and blue and drab saying loudly, "hit's 'ot, you know, hit's never so 'ot at the Derby in H'England, mam, you see," as she gave them her horses' heels.

And at Eighty-fourth Street and Harlem Lane, Phoenix was waiting with his fastest pair of trotters and a new racing cart. Marie winked at Stobo and tightened her grip on the reins. Stobo rode up close and all at once the swan necks were loosed and stretching out—dust was flying and everybody was shouting as Phoenix wheeled alongside of Marie's team and began to extend his horses with the whip. Mud, dust and chickens flew as they dashed side by side all the way to Ninety-second Street. By then it was obvious that Marie was the better driver and had the fastest horses and that she was going to leave Phoenix far behind. But suddenly she began to bring her gray and her bay in and lifting her hand she blew a kiss at Phoenix and together at a clattering pace they went over McCoomb's Dam Bridge and straight into Jerome Park. They had their programs so the Steward at the bridge let them enter at once. Phoenix's man, in a fancy hatband and a bright garment, brass-buttoned to the throat, was waiting to take his master's horses. He directed Stobo to come with him, leading Marie's rig, to the Whitney Stables.

The band was playing a melody of Meyerbeer when Marie and Phoenix sauntered boldly up to the Clubhouse together. "Now tell me, so I'm sure you've got it straight, just what you're going to say when you get home late."

Marie pulled down the corners of her mouth and said, like a child saying her grace, "Sir, the wheel of my carriage came off and I stopped to get it fixed and Miss Fish came along and—"

"That's enough—oh—don't let go my arm. Hold it tighter. Now let me see which do I want in the first race?"

Arm in arm they made their way, through the milling thousands crowding to be seen and to bet and look. Just as they were leaving the circle a voice called from the grandstand, "Marie Boozer!"

"Lord—Buck Preston!"

It was Buck. Wearing a short, silk driving dress with a black Amazon hat with a white feather curling over her dark chignon. How chic and grand she looked.

Marie felt sick and for an instant she was back on Secession Day and Buck was starkly perfect in a black velvet habit and she—she—was wearing a flossy swan's-down cape and on ostrich plume hat.

"Miss Preston, this is Lieutenant Phoenix. Oh, no, I'm married to Mr. John Beecher. He and Lieutenant Phoenix are fellow Union Club members. Mr. B. is in the Clubhouse or will be soon. We were just going to see about our horses." Then, reluctantly, "Come with us."

And so it happened that at the end of the third race, Evie, distraught and tearful, and a red-eyed, very drooping-shouldered Mr. Beecher came on Marie and Mistress Preston and Mrs. O'Connor sitting innocently together in the Clubhouse wagering gloves and finger rings and scarves on the horses.

And Phoenix? Returning from the pool temple where he had just placed a thousand on Red Dick ridden by William Henry to win over Metairie, Patsy Hennesy up, Phoenix spied the arrival of his fellow club member and made a hasty retreat, leaving a note with Stobo to give Marie.

Phoenix spent the rest of the afternoon along the rails with some of the Irishmen from the sixth ward and drank his share of their whiskey and had a fine time. Today's plan to seduce *la belle* had evaporated. But he was more determined for this to happen than ever. The memory of her strong graceful back as she flashed in front of him at Ninety-first Street was enough to set any man on fire. The surprise at discovering she *had* been somebody in Columbia before—(why *everybody* knew who the Prestons of South Carolina were.) And Buck Preston had called to Marie first. They had laughed over their school days together and Marie had been eager to hear of former friends in Columbia. It made Marie more desirable a prize. And she had been jealous of the way he had commented on Buck's Parisian costume. A woman of taste and refinement, definitely, but cold as ice. However, it never hurt to make the warm gold ones jealous of the cool dark one.

Not until Mr. Beecher and Evie were out of sight in the barouche did Stobo come and tell Marie that her horses were ready to drive home. He stepped up to her, still with Buck Preston, and noticed her eyes were wide open, shiny with tears, but she was smiling steadily.

Stobo bowed, "Your team is ready, Miss Marie."

Marie kissed Buck on the cheek and said, "I'm sorry you're sailing for Liverpool tomorrow. I wish you could have come to dinner with us. I *knew* you'd like Mr. Beecher. I'm glad you met him. And he liked you."

It was lovely driving home in the late afternoon. The gray and the bay were as smooth as silk. The students at Columbia College were celebrating the Burial of the Ancients. They whistled and catcalled after her and she waved gaily at all of them. Oh—she was happy!

She had never been so happy. Strains of Offenbach and Strauss were heard here and there throughout the park. Birds twittered sleepily. Carriages of young people passed, singing "Softly On The Window Pane" and "When You Win A Maiden's Heart," from *The White Fawn*. She and Phoenix had seen *The White Fawn* together six times. Side by side in the dark together. Holding hands.

The delicious note Stobo had reluctantly given her, had read:

Not Race Week. I must have been out of my mind. Be wise and fetch Mr. B. with you to the Park tomorrow and the next day. By the last day he'll be fed up and convinced you have nothing in your pretty head but horses. The Yacht Club is having a Regatta on June the nineteenth. Circle it with gold ink on your calendar. *That* will be *our* day.

P.

Just before the supper bell rang in the Beecher household, Marie went upstairs to Amelia's room. She opened the door and said, "Get up and come and carve the mutton."

"No. Mr. Beecher was horrid to me when he returned from the Races. He said all kinds of dreadful things. No man ever accused me of being a trouble-maker before. And after all I've done for him. For both of you. What did you say about me to cause Mr. Beecher to behave so ungentlemanly?"

"I told him that you were a mean woman and had a suspicious nature. To keep him from suspecting me. Mr. Beecher had to believe either me or you. The idea of you sending him haring out to the Race Track to try and catch me flirting with Lloyd Phoenix. That was a pretty dreadful way to treat a daughter."

"Just because I don't countenance your fast behavior makes you say I don't treat you like a daughter."

"Big Dave and Papa Feaster treated me like a daughter. They wanted me to be happy."

"Foot," jeered Amelia, "those two ninnies."

"They were good to me. Better than anybody else has ever been."

"You," Amelia said darkly, "weren't married to them."

"And you," Marie said, keeping her voice soft, "aren't married to John S. Beecher."

"Well, you'd better not fall in love with Lloyd Phoenix. You'd better try and keep what you have—a rich husband. I never saw anybody like you. Thinking you can break all the rules and come out on top."

Marie said mercilessly, "What about you?"

It suited Amelia to disregard this. "What I can't understand is what you'll gain by setting Mr. Beecher against me."

"It suits me to have him on my side rather than on yours. What a bad humor you're in. I'm the one who has been wronged and I'm in a grand humor, or I was until I came up here. Why did I come anyway?"

"To tell me it was time to carve the roast. Well, it's your house. You carve it. I'll eat upstairs on a tray. All of you are against me. None of you love me."

Marie said, "Love has nothing to do with mutton. Leave off the powder and put on some rouge. And remember—don't try any more of your sly tricks with me *or* Mr. Beecher. It *is* my house and I'll put you in the street without a penny if you ever so much as comment on the way I choose to live my life."

Later, when she was standing by the sideboard expertly carving the leg of lamb and serving the new June peas and the rice and mushroom curry, Amelia thought: this is the worst hand I've drawn yet—that Mr. Beecher is now my enemy. Until today I was confident he and I together could control Marie. This is an irrational set of circumstances; the single event that was not inevitable but which I brought about by using my fear instead of my brain. This is a joke of the devil on me. She sighed, listening to Marie talking sweetly to the exhausted, irritable Mr. Beecher.

"But, honey, I just won't go to that old horse race tomorrow if you don't come too. We can have Stobo drive us in the barouche and take a lunch and have a picnic in the park all by ourselves. Oh—I'd just adore that, wouldn't you?" Marie lidded her eyes at Mr. Beecher and gave a voluptuous sigh so deep it seemed positively vindictive.

Mr. Beecher was many years her senior and she had
(as might have been expected in one of her tempera-
ment) grown weary of him.

THE COUNTESS POURTALÈS,
by "Felix Old Boy"

37

At the Sunday morning breakfast table, Evie, who was
an avid newspaper reader, was droning away, to the
family, the latest about President Johnson's impeach-
ment and the baseball scores of the games at Mount
Morris Square and the awful way the Negroes were behaving in the State House in Columbia and the Ku-
Klux Klan riding around at night in South Carolina to
scare the Negroes and to protect the white women.

"They used to call themselves the Invisibles," Amelia
said thoughtfully. "I remember during the heat of
Secession—"

"Don't," said Mr. Beecher testily, "I am enjoying
these buckwheat cakes and smoked beef too much to
risk an attack of indigestion."

"Read about the Paris fashions." Marie, in a pale-
pink muslin wrapper over a deep-rose muslin gown,
picked up a broiled woodcock in her fingers and began
tearing the meat from the bones with her sharp teeth.

Mildly, Mr. Beecher said, "Please, Mrs. Beecher,
learn to cut your game daintily. You're eating as if you
were at the court of Henry the VIII."

"Honey, don't be so cross," Marie leaned back sen-
suously in her armchair and the angel sleeve of her
wrapper fell off her shoulder and bared her pearly
skin. She smiled sleepily up at the painting of hanging
dead ducks over the chimney piece. It was the only
picture in the darkly paneled dining room.

A shaft of sun coming through the windowpanes,
which were done in tinted tracery embossed on a gold

ground, fell on Marie who began dutifully and skill-
fully disjointing what was left of the bird on her plate
with an ivory-handled knife and silver fork. The gar-
ish light made Marie look like an actress on a stage.
Marie was playing a part and Evie suspected it. She
knew it when, after breakfast, Marie sat in Mr. Beecher's lap and pulled his mustaches and tickled him until
he hugged her and laughed like a schoolboy.

"Go on, read about the fashions," Amelia said
mechanically.

Evie turned to the "Report from Paris" in the June
fourteenth, New York *Herald*.

"It says 'the races at Longchamps were a crush of
muslin, waves of soft foulard, a shimmer of turnouts,
shakings of rice powder.' "

"Hah!" Marie sat up and Mr. Beecher jiggled her up
and down on his knee singing softly, *This Is The Way
The Ladies Ride*. "I knew I was dressed correctly last
Monday. And you wanted me to wear a plain, short
silk like Buck Preston."

Evie continued to read:

But why have the elite taken to acacia shade and abandoned the green shores where their vaporous robes floated
so effectively near the floating gondolas of the lake?

It is Cora Pearl's fault. This most determined female
innovator—who, as I have before observed, wears her
diamonds on her satin shoes—having got tired of driving
ponies ahead of the fastest phaetons and of propelling
minors to the roulette tables, fancied her fair proportions
would look well if she propelled herself and sat to advantage astride a velocipede, and thus mounted, fair Cora went
round the lake, but all the *gamins de Paris* shouted after
her. Among these irregulars of the social world stood fore-
most and loudest a schoolgirl. On her Cora's indignation
centered. She begged one of her admirers to lay hands on
the girl and lovely Cora had the offender whipped—yes
whipped. The scandal may be fancied from here to New
York. The case came before a magistrate. Cora had a fine
to pay and the genteel have ever since turned their
flunkey's backs to the now desecrated resort. Drive
through it they must, however, for the Empress does so,
and if she is not afraid of catching a velocipede, others
less high need not fear getting worse. Paris, May 29,
1868.

"Stop reading about bad women, Evie." Mr. Beecher glowered at his sister-in-law. "I loathe Paris and can't see for the life of me why a decent paper would print such disgusting vulgarity about a, well—a second-rate actress. Don't you agree, Mrs. Beecher?"

"I rather liked it until the part where she had the girl whipped."

The clock out in the hall began to strik ten but stopped after seven strokes. Marie smiled at Mr. Beecher.

"Oh, dear, I've forgotten to wind the clock," he said, going toward the hall. "Thank heavens, Race Week is over. I can settle down now and attend to my business with a light heart. Some important Englishmen will be here for the next few days. Tea people, familiar with the Indian market. I'm giving a bachelor dinner for them Thursday at the Union Club. You won't mind my neglecting you a little, will you?"

"No, sir," said Marie. She sank into the chair he had vacated with an enormous sigh. "I intend to shop for summer dresses most of the week. Until Thursday."

"And Thursday?" Mr. Beecher was winding the clock noisily with its big brass key.

"Oh—I'm going with Miss Fish to the Yacht Club Regatta. I'm sorry you can't come. There's a dance afterwards at Staten Island at the Clubhouse. What a bore. I wish it was another horse race."

But the generous tea merchant being of a forgiving
disposition . . . tried to forget what, he said to himself, might after all have been only a thoughtless and
not a guilty affair on her part.

THE COUNTESS POURTALÈS,
by "Felx Old Boy"

38

On Thursday Marie awoke at dawn—eager for the day
to hurry along. When Stobo brought her a breakfast
tray and said Mr. Beecher regretted having had to go
downtown without telling her good-by and had left
word he would not be home from his club till after
midnight, she jumped out of the bed and danced in
her nightgown around the room singing *When Husbands Go To Crete You Know.*

Evie helped her slip into a long-sleeved, straw-
colored muslin with a frill at the armhole and a frilled
fichu overskirt plain in front but hooked up in back by
means of tapes sewn from the waist. From her wardrobe she took a floppy straw hat with a single red rose
and tied it on with a length of blond gauze veiling and
was waiting at the foot of Desbrosses Street by eight-
thirty with Mrs. O'Connor when the little steamer,
Yankee, that was to take the press and the officials and
their guests, puffed up to the wharf.

All the time Phoenix was bustling about talking to
the reporters and opening champagne and pointing
out the racing craft and telling Miss Fish that her
shirtwaist was most becoming and Miss Bacon that she
must let him show her his schooner, Marie was aware
that her presence had agitated him and that he was
as excited about the outcome of the day as she.

There were ninety-three on the little steamer and
the orchestra aboard played and they all sang *Le Sabre*

de Mon Père while they followed the white-winged craft toward Staten Island.

It was a glorious sunny day although the south-westerly breeze was light and rather fickle. As was the custom, the competing yachts were moored in a double line. The race was due to start at 10 A.M. and more than a hundred vessels of all kinds had turned out to follow it. All the competitors had their flying kites aloft and the schooner *Magic* was sporting a new flying jib made for her by Ratsey. Each yacht had set her largest topsail and altogether it was a brave sight for the spectators. When the starting gun was fired at 10 A.M most of the yachts got off smartly and in a few seconds the sloops, *Gussie* and *White Wing,* and eight schooners were under way.

Off Staten Island everything was lovely. In the foreground the glancing hulls of yachts cut through the glittering water while in the distance the snowy sails of the racing craft waved to and fro protesting the feebleness of the wind. Small boats hurried from point to point and gaily decked steamers full of singing and laughing spectators of all sorts ploughed the waves in all directions. The shore line of the Island was fringed with spectators too—the bright-green lawns of the great mansions sprinkled with flowery muslins and all the roofs decorated with flags.

After about an hour, however, the breeze fell very light and a thick sea mist enveloped the yachts. The *Yankee* lost all except two of the schooners, the *Rambler* and the *Magic,* but by one o'clock they were enveloped in the mist also and word reached the celebrants aboard the *Yankee* that the racing craft were all becalmed and the official race had been postponed until the next day.

"But what about the ball?"

"Oh—that will take place at Staten Island Clubhouse tonight as planned."

"But what will we do until then?"

"Let's ride back and forth between here and New York all afternoon!"

"Why doesn't Phoenix take us aboard his schooner and show us his sinful gilt and velvet quarters and

serve us high tea and then we can all come back to
Staten Island on the *Yankee* to the ball?" Mrs. O'Connor suggested.

"A capital plan," Phoenix agreed, and whispered
in Marie's ear as he escorted her from the *Yankee* onto the wharf, "When I take the ladies into my cabin
come with us. But when they leave the main cabin—
make an excuse that you've got to tie your sandal—
there is a little closet behind the bed. Slip into it. I'll
say you were taken suddenly ill and got a carriage
and drove home. Then I'll make an excuse about not
going back to the ball—I'll say that as an official I must
go in a steamer and check on the participants."

Because of the heat, Marie nearly died in the little
closet. She could hear Miss Fish laughing and Miss
Bacon saying where did Marie go? And Mr. Morton
said—someone said she'd got a perish and taken a boat
back there on the wharf. And Mrs. O'Connor said
but I could have sworn she was here in this cabin
not ten minutes ago.

And then Phoenix was making his regrets and
they were clattering away and she heard the whistle
of the little steamer toot shrilly and the band playing *Le Sabre de Mon Père* and a champagne cork
popping.

He flung open the door. Phoenix—in his shirt sleeves
—a bottle of champagne in one hand and reaching for
her with the other and she was laughing and he was
kissing her and pulling her down onto the bed with
him and then not kissing her and holding her against
him, making her drink some champagne out of the
bottle and then he drinking some and leaning over and
she opening her mouth and he spurting champagne
from his mouth into her mouth and—

Now it was almost midnight. If she let him sleep—
if she didn't rouse him why then—in the morning people would find them and he would have to marry her.
Oh Lord in heaven—no he wouldn't. She had been no
virgin. Almost but not quite a virgin. And Phoenix was
so violent and smooth at the same time. So sensitive to
what made her moan with delight and yet he was
cruel too and demanding.

"Phoenix—Phoenix—darling—it's time to take me home."

He was wide-awake instantly and up on his elbows looking down into her face. His hair was falling onto his forehead and his bare chest glistened in the starlight.

He murmured, "You do love. me. O what a night! O what enormous eyes you get after you make love! O what are we going to do?"

"It's time for me to leave," she whispered, drowsy and warm and moist. She put her arms around his neck and said she would kiss him just once more and then he would have to hook her up, that is if he hadn't torn all the hooks when he—

"Let's see."

He got up and took the rumpled froth of muslin off the floor and shook it out. She stood up and yawned and stretched and he said—slip into it. And she said without any underclothes? And he said—just so we'll know the hooks are still there. Turn around. Let me look at your pretty back. I never saw but one that could compare with it.

"Whose?"

"Are you jealous?"

"No. Merely curious."

"Someone you never heard of."

"Who?"

"A Parisienne—Cora Pearl."

"You mean that second-rate actress who wears her diamonds on her shoes and rides a bicycle?"

"Really, my dear! Here—hold the candle while I open one more bottle of champagne to give me the strength of character to take you home."

She held the candle high. Phoenix suddenly stopped in the middle of opening the champagne bottle. Pale with passion—Marie in the misty muslin with nothing on underneath—holding the candle high above her tangled golden hair—her breasts thrusting with a yearning to have him take her again—her eyes—those great luminous grateful eyes—

He quoted softly:

A slight sublime, a dream, a miracle;
A little goddess from some luminous field
. . . . Nay, wherefore shame?
And I, ah, who shall blame me, who shall blame?

The champagne cork popped and the champagne fizzed and spilled out. But Phoenix and Marie were lost in each other's arms.

"Oh! the back of your dress is wet from the wine. We'll have to let it dry. Put down the candle—it is burning me."

"Let me go—you are hurting me!"

"No—no—stay! Just once more—"

He pulled her onto his lap and began unloosing the damp hooks.

"I am doing wrong to let you persuade me to stay!"

"Very well," he said hotly, "I'll fasten you up again." And he pressed his hand inside her dress on her bare back and pulled her in to him.

Her heart raced. She tried to think of poor Mr. Beecher; but her marriage, her future, her past had disintegrated and faded into a faraway dream. After all, who was Mr. Beecher? What did she owe Mr. Beecher? Had there ever been a Mr. Beecher? Was this not truly her first time?

The delicate muslin crumpled away from her body onto the floor. She threw back her head and with her special voluptuous sigh gave herself up entirely to delight.

Dawn was definite when Marie let herself into the dark hall of the Beecher house. Mr. Beecher, sick with fear that she was gone forever, was standing on the bottom step of the stairs. Amelia, looking like a death angel, was lying on the sofa in the parlor. Evie, gnawing her nails, was sitting beside her mother and Stobo was half hidden behind the dining room portière.

They all rushed forward together to meet her—we were sure, they chorused, you were in an accident or drowned or kidnaped or murdered in the street. Where —where—where have you been?

Marie looked from one wretched face to the other all gray and drawn in the light of sunrise; all spinning around her, twitching and flickering.

"I," she began hesitantly, swallowed and planted her wet sandals firmly in the Brussels carpet to hold her steady. "The propeller came off and we stopped to have it fixed and Miss Fish invited me— Miss Fish—"

She couldn't go on. Not when she saw Mr. Beecher's believing eyes. She must not tell him a lie. She must tell him the truth. She must admit everything to him.

But when she felt his drooping wet mustache against her throat, his tears of thankfulness that she was safe and at home with him, she burst into a wild weeping.

"What happened, little one, little baby-girl?" he asked, tender as a father. "It's all my fault for not having gone along to look after you. For putting my business ahead of your pleasure. Those wild Yacht Club people never consider time. Only tide. I might have known they'd not take the proper care of you. Never mind! You are home now."

He was so gentle and kind and his arms around her so sheltering that she was too ashamed to tell him.

"I tried to get you word. But I couldn't," sobbed Marie, and hid her red face in his neck.

Mr. Beecher cradled her in his flabby arms and smoothed her hair. The weight of Marie against his chest removed all the frightening suspicions Amelia's gloom had aroused. He said irritably to his mother-in-law, "Go upstairs, Madame. You too, Evie. Hush, Marie, hush now."

He led her into the kitchen and while he was fussing around the stove and buttering bread Stobo came up to Marie and started to speak but she looked up at him guiltily and pleadingly and he went, sadly, silently, out to his meagre room.

Mr. Beecher sat across the table from Marie. "There—drink your hot milk, my poor baby."

She drank two glasses and hungrily devoured three roast beef sandwiches and Mr. Beecher kept patting her arm and looking at her with adoration.

Mrs. Beecher and Phoenix met after their first acquaintance and their intimacy caused gossip. . . .

SAN FRANCISCO CHRONICLE

39

A wild, hot summer followed that typified Marie's mood. Heat without kindness; sensuality without sentiment. Voluptuous impatience was the byword and excitement its key. Their perfect rapport made her enslavement to Phoenix as necessary as opium is to an addict.

Vehement, cruel quarrels with Amelia, who continually voiced her anguished premonitions, were the first primary consequence of this violent love affair. The final descriptive title that Amelia let fly at Marie left Amelia herself so shocked that Stobo had to fetch the doctor to administer laudanum to her. Throughout this unpleasantness, to Evie's nervous questions, Marie laughed unconcernedly. That! she snapped her fingers, for Amelia! And That! That! for the future.

In the autmun the "goings on" aboard the *Intrepid,* made fast at the foot of Beekman Street, began to be whispered in the various clubs and opera boxes and boudoirs and ballrooms of New York. Marie avoided her former friends and Mr. Beecher fretted over their being left out of dinners and soirées to which they had formerly been invited. But Mr. Beecher still refused to listen to rumor or to have it out with Marie. Why should he? What would he gain?

Marie's eyes shone like stars, she danced up and down the stairs, she sang gay, silly songs as she lay pink and luscious in her porcelain tub before the dressing-room fireplace; his dear darling wife was the merriest, prettiest, kindest lady in New York.

And she was so thoughtful of his health (darling,

Mr. Beecher, why don't you go on home after Mr. Dickens finishes reading *Dr. Marigold?* You're tired. I'll come later with Miss Bacon, or Miss Fish or Mrs. O'Connor. Or—poor, dear Mr. Beecher, I know you don't want to go and sit through *The Black Crook* at the theater this afternoon. It's Thursday—your card day at the Club. Or—it's Monday—why don't you go and spend the afternoon at the Club, as you love to do, sitting with Mr. Schermerhorn counting the Negroes who go up and down Fifth Avenue? I just passed a Negro funeral below Bleecker Street headed up the Avenue. You take the "up" side this afternoon and you'll win a fortune from him. Make haste and you'll be settled in your chair long before the funeral passes in front of the Club's windows. Me? Oh—Stobo will drive Evie and me to a tea party on a schooner.)

And in contrast to poor Mr. Beecher, Phoenix was so healthy. He enjoyed the same things Marie did. They spent much of their time in the out-of-doors. They drove fast horses up St. Nicholas Avenue (Harlem Lane renamed) and galloped thoroughbreds along the forest roads of Central Park. In the winter when the flag was up on the Mall they flew about the frozen lake in Central Park on skates and drank champagne in the shadow of the frozen fountain with the spread-winged angel as their guest. In the spring they picnicked on his family's acres in Westchester and drove to his shooting lodge where Marie showed him how ladies from South Carolina could outshoot any of Admiral Farragut's officers.

However, "I just wish I was certain that you loved me as much as I love you," was her constant cry.

Ironically enough, it was on a day that she had been the most convinced that he loved her madly that Phoenix announced to her that he and his father were planning a cruise. It was an early June afternoon and they were at his shooting lodge. It had been noised, he declared, in his mother's parlor, that he had given Marie the family jewels. A search by his father had taken place in all the lock boxes at the bank. Things had come to a head naturally. Then the jewels had been found.

Marie said uncomprehendingly, "Why do people say such malicious things?"

"For months, Marie, you are aware we've been talked about. According to my father we are the scandal of the Union Club, the Union League Club, Delmonico's, Trinity Church and the New York Yacht Club. I don't mind about the others but I hate to have been discussed at the Yacht Club."

Marie said, "So now you're running away on a cruise.

"Now," said Phoenix, "it has to be faced."

Marie's face was flushed. She said, "I don't believe we've been talked about that much."

"For my family's sake and my own reputation we are going to be far more cautious in our meetings."

"But I don't want to be cautious," she cried impatiently. "Instead I intend to——"

"Why, what?" said Phoenix.

Marie put her arms around his knees and mischievously looked up at him. "Get a divorce." She was sitting on the grass between his feet. Her hair was loosed from its net and had tumbled over her neck and shoulders.

"You are a madwoman," he said, laughing and tangling his fingers in the goldy strands. "I'll never understand you." What he did not understand was why she had such a determination about such a simple love affair. Why she had such young illusions. Or, to be more exact, delusions about love. She wanted love to be permanent—serious—an intoxication of the soul and the morals as well as of the body. He wasn't ready to break loose from her, but if he was not clever she could become overdemanding and tyrannical.

Deciding that ruthlessness was necessary, Phoenix said, "A woman can't afford this kind of celebrity. And I don't like sharing the blame. My mother has suggested that you and I *both* go away for a while and somebody else will fall in love with somebody else's wife and we will be forgotten as the number-one New York scandal of 1869."

Marie said vaguely, "I think I'll go ahead and divorce Mr. Beecher anyway."

"No, dear." Phoenix's eyes were merciless.

Marie said grimly, "Don't you want me to?"

"I want *you*," Phoenix said almost protestingly. "But I don't want to hurt poor Beecher or my mother and father. I'm convinced mother's idea of our taking a trip is the correct thing."

"Where would I go? To Paris—London—Madrid?"

"The new overland railroad has just been completed to California. Mr. Beecher has probably never been out West. Take him to San Francisco. They say it's fascinating. All kinds of gorgeous haciendas and Spaniards serenading you at night and bulls—"

Marie was bitter. "You must be sailing to Cowes or to Havre."

In a rather thickened voice, Phoenix said, "Wait a minute—what do you mean by that?"

"You mean you don't want me trailing all over Europe after you, is that it?"

"New York is really a small town when it comes to people gossiping. What I mean is that we must let New York forget that our names were ever linked together. People will find out you went West with Mr. Beecher. That will hush them up."

"He'd rather spend the summer at Newport."

"Newport then. Anywhere so long as he's with you."

Marie was hurt. She said, "I suppose you're right. Well, fetch the horses and let's ride back to town."

"You mean now? O no! O never! We've not drunk our champagne. I'm dying to have you this minute. Right here on the grass."

"No. If you're going on a cruise this is as good a time to say good-by as any."

"But I can't leave you without—"

She had risen and was running toward the horses. "Damn," he said to himself, watching her as she went. He had never desired her this way. So that he could hardly breathe as he went running after her. "I won't go. I promise. I can't give you up."

"But you must. You said your mother told you you must." Her eyes were full of fire.

"I'll do anything for you. Anything!" And he threw her down on the grass not waiting for her response in the haste of his lips to take her mouth.

But the next month the same scene was re-enacted. Only with less ardor on Phoenix's part. And he and his father sailed to the Indies on the *Intrepid*. For Marie *was* growing bold and demanding. She did all kinds of reckless things to shock people. At last even Mr. Beecher was forced to suspect his wife of not being faithful to him. He no longer called her his baby girl and, pathetically, in his timidity to have it out with her, he behaved as if he were the guilty one. At night he no longer turned out the lamp and frolicked goatishly about the bed. He whined for her favors.

Marie drove to Phoenix's house in broad daylight when she learned he had returned. He was in a good humor and they were very merry, but the next day she arrived and his mother was there and he ran out and told her to be off and *never* to come to his lodgings again. He spoke to her as though she were a street girl and she replied to him in the same way.

What had become of the proud Marie?

She was so truly lost in love that pride had fled, red-faced, from her brain and heart.

But the same scenes were re-enacted until the outraged husband (who could no longer deceive himself)
became thoroughly exasperated at the conduct of his
pretty wife.

THE COUNTESS POURTALÈS,
by "Felix Old Boy"

40

Marie was at the zenith of her impropriety during the
next two years. She was like a young tree tortured and
twisted out of all its original shape by a hurricane,
and with as little power or will to move from the center of the storm.

After that summer spent apart, Phoenix never took
her to Delmonico's any more nor skating in the park,
nor did they ride horseback in the park, nor come
along "the road," nor go to the Academy of Music nor
to the better theaters.

Always to the noisy, racy spots frequented by the
demimonde.

Such places as Niblo's Garden where they watched
The Black Crook, a musical spectacle of unveiled female figures and shameless sensuality; or the new-
fashioned burlesque shows; or Tony Pastor's Opera
House, on the Bowery near Prince Street; or Harry
Hill's dancing hall; but mostly to Morrisey's gambling
house on Twenty-fourth Street.

The bearded, suave Morrisey, flashing his diamond
rings, would greet Marie gaily and say, "Just saw Mr.
B. pass and go inside the Union Club. All's clear. Mr.
P. says will you join him at the rear table in the supper room? He's ordered Napoleon *Cabinet* champagne
for you tonight. My—but he's a rare picker!"

She dropped all of her former friends including Miss
Fish and Mrs. O'Connor and the horsy set. The only
people on whom she called now, strangely, were the

Bostwicks of Columbia and Mary Preston Darby. Often she went and took them packages of Mr. Beecher's fine teas or brandies and sat for a half hour hungrily asking for news of her former friends in Columbia. Mr. Beecher refused to have these Southerners in his house and she, in turn, refused to accompany him to his club functions. Why should she? There were other more exciting places to meet Phoenix.

From Morrisey's, the next place Phoenix introduced to her was the Louvre—a concert saloon that was famous as a resort of the most fashionable and expensive *chere amies* in New York. It was a show place with crystal chandeliers add tall marble columns and walls paneled in gold and emerald and frescoed with baskets of juicy fruits and the prettiest waiter girls in the city.

And it was here at the Louvre on her twenty-fifth birthday that the first blow fell.

The Louvre was on Broadway and Twenty-third Street, a few steps from Mr. Schermerhorn's marble mansion. Stobo pleaded with Marie not to make him hand her out of the barouche at this place but she wouldn't listen. His eyes hooded and his mouth poked out in disapproval, he was just driving away when Marie discovered she'd left her reticule in the barouche.

"Stobo," she called loudly. As she held up her arm to motion him to come back, she saw Mrs. Schermerhorn looking out of the lighted window at her. Then Mrs. Schermerhorn pulled Mr. Schermerhorn to the glass and pointed out at her. Mr. Schermerhorn put on his spectacles to be positive. And Marie lifted her long dress a trifle in the back in an impudent gesture in their direction and walked gaily into the saloon.

But her evening was ruined for when she laughingly described the shocked Schermerhorn faces peering through the lace curtains at her Phoenix was angry.

"You are too intelligent to have flouted the Schermerhorns. You are becoming notorious for foolishness. You know that society demands certain things of a woman. Now with a man, it's different."

"I thought you loved me especially because I wasn't like other society ladies," Marie pouted.

Phoenix looked reflectively at her. What a woman she was. Here he was trying to get loose from her. Had been trying for two years and yet the attraction she held for him was still formidable. In spite of her violent outpourings of love and demands for his love. In spite of the fact that now he rarely came from loving her without being furious with her and himself; and lately he had spent the hours at every ball he had attended trying to fall in love with some one of the girls his mother brought to his attention; or with some one of the bored and beautiful married ladies who brought themselves to his attention. He wanted to break up with Marie, but he did not have the will or the courage to say never again will I make love to you.

Yet he had no intention of ruining his life because of her. Suppose Beecher came storming to fight a duel with him or sued for alienation of affections? It would be all over New York in a day. It would kill his mother. He would be invited to resign from the New York Yacht Club! Mr. Beecher and Schermerhorn sat side by side at the Union Club. If Schermerhorn took a notion to discover just who was aiding Marie in cuckolding his good friend Mr. B. he had merely to step across the street to get to the Louvre and tomorrow he would consider it his duty to inform Mr. Beecher.

"Marie, you must return home at once."

"Heavens, I'm starved. I ordered a truffle soufflé and maraschino sherbet *and* asparagus. I wouldn't dream of leaving."

"I'll get you a hack. I'm positive Mr. Schermerhorn followed you here."

"Oh all right, if you insist on being so mean. But I think you are making all this up just because you're flirting with one of the waiter girls."

Phoenix is so handsome and I love him with all my heart and I am suddenly terribly frightened he is going to leave me. With these feelings, Marie wrapped herself in her sable cloak and left the Louvre.

The next afternoon Mr. Beecher demanded an explanation from Marie. Mr. Schermerhorn had told him all about seeing her go into the Louvre the night before, having followed her. Marie, having no gift for reconciliation nor inclination for it, laughed and pooh-poohed the whole affair. For the first time, Mr. Beecher did not bow before her loveliness. For the first time, he did not care how many of her favors she might withhold from him. He could not, nor would he, have his wife's name, *his* name, brought up in the Union Club as Mr. Schermerhorn had done publicly, today. And, Mr. Beecher's thick blond eyebrows drew together in a heavy scowl, after their conversation Mr. Schermerhorn had requested the Club steward to move him permanently to another chair in front of another window. Far from John Beecher's customary chair. It was a dreadful humiliation.

Mr. Beecher said in a shrill voice, "You know what a horror I have always had of you being seen in the wrong place or with the wrong company."

"I went in alone."

"No lady, for that matter, no fancy woman, goes into the Louvre to be alone. Not even the waiter girls. I know it was Lloyd Phoenix you were meeting. Mr. Schermerhorn saw you with him."

Marie opened her mouth to tell Mr. Beecher exactly how his padded shoulders and tapered hips; his stooping mustache; his old-maidy ways compared with Lloyd Phoenix's.

"You old—"

"Well?"

But she'd promised Phoenix not to let friction develop between her and Mr. Beecher until he gave her permission. She'd given Phoenix her word. Phoenix—

Mr. Beecher leaned forward and his angry green eyes bored into hers. "Well?"

She'd been foolish to insult the Schermerhorns. Knowing how Mr. Beecher doted on the Union Club.

"Well—I'm just sorry. That's all. Sorry."

Mr. Beecher's stiff grip on himself relaxed. Ah— maybe—maybe— "Will you promise me to stay home tonight? Not to go to that place again?"

"Yes." She'd not liked it there anyway. There was one particularly pretty waiter girl with smooth hair she'd caught winking at Phoenix.

"You aren't even paying attention to me." Mr. Beecher grabbed Marie by the shoulders and shook her. But not very hard.

The very timidity of his gesture infuriated Marie. She slapped Mr. Beecher's face. Hard.

Mr. Beecher turned and walked unsteadily out of the parlor and up the stairs. Later, Stobo told her Mr. Beecher had cried and then said he didn't want any supper but would go down to Downings for oysters and ale and on to the Club for a game of whist.

Still later, Amelia came to talk to Marie in her bedroom. Evie had just finished helping Marie lace her corset. Marie's yellow hair was all fluffed out and hanging around her bare shoulders. Amelia sat down on the purple velvet ottoman in front of the fire and smoked in quick puffs. Marie watched her out of the corner of her eye and, bending over, began to brush the back of her hair, hiding her face. A hundred strokes. Still Amelia puffed and tapped one of her long, skinny feet on the brass fender and smiled in a strange gloating way.

"Mama, why don't you say something?" Evie asked, all in a flutter.

Too mildly Amelia said, "Overmuch has been said in this house lately. Do you realize, Marie, that in one burst of irresponsibility you have destroyed all of the schemes I have laid so carefully for us since your birth?"

"It's my affair."

"Oh—no—it's mine and Evie's as well. What will we do? Where will we go?"

"Nobody's going anywhere."

"Mr. Beecher is through with you. He's not even infatuated with your good looks any more. You've been a fool, a fool! Do you expect Phoenix to marry you? I wouldn't call *him* a marrying man."

Evie giggled nervously. Marie did not answer but began savagely jabbing tortoise-shell pins in her lively hair. It wouldn't stay in its net. It wouldn't even wind in a figure eight or a French twist.

Her eyes burning in her skull-like face, Amelia went on, "Where are you going tonight? I thought you promised Mr. Beecher to stay at home."

"Foot! for promises."

"Phoenix has certainly changed you from the good girl you used to be. It's shameful."

Marie flushed, but bit her lips to hold down her temper. She must keep calm so that when she told Phoenix tonight that he and she must—simply must be married.

Amelia had finished her cigar. She threw it in the grate, saying, "If you're planning to keep a rendezvous with Phoenix, you might as well unlace your corsets and give up trying to make your hair lie smooth and close. He'll not be there."

Marie jerked at a length of her curly hair. "Oh? Did your astrologer tell you?"

"No. I sent Phoenix a note saying you were taken ill with cholera morbus from something you drank last night. You know how well I can copy your handwriting. I don't think even you would suspect you hadn't written it."

Amelia's voice wavered on the last sentence. Marie's eyes! What had happened to Marie's eyes? Had they turned to glass? Or ice? It was only as she comprehended Marie's eyes that Amelia realized she'd played the wrong card. And this was the big game. The stakes were high. Too high.

Marie was saying contemptuously, "You are insane." Marie's thick gold eyebrows were contracting ominously. They two, she and Marie, had had many quarrels but this was the first time Marie had looked like this—so still—so icy—so controlled.

Amelia put up her hand as if she were about to cross herself. She became limp and weak. Her mouth worked frantically. "Evie—Evie!"

Evie fetched a vial of smelling salts and held it under Amelia's nose. Marie watched, cold and still as stone. Marie said, "This is the last trick, Mama. Pack up and get out of my house. Tonight."

"No, Marie," Evie looked at her sister with amazement and fright. "Mama is sick. You don't mean what you're saying."

"I'm ready to get out," Amelia sighed. "This is torture."

"Yes, of course it is. I am the evil force and you are the victim. Of course! How dared you? It's worse than when you stole Willie's watch. A thousand times worse. My love for Willie was a young girl's love. My love for Phoenix is a woman's love."

"Love—you dare talk of love?" Amelia covered her face with her thin fingers. "Help me up, Evie, let's leave at once."

Marie said, "Don't listen to Mama, Evie. She'll ruin your life too. Stay with me. Oh, this is terrible!"

Amelia was crying raggedly. But she was thinking: Marie's frightened now. She's warming up as she always does. Tomorrow she'll beg me to come back and look after her. She's afraid Phoenix has grown weary of her. The wise move is for me and Evie to actually get out of the house. Leave her alone here. Why, by noontime tomorrow she'll have sent Stobo for us and be so contrite I will be able to do anything with her from now on.

"Poor girl," Amelia said, too tired to make her voice have the ring of pity she wanted it to hold. Too tired for much pity even—or affection—or anything.

She went to the lodgings of her friend Phoenix and found him preparing to attend a ball. . . .

A CHECKERED LIFE,
by "One Who Knows"

41

For a long time Marie sat in front of her dressing table staring at the cold-eyed stranger with the wild, light hair who looked back at her from the beveled glass. The maid came and said supper was ready but Marie shook her head. She heard Amelia and Evie descend the stairs and Stobo and the maid bump down after them with luggage. She heard the barouche drive off and she heard the chiming of various church bells throughout the city.

At eight o'clock she put on her warmest woolen dress and fastened her sable cape around her shoulders. She studied her sable muff for a few minutes and then ran downstairs to Mr. Beecher's study. She knew where he kept his pistol. In his bottom desk drawer. She found it, checked it carefully, discovered that it was fully loaded and tucked it in her muff. To walk alone down to Thirteenth Street where Phoenix lived was dangerous at this hour of night. She would probably be accosted by rough men. With the pistol she was prepared to deal with them. The main thing, now that she was recovering from the shock of her showdown with Amelia, was to reach Phoenix and let him know she was not ill and that she loved him very much.

As she walked along Fourth Avenue, the night had grown colder. The paving stones were slippery with ice. The wind was blowing from the north. She thought, it will snow tomorrow.

A light glimmered in the hallway of Phoenix's Thirteenth Street brownstone house. The house appeared grim and disapproving. Marie began to question the tactfulness of the situation. A clock struck nine with a harshness that increased her need for his understanding and love.

A man called to her from the shadows down the street. She tightened her fingers around the warm steel of the pistol and fled up the steps. On ringing the bell she began to shake as if she had a chill. An insolent, whey-faced English valet with gray, mutton-chop whiskers peered at her through the side glass, but made no motion to open the door.

Marie pushed the bell frantically. He opened the door a crack and gave her an impudent look, " 'E's not 'ome."

"Tell Mr. Phoenix Mrs. Beecher is calling on urgent business."

"Not at 'ome. Can't you 'ear?"

"Tell Mr.—"

"Not at 'ome. Ow—don't point that weapon at me. You're 'urting me chest. All right—'e's upstairs in 'is room, dressing to go to a ball. 'E'll give you wot for, all right. No—this way—"

Phoenix was standing in the upstairs hall. Under the gaslight his brown hair shone like metal, his mustache was waxed razor fine. He had on full evening dress. His black broadcloth coat with long satin lapels turned down to the second of three buttons showed his snowy, pleated, white cambric shirt with a central band of embroidery and a waistcoat of embroidered white silk.

With her usual impetuousness, Marie did not notice his outraged expression but rushed toward him and flung her arms around his neck.

Phoenix's smooth, brown skin reddened. "What the hell are you doing here? I told you never to come to my house again. Suppose you were noticed?" Every word was a slap in the face. "Last night taught me a lesson if it didn't you. There's nothing that irritates me so much as a woman who makes scenes."

What Phoenix meant was that when a man had finished loving and a woman still desired to be loved it was a hateful situation. And he knew, too, that, suspecting she was losing him, Marie was frantic to keep

him. Her frightened eyes pained him, but he dared
not say anything that might reassure her.

"I am on my way to a reception to celebrate the
opening of the new Art Gallery and then to a special
performance of *Hamlet* at the Booth Theater. I am already late. Higgins, call Mrs. Beecher's carriage."

And on that he turned abruptly in his patent-leather
dress boots and left the hallway.

Marie realized too late that she had played the fool
in coming here. That she was making a nuisance of
herself. She gripped the stair rail. For a moment she
could not trust herself to move or to speak. What if
she cried? Oh—no—tears would never move *him*.

He was straightening his white silk tie when she entered his room.

"Who is it?"

"Whom did you expect?"

"Oh—I thought you had gone." He picked up a pair
of new, white-kid gloves and began pulling them over
his strong hands. "Higgins—fetch my cape and cane
and be sure and sweep the room after I leave."

As he put on his tall silk hat and held out his arms
for the cape and cane, his and Marie's eyes met. For a
cold minute they studied each other. Realized each other. Then the report of the pistol roared through the
house. Higgins screamed. Marie, still holding the smoking revolver, leaned weakly against the table, fascinated.
Phoenix was holding a white linen handkerchief against
his ear.

"Get some cloth and court plaster and bind up this
scratch," he said, his voice shaking with a rage that
now transcended Marie's desperation.

"There are four shots left," Marie said. "I aimed for
the lobe of your ear. Next time—I will spoil your shirt
front."

There was a spot of blood on his cheek. She yearned
to wipe it away. She had barely nicked the lobe of his
ear. Higgins wiped off the blood and a spotty darkness of gunpowder. Phoenix furiously finished putting on his gloves and, taking the cane, bowed to Marie
as to a total stranger.

"I'll come back tomorrow," defiantly Marie declared this. Then bending quickly forward, she kissed him on the cheek and fled ahead of him down the steep, gas-lit stairs.

She ran up the street, then all the way over to Lexington Avenue. The Bostwicks! They were from Columbia. They would not treat her like trash to be swept aside. They would welcome her. Locating their house she burst past the wide-eyed Negro maid and into their cozy parlor. She was crying so hard and was so incoherent and hysterical that nothing could be got out of her except that Amelia and Evie had left her—had moved out—had been shot—

Finally, Mr. Bostwick walked over to the Beecher's residence and fetched Stobo with the barouche and Stobo drove Marie home. He refused to speak to her, but he brought hot water and filled her tub and then came back with a pitcher of warmed milk and brandy and a butter and sugar sandwich which she gobbled hungrily.

When he had gone down again and fetched her another sandwich and a piece of chocolate cake, he said a grumbly good night. Then: "You might as well begin to make plans, honey. You is just as finished in this here town as you was in Columbia. You just can't seem to learn a thing. Your ma turned out to be mighty true when she said you haven't in no way played your cards right. Not a single solitary hand that the good Lord has dealt out to you."

Later, bathed and wearing her simplest linen nightgown, Marie plaited her hair in two childish braids and climbed onto the feather mattress and pulled two pink-satin down comforts over herself. She was alone in a house for the first time. But she refused to think or feel or weep or remember. Outside it had begun to snow and the clatter of the milk wagons and the wheels of carriages of late revelers and occasionally one of the white-topped omnibuses came and went with muffled insistency. As she listened, her breath gradually rose and fell with the thrumming.

She dreamed that she was back in Columbia in the cold graveyard of the Catholic church. Evie had disappeared from the gravestone on which she had been lying. Fire was roaring everywhere except in the freezing graveyard. Marie took a step and stumbled and fell on a pile of fresh earth. She had to grab handfuls of earth with her hands to keep from falling into an open grave and down in the grave was a coffin without a lid and in the coffin lay—was it Amelia? No—it was Preston Hampton with his face shot away. She could smell the smoke very clearly—it was not the smoke of a burning city but a million cigars—

"Mama! Mama!"

Her own screaming waked her. The smell of cigar smoke was thick in the room. The fire in the Franklin stove was burning brightly. Mr. Beecher in his bathrobe and nightcap was reclining on the chaise longue in front of the fire smoking a cigar.

Sighing, Marie put her head under the covers. She waited for Mr. Beecher to bounce into the buoyant cloud of feathers beside her. She waited a long time. The fire in the stove died down. The smoky odor disappeared. She could hear him snoring. He'd catch a cold and maybe have pneumonia if she didn't wake him and tell him to come to bed.

She got up and took one of the pink-satin comforters and bundled Mr. Beecher up in it. He looked such a nice old man.

"Poor thing," Marie whispered and went back to bed and slept restlessly off and on till morning.

The persevering Marie determined to follow her
recreant lover and took passage in the next steamer
for Europe.

A CHECKERED LIFE,
by "One Who Knows"

42

Sponsored by the Art Committee of the Union League
Club and headed by the publisher, George Palmer Putnam, the Metropolitan Museum was opened the next
day with a private showing for Union League Club
members in a rented brownstone building on Fifth
Avenue near Fifty-third Street. Though he had a
fresh and heavy cold, Mr. Beecher was determined
that he and Mrs. Beecher should be seen together at the
exhibition.

Wearing a black Neapolitan hat trimmed with black
and gold medallions, a set of cameos in her ears and
around her throat, a gown of gold taffeta shot with
brown threads, much bustled in the rear and drawn so
tight across her stomach that bystanders swore she had
to have been sewn in the dress after putting it on,
Marie was so stunning-looking that whenever she
stopped in front of a picture all eyes were on her and
not on the canvases. Not on the shocking sketch of the
nude lady lying in a field of clover; nor on Eastman
Johnson's new *Wounded Drummer Boy;* nor on
Nichol's *Disputed Boundary.* On her, Marie Boozer
Beecher, who dared come, looking like a queen, to
this respectable event. She who just last night had
boldly drawn a pistol from her sable muff and shot off
the ear of one of the most respectable scions of society!
They knew all about it. At the reception the night before, Phoenix had sported his bandage and jokingly
told everybody about his narrow escape from that
Beecher woman.

Mingled with voluble disapproval, went an undercurrent of angry comment. This was the second time New York society had been taken in by this Southern refugee. If they all united in snubbing her over this, no doubt it would be the end of her!

Phoenix arrived, while Mr. Beecher was asking the price of the Eastman Johnson. His and Marie's eyes met, and he grabbed his hat back from the attendant and immediately quitted the exhibition.

Marie had been unhappy enough all day. Now her misery increased. Pleading a fever, she persuaded Mr. Beecher to take her home and himself return alone to the exhibition. His suspicions keenly aroused now, Beecher did just that and immediately hired lawyers and detectives and began his own investigation to discover just what *had* gone on the previous evening that his fellow club members had been whispering in his deaf ear whenever he gave them his attention.

Back at home, Marie wrote and had Stobo deliver a note to Phoenix:

> Do not desert me. Give me a sign that you forgive me. Write me just a little letter. If you are afraid to write— tell Stobo where I can meet you. At once—at once—

The next day:

> Although you refused to send me a word I intend to keep on writing you until you break your silence. I will continue to behave as if nothing has happened between us. I will be merry and wear my prettiest dresses and be always ready to come to you wherever you are. I don't care how bad a place. I will come for I love you.

And three days later:

> No word from you. If this strain continues I will come again to your residence. And if you do not wish this you will tell Stobo where to fetch me. Do you hear? And if this ardency bores you, remember you taught me to answer the urgence of passion. Send for me at once—at once.

And on the sixth day the English man-servant, with keen relish, informed Stobo that his master had sailed for Liverpool that very morning on a Cunarder and he would suggest that Mrs. Beecher be more careful of her supply of stationery. Someday she might have need of it.

The scandal of the shooting and the reason for Phoenix's hasty departure for Europe was now spreading all over New York. The shock to Mr. Beecher, having finally learned the whole truth, was so great that he had an attack in which all power to speak or move his arms and legs left him and it was several days before he could summon the strength and his lawyer to announce to Mrs. Beecher that he had filed papers for divorce.

But by then, Marie was on the high seas on a Cunarder too. She left a note to Mr. Beecher:

I have gone for good. There is no use in continuing the delusion that you and I were meant for each other. I am taking my jewels and fortunately my bank account is still fat enough to care for me properly until I make other arrangements. I imagine you will divorce me. Do it on any grounds that might make such a step less painful to you. Poor man! You never should have got tangled up with Mama. None of this would have happened. I was mad to marry you. I am sorry it was such a disappointment to both of us. All my compliments to you and acquaint your lawyer that he can write to me at the ———— Hotel in Paris where I expect to reside for some months hence.

With some affection
Marie.

And sent one by Stobo to Evie:

Dearest Sister:
I have gone to Paris after Phoenix. He is ahead of me on this ocean sea by a week only. Wouldn't it be a laugh if a storm delayed his vessel and we arrived simultaneously at Le Havre? I want you to go to Mr. Beecher's house and pack up any of the good clothes I may have left. Fetch them and your sweet self to me at the ———— Hotel on Rue ———— in Paris, France, instanter. You'll die in a boardinghouse with mean old Mama. I'm sure Pheonix will be eager to make up when he sees me. He will take you and me to all sorts of divinely wicked places and introduce us to the gayest spots in Paris. How different it will be, compared to the last time with Mr. B. He was so

afraid a girl might try and pick him up on the street that he
would not budge from the hotel unless I accompanied him!
You and I can rent bicycles and ride in the Park. I bet I
can outride Cora Pearl any day and I know my backsides
are as good as hers. At least my face is better looking. Or I
think it is. And at twenty-five there are so few good years
left I intend to make the most of mine. If Stobo comes
asking for money, don't give him any. I gave him a
thousand dollars to open a saloon back in Columbia. He
says the carpetbaggers and the colored people are having
a field day there. Oh dear—even writing the word Columbia makes me blue. And I've determined not to be. I
wonder what Willie would think of me if he knew about
some of the things I've done these past years? If I
weren't all packed, with my ticket in my reticule, and
my luggage aboard ship I might change my mind and
go home and see if he ever married anybody. Go and ask
Mary Darby. I've wanted to, but never dared. No don't
go. Forget it. I'm just feeling a bit shaky at setting off
for Paris all alone. More of this and I'll cry. So make
haste and join me in the acacia groves of the Bois.

A bientôt,
Marie.

PART FIVE

EUROPE

1872

Don Piatt met the Columbia beauty on a railway trip (in France) and thus accurately describes her appearance at that time: Looking through the triangular glass that exists between the compartments, one saw Phoenix sitting on a seat opposite, coolly smoking a cigarette. Mrs. Beecher wore a gray ulster, a peaked hat, with gloves and boots to match, and was, as well as we could determine, about twenty-five years of age. Her eyes were large, lustrous and either dark gray or hazel, which we could not determine . . . the whole face told of a Judith who would go in on Holofernes with assurance of distinguished consideration.

SAN FRANCISCO CHRONICLE

43

Marie caught up with Phoenix on the little boat that regularly crossed the English Channel. He had stopped a few days in London to have his tailor measure him for a new yachting outfit and to spend a week end in the country with Lord and Lady Yarborough. There he was standing by the rail, watching the cliffs of Dover slip into the background. Marie, coming up on the deck, saw him and rushed forward crying, "Phoenix! Phoenix!"

"Oh Lord! Where did *you* come from? Don't you realize that I am running away from you? I've come this winter journey from New York just to escape you. Surely you are aware that I am terribly angry with you." His voice was anything but angry. Who had ever looked so lovely as she?

"But listen to what's happened!"

And she told him everything, spasmodically, in haste. She almost danced in her excitement, exaggerating the facts, pretending it was she who was divorcing Mr. Beecher for adultery, and that she had been deserted by her mother and sister and now was all alone and comfortless and practically in a decline. On the boat coming over, she'd not been able to leave her cabin at all.

"You've never looked healthier or happier."

"It's just seeing you again. Oh now everything is wonderful!"

She tucked her hand in his. His fingers clenched into a fist against her. Sudden tears came into her eyes that, reflecting the heaving sea, were a kaleidoscope of green and blue and gray, flashing like fire under the waves. A pulse in her throat throbbed. Color came and went in her cheeks. Her physical beauty had never excited Phoenix more sensually. So that he lost his head and took her in his arms, not caring who saw him kissing her. For the moment she had triumphed.

"We'll talk about it in Paris," he said hoarsely.

"We'll stay at the same hotel—" she bubbled joyously.

"But—" Phoenix looked lost.

"Nobody will know. And the day the divorce is finished—"

They were lovers again, and as February turned into early March and tulips blossomed in the Tuileries gardens and the skeleton-topped chestnut trees along the Champs Élysées changed to a soft feathery yellow-green, Marie knew she was the happiest woman in the world. She was at the apogee of her beauty. Wherever Phoenix took her, she was the center of admiration. Tooling through the Bois in her trim cabriolet handling the ribbons herself, racing the English *demimondaine,* Skittles, in her "pony chase, with a pair of black cobs and two grooms on coal black cattle behind"; or passing Cora Pearl, wearing canary-colored hair, leaning indolently back on a yellow satin swan's-down seat in her blue carriage. Or Cora Pearl again, wearing her own red hair and riding in a yellow barouche with a crimson swan's-down seat. Cheering La Goulue in the red-and-gold Seize room of the Café Anglais as she lifted her frilled froufrou petticoats and waved her black-stockinged leg wildly in the air in the new dance—the cancan. Herself practicing the cancan with the girls in the Foyer de Danse of the Opera House during their exercise periods. Adoring Adah Menken, riding the white horse at the Gaité. Dancing with Phoenix in Jardin Mabille and gathering more spectators to watch them waltz than the velvet-eyed English beauty, Mabel Gray, and her Russian duke.

Each day passed with some new sweetness or excitement. She made promises to Phoenix. She told him about her past life. Phoenix hushed her with hot embraces and she, looking up at him with eyes grown enormous from love-making, would plead with him to declare he loved her above all the world.

Had she not been so pretty, so intriguing in her responses, so possessed by love, not by mere lust; she would not have held such an enchantment for him.

And then one evening in early March, when she was dressing to go with him to a dinner at Cora Pearl's house in the Rue de Chaillot, Marie said, "Apparently you know all the fast women in Paris, but when we are married I don't think we ought to go with people like Cora Pearl and Skittles and those."

"What do you mean by 'those'?"

"You know. Women who let men keep them without being married."

"And you?"

She flushed and shrugged her shoulders in annoyance. "That's not fair. You don't 'keep' me. I'm rich and as soon as I hear from Mr. Beecher's lawyer we are going to be married."

"Hum!"

"What did you say?".

"I said that in that pearl-colored velvet and with your hair done à la Pompadour you look like a countess."

"I've wanted a mushroom-colored velvet ever since I went to my first ball at the Prestons' in Columbia and Mrs. Preston wore one. Oh—I was frightened! It was Secession Day and—"

Phoenix looked at Marie queerly in a tender way.

"You always grow sentimental and sad when you speak of Columbia. Perhaps you should move back there when your divorce is final."

"Oh—no—no—you wouldn't like it. Reconstruction has been awful in South Carolina. The colored people are in full control and all the white people, I mean the nice white people, are terribly poor. Only the carpetbaggers have any money. And where would you keep your yacht?"

"How precious you are," he cried, kissing her hand. In the pale velvet with the train and the heart-shaped corsage filled in with point lace and ornamented with pearls she did indeed look a great lady. "Let's not go to Cora's tonight."

"You do love me," she said happily. "But you've accepted Cora's invitation. We'll go this once. It might be fun."

That night at Cora Pearl's, Marie met the Prince of Wales and the Marquis de Vellavieja and the Duc de Mouchy and the Duc de Gramont-Caderousse. Prince Jerome Napoleon, who had set up the elegant establishment, being an expulsé since the beginning of the Franco Prussian War was, alas, not present. Young Alexandre Duval, who was currently buying Cora's jewels and caviar, acted as the host.

Among the women to whom Phoenix introduced Marie was the soft-spoken Courtois, said to be the best dressed woman in the world, Mabel Gray, the sweet and evil, and the cultivated Leblanc, wearing the Hope Diamond.

"Why does everybody call these ladies just one name?" Marie whispered to Phoenix over a bowl of lobster bisque.

"It's politic," Phoenix whispered back.

"I don't understand."

"Sh-h-h—here comes our hostess whose real name, by the way, is Eliza Elizabeth Crouch. Crouch, translated into French presented an *équivoque* to Eliza Elizabeth, so she christened herself Cora Pearl!"

A single violin played *Kathleen Mavourneen* (composed by Cora's father in England long ago). Then the door was flung wide—a trumpet tootled from the kitchen and four footmen in scarlet livery came staggering in with a gargantuan, covered silver dish.

"It looks like a silver coffin," Marie said low to Phoenix.

"She'll be wearing her red hair tonight," Leblanc said. "To match the roses."

The servants heaved the silver platter in the middle of the long table which was strewn with bunches of hothouse grapes and red satin roses. They took off the silver cover and there, on a bed of grape leaves, lay Cora Pearl entirely nude. Her red hair was brushed in flames out from her clown face. Her small eyes sparkled in answer to the gasps of admiration that flew up and down the table as her angel's body was loudly acknowledged, by the connoisseurs gathered there, to be the most beautiful body in all the world. Which it most undoubtedly must have been.

Back at their hotel, Marie stopped at the desk and received a packet of letters from the clerk. Phoenix followed her to her room and she read them to him, aloud.

The first was from Mr. Beecher's lawyer:

The proceedings are going forward with dispatch. It but remains for the post to reach here from there with the name of the gentleman with whom you are currently being seen constantly in Paris for Mr. Beecher to name the co-respondent. He has been hesitant about naming one of his fellow Union Club members and it is with great relief that he has learned of your constant escort in Paris. Within a month, Madame, you will receive papers to sign and on so doing you will be free to pursue any path that you desire in the future.

The second was from Evie:

Mama refuses to allow me to join you. She is very sick, I think, but she won't see a doctor. She insists that I return to South Carolina and pay Papa a visit. I have written and he has sent me a ticket. I am glad for I don't like this boardinghouse. It is very shabby. I think you should send Mama some money. I think she misses you. I will write you from Winnsboro. Do you remember the man in the coffin? I think his name was Mr. Manigault. I will put some flowers on his grave. I am glad I am going. Why don't you come back and make up with Mr. Beecher so we can all be together again?

Midnight struck as, with trembling fingers, Marie folded up Evie's letter.

Phoenix said, "Let's not discuss these letters now. We've eaten and drunk too much. Kiss me good night. Tomorrow we will make plans." He walked unsteadily to the door.

Assuming a gay air, Marie said, "You realize what all this means?"

"Yes."

"It means that in a very few days I will be free."

"Naturally."

"Will you join me downstairs for breakfast in the morning?"

"No. Some new Americans arrived in the hotel this afternoon. Possibly from New York. I didn't learn their names."

"When we are married we won't have to worry about things like that. Speak to me—you look very pale."

"The lobster bisque has soured on my stomach."

"Shall we lunch at Les Trois Frères? I'm hungry for some of their *boeuf à la mode*."

He nodded and Marie, standing in her doorway, watched him walk quickly down the long, crimson-carpeted hall in the dim light of the gas lamps. As he began to ascend the stairs to his floor, she ran to the foot of the stairs and looking up, cried, "Tomorrow!"

But he was lost in the shadows and she could hear his footsteps diminish up the plush stair carpet. She walked slowly toward her big, empty room. It had been an unfortunate evening altogether.

And Phoenix looking back from the top of the stairs saw Marie, in her moonlight-colored dress, melting into the dim distance of the corridor like a lost dream. For a minute he was tempted to run after her and take her in his arms. But he didn't—he just held tightly to the stair rail so that he would not stumble and make a sound.

"Oh damn! Oh damn!" he swore to himself. What a farce! This is going to make me ridiculous. Mother will be livid. A corespondent in a New York divorce case! It will be in all the papers. Marie has made me a lively mistress and a pretty one but what could I do with her? I don't want to marry her or anybody. It would be too dull. She'd make a scene whenever I wanted to take a cruise without her. Look how she shot me when I tried to free myself from her in the winter. Well, it *has* been pleasant having her again for this spring. But— here—I'll ring for the valet and have him pack my things at once. Constant escort in Paris, indeed! Let another fellow play Beecher's cuckold. I'll take a cab to the station and sit and wait for the next boat train. Can't risk her running after me another time. I'll go straight to Harwich when I arrive in England. It's spring —old Ashbury will probably have the *Cambria* in racing shape. P'raps I can persuade him into a speedy voyage. Marie'll never catch *me* again. By summer she will have a new *bel ami* and it will be time to sail my precious *Intrepid* to Newport for the season and then the races and after that—

So reasoning, Phoenix sat down and quickly dashed off a farewell note to Marie, smoked several cigarettes and drank some warm brandy while the sleepy porter packed his luggage. When the last strap was buckled, he put on his summer-weight short cape and his tweed cap that had a bill before and behind and, executing a few gay jig steps after he had slipped his letter underneath her door, departed from Marie's life for forever.

After a brief residence in the gay city (Paris) Marie,
Cora Pearl (Prince Napoleon's "friend") and an-
other equally sensation-loving female went on a
trip . . . visiting Moscow and St. Petersburg. . . .
One of the party so completely snared a young
Russian Grand Duke that. . . .

A CHECKERED LIFE,
by *"One Who Knows"*

44

The Grand Duke Vladimir of Russia was to be married in the autumn of 1872 to a German princess
who had seen the gay, fun-loving young brother of the
Czarevitch in Germany the previous autumn and had
decided that he was her destiny. But, having the summer to enjoy before the said fate came upon him,
Vladimir invited a few of his gay companions from
Paris to attend a ball in St. Petersburg in July.

Cora Pearl arranged the group from Paris. Herself
and Fanny Lear (originally of Philadelphia) and the
rich young American who resided at the ———
Hotel and who, since being deserted by her "amor,"
had added zest to the Paris scene during the past few
months. Oh, she drank too much champagne and
brandy most evenings, but she was a beauty and quite
mad and Vladimir had inisted on "a pretty new one
full of fire that none of us have ever seen before."

Cora Pearl's invitation to accompany her to Russia
was delivered to Marie with all the ostentation of a
court summons. As she had done with Phoenix's letter,
with its underscored "nevers" and "forevers" (signed
—not with love and devotion, but with a great over-
sized *"P"*), she tore up Cora's letter and threw the

shreds out of the window. Then she picked up a bottle of cognac on the candlestand, poured a goblet and began to sip it desperately.

In her desolation she had passed far beyond self-pity or loneliness. It would be as easy to go to St. Petersburg as to return to America. She would laugh and drink and be merry and noisy all night and sleep all day. But she needed some new dresses. Daring ones. No more creamy velvets and point lace for Marie! She would have Monsieur Worth make her a red-and-white organdy with yards and yards of red froufrou petticoats, and an orange taffeta with great clouds of gold lace petticoats and a wide girdle of yellow marabou. She grinned at a sudden thought of how they would horrify Amelia with her infallible sense of the dramatic but elegant. Well—she'd be dramatic all right. As eye-catching as ever Cora Pearl would be naked on a silver dish.

St. Petersburg was reached in early July and Cora announced that the great ball would not take place for a week. Until then, there would be dinners every evening and entertainments with the old men and different ones with the young men, and drives along the Neva in open droshkies and picnics and—

Marie hardly heard her. Anticipation of these festivities was now as bizarre as her environs. Her one idea was to keep moving about and sipping brandy so she would not think of or remember anybody or anything that made her sad. She had a superstitious fear of conjuring up anyone she had ever cared about. They were all responsible for and part of her present wretchedness. If one of them—the little boy Willie in a bowler hat giving her both chicken wings from his lunch basket; Amelia picking a card from a much used pack and hypnotizing her with glittery black eyes; Evie gnawing her nails and begging not to be left behind; Phoenix with his hard allure teaching her to delight in his sensual touches; Big Dave fondling her tangled hair—insisted on appearing, she drowned them immediately in a glass of brandy or a pint of champagne. They went down protesting and gurgling. And when they were gone she could laugh again and dance the cancan high and madly as ever La Goulue had done one night she and Phoenix—

Had Marie been less confused, St. Petersburg would have delighted her. She drove about with princes and dukes in swift carriages and saw a fairy-tale town with the face of a Titan, not one of the Graces. It couldn't be real. Nothing was any more. Everything was part of the opera bouffe in which she was playing a leading role.

The great bazaars jammed with crystal and gems from Siberia and India, wax tapers and sacred pictures and lamps to burn. The merchants drinking tea and, on a small frame filled with ivory balls, reckoning their accounts. The crooked streets paved with flinty stones. The churches and palaces and pink-and-yellow washed cottages jumbled together. The picturesque domes and towers against the sky. The drays and country carts driven by peasants in pink calico blouses (that went ill with their florid faces), wide trousers tucked into high boots or their feet in shoes of plaited reeds or strips of lime-tree bark and though it was warm, wrappers of greasy sheepskin, their yellow hair bound in fillets and huge beards reaching to their waists.

In open spaces, coaches stood for hire, the coachmen in low, broad-brimmed, black hats and long caftans of dark cloth uncollared and padded at the hips and white gloves secured at their waists by the thumbs.

There were hucksters running around crying salted cucumbers as a relish for black bread. Clerks sitting in shop doors playing chess or dominos. Soldiers, dark gypsies, Tartars, Persians, Jews thronging the streets. And the women! The way they stared at Marie in her wide-brimmed, pink straw hat tied under her chin with yards of cherry-colored veiling, at her tiny parasol of black lace, her rosy muslin dress and the absurd, pink-flamingo feather shawl. The way Marie stared at them —those flat-faced women in long sacques of wadded cloth and thick handkerchiefs covering their dull hair.

And everywhere music—in the parks, at the banquets, picnics and masked balls. Princes and dukes, generals and dignitaries, old and young coming and going with the various entertainments. Cora Pearl wore different colored hair each night and grew progressively bolder and coarser as the ever flowing vodka took control of her senses; Fanny Lear, whispered here to be a Rumanian princess, fell in love with a young palace guard and was forbidden to attend the Grand Ball at the Imperial Palace. Whenever Marie came near a certain member of the royal household she allowed him to take her in his arms and the music and the drumming of her blood drowned out the protestations of her heart.

On the night before the Grand Ball, Marie, wearing a black mask over her eyes and a swan's-down *sortir de bal* over the white organdy with its seemingly limitless froufrou petticoats of red satin that M. Worth had designed for her in Paris, arrived at a banquet after the dinner had begun. She was slightly tipsy and her cheeks were flushed but the powdered, gold-laced footmen bowed much lower to her than they had to the others. And when one of them took her swan's-down cloak and saw the froufrou petticoats, he bowed again and when another came up to announce her as she entered the banquet room, his eyes bugged open and his lips moved as he counted red petticoats.

The room was gilded and hot and the Grand Duke came forward and took her hand and all the younger men, dukes and princes and colonels, rose and put their feet on the table and raised glasses of vodka and cried—"La Belle!" And there was such an excess of frenzied shouting and toasting when they saw her costume that Marie felt giddy from the noise and the heavy scent of lilacs and wines and cigar smoke.

Then at a signal from the Grand Duke, the orchestra struck up the section of Offenbach's *Orpheus in the Underworld* to which the cancan is danced and everybody yelled and demanded that Marie perform and she lifted up her skirts and jumped up on the table and did such an enthusiastic cancan that soon all the men were stamping and the ladies who'd worn fashionable bustles or cramping crinolines did the best they could and the whole scene was a riot of noise and revelry.

After the banquet, they had races along the Neva in open droshkies and swift carriages. The Grand Duke took Marie back to her hotel at dawn and the following night he personally escorted her to the Grand Ball in the Imperial Palace.

This night she wore white satin. Close, fine white satin with no ornament except a water lily at her breast and another in her hair. The change from the evening before was dramatic. In the middle of the evening, the Grand Duke led her upstairs into a cosy little room. She sat on a bench by an open window and looked out at the sky and began to cry for no reason. She did not hear the Duke return but she responded to his arms when he slipped up behind her and clasped an emerald-and-diamond necklace around her throat—pinned a great mass of emeralds on her breast and tore the water lily from her hair, smoothed it again, and placed a diamond tiara on her head.

Marie had drunk much too much vodka, and catching a glimpse of herself in a mirror decided the tiara was slightly crooked but not wanting to hurt the Duke's feelings she kissed him hotly and eventually agreed with him that she looked very imperious.

Soon after he took her back down to the dancing, the orchestra struck up the national hymn and who should condescend to appear with the young Princess Dolgorouky but the middle-aged Emperor himself.

Marie dropped herself in a low curtsey of which Madame Togno would probably have criticized the extravagance. But what was this? Who was the Emperor calling so angrily? Whose arm had replaced the Duke's around her waist? She looked up. Two sets of rough arms had replaced the Duke's. She was in flight. High dignitaries were rushing her from the room. Her little feet waved to and fro trying to run in the air. Rough hands unclasped the necklace from her throat, fumbled at her breast, jerked the tiara from her head. Rough voices said in French that she had been noticed leaving the dancing and going upstairs to the Empress' apartments. She had been seen wearing the Empress' jewels on her descent of the stairs! Ergo—she was a thief.

Marie looked around. Everything was very fuzzy and Vladimir had entirely disappeared. He must have gone to tell the Emperor that he, not she, had taken the jewels.

But he hadn't. He had simply left her to take the consequences of their *amourette*.

The next day, Marie and Fanny and Cora were subjected to hours of questioning and rude interviews by the secret police and high-ranking army officers and personal representatives of the Emperor. Marie declared positively she had not stolen the jewels but she couldn't deny she'd been in a mighty sumptuous little room upstairs in the palace. Nor could she deny that she'd come downstairs wearing the emeralds. Nor that she and the Duke had—

Had what? the Minister of the Secret Police asked, over and over. Stolen the jewels?

No, not that.

But she had been wearing the emerald tiara and the necklace and the brooch when the Emperor saw her?

Well, yes, but—

The Minister of the Secret Police threw up his hands. What could one say to this lovely, gentle creature who had the bearing and features of a grand duchess? The Minister got himself in hand and said: "If you and your cohorts are not aboard the train leaving the Russian boundary tomorrow, you will be confined at once in a prison. This scandal will be in all the papers. You will be ruined wherever you appear from the results of this affair. If the German princess hears of this she may even refuse to marry the Grand Duke! No—that must not happen. Madame Beecher, Madame Beecher, are you listening? Do you hear me?"

"Yes, sir," Marie said softly. "I'm terribly sorry."

45

And now here she was again, pursuing Phoenix with all the ardor and anxiety and nervousness of the first time. Her fingers shook as she brushed her hair in the boat cabin just out from Dover. Make it lie smooth, she told herself, you're not quite sober after all the brandy you drank last night. Why on earth did you do it? But he must not suspect that you've let yourself go to pieces. You must at least look like a lady.

"How do you know Phoenix is in England?" she asked Cora for the dozenth time.

"I read it in that newspaper the man had in Havre. He was weekending with Earl Yarborough at Brockelsby Hall. Plon Plon was a guest there too, and if he's left the Hall Plon Plon will tell you where you can find him."

And if she found him? Marie went over and looked out of the porthole at the shining water. How Phoenix loved the sea! He had loved her too. He had loved her like a madman. Surely he would again if she could just let him understand that she could not live without him.

Never! he had written, Never! Never! But she hoped he would. She must continue to hope. She couldn't live without hoping. Not to hope made everything she had ever done seem senseless. Not to hope meant accepting the ultimate humiliation. She had been such a gay, proud child. She had been surrounded by so many people who loved her and cherished her and expected high things of her. I never appreciated my life, she whispered to herself. Why, even Mama loved me in her twisted way. She thought I was an extraordinary person and that the cards predicted a rich future. And look at me. Look where I am. Look who I am traveling with. Listen to her—common as pig tracks.

Cora Pearl was saying, "I'm sure the diamond and emerald scandal has made all the British papers."

"I'll die if it has."

"It will only make you a more desirable mistress for Phoenix. Um-m-m infatuating the Grand Duke to the point of his letting you wear his mother's tiara! It makes you first water, actually. I only infatuated a stuffy old general who belched and complained of his bunions. And look at Fanny Lear—a mere guardsman. And we're professionals and you—"

"I?" Marie didn't like this conversation. As a matter of fact, she didn't like Cora Pearl. But Cora *was* a gay hoyden and somebody to be with and didn't mind when Marie poured herself another drink, as now. With shaking fingers Marie held a glass of brandy to the porthole light and then downed it quickly.

"You'll learn all the tricks of the trade someday. Now your looks are enough. But you'd better stop drinking so much brandy. It shows in your eyes and on your hips."

Marie looked across the cabin at Cora. She couldn't be more than thirty-one or two, but Cora's face in the harsh light from the porthole looked at least forty. Only when she walked around without any clothes on, did Cora exude youth and fire. And then—well, there was something not quite normal about her. She was possessed of some kind of mystic physical essence that made you forget her ugly face and her coarse vulgar talk and her—

She'd pour one more tiny little drink. And then she'd not have another for a long time. Maybe never. She would arrive in London and take a bath in a nice tub at Brown's Hotel. Then she'd hire a horse and go for a gallop in the park. She needed exercise. She *had* put on some flesh around her middle. Phoenix wouldn't like that.

She said to Cora, "As soon as we get in the train I'm

going to sleep all the way to London. When we arrive I'm going to take some exercise."

Cora said, "A good idea. In this light you don't look like yourself."

Marie was dismayed. She put on her gray-peaked traveling hat with a pale green veil. The veil came down over her face. She tied it tightly under her chin. Now—she looked better—less puffy and yellow.

That morning the train to London was crowded. Two young government clerks shared their compartment. Soon the four were chatting and Marie produced a bottle of brandy she'd tucked in her basket, just in case she felt a little faint along the way. And by the time they reached London, she had decided to spend the evening with Cora and the boys. Tomorrow would be plenty of time to go after Phoenix.

Cora insisted that they go to a small hotel in Soho instead of Brown's.

"Let's make a night of it. To celebrate being in England. This place in Soho is perfect. We can move to Brown's tomorrow. Rather I'm going to find Plon Plon. You can move to Brown's."

"I don't like this hotel." Marie felt truculent and argumentative. The clerks came in with some Irish whiskey and a bottle of sweet red wine. Marie threw the red wine out of the window. They decided to drink the whiskey, then hire a cab and drive in the dusking to see the sights of the city. At sunset one of the clerks said let's drink one more bottle before we go out.

While he was away purchasing the spirits, Cora ordered a huge supper sent up from the kitchen. A steak and kidney pie, fish and chips and a boiled cabbage. She declared loudly and often how hungry she was for some good old home cooking. Tired of all that sauce and spice she had to eat in France. Just to think of it made her hot. She removed her dress and shoes and postured up and down the room in her petticoat. The clerk came back with a bottle of French brandy and another bottle of Italian wine. Marie threw the wine out of the window.

This time they were delighted with the noise it made

and Cora threw a chair out of the window. It hit a cat and a dog began barking and a child screaming.

Someone knocked on the door. Marie, half of her hair escaped from its net, her peaked hat falling over one eye, opened the door and the landlord came in and asked them to be quiet. He was an old man with white hair cut round on his head and big, kind blue eyes. He walked with a cane. One of his knees was stiff.

Cora picked up the steak and kidney pie and jammed it on the old man's head. The clerks howled and whooped at his startled face with brown gravy running down his cheeks and the bowl just fitting his head like a greasy brown cap.

Marie lifted her skirts and humming a bit of Offenbach turned her back and began to dance a cancan. She didn't like the way the old man looked with that mess on his head. He was begging the two young men to get out or behave themselves. They said rude words and made vulgar noises. Then he said he was going to call the police and have them thrown out. The two clerks grabbed him by the arms and shoved him into the hall and slammed the door. He beat on the door with his cane. Cora called, "Shut up!" Marie began to weep. She had turned one of her ankles. The old man kept calling and yelling to them to open the door.

Cora, still in her petticoat and bare feet, opened the door. Marie limped over and said to the old man, "Go on away. We'll be quiet."

But Cora said, "Like hell, we will." And the clerks said, "Beat it off, old man, or we'll kick you down the stairs." And Marie said, "If you do I'll kick both of you." Cora laughed and took off her corset cover.

"If any kicking's done, Cora will do it." So saying she roughly pushed the old man to the head of the stairs and gave him such a kick that he crashed headlong all the way down, to the yelling delight of the clerks and Cora. The three of them went back into the room and opened the new bottle of brandy and began shouting and jumping about more violently than ever.

Marie, however, crept down the stairs. He was dead.

She knew he was dead. He had to be dead, bumping down as he had. One step at a time. The steps must have come loose for they wouldn't stay still. Or was she still aboard ship? But what ship? The *Weybosset?* Out of Wilmington? No. No. That was another Marie entirely. And the old man—was it Big Dave—with those blue eyes full of tears, moaning and picking himself up? Thank you, Lord, for not letting him be dead. Where was his cane? He'd had a cane. Marie crawled back along the stair rail and found his cane. Then she made her way down to him carefully, wary of the writhing stair rail. He was sitting on the bottom step with his head in his hands. He was crying. She helped him up and then he held her steady until she got her balance.

She gave him his cane. He said, "She'd no call to do that."

Marie said, "She had a little girl whipped onesh in Parish jush for laughing at her riding an old byshickle. She'sh a bad woman. Worsh than mama."

He said, "I'm going to the police. This very night."

And Marie said, "Yesh. Thash's wha' you mush do. Right away. She'sh a bad, bad woman. A real mean old woman."

The man went out and Marie took his place on the bottom step of the stairs. The dingy, gaslit hall was going round and round. And upstairs those people were making so much noise. The whole house was heaving. But the noise soon got very far away. Farther and farther away. She was asleep.

The next morning the quartet appeared in court. They were all sober and serious now. Even Cora Pearl was quiet. She looked like an old woman and bilious, too.

The police magistrate couldn't take his eyes off Marie. She kept crying in a lacy handkerchief. Her traveling clothes, though rumpled, were of the finest cut and material. Her voice was low and sweet and cultivated. Her manner was gentle and appealing. She seemed heartbroken about the whole affair. He noticed the way she was with Cora Pearl and the clerks. Very stiff and formal and haughty. How had she ever got mixed up in such company? Such a pretty, lady-like little thing? And from fine, rich New York people. She said so.

He fined them each fifty pounds and released them on the condition that they at once leave London—the alternative being three months confinement in Bridewell prison.

46

Marie returned immediately to Paris. Her one idea was to pack her things and go home. She remembered now that she'd not sent Amelia or Evie any money. And Evie had written that Amelia was very ill. That she loved Amelia or didn't love her wasn't the point. The point was what kind of a person had she, Marie Boozer, become? The numbness that had frozen her heart back at Solomon's Grove was all gone now. Her heart was beating again all right. And such a shame was on her. Such a black, terrible shame.

Again she asked herself. Love? Did one ever love but once? Had she truly loved Phoenix? Or Willie? Was she even capable of love?

I'll be gay, Mama, she had said, sailing down the river toward Wilmington away from Willie. I'm going to have so much fun—

But had it been fun? Had it?

The hotel clerk in Paris was glad to see her. Thank heaven somebody was glad to see her. He handed her a pile of letters. One of them was marked *"Very Urgent."*

She sat down by the window in her same bedroom and looked out over the Tuileries Gardens. She and Phoenix used to stand here and watch the leaves turning green. Ah, Phoenix. Now it was late August and the heat shimmered over the gardens and the children cried out their delight in the little boats and the pony carts and the Punch and Judy. If she and Phoenix had just had a baby why then he might not have left her. Oh, but he would have. Her Mama had been right.

She opened Evie's letter first. It was postmarked a month ago and had been mailed in Columbia!

Well, look where I am! And guess who I saw uptown this morning? Yes—old Willie C! He didn't recognize me but I did him. He is a brakeman on the railroad and he had on his working clothes. He is still mighty good-looking and they say all the Columbia girls are after him. The next time I see him I am going up and talk to him. I wonder why he hasn't gotten married. Maybe he'll marry me!

Jay is a big boy. Papa wants so bad to send him to college. I told him you might help. But he says no, we can't take any help ever from you or Mama. Mrs. McCord asked about you at church last Sunday and I didn't tell her about the divorce because I knew it would make her sad.

Oh—guess what? Two years ago Papa and Jay were so poor that he put his pride in his pocket and went to Mrs. Elmore and asked if he could have the old "showbox" back. She was glad to get it out of her carriage house. Papa has sold bits and pieces of it and what do you know —the silver lamps and the crystal windows adorn the carriage of the fanciest yellow woman in town! The blue satin seats were bought by a carpetbagger for his carriage; and the Governor had the painted door fitted onto his coach! The potbellied body was bought by a butcher and I see it every day going around from door to door, pulled by a flop-eared mule, and full of fresh beef.

Everybody is very poor but we have parties and drink lemonade and eat biscuits and blackberry jelly. I think it tastes better to me than all that wine and caviar you and Mr. Beecher were always serving. And nobody really liked us up there. People here ask about you but never about Mama. I hope you sent her some money for she was real poorly when I left. She was mighty mean to me at the end and didn't act like she cared at all when I went away. Papa is not mean to me at all. But Auntie hopes I'll get married soon and be off her hands. There's going to be a picnic at the park next week. Maybe I'll see Willie again, dressed up. I hope so. I always was jealous of you and Willie. I wish you'd send me some white-kid gloves from Paris. Nobody here has any but cotton ones and I'd be something special with Paris gloves.

Love from Eveline.

"Damn Evie," Marie said through clenched teeth and threw the letter in the waste basket.

She tore open the *urgent* letter—it was from Mr. Bostwick.

Thank heavens I have at last got your address from your stepfather who had it from your half-sister. It is of the utmost urgency that you return to New York at once. The devil with your divorce case. And the devil with Mr. Beecher. Your mother is in a charity room at the Woman's Hospital at 83 Madison Avenue. She is dying of cancer. She assures everybody that you were not aware of her condition when you left New York. She is a proud woman and will not accept help from anyone. Not that there has been any. Beecher refuses even to listen to a word concerning her. Mr. Feaster writes that he is sorry but he is in an impoverished state and your half-sister has told him you would surely send your mother money. That black rascal, Stobo, so far, has paid all of her imperative expenses. He goes to the hospital to see her every day. I think he works at the new railroad depot as a luggage porter. I don't know why I bother, you all having proven such traitors to the Confederacy. But I hope you will respond to this plea and come at once.

In Haste,
P. Bostwick.

Like a low web the September afternoon sky was loose over the quai. The *Java* looked shiny and white in the cloudy mist. And it was so hot. There must be a storm blowing somewhere in the Atlantic Ocean.

Marie untied the satin strings of her new, fawn-colored, summer ermine scarf and wanted to unbutton the mushroom flannel jacket of her traveling suit but she didn't dare. M. Worth had assured her she would be the most fashionable lady sailing from Havre and she must play the part carefully. She was starting at the bottom again toward being a belle. Poor Stobo! Thank heavens he would never know about the disgraceful summer that was ending. Nobody would ever know. And she—she would never remember it. She had turned over a new leaf. From now on—

A porter struggled by with some unusual and handsome luggage. A man's luggage. Marie had seen luggage like that before. It was made by an exclusive craftsman on Broadway. It had a special form of handle. Where had she seen such luggage? Why, in the cabin of the *Intrepid!* Many times.

Though her eyes had been the dull gray of the woolly sky a moment ago, now, focused on the rare leather, fire as under water began to burn in their depths.

She put her chamois-gloved hand behind and made sure that her bustle was not on crooked. One's tiara might get by with a slight slant but never one's *derrière*. Not if one's heart was suddenly throbbing as if the whole world was coming to an end.

For the past two weeks she had worked frantically to get a new fall wardrobe assembled, her affairs in order, her luggage packed so that she could proudly return to New York in the grand manner and nobly look after Amelia. She had mailed Amelia money immediately but she knew Mr. Bostwick was going to reproach her for not having herself come by the first ship. But something had told her to take passage on the *Java.* And she had thought Phoenix was in England! Or had returned to the States in time for the racing season off Newport.

What should she do to catch his notice? Where was he?

She looked around and saw the luggage piled near the gangway. And to think, she had resolved never, never to run after him again. And here she was practically fainting with excitement at the prospect of meeting him face to face. And he—surely when he saw how well she looked (not a single drink since the nightmare in London; all the fat gone from her hips); rested, and her hair lying in a smooth, smooth coil on her neck under the tiny, tan, plumed Eugénie hat. Oh—he would be happy too. She just knew it—

She could scarcely breathe. Her pulse was leaping from her throat. Her knees were going to buckle under her. She bit her lips and lifted her hand in nonchalant greeting.

He was running forward to take her hand—Count Pourtalès—the funny, ardent little Frenchman—and saying—"Ah—I would have known you anywhere— the little loyal refugee! And you embark on this voyage? *Ce soir* you dine with me? *Et tous les soirs aussi?*"

"How delightful of you to recognize me! I took you for somebody else. But I'm glad you are sailing on the *Java* too. I will be happy to dine with you," Marie answered quietly, her eyes entirely gray again but soft with winked-back tears. The luggage maker on Broadway was very famous. Why should she ever have dreamed— With a graceful gesture she gave Count Pourtalès her hand and let him lead her up the gangway.

And that night she lay awake and wept while the foghorn mourned its disappointment to the rising waves and the wind shrieked and howled derisively in the shrouds. Somewhere on this ship the man with the familiar luggage was sleeping happily. But where was the other one who had signed that cruel letter with the great flourishing "P"? Wherever he was, she was certain now that he would never return to her. If she was wise and, for a change, played her cards right she knew without a doubt she could be a countess. She had explained to Pourtalès that she was divorced, poor dear Mr. Beecher having lost his mind entirely, and that she was rushing home to be at the bedside of her dear, darling Mama who was dying. The Count had patted her hand and murmured sympathetic things. But when he said good night, he had kissed her hand passionately and looked up at her with utter infatuation. It had been hard not to laugh at him.

Now she didn't feel like laughing. She felt like screaming. But when she thought of returning to New York and Paris and London and Columbia, especially Columbia, as the Countess de Pourtalès—of all the wonderful, wonderful life ahead of her—the tiaras and the castles and the balls and the kings and queens—she knew that this time she *was* going to play her cards well. And Amelia—why she'd be like the cat who swallowed a whole flock of canaries. The mother of a countess! Marie could almost hear Amelia chuckling and saying, "Well, honey, you made it. Mama knew you would."

EPILOGUE

NEW YORK

September 1872

There is a wild wind blowing outside. A hurricane is passing New York Harbor en route to Newfoundland. Amelia listens to the wind and thinks she is back in the boardinghouse on Richland Street in Columbia and the pain that is eating her up will soon terminate in a beautiful experience. A warm, golden, glowing experience.

Then she hears the nurses walking up and down the hall and the woman in the next bed moaning and the omnibuses on Madison Avenue and the street cries and the clanging bells and all kinds of noisy clatterings. And she knows she is far away from Columbia. She is in New York and she hates New York. She hates everything that has happened to her in New York.

A nurse comes in and asks if she needs more opium. Amelia nods her head and laughs a little. But she doesn't bother to open her eyes. She reaches up and scratches her nose with a bone of a forefinger. She hopes the dreaming will soon begin. The sweet scents, the soft music, the lovely people.

"The dress had such pretty white lace on it," Amelia murmurs, "and real gold buttons. I wore it to Big Dave's funeral."

"What did you say?" The nurse counts Amelia's pulse and listens to her breathing. "How old are you?" she asks trying to discover how aware Amelia is.

"Forty-two," Amelia whispers. She laughs girlishly, "Real gold buttons. Solid gold."

The nurse speaks, "Isn't there anybody I can send for to come and see you? Or that I can notify when—"

"My daughter is coming. Soon. I can almost hear her voice out in the hall." Amelia knows very well what the nurse means by "notify." She means that if there isn't anybody she will be buried in Potter's Field. So she tries to tell the nurse that Marie is coming to give her a grand funeral the likes of which New York has never seen. How Amelia hates New York!

Her chest begins to pant from her hating. How she hates the way those omnibuses keep rattling over the paving stones. How the wind shrieks. How the lamp grows dim and the candle flickers. Amelia does not realize that it is she shrieking in agony. That the rattle is her own death rattle. That the dimming lamp is her own consciousness fading into darkness. The flickering candle her own heart.

Suddenly a door opens and she hears Marie's rippling laughing and she smells the haunting sweetness of Marie and Marie's husky voice is calling, "Mama! Mama!"

Amelia raises herself convulsively, her back arched, her black hair streaming, her eyes glazed, staring at the vision of golden liveliness that is running toward her.

"Marie! My beautiful child!" She screams and falls back upon the cot in a final convulsion.

The nurse bends over the bed and calls frantically for help. Amelia is dead. She is all alone somewhere, far from the vision of the only person she ever really loved.

WHAT HAPPENED AFTER

Shanghai, China, July 1, 1878

My dear old friend:[1]

Yours of the 15th May, reminding me of my promise to
furnish "my experience" and a summary of my "checkered
life," came to hand in due season. I had commenced it
it several months ago, but have been delayed by one thing
and another—writing only at such times as when the
Count was out of the way, which is not often or very
long—for, as a noted Columbia lady used to say of a
celebrated physician, (since resident of California), "he is
perfectly enamored of me"—I quote from a story you
used to laughingly tell us. I have finally given up the
attempt—at least, for the present. We have traveled a
deal about this God-forsaken, no-railroad country, (where
the men are almond-eyed and the women clubfooted and
otherwise malformed), and the passage, as you are aware,
must necessarily be slow. The Count is very kind, and I
give him no cause for jealousy; the fact is, this is a great
country for jealous lovers or husbands, as the women
are compelled, owing to the laws and the peculiar male
population, with their dirty persons and ways, (ugh! it
makes me shudder now to think of them), to keep much
within doors. It is a stupid sort of life we have been
leading in China, but I don't think we will remain here
many months longer, as the Count's family and friends
(he says and thinks so, at least), are becoming reconciled
to his departure from the customs of the old French
families—connecting himself with one beneath him; I bet
I'm as good a woman, in every sense of the term, as any

---

[1]This "Old Friend" or *"One Who Knows"* to whom Marie wrote
this letter was Julian Selby, Editor of the *Daily Carolinian*, the
offices of which were just across the street from the Feaster house
in Columbia when Marie was a girl. After the war Mr. Selby edited
the *Phoenix* (risen from the ashes, not Lloyd), a daily paper in
Columbia.

of them—if I haven't mothered half a dozen children; much the better for me and the children, too, as you'll agree. We have no stirring adventures nor excitements, but I ought to feel satisfied, as I have had my full share of them elsewhere. I had another picture taken to send to you, but it makes me look like such a guy, that I would not forward it. I'll have another trial soon, and if it is any better than the last, it will be sent. I like to hear about the Columbia people, but have no desire to see the place again; it is too small a town (city—I beg pardon!) to live in, as everybody seems to know everybody's business, or at least tries to find it out; we've had some good times there, though, haven't we? but it's not necessary to specify. [Here follow inquiries about a number of individuals, many of whom have long since departed.] I hope your "ship will soon come in," so that you can pay me that much-talked-of visit, when we could knock around and see what Kang-kow, Whang-ton, Ting-re and other delicately spelled places look and smell like—I've been among a few of 'em. The Count knows you—by reputation, at least, (and you can bet all your spare change that I gave you a good one.) Write me a good long letter—bother the postage.

Asking pardon for my noncompliance with your request, I remain, as ever yours,

Marie.

P. S.—Recollect, you are to let no one peruse my letters; you can detail such portions of their contents as you please. M.

This letter was the last word to reach Columbia directly from Marie. What ultimately happened to her has been a source of never-ending interest and conjecture. It was generally believed that Marie divorced the Count and married the Caliph of Baghdad and that he was so afraid she would grow weary of him and leave him that he had the tendons in her heels cut so that she would not be able to run away. From then on, she was carried everywhere on a gold velvet cushion by two Nubian eunuchs. As a consequence of no exercise she became enormously fat, much to the Caliph's pleasure, and toward the last it took four giant Nubians to fetch and carry the beauty on her golden cushion.

Yet several Americans who were in Paris in the late 1870's have written of seeing Marie there riding with a gigantic, bearded man in the Bois in a showy Russian equipage that attracted considerable attention.

Simkins and Patton in *The Women of the Confederacy* believe the Augusta *Chronicle's* obituary article is the true story:

The Augusta *Chronicle,* September 18, 1927, reprinting an undated obituary article by D. A. Dickert of Newberry, S. C., wrote: "The subsequent career of Mary Boozer, according to this authority, was even more glamorous than her war-time activities, and doubtless without parallel in the annals of the women of South Carolina."

The article described her years up to the time she married the Count de Pourtalès and then went on to say . . . "She continued her daring adventures in Japan, whither she and her husband soon sailed, her charms ensnaring a number of important officials in the Mikado's government. Divorced by the French ambassador, she married the Japanese prime minister, who, finally wearying of her continued indiscretions, had her thrown into prison and beheaded."

Not so. No bad end suddenly for our heroine. For the truth is that Marie lived happily ever after and her husband, Count Arthur de Pourtalès-Gorgier had a distinguished career in the French foreign service.

To prove it the Almanack de Gotha, 1900, gives as Count Pourtalès' wife, an American, Marie Bossier. Ruvigny's *The Titled Nobility of Europe,* 1914, p. 1172, gives Arthur, 3rd Count de Pourtalès, born at the Chateau de Gorgier, Canton Neuchâtel, Switzerland, 1844. His second marriage: Baltimore, May 2, 1876, to Marie Boosier, the most beautiful of Countesses who died in her castle on January 30, 1908.

BIBLIOGRAPHY

"One Who Knows" (JULIAN A. SELBY), *A Checkered Life*, being *A Brief History of the Countess Pourtalès* formerly *Miss Marie Boozer of Columbia, S. C.*, Columbia, S. C. Printed at the office of the Daily Phoenix, 1878.

"Felix Old Boy" (YATES SNOWDEN), *The Countess Pourtalès*, S. & H. Publishing Co., December, 1915.

O'NEALL, JOHN BELTON, *The Annals of Newberry*, Newberry, S. C., Aull & Houseal, 1892.

CHESNUT, MARY BOYKIN, *A Diary from Dixie*, New York, D. Appleton and Co., 1905.

LEIDING, HARRIETTE KERSHAW, *Historic Houses of South Carolina*, Philadelphia, J. B. Lippincott & Co., 1921.

BATEMAN, JOHN M., *A Columbia Scrapbook*, Columbia, The R. L. Bryan Co., 1915.

SELBY, JULIAN A., *Memorabilia*, Columbia, The R. L. Bryan Co., 1905.

SCOTT, EDWIN J., *Random Recollections*, Columbia, Charles A. Calvo, Jr., Printer, 1884.

WILLIAMS, J. F., *Old and New Columbia*, Columbia, Epworth Orphanage Press, 1929.

SIMMS, WM. GILMORE, *Sack and Destruction of the City of Columbia, S. C.*, edited by A. S. Salley, Oglethorpe University Press, 1937.

GIBBES, COL. JAMES G., *Who Burnt Columbia?*, Newberry, S. C., Elbert H. Aull Co., 1902.

SNOWDEN, YATES, *Marching with Sherman.* A Review of The Letters and Campaign Diaries of Henry Hitchcock, Major and Assistant Adjutant General of Volunteers as Edited by M. A. De Wolfe Howe and published by the Yale Press, New Haven, Conn., 1929.

TREZEVANT, DR. D. H., *The Burning of Columbia, S. C. A Review of Northern Assertions and Southern Facts*, Columbia, South Carolinian Power Press, 1866.

HAMPTON, WADE, *The Burning of Columbia*, Letter, June 24, 1873, with Appendix, Charleston, S. C. . . . . 1888.

SHERMAN, WILLIAM TECUMSEH, *Memoirs of General W. T. Sherman*, 2 vols., New York, D. Appleton & Co., 1875.

SHERMAN, WILLIAM TECUMSEH, *General Sherman's Official Accounts of His Great March Through Georgia and the Carolinas,* New York, Bunce and Huntingdon, 1865.

"WHO BURNED COLUMBIA?—General Sherman's Latest Story Examined," Southern Historical Society Papers, XIII (Jan.-Dec. 1885), 448-53.

TAYLOR, MRS. THOMAS (ed.), *South Carolina Women in the Confederacy,* 2 vols., Columbia, The State Co., 1903.

SIMKINS, FRANCIS B. and PATTON, JAMES W., *The Women of the Confederacy,* Richmond, Garrett and Massie, 1936.

SMITH, DANIEL E. HUGER, HUGER, ALICE R. and CHILDS, ARNEY R. (ed.), *Mason Smith Family Letters,* Columbia, University of South Carolina Press, 1950.

LECONTE, EMMA FLORENCE, *Diary,* 1864-1865, 1 volume in the Southern Historical Collection, University of North Carolina.

WARING, JOSEPH FRED, *Diary,* 1 volume in the Southern Historical Collection, University of North Carolina.

CHILDS, ARNEY ROBINSON (ed.), *The Private Journal of Henry William Ravenel 1859-1887,* Columbia, University of South Carolina Press, 1947.

Battles and Leaders of the Civil War, Vol. IV, Part II, New York, The Century Co., 1884.

CHISOLM, A. R., "Beauregard's and Hampton's Orders on Evacuating Columbia—Letter from Colonel A. R. Chisolm," in the Southern Historical Society Papers, VII (May 1879), 249-50.

ALDRICH, A. P., "The Oakes," *Our Women in the War.* The Lives They Lived; the Deaths They Died. From the Weekly News & Courier, Charleston, S. C., ed. Francis Warrington Dawson (Charleston: News and Courier Book Presses, 1885).

CONYNGHAM, DAVID POWER, *Sherman's March Through the South with Sketches and Incidents of the Campaign,* New York, Sheldon & Co., 1865.

LAFAYETTE MCLAWS PAPERS (small volume of war orders 1865) in the Southern Historical Collection, University of North Carolina.

LECONTE, JOSEPH, *'Ware Sherman,* Berkeley, University of California Press, 1938.

HARWELL, RICHARD B., *Confederate Music,* Chapel Hill, University of North Carolina Press, 1950.

BROOKS, U. R., *Butler and His Cavalry,* Columbia, The State Co., 1909.

BROOKS, U. R. (ed.), *Stories of the Confederacy,* Columbia, The State Co., 1912.

WELLS, EDWARD L., *Hampton and Reconstruction,* Columbia, The State Co., 1907.

WELLS, EDWARD L., "A Morning Call on General Kilpatrick,"

Southern Historical Society Papers, XII (March, 1884), 123-30.

BARRETT, JOHN G., *Sherman's March Through the Carolinas,* Chapel Hill, University of North Carolina Press, 1956.

TATUM, GEORGIA LEE, *Disloyalty in the Confederacy,* Chapel Hill, University of North Carolina Press, 1934.

KIRKLAND, THOMAS J. and KENNEDY, ROBERT, *Historic Camden,* Columbia, The State Co., 1926.

MORRIS, LLOYD, *Incredible New York,* New York, Random House, 1951.

LYNCH, DENIS TILDEN, *The Wild Seventies,* New York, D. Appleton-Century Co., 1941.

THE SATURDAY BOOK, 8th year, 1948; and 16th year, Hutchinson & Co., London, 1956.

Museum of the City of New York—The Edward W. C. Arnold Collections; Women's Fashions of 1867, by Goddard; Frank Leslie's Illustrated Newspaper 1865-1866. The J. Clarence Davies Collection: *Shopping in 1870* by William L. Myers, from *Harper's Bazaar, Fast Trotters on Harlem Lane; Skating in Central Park,* etc.

New York Historical Society—Biographical sketch of Lloyd Phoenix.

Log Books and Diaries of Lloyd Phoenix. Courtesy of G. W. Blunt White of the New York Yacht Club.

Union Club of the City of New York, Officers Members Constitution Rules, N. Y. Public Library, 1866-1874.

TOWNSEND, REGINALD, *Mother of Clubs,* Being the history of the first hundred years of the Union Club of New York 1836-1936, The Printing House of W. E. Rudge, 1936.

Address of the President of the Union League Club, June 23, 1866, New York, 1866.

Union League Club New York Annual Reports, 1863, 1865, July '65 Charter and list of members, May, 1868.

IRWIN, WILL; MAY, EARL CHAPIN; and HOTCHKISS, JOSEPH, *A History of the Union League Club of New York City,* Dodd Mead & Co., 1952.

Union League Club New York *Scrapbook,* New York Public Library.

BELLOWS, HENRY W., *Historical Sketch of the Union League Club of New York,* Its origin, organization and work 1863-1879. For private distribution. New York, Henry Putnam's Sons, 1879.

VIZETELLY, E. A., *The Court of the Tuileries* by "Le Petit Homme Rouge." London, Chatto & Windus, 1907.

PEARL, CYRIL, *The Girl with the Swansdown Seat,* Indianapolis, The Bobbs-Merrill Co., Inc., 1955.

VASSILY, COUNT PAUL (EKATERINA RADZIWILL), *Behind the Veil at the Russian Court,* New York, John Lane Co., 1914.

ALDANOV, MARK, *Before the Deluge*, New York, Scribner's Sons, 1947.

GRAHAM, STEPHAN, *Tsar of Freedom*, New Haven, Yale University Press, 1935.

NEWSPAPERS:

Columbia Phoenix, 1865.

Hillsborough Recorder, February 15, March 22, March 19, March 29, 1865.

Wilmington Herald of the Union, March 14, 1865.

Wilmington Daily North Carolinian, 1865.

New York Herald from April 6, 1865—February, 1866; from April 1868—January 1874.

New York Times, 1867—1870—1873.

New York Times, April 1, 1926.

Philadelphia Times, September 20, 1880.

The San Francisco Chronicle account of Marie Boozer was copied, undated, in *The Countess Pourtalès*, by Yates Snowden.

I would like to acknowledge information and help given by Julian Bolick, Thomas N. Pope, Mrs. Eva Gittman, Samuel Gaillard Stoney, Peter Manigault (for reading the manuscript), Melville Stone, and G. W. Blunt White, of the New York Yacht Club; and, fortunately and rewardingly, Dr. John Hunter Selby, of Washington, who has permitted me to reveal the mysterious "One Who Knows" as his father, Julian A. Selby.

ABOUT THE AUTHOR

ELIZABETH BOATWRIGHT COKER was born in Darlington, South Carolina. Her marriage to James Coker in 1930 joined two of the oldest and most aristocratic families in the South. Mrs. Coker is the author of seven bestselling novels, including *Daughter of Strangers, India Allan* and *La Belle,* which are all set in the South of the Civil War. Her books were book club selections and have been translated into half a dozen foreign languages. She now lives in Hartsville, South Carolina, the seat of Coker College, established by her husband's grandfather.

a Special Preview of
the colorful opening pages of
the newest novel by
the author of LA BELLE

BLOOD
RED
ROSES

by Elizabeth Boatwright Coker

One

Everything was upside down at Cedar Grove Plantation in Albemarle County, Virginia, on the 13th day of October, 1860. My whole delightful, wonderful world was about to come to a bad end suddenly as Aunt Dell had constantly warned me it would when I was over-excited as a child. Ironically this was going to happen because of my noble gesture: agreeing to Aunt Dell's velvet-veiled suggestions that I immediately marry a rich man who will adore me enough to pay off Uncle Jim's tobacco and racing debts, saving his honor as well as the plantation.

It was my duty to do this awful thing. Papa put me in Aunt Dell's arms minutes after I was born. Barely hesitating to give the farewell kiss to her younger sister's corpse, Aunt Dell rushed out of the room, to show me to Uncle Jim, who was Papa's elder brother. I don't believe it ever occurred to them thereafter that they hadn't conceived me themselves.

Oh, how I will hate that rich husband. Aunt Dell insists that if he isn't a thoroughly bad hat I will learn to like him well enough after the children start coming. My precious little half-sister, Amun, who is frail, can be the one of us to marry for love.

Misfortune struck The Cedars this past May when Uncle Jim wagered a great part of the plantation on one of his racehorses. In the match the gallant animal broke his leg and had to be destroyed. In July the tobacco crop was shredded by hail. Then in August the cider house burned down and the apple harvest rotted on the ground. In September a heavy storm broke in the night. The

James River roared like the ocean and went over its banks. Rain filled the outbuildings and barns and fields. The boats were all swimming in the boathouse. An enormous oak tree upended and crushed the whiskey still. Six skilled tobacco field slaves ran away.

To cap his bad luck Uncle Jim was so exhilarated by the way the "Chosen," wealthy Mr. Monk, of the Eastern Shore of Maryland, looked at me at supper last night that he drank so many bumpers of wine on top of brandy, hallooing and toasting first the hunt, then jolly Mr. Page, the Master, then Mr. Monk's racehorses, one after another, that on finally setting out to resume his chair at the head of the table, he misjudged the distance and fell hard on the floor.

After silently watching him make a few unsuccessful tries at rising, Aunt Dell languidly summoned Great Peter, our head house Negro, to carry him off. Great Peter laid him on his four poster bed from which in this October daydawn he was shouting orders.

I was dressed in my expensive new green velvet riding habit, determined to make the most of Mr. Monk's interest, even though he is a full head shorter than I and one of his eyes rolls around in its socket.

Mr. Page, Uncle Jim's best friend, aware of his financial difficulties, arranged this hunt today just so Mr. Monk could watch me take Parasol, my peppery mare, over the fences. If anything will sell me besides my looks it will be my horsemanship. I am more exciting in the saddle than in the waltz for, though fine-boned and graceful, I am almost six feet which is a trifle too tall for most gentlemen to be able to look down into my eyes.

As I finished adjusting my plumed hat and a sheer veil over my face I heard our horsekeeper, Jason Jenks, in Uncle Jim's room. I flew down. Jenks was saying it had to be today or never. Bonnie Bet had fooled him. This could be the end of her heat, not the beginning. He'd turned the teaser horse into the next run to get her frolicky and excited, ready for *her* chosen: the big bay stallion, which Uncle Jim had mortgaged the now-extinct tobacco crop to obtain to stand for a season. The bay was in the pen raring to go, said Jenks. A wonder we hadn't heard him neighing in the night.

"What's happening?" In my haste I stumbled over my long skirttrail.

"You're supposed to hook it over your wrist," Aunt Dell's voice came from somewhere in the dim room.

Uncle Jim shouted, "What's happening indeed! This clod, Jenks, has had the gall to suggest that if I can't walk, you give up hunting and cope with the teaser when Bonnie Bet is taken from him to the bay. My proud beauty! What villain would deprive the huntsmen of such a vision?"

Jenks stood staunchly on his thick young legs. "There'll be two hunts a week, Mr. Burwell, from now until late spring. Miss Angel's the only one the teaser won't harm at such a time as today, you excepting, of course, sir."

"Just give me a minute to take off this endless riding habit, Jenks."

"Do." Uncle Jim wrathfully lifted his bushy salt and pepper head from the pillow. "I've changed my mind. If we miss breeding Bonnie Bet we're out of the racing and the tobacco business."

"Don't fret, darling. I'll enjoy taking part." I was already unpinning my hat.

I could see Aunt Dell now, rocking in a cane chair by the wood fire, nightcapped and wrappered in flowered flannel. She said how could I, her own niece, think of taking part in a going-on like that. I said I didn't intend to take part in the actual going-on but what if our teaser got out of control and jumped the fence and got to Bonnie Bet as he was so capable of doing? Was Aunt Dell eager to go to the poorhouse?

Uncle Jim said, "Don't argue with that fool girl, Mrs. Burwell. She's well aware of what's expected of her. But the crazy way she is about the teaser she'll probably open the gate and slip him to Bet first. Her pity for the underdog will be the ruin of her yet. Help me up, Jenks. God damn you—my back's broken for sure." He fell back, groaning.

Great Peter tiptoed in with a silver mug of warm rye

whiskey and sugar water and supported Uncle Jim while he drank. "Be gentle now, Master. Miss Angel knows what's fitten for a lady. She won't go no further than the run; not Miss Angel."

Jenks, his yellow whiskers standing out from his rosy cherub cheeks, spoke to me across the bed. "He's slipped a joint, Miss Angel. This ain't the first time. Usually he manages to hide it from you all. We rub him with liniment at the stables and loosen him up. But today he's worse than I've ever seen him. You take off that pretty green skirt and put on something real old. The runs are a bog of mud."

Uncle Jim waved his hand. It was trembling. I took it and squeezed it hard, saying, "Mr. Monk wouldn't do for me, Uncle Jim. You might as well know that I saw him nodding when I played the Chopin waltzes after supper. I'll be very careful around dear Teaser."

"I don't trust you, Angelica. Not when your emotions are involved. You're too much like your father. He could always be counted on to behave rashly and grieve about it later."

"If you don't trust Angelica, Mr. Burwell, tell her to pin her hat back on and gallop to the Inn where the hunt is this minute assembling." Aunt Dell had risen and put her arm around my waist. She was a tall listless looking lady with marked remains of beauty. She was listless because she never took any exercise. Her green eyes glittered when lighted with interest, which was seldom. Most of the time she had a vague stare whether she was talking or not. Today was no exception.

Jenks was going out through the door into the hall. "I say, Mr. Burwell, I'll not let Miss Angel nowhere near the pen. The teaser needs her."

"And *I* say, Mr. Burwell," Aunt Dell's eyes were staring at nothing in the fringed bed canopy, "Mr. Monk and his money are more important to Angelica *and* us than the teaser."

Assuaged by his hot toddy, Uncle Jim raised up on his elbow, "And *I* say, Mrs. Burwell, that unknown to you I've wagered everything on a successful crop of foals next year. A get of Bonnie Bet and the Sir Archy bay, unrun, will bring enough to pay off the wager on The Cedars. Once the colt runs, Angelica can be an old maid and spend her life with the teaser if she so chooses. Hurry, girl, they are waiting for you at the stables."

A light frost had fallen in the night. The ridge horizon was robed in a haze of dream-stuff blue. I heard the melody of the huntsman's sweet-toned copper horn and the belling of the hounds. As the hunt distanced I thought, well, there goes the best chance I'll probably ever have to pay the bills for my fine coming-out clothes and help Uncle Jim settle his debts. When Mr. Monk vanishes there's nobody around here rich enough for me to set my cap for. We'll be bankrupt by New Year's whether we breed Bonnie Bet or not . . .

Teaser had impeccable bloodlines but Uncle Jim had a horror of a white colt with blue eyes. Teaser had been an accident that befell Silver Star, full sister to Kitty Fisher. Silver Star was one of Uncle Jim's most prolific grey brood mares. Five years ago, a grey hunter of Mr. Randolph's ran away and vaulted the six-foot fence surrounding the east pasture where Silver Star was trotting along with her two-week-old black filly. Jenks had found her and the hunter there grazing together but no one suspected what had gone on before until Silver Star began making nests in the hay in her stall a week before she dropped Teaser.

One look at the poor shivery little creature had been enough for Uncle Jim. The two greys had made an albino! The best fate I was able to bargain for him doomed him to frustration whenever the breeding pen was active.

But every now and then I loaned him to Farmer Grundy, who considered himself lucky to get, free of charge, white colts descended from the great Eclipse. Teaser was the swiftest moving, boldest jumper in our entire stable.

There was a lot of commotion beyond the near barn where the breeding pen was set up. This was the nearest I'd ever come to the "going-on" as Aunt Dell called it. Hog killing and horse breeding were secret rites. Ladies and children stayed behind drawn curtains at such times.

If Jenks saw me so near he'd order me back to the house. I picked my path through the mud and into the barn, staying close against the stalls.

Through the light at the end of the runway I saw Jenks and four black men coming with the big bay. The stallion was plunging and throwing his head, snorting clouds of steam through his dilated nostrils. His eyes were fiery, his breathing loud. He struck the soft earth with his hard hoofs. Bonnie Bet, held by two black stablehands, was kicking with her back feet and thrashing her well-set flaxen tail back and forth in the stallion's face; suddenly she threw her tail far to one side.

He was just about to——

"Angelica! Hurry!"

I could have killed the beloved caller. "Amun! What are you doing here? Don't you know what's taking place? Get back to the house."

"Aunt Dell and Uncle Jim want you at once. It's an emergency."

I caught the hand my tiny blonde half-sister held out and fled with her to the rambling old strawberry-colored brick house . . .

Amun kept chattering about a letter as we ran through the weedy, formal garden hedged with unclipped cedars. I hadn't listened but was aware that great news had come when I saw Aunt Dell in a close-bordered tarleton cap, seated at the head of the dining table. She was wearing her widest hoop under her least-shiny grey taffeta day gown. Her green eyes glittered as she waved some rumpled sheets of paper in my direction.

"We're saved!"

"Let's go into Uncle Jim's room. I'd rather hear about it when he does."

"He's savored every word already. Great Peter is shaving him now. He's going to make an heroic effort to put his trousers on and be brought out into the drawing room."

Two

My dear Adelia,

There is only one subject discussed a days in Charleston, SECESSION! The resolution to quit these United States consumes everybody. Throughout South Carolina men of all stations in life sit together under spreading oaks talking about it. I doubt you could find more than a handful of Up Country souls who agree with Mr. Pettigrew and Mr. Calhoun that we should put up with Yankee meddling in our private affairs any longer. What impudence! In *their* sailing ships *they* fetched the blacks here from Africa. Now that they've pocketed *our* money their pious preachers demand that *we* set them free! To the devil with them, as dear Papa would have said. . . .

Baynard Elliott Berrien of Cotton Hall Plantation on Hilton Head, S. C., sailed into town about a month ago and took up residence at the Charleston Hotel. He resembles his late father, our Cousin Hazzard, being six and a half feet high and considering Hilton Head Island more important than Charleston. Have you ever known such gall?

But, lacking Hazzard's rude conceit, Beau, as he is called, possesses an almost royal presence heightened by the rufous coloring and the bold hooked nose that have been in the Berrien family since the Crusades. His fiery brown eyes give him alternately the look of a sly fox or a swooping hawk. It's difficult to describe him. He's different from anybody we ever had in the family before.

The ladies flock after him, those from the uptown back streets as well as ones of our kind. Tales of his wildness where wine and women (including his young stepmother) are concerned have been whispered behind fans ever since he returned from his studies at Harvard College six years ago. He never noticeably refuses the role gossiped about; if folks choose to be shocked he generally obliges. But since his father's death and his inheritance of the Berrien fortune, his eccentricities are called quaint and amusing. His friends say that under the dwindling bouts of carryings-on he has improved, changed considerably, except for being unpredictable.

Aged twenty-five, he plants cotton on Hilton Head Island and St. Helena Island and Fripp Island and along the River May. Lord knows the extent of the Berrien holdings in blacks *and* cotton land in Mississippi.

He possesses parts as well. His peers speak him as the finest deer and waterfowl shot in the Low Country, a magnificent horse rider, a careful father 'in locus' to his three younger brothers, and properly proud of his Huguenot heritage.

Did Beau hold the reputation for being too often in his cups or for cruelty to his slaves as did his father I would not be writing you. As you know, our Cousin Julia, this boy's mother, broke her heart and health over it. They say the second Mrs. Berrien knew how to cope with Hazzard. She rarely, if ever, set foot on a sea island plantation, and let her husband lie wherever his drinking flung him. Beaufort keeps an aloof distance, she having managed to make enemies of every family connection. So far as I know Hazzard only brought her to one Ball in Charleston. I was serving the oyster stew that night so merely glimpsed her. Mainly I remember that she had too much hair and the way she kept fidgeting with her diamonds and her raspy Northern voice complaining that Southern ladies didn't appeal to her.

I mention this because it struck me as odd for Beau, on his first visit, to bluntly state his reason for calling: I must help him find a suitable bride! Have you ever? He is anxious to marry and settle down before war clouds darken the horizon.

"War?" I asked.

"Of course, Madame," he answered firmly. "You aren't under the illusion that the North will let South Carolina depart in peace, are you?"

Not caring to pursue unpleasant subjects I returned

to his request. "Why me, rather than your stepmother?"

"Frankly because I don't want Elsa to know a damn thing about it."

He chose me as his mentor having often heard his mother speak of me as THE Grand Dame of Charleston!

Flattered, I arranged dinners and teas for him in the best houses and he went through all the motions of the proper courtier. Ten days ago he gave me his reaction to the Misses Ravenel, Middleton, Chisolm, Prioleau, Stoney, Heyward and Alston: though Miss R had gorgeous blue eyes she also had brown spots on her teeth; Miss M fell off her horse and cried; Miss C affronted him, reading aloud vulgar poems by a fellow named Whitman; Miss P pretended to faint when he bit the tip of her ear as they were waltzing; Miss S constantly fanned and giggled; Miss H had an offensive odor; and Miss A had thick ankles.

I was about to send him packing. After all I'd spent the better part of a month at his disposal and so far he'd only presented me with a silver rice spoon. But suddenly I thought of you. Angelica's heron-like beauty has been carefully reported in Charleston by several young gentlemen who have recently hunted in your area. Already I have received six requests for the pleasure of escorting her to my Oyster Roast at the Cooper River Plantation in February!

However, knowing that things have not gone well for you and Jim of late, I have given Beau Berrien directions about arriving at The Cedars and have been advised that he left on the cars for Richmond October 6, thinking to procure a mount from his Cousin Harrison there and ride on to you. Expect him on the 13th or 14th . . .

> Fondly,
> Rebecca Bacot

"Your mother and I played with Beau's aunt in his grand house in Beaufort when we were children. I would love for you to be mistress there."

I could feel my hair slipping down from its net. "I simply *must* put Teaser into his stall."

"Don't go back out there, darling, you look worn out."

"I've been running ever since dawn. What time is it now?"

"Ten o'clock. Do make haste. The South Carolina Hamptons are stopping by for dinner on their way from White Sulphur Springs after visiting the Prestons. Mr. Page has sent word that Mr. Monk was so disappointed at your not showing up for the hunt he's going to stay over and hunt tomorrow. They will be here for dinner, along with Azilee and Lizora Bizarre. You'll have to watch out for that Lizora. She looks stunning in riding dress and she's poor too. Oh, everything is working out perfectly. The Walkers are here already, playing whist in the drawing room."

"Lizora Bizarre makes me feel awkward. She knows it and always stands close to me to show off my tallness by her littleness."

"That makes thirteen people at table, Aunt Dell," Amun said.

"Then you'll eat in the kitchen, Miss Puss."

"If the rich fox gets here in time *he* will save me." Amun nodded her round little head shining with cropped flaxen hair, she having had typhoid fever last summer.

Aunt Dell airily waved a silver teaspoon. "He'll get here. I've got one of my hunches. If he isn't here by three I'll delay dinner till four then five then six o'clock. I've ordered Great Peter to fill the gentlemen up with grog and the ladies with a concoction of brandy and sugar water. Competition between Beau and Mr. Monk will turn the trick. You must wear Mrs. Meriweather's blue silk, Angelica. It makes your eyes glisten like morning glories."

I had never seen Aunt Dell so enthusiastic. Nor have I ever felt more wretchedly desolate. "He won't like Chopin and I don't like pompous asses."

"His mother played for Chopin in Paris when she was a girl. And Chopin listened! He rarely did, you know."

"I'll tell Dinah to fix you a bath in the big tub. You've got to smell good. You smell pukey now." Amun was jigging around excitedly on her skinny legs.

"You go on like a jackanapes." Aunt Dell tapped

Amun's sharp little shoulder with the spoon. Her eyes took on the glittery look again. "Hepzibah is boiling our last three-year-old forty-pound ham. There's a white-faced sheep on the fire and all those wild geese and ducks you and Jenks shot day before yesterday; *and* a turkey gobbler and a dozen pullets and hominy and sweet potatoes and syllabub and lemon ice cream."

I couldn't stand any more. I rushed away through the kitchen, which was filled with chattering black women and quick little mulatto serving boys in white long-sleeved aprons, with red and white turbans on their heads. They were egg whipping, butter creaming, meat basting, raisin stoning, salad chopping, sugar pounding, biscuit beating, fowl picking, silver polishing, napkin folding, wine cooling and things like that.

There was no doubt about it, Aunt Dell had executive talent. She had put everybody, except me, to a task they could happily accomplish. In her book, today was one of life's great occasions to which, without appearing to do anything at all, she planned to rise superbly. It was maddening.

When I reached the lot it was obvious that Teaser was determined not to be put into his stall. His game of catch-me-if-you-can had a peculiar effect on me. Being on the edge of hysteria, I burst out laughing. Recklessly jumping up to catch his halter I stepped on my skirt and tore it half off. Still laughing I admired my shapely leg and didn't duck away from a clod of mud Teaser's forefoot kicked up. It smeared all over my forehead. This was the last straw.

"Come here, you damned demon!"

The unfamiliar, screaming tone of my voice arrested him. He quieted, nuzzling my shoulder with his long soft lips.

"You funny old horse." Exhausted, I leant my cheek against his lathered neck. "You poor funny old horse."

Three

"No funnier than you."

I recognized him immediately up there against the sky, looking like an over-life-sized equestrian statue in an exaggerated stovepipe hat. Did he go all the way up into the hat? Apparently he did for when he lifted it off he was still the tallest human I'd ever seen in a saddle.

Dismounting, he bowed smartly, "Baynard Berrien, at your service, dear lady."

Teaser tensed, pricked up his new-moon ears and neighed angrily. As the giant secured his mount to a post and, waving his hat, headed toward the gate, Teaser wheeled away from me and galloped along the rail, sending mud and stones flying right and left as he went.

"Climb through the fence quick, you idiot. I've panicked him."

The gate opened and Teaser made for the space to escape.

"Hoa, there. Hoa, you scoundrel," the newcomer roared, jamming his hat back on.

Teaser was on his way to freedom. I kept running and calling, "Mr. Berrien! Mr. Berrien!" knowing Teaser saw only the open gate and not the man blocking his escape.

The thought of those powerful hoofs and huge hard teeth crumbling that magnificent specimen into a muddy-bloody mess undid me. I kept on shrieking and screaming. Teaser was upon him. I froze, paralyzed. For a few seconds of hideous noises it was man against horse. Then a yell; then a squeal; a jerk; and it was all over.

Teaser snorted and kicked and snapped his teeth like castanets. Flecks of foam exploded from his nostrils.

The Chevalier Berrien, his whole powerful body turning flexibly, iron arms taut, Wellington boots planted ankle-deep in the mud, hung on to the halter as the stallion plunged and reared.

"You're killing him," I gasped, stumbling and slipping as I ran, "you're killing him."

"Better him than me," he shouted. His linen shirt frill was ruined; his cravat gone; his sleeves torn from the shoulder seams of his tight fitting fawn broadcloth coat.

As I reached up to snatch the rope away from him my hand came in contact with a hairy wrist above a sodden chamois glove. Flame from the bare reddish flesh darted into my fingers, ran up my arm, through my armpits, tightening and thrusting my breasts toward this wild man. He was the fox! I heard his rapid heartbeats; and mine.

"What in blazes were you doing fooling around with this crazy stallion. Do you work here?" he asked, breathing heavily.

He thought I was a stable hand! My weariness vanished. My audacity and courage returned. "My uncle works here. I was on a special assignment to lock up the teaser. They're breeding the finest Burwell mare over beyond the big barn. Teaser wouldn't hurt me. He loves me."

"Which goes to show you know nothing of the male sex when he is deprived of his rights. Where the hell are my cigars? In the mud, dammit. Come on, I'll lock him up. Lead the way to his stall. He won't make any more trouble. He's met his match and knows it."

Teaser did too. Capriciously he snapped at a mass of flying russet hair. My rich prospect was about to be scalped! But, not liking the taste, Teaser let go and whickering, head down, gave a playful hoist of his back feet and lightly picked his way behind us through the muck toward his stall.

As the bolt dropped into place the newcomer said, "Even in this disheveled state I must present my compliments to the Burwells. First, I'll stable my dull mount, than I'll look in on the breeding. See if the horses are as ill cared for as the land. Then I'll be forced to endure an endless dinner full of conversation about Virginia people I never heard of. After that I'll slip away and take tea with you."

"How will you find me?"

"Your uncle will direct me. I'll make friends with him

at the breeding pen. Don't worry; I'll not divulge my wicked designs on you. I'll tell him I might drop in on him later and talk horses."

"You can't miss him. He has yellow hair and bushy yellow sideburns. His name is Jenks. The stall on the end is empty. I'll see that your horse is fed."

Angelica's meeting with Beau leads them to build a life together. However all of their plans are threatened by the onrushing events of the Civil War.

The complete Bantam Book will be available May 24th, on sale wherever paperbacks are sold.

DON'T MISS
THESE CURRENT
Bantam Bestsellers

Bantam Book Catalog

Here's your up-to-the-minute listing of every book currently available from Bantam.

This easy-to-use catalog is divided into categories and contains over 1400 titles by your favorite authors.

So don't delay—take advantage of this special opportunity to increase your reading pleasure.

Just send us your name and address and 25¢ (to help defray postage and handling costs).

BANTAM BOOKS, INC.
Dept. FC, 414 East Golf Road, Des Plaines, Ill. 60016

Mr./Mrs./Miss_____
(please print)

Address_____

City_____State_____Zip_____

Do you know someone who enjoys books? Just give us their names and addresses and we'll send them a catalog too!

Mr./Mrs./Miss_____

Address_____

City_____State_____Zip_____

Mr./Mrs./Miss_____

Address_____

City_____State_____Zip_____

FC—6/77